UNWAVERING HEART

I0876626

THE MATRIARCHS

2

Unwavering Heart

The Story of Rebekah

Angela Hunt

BethanyHouse
a division of Baker Publishing Group
Minneapolis, Minnesota

© 2026 by Angela Hunt Communications, Inc.

Published by Bethany House Publishers
Minneapolis, Minnesota
BethanyHouse.com

Bethany House Publishers is a division of
Baker Publishing Group, Grand Rapids, Michigan

Printed in the United States of America

All rights reserved. No part of this publication may be reproduced, stored in a retrieval system, or transmitted in any form or by any means—for example, electronic, photocopy, recording—without the prior written permission of the publisher. The only exception is brief quotations in printed reviews.

Library of Congress Cataloging-in-Publication Data
Names: Hunt, Angela Elwell, author.
Title: Unwavering heart : the story of Rebekah / Angela Hunt.
Description: Minneapolis, Minnesota : Bethany House Publishers, a division of Baker Publishing Group, 2026. | Series: The matriarchs ; 2
Identifiers: LCCN 2025046748 | ISBN 9780764245183 paperback | ISBN 9781493455409 ebook
Subjects: LCSH: Rebekah (Biblical matriarch)—Fiction | LCGFT: Bible fiction | Christian fiction | Historical fiction | Novels
Classification: LCC PS3558.U46747 U59 2026 | DDC 813/.54—dc23/eng/20260105
LC record available at https://lccn.loc.gov/2025046748

Scripture quotations are taken from the Tree of Life Version. © 2015 by the Messianic Jewish Family Bible Society. Used by permission of the Messianic Jewish Family Bible Society.

This is a work of historical reconstruction; the appearances of certain historical figures are therefore inevitable. All other characters, however, are products of the author's imagination, and any resemblance to actual persons, living or dead, is coincidental.

Map is copyright © Baker Publishing Group.

Cover design by Peter Glöege, LOOK Design Studios

The Author is represented by the literary agency of Browne & Miller Literary Associates, LLC.

Baker Publishing Group publications use paper produced from sustainable forestry practices and postconsumer waste whenever possible.

26 27 28 29 30 31 32 7 6 5 4 3 2 1

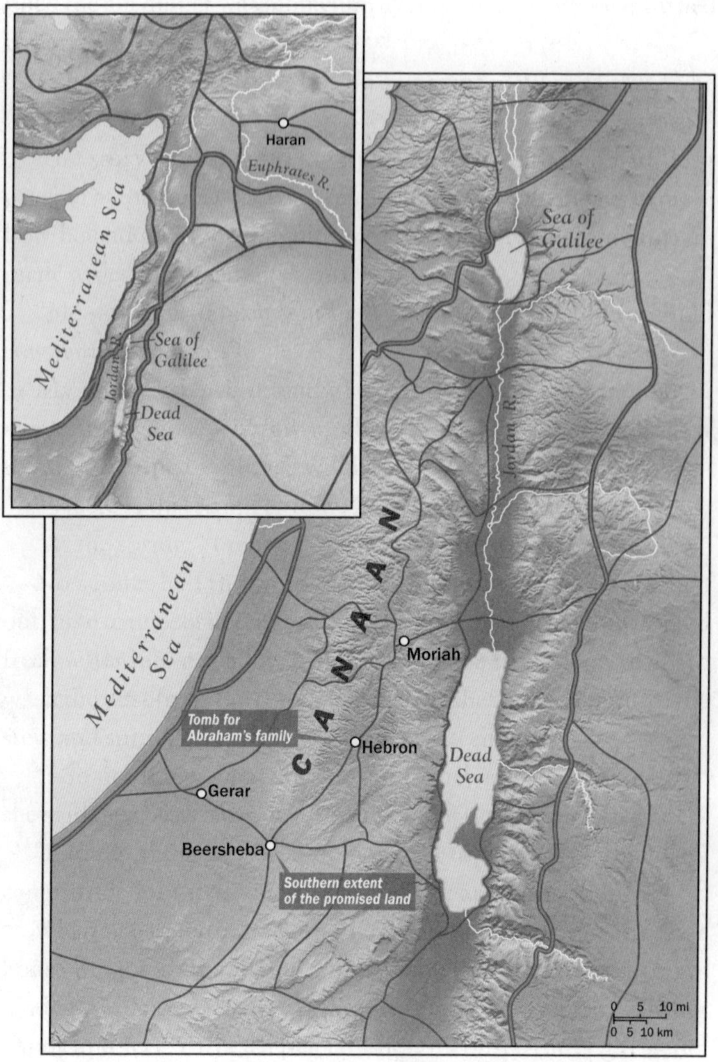
Haran
Euphrates R.
Mediterranean Sea
Jordan R.
Sea of Galilee
Dead Sea
Sea of Galilee
Jordan R.
CANAAN
Mediterranean Sea
Moriah
Tomb for Abraham's family
Hebron
Dead Sea
Gerar
Beersheba
Southern extent of the promised land
0 5 10 mi
0 5 10 km

Introduction

Once you've read a few pages of *Unwavering Heart*, you may find yourself thinking, *Wait, that's not in the Bible.*

You'd be right. The Bible gives us pencil sketches of particular events, but a novelist's job is to flesh out those sketches by adding color, texture, and context, both through research and imagination. I'm not at all attempting to rewrite the Bible; I'm attempting to show you the full story as it *might* have happened.

You may be surprised to learn that many of the scenes in this novel have been adapted from either the Bible, my primary source, the ancient Book of Jasher (mentioned twice in the Scriptures), or the Book of Jubilees, another ancient Jewish text. The latter two books never claim to be inspired or inerrant, but they certainly provide interesting context surrounding the lives of Rebekah and Isaac. If you have questions while you're reading, the author's note at the end of the novel may provide you with some answers.

So settle into your favorite chair, brace for the unexpected, and enjoy this story of the second matriarch of our faith.

The heart of a mother is a deep abyss, at the bottom of which you will always find forgiveness.

—*Honoré de Balzac*

Book One

HARAN

Now Abraham was old, advanced in years, and ADONAI blessed Abraham in everything. Then Abraham said to his servant, the oldest of his household who managed everything that belonged to him,

> "Now put your hand under my thigh, so that I may make you take an oath by ADONAI, the God of heaven and the God of earth, that you will not take a wife for my son from among the daughters of the Canaanites among whom I am dwelling. On the contrary, to my land and to my relatives you must go and get a wife for my son Isaac."

So Abraham took a wife for his son Isaac, and her name was Rebekah, the daughter of Bethuel, the son of Nahor, the brother of Abraham.

Genesis 24:1–4

Chapter 1

THE DRY AND STUBBORN earth seemed reluctant to receive the body of my esteemed grandfather. Behind the gravediggers, the hired mourners keened, their voices weaving a sorrowful lament to honor Nahor, son of Terah. I stood among them, my fingers tight around the edge of my shawl. Dust clung to my skin, mingling with the sweat at my wrists.

My father, Bethuel, stood at the head of the grave, his face like weathered stone. The mourners fell silent when he lifted his hand. He spoke the traditional words of parting, calling upon the gods of our ancestors, but I barely heard him. My thoughts churned with a matter more pressing than grief. My grandfather had spoiled me, but my father was more pragmatic. With Nahor gone, my father was now the head of the family and would be eager to make decisions. And what more crucial decision could he make than to select a bridegroom for his daughter?

I shifted my gaze to Laban. My brother, three years my senior, seemed lost in the ritual, mouthing prayers as he studied the other men. He would not be concerned about my fate. As the favored child, he never worried about anything but his own appetite.

The specter of my future settled over me like the dust covering my grandfather's shrouded body.

The sun climbed higher, nearing its zenith. As the burial party broke apart, murmuring among themselves, my father approached.

"Rebekah." He pitched his voice for my ears alone. "Tomorrow night we will entertain five guests at our table. Everything has been arranged, so you must be ready."

The words struck like a blow. I knew what he meant. I knew why they were coming. With my lenient grandfather gone, my father had wasted no time.

Five men. Five possible futures. And not one of them the future I wished for.

THE FIRE CRACKLED at the hearth, its golden light dancing across the mud-brick walls of our kitchen. From the tall window, the closing calls of nearby merchants quieted as the city prepared for rest.

I sat cross-legged on a reed mat, my right hand turning the upper stone while my left hand dropped barley into the hole at the grindstone's center. With each revolution, coarse meal spilled from between the stones, releasing a nutty aroma that mixed with the smoke of olive wood in the fire.

My shoulders ached, both from the stress of the funeral and the day's labor at the well. I had made twelve trips with a clay jar balanced precariously on my head, water spilling over my neck despite my best efforts. Father's six goats had returned to their pen, and the animals were thirsty. And Mother was quick to commandeer my services rather than Laban's.

The curtain between the cooking area and the courtyard lifted, and Laban appeared, his athletic frame silhouetted against the fading day. Even in the dim light, I could see smudges of dirt on his face and elbows. While I trudged back and forth to the well, he had played kick-the-pig's-bladder with his friends.

"There you are," he said, moving toward the clay pots near the fire. "I'm starving. Does any of that honeyed bread remain?"

I jerked my chin toward the small table, where Mother had left a cloth-covered basket. "Take only one piece. The rest is for Father."

Laban grinned, stuffing half a piece into his mouth. He took a second piece, too, knowing he would not be reprimanded for being greedy. Father never scolded Laban the way he scolded me.

My brother plopped down on a bench, leaning back against the table with the ease of a young man who never fretted about disappointing his parents. Honey glistened on his fingers as he stretched his legs, nearly upsetting my bowl of grain.

"Why do you look like you have been drinking vinegar?" He spoke around a mouthful of bread, his eyes lit with mild curiosity. "You scowl at the grain as if it insulted our ancestors."

I pressed my lips together and turned the stone faster. "You would not understand."

"Try me." When he reached over to pluck a few kernels from my bowl, I slapped his hand.

"You are a man," I said, the words bitter on my tongue. "Everything is easier for you."

Laban barked a laugh. "Easier? I spent the entire afternoon helping Father count the new lambs."

"When you were not playing games." I looked up. "When was the last time Father asked me to go out to the fields? When was the last time he looked at me like I sprinkled the sky with stars?"

"Men are supposed to care for the livestock."

"Mother and Father spoil you," I said, attacking the quern with more force than necessary. "Who has to help the servants? I do. Who has to serve the men at meals? I do. Whose birthday is celebrated every year with a grand feast? Yours, not mine."

"You want a feast?"

"For my birthday dinner Mother gave me an extra portion of

stew, but Father barely acknowledged the day. For *your* last birthday, they slaughtered a calf and invited half the city."

Laban grinned, honey glistening at the corner of his mouth. "What is wrong with that? Men are more important than women."

I stopped grinding. "So you are more important than me?"

He shrugged.

The silver anklet Mother had given me as a birthday gift—my only piece of jewelry—suddenly seemed a paltry consolation compared to the ornate knife Father recently presented to Laban for no reason at all.

"It is not right," I said, my voice low. "Without women, men would not exist."

He reached for another piece of honeyed bread. "And without sunshine, we would have no grain. But if you are hungry, can you eat sunshine? No, and you cannot have women without men to sire them."

I scowled, irritated at his insistence on having the final word.

"They love you more," I said, the words escaping before I could trap them. "Mother and Father favor you more than me."

For an instant, my brother's smile faltered. Something like discomfort—or guilt—flashed across his stubbled face, but the look vanished as quickly as it had appeared. "That is how the world works, Rebekah," he said. "The firstborn son is the heir. The daughter marries and becomes part of her husband's family. You will understand when you have a family of your own."

His glib words reminded me of Father's plans and brought tears to my eyes. I blinked them away, for I would not give Laban the satisfaction of seeing me cry. Instead, I went back to work, channeling my frustration into the grindstone.

"Have you nothing else to do?" I asked, not looking at my brother. "Surely somewhere someone is throwing a party for you."

He left me to my work, but I could hear his laughter as it reverberated through the hallway.

Why did my parents favor him above me? He was the firstborn

and a man, but I was not born a slave. Women had worth, and surely the second born should be as cherished as the first.

When I had ground all the grain, I straightened my aching back and made myself a silent promise. If I had to marry, I would marry someone who valued me above all others. Someone who would see me—*truly* see me—not as lesser, but as worthy of the kind of love that flowed so easily toward my brother.

Was there such a man in Haran?

I WAS ON MY WAY to my room, my heart still heavy from the day's events, when I came upon my childhood nurse near the hearth. The amber light of dying embers flickered over her face as she wove a basket from slender reeds. I sat next to her, then confessed something in a quiet voice: "Deborah, the thought of tonight's dinner fills me with dread. I do not think I will want to marry any of the men Father has invited."

"Why not?"

"Because I cannot help feeling that Father intends to offer me as he would a prize ram. I do not want to be considered in such a way."

She looked up, her compassionate eyes meeting mine. "My precious pet," she said, keeping her voice low, "you have always known that a marriage would be arranged for you. You are fortunate that you were not betrothed long before this."

"I was not ready before this," I mumbled, reminding her of the recent changes in my body.

Deborah shrugged. "Still, some girls are betrothed as infants because marriage is part of life. Husbands and children can be good things."

"Yours were not." I bit my lip, instantly sorry that the words had slipped from my tongue.

"My master in those days did not allow me a husband," Deborah said, correcting my impression of her past. "And my baby died before it could walk. But the gods were merciful. Because my child had not been weaned, I became your wet nurse. You have filled the void in my heart ever since."

"I am sorry." Overcome with love for the woman who had always been my comforter and encourager, I squeezed her hand. "I do not know what I would do without you."

"You would be fine." Her words, though warm, held a note of resignation. "As you will be fine when you are married. But do let your father know your concerns. You do not want to find yourself married to an evil man."

"How can I tell if a man is evil?" I hugged my bent knees. "And why does my mother not speak to me about these things?"

"Your mother is busy helping your father." Deborah sighed, set aside her basket, and took my hand, her warmth a comfort against my chilly apprehensions. "Your mother accepted her role and expects you to do the same. Women are not always able to choose, but they have the gift of influence, so use yours carefully. Study the men your father presents to you and listen carefully to their words. Because once you are married, you will assist your husband in his work and bear his children. This is the way things are, the way they must be."

As she spoke, I could not help but think of my grandmother Milcah, who bore eight sons and three daughters, then smiled when Grandfather took a concubine and sired even more children. Grandmother took care of all of them until the day she died.

"I want to do more than what my mother and grandmother have done," I said, my voice trembling. "I do not want to spend my entire life in Haran. Grandmother told me about her sister Sarah, who traveled the world, met kings, and was mourned by princes when she died. She and Abraham worshiped a God called ADONAI, who worked miracles for them—"

Deborah cut me off with a warning finger. "Stories have a tendency to grow in the telling," she said. "Do not wish for what you do not know to be true."

The room seemed to shrink around me, the aroma of baking bread and herbs intensifying as if to remind me that I might never escape this house and the city surrounding it. Then a worrisome thought slammed into my awareness: marriage involved children and childbirth.

I shuddered at the thought. "How can you wish me married," I asked, "if I might die when I attempt to bear a child?"

Deborah's hand squeezed mine, a silent acknowledgment of the risks women bore. "Life, my pet, is unpredictable and dangerous," she said, her voice gentle. "That is why we do not neglect our prayers and sacrifices to the gods. They alone can protect us . . . if they choose to do so."

Her words filled the quiet room, yet they did little to comfort me. I whispered a ritual prayer designed to ward off evil, in this case the evil of death. But which god could answer my request?

"Which?" I asked. "When you need a powerful god, to whom do you pray?"

Deborah lifted one shoulder in a half shrug, then the corner of her mouth rose in a smile. "The only God who seems to work real miracles is Adonai. They say Sarah's husband was entirely devoted to Him and would worship no other."

"Adonai." I whispered the name. "My grandmother said He was responsible for giving Sarah a son in her old age." I squeezed Deborah's hand. "Have *you* ever prayed to Adonai?"

She shook her head, but her smile broadened. "I would not know how to sacrifice to a God who cannot be seen, but if He is as mighty as they say, I would be willing to learn."

TORCHLIGHT DANCED over the walls and burnished the polished bronze of the dinner platters. The scent of roasted lamb and coriander filled the room, mingling with the sharper, acrid smell of incense. I sat beside my father, my hands folded in my lap, my lips pressed together, and my pulse steady . . . only because I willed it so.

Five men sat before me. Five men who had presented themselves as potential bridegrooms.

The oldest was Nadab, a widower with three grown sons. His spice caravans, he informed us, traveled as far as Egypt, and his prosperity was evident in the fine linen of his robes and the gold rings that adorned his fingers. He looked at me with kind eyes, but those eyes still held the shadow of his dead wife. I would forever be compared to a ghost.

Next was Kemuel, the wine merchant whose laugh was too loud and whose breath reeked of his wares even before the meal began. His fingers lingered too long on my arm when I poured his wine, and the thought of those hands in my bed made my skin crawl.

Aram, the trader in dyed cloth, was soft-spoken and appeared gentle. Of all of them, he frightened me the least. But his eyes were dull, revealing a lack of spirit that made me wonder if life with him would slowly extinguish whatever fire burned within me.

The fourth man, Ephron, dealt in copper and bronze. His rough hands were scarred from fashioning and handling metals. He spoke little during the meal, but watched me with calculation in his eyes, as if measuring my social skills to determine if I was worth the bride price.

Zimran, the chief priest of Sin, was the last to present himself. He watched me with shrewd, kohl-lined eyes, running his fingers along the rim of his cup as he spoke of omens and lunar blessings. His appearance was striking, but his smile never reached his eyes, and his manner reminded me of a desert jackal sniffing out its prey.

When the men had finished eating, Father asked me to sit, so I did.

I listened. I nodded. I smiled when expected. But none of their words moved my heart.

"Rebekah is skilled in weaving," my father said, his voice ringing with pride. "Her fine woolen cloth elicits envy from our neighbors."

"A woman who can weave makes a fine wife," the cloth merchant remarked, tilting his head as if calculating how much fabric would be required to clothe me.

"She also sings like a nightingale," my father added. "A gift from the gods."

"The gods," the priest of Sin echoed. His gaze lingered on me, heavy with expectation. "Tell me, girl, which god calls to you?"

I hesitated. I knew what he wanted to hear. I could bow to the customs of my people and give an acceptable answer. But my heart yearned for something greater than the gods of Haran.

In that moment, more than anything I wanted to know ADONAI, the God of Abraham. But to speak my desire before these men, before my father, would be to invite scorn, perhaps even disgrace.

So I lowered my eyes and sipped from a cup, letting the question hang in the air.

The night stretched, filled with voices that spoke of futures I did not desire. In the flickering lamplight, I clenched my hands beneath the table and prayed I would not be like my mother or grandmother, who were married to Haran as much as to their husbands.

Somehow, I wanted to walk a different path.

WHEN THE MEN had gone and the house had fallen silent, I lay in the dark, too troubled to sleep. My chamber was silent but for the whisper of the wind slipping through the narrow window and Deborah's light snoring. I rolled out of bed, my bare feet cool against the stone floor. I stepped lightly, careful not to wake my nurse, and moved to the wide window that looked out into the courtyard.

The night sky stretched vast and unbroken before me, the stars glinting like scattered silver coins. I rested my arms on the windowsill and studied the inky heavens.

"Adonai," I whispered, the name unfamiliar on my tongue. "I do not know you, yet I know you are there."

My grandparents had told me so many stories, and I wanted to believe all of them. Of Sarah, barren for decades, who bore a son at the age of ninety. Of how she was transformed, her body made youthful again, so she could nurse her son and dance with her husband.

I had heard how mighty Pharaoh feared Abraham and lavished him with slaves, cattle, and camels. How the king of the Philistines had done the same. The people of Canaan called Abraham a prince, a man of wisdom and favor, all because of the God he served—the One he called Adonai.

My fingers tightened against the stone ledge. How did one speak to a God who worked miracles? A God who was not bound to a temple, not carved of wood or stone, but who moved unseen, shaping the world with His will?

"How do I find you?" I asked. "How do I call upon a God who does not dwell in houses built by men?"

I waited, listening. The wind shifted, blowing cool against my face. No voice answered, no sign appeared. Yet something within me steadied, as if the silence itself had spoken.

"I will wait," I whispered. "And I will listen for your voice."

Then, with a heart both restless and resolved, I stepped away from the window and returned to bed, cradling the name of Adonai within me like a precious gift not yet unwrapped.

Chapter 2

THE SCENTS OF warm hay and camel musk thickened the air as the morning sun cast long shadows over the tents of Abraham's household. The desert wind stirred the edges of the goatskin panels, a whisper disrupting the stillness of dawn. Eliezer stood before his master, his aged hands clasped before him, his eyes steady upon the man he had served throughout his lifetime.

Nothing remained but this required ritual of responsibility. For some time Eliezer had known what would be required of him, and he had made the necessary preparations.

Abraham, now old and heavy with years, sat beneath the awning of his spacious dwelling, his face lined like the cracked earth after the rains had gone. Yet his voice, though weakened by time, still rang with authority.

"Swear to me, Eliezer," he said, his voice hoarse, "that you will not take a wife for my son from among the Canaanites, but instead you will go to my kindred in Haran. Find a bride for Isaac, one willing to leave her home and come to this land."

Eliezer knelt, sliding his hand beneath his master's upper thigh in the custom of sacred oaths. "Master, I swear it. But what if she will not come with me? Should I bring your son to her?"

Abraham's eyes darkened. "No. Isaac must not return there. ADONAI has promised this land to my descendants, so the woman must come willingly."

A gust of wind lifted a flap of the tent, sending a whirlwind of dust into the morning light. Eliezer bowed. "I will fulfill your will, master."

"Everything has been prepared for your departure. May ADONAI go with you."

Eliezer turned. From the shadows, the camel singer approached with a line of ten camels, their saddles draped with tapestries and their baskets laden with gifts: jewelry, fine garments, and other precious items from Abraham's household.

Eliezer took the reins of the lead camel. The burden of responsibility settled on his shoulders as he ordered the animal to kneel and mounted the beast.

As the rising sun warmed the hills surrounding Beersheba, he commanded the camel to rise and set out on the long road to Haran.

ELIEZER CLUNG TO a strap on his swaying camel, the back of his hand dotted with perspiration. For two days they had been traveling toward Haran, and dust coated his sandals and garments. Behind him stretched the caravan, the ninth camel walking unburdened save for water jars and a saddle for its intended rider, the unknown bride.

"Sing, Rafel," Eliezer called over his shoulder. "The beasts grow sluggish."

Rafel, Abraham's renowned camel singer, cleared his throat and launched into a particularly grating melody. While the other servants groaned, the camels pricked their ears and quickened their pace. Eliezer had insisted on bringing Rafel for precisely this reason, as the camels responded to his awful singing with vigor, as if they, too, were eager to escape the sound.

As they traveled the King's Highway, Eliezer pondered the task his master had given him. Finding a bride for Isaac was no small responsibility. Abraham had been specific: the woman must come from his kindred in Haran. Beyond that directive, the choice rested on Eliezer's shoulders. For his part, Eliezer was content to leave the choice to ADONAI.

Eliezer squinted at the horizon and wondered what kind of woman the Lord would select for Isaac. Would she possess the quiet strength of Isaac's mother? Sarah had been beautiful, even in her advanced years, with her beauty matched only by her formidable spirit. She had managed Abraham's large household with quiet efficiency and maintained her dignity in the courts of foreign kings. She had even managed Abraham on a few occasions and freely spoke her mind.

Perhaps ADONAI would choose someone entirely different—a young woman with a cheerful disposition who would bring laughter to Isaac's somber face. Though a mature man of forty, Isaac had not fully recovered from his experience on Mount Moriah. Something in him had changed that day, something that could not be completely explained by his grief over his mother. No, the young man's personality had become more reserved, more contemplative. He needed someone who could draw him out of his brooding silence.

As the afternoon sun assailed the caravan, Eliezer's concerns multiplied. Would the bride be adaptable to life in Canaan? The life of a nomadic herdsman was not easy, especially for someone accustomed to a bustling city like Haran. Abraham's household moved with the seasons, following water and grazing land. Their goatskin tents were comfortable but simple. How would a city dweller adjust to life under the open sky, to sandstorms and water shortages?

What if the bride was spoiled or prone to complaining? Such a woman would make life difficult, not only for Isaac but for the entire household. During his tenure as steward, Eliezer had seen how a dissatisfied wife could sow discord throughout the entire camp. Many times Abraham had sent him to tell a lingering guest that the hour had come for his party to move on.

Rafel suddenly released a piercing high note, raising the hair at the back of Eliezer's neck. The camels lurched forward with renewed energy, and Eliezer clung to his saddle.

"Not so fast, Rafel," he called. "We still have many miles to go."

As their mounts settled back into a steady rhythm, Eliezer's thoughts returned to his task. How long would this mission take? If he found a suitable bride right away, they might return to Canaan within a fortnight. But what if the girl's family insisted on a lengthy betrothal? Abraham was not a young man; he yearned to see his son become a husband and father before his death.

Eliezer frowned, realizing he might have underestimated his task. Would this young woman come willingly, or would she find excuses to delay? Abraham would not want Eliezer to coerce a woman into marriage. Their union must begin with willingness, even eagerness, on both sides.

What if the bride was reluctant? Some women might balk at the prospect of traveling so far to marry a man they had never met. What if she insisted on an escape clause should she be displeased with Isaac's manner or appearance?

And what of Isaac himself? What if he did not care for the woman Eliezer selected? Isaac had always been obedient to his father, but marriage was a lifetime commitment. If Isaac found his bride displeasing, what could he do? Would Eliezer have to return her to Haran? If that happened, the woman would be viewed as rejected, unwanted. She might not overcome the shame.

"ADONAI, God of my master Abraham," Eliezer prayed as the caravan approached an oasis, "direct my path. Show me the woman you have selected for Isaac. Make my way plain and clear."

As the servants watered the camels and began to prepare the evening meal, Eliezer removed himself from the others and watched the sun sink toward the western horizon. Tomorrow they would reach the outskirts of Haran. Soon he would stand at the city well, watering the camels and asking ADONAI to reveal the woman who should become Isaac's bride. The woman who, like Sarah, would become the mother of multitudes.

The responsibility of his assignment weighed heavily upon him, yet quiet confidence lay beneath his concern. The God who had guided Abraham from Ur to Canaan, and who had given him a son in his old age, would surely guide Eliezer now. He would not fail. Somehow, he would recognize the right woman when he saw her.

Chapter 3

THE SUN HAD not yet risen when Father came to wake me. His sandals scraped against the tiled floor, a soft accompaniment to the distant bleating of sheep and Deborah's gentle snores. I had been awake for some time, studying the ceiling as darkness gave way to the first pale hints of dawn.

"Rebekah." Father's voice was firm, like the hand with which he jostled my foot. I lifted my head to look at him, and even in the dim light I could see the lines of concern etched into his face. "We must speak."

I sat up and pulled my wool blanket around my shoulders. I knew why he had come.

"Your suitors grow impatient," he said, settling himself on the edge of my bed. "All five have sent word asking for your reply. They will not wait forever, and you are of age. I must give them an answer."

I swallowed over the lump in my throat. "When?" I managed to ask. "When must you tell them something?"

"Tonight." The word fell between us like a stone dropped into a well. "By nightfall you must choose one of them to be your husband."

The finality in his voice sent a shiver through me. I had been dreading this moment since the dinner where all five men appraised me like a ewe at the market. Perhaps I could persuade Father to wait.

"Father—" I began, but he lifted his hand.

"No more delay, Rebekah. You are fortunate to have such prospects. Any one of those men would provide well for you. Five suitors, and all are men of means! You will be married to wealth, and that is not a thing to take for granted. Your mother and I could never have imagined such fortune when first we wed." He stood, his knees creaking. "Spend the day in thought and prayer. By sunset I will expect your decision."

"And if I cannot decide?"

"Then I will decide for you."

After he had gone, I remained in my bed, watching Deborah sleep. I could hear the household stirring outside the door: the scrape of the quern as Mother prepared flour for bread, the splash of water as someone drew from the household cistern, the clatter of cooking vessels.

I pressed my palms against my eyes and the tears that threatened to overflow their banks.

Five men. Five futures. And I wanted none of them.

ONCE DEBORAH AWOKE, I rose and dressed, then allowed her to tie back my hair and secure it beneath a scarf. "What troubles you?" she asked, tucking stray hairs beneath the fabric. "You are trembling, pet."

I shook my head. I loved Deborah, but I did not want to hear her thoughts about the men who waited for my answer. Since she would likely go with me to my husband's house, she was not exactly impartial.

"I am anxious," I admitted. "How can I be calm with my father pressuring me to make a decision by sunset?"

I slipped out of my chamber and walked into the central courtyard of our home. The cool morning air carried the aroma of freshly baked bread. Mother glanced up as I passed, her eyes questioning, but I could not bear to speak with her yet. She had been so pleased by the attention shown to me, especially from Nadab, whose riches would elevate our family's standing considerably.

I made my way to the cistern at the end of the courtyard, then drew water to wash my face. The cool liquid helped clear my thoughts. I closed my eyes, letting droplets trace paths down my cheeks.

"Adonai," I whispered. My father occasionally mentioned this God along with other deities, probably more out of respect for his uncle than true faith. But something in me had always been drawn to the stories of the invisible God who spoke to people, made promises, and kept them.

"Adonai, if you are real, if you can hear me . . . show me what to do. I am afraid."

I heard nothing but the cooing of doves in the nearby palms. What had I expected? A voice from the heavens? A sign reflected in the water? The God of Abraham lived in Canaan, not in Haran. The old gods held sway here.

The day stretched before me like an unfinished tapestry, its patterns not yet woven into place. I went about my chores mechanically—grinding grain, carrying water, helping Mother and Deborah prepare the midday meal. All the while, my mind churned with thoughts of my five possible futures.

Would I be a respected widow's replacement, managing Nadab's household with dignity but without being loved? Would I spend my nights avoiding Kemuel's drunken advances? Would I slowly wither beside the passionless Aram? Would I be merely another possession to Ephron, like his copper ingots? Or would I be forced to support Zimran as he conducted his priestly rituals for a pantheon of gods?

By midday my head ached from the pressure of foreboding thoughts, and anxiety squeezed my heart like an olive in the press. I sought refuge in the small storage room where Mother kept the winter grain, sinking to the floor between a pair of heavy clay jars.

"There you are." Laban's voice broke the silence. He stood in the doorway, his broad frame blocking much of the light. "Mother is looking for you."

I nodded but made no move to rise.

Laban crouched in front of me. "Father told me about the urgency of your decision." His voice held none of its usual brashness. "What will you do?"

I stared at my folded hands. "How can I choose? I feel no more than polite regard for any of them."

My brother clicked his tongue. "Marriage has nothing to do with feeling, sister. It is about survival and security. You are fortunate to have such prospects."

"So Father has said," I replied, unable to keep a note of bitterness from my voice.

Laban took my hand in his. "I do not know if this is helpful, but I think you should choose Nadab. He is old, yes, but he is greatly respected. His sons already manage much of his business. He would treat you with dignity, and"—Laban shrugged—"he will not live forever."

I drew back, surprised by his candor. "You think I should choose based on how soon a husband might die?"

A wry smile twisted Laban's lips. "I think you should choose the path that gives you the most wealth and freedom. As a widow of means, you would have far more choices than you have now."

His pragmatism both shocked and comforted me. At least he was being honest and not dressing up the transaction with ridiculous words about love and devotion.

"Thank you," I said. "I will consider your advice."

Laban stood. "Always consider your prosperity first. With wealth, you are certain to be happy."

After he had gone, I rested my chin on my knees and pondered my brother's words. Was Nadab my best hope? Should I marry an old man and wait for widowhood to gain a measure of independence? But after that, what would I do with my life?

"ADONAI," I whispered into the stillness, "my heart is not moved by any of these five. Is there no other man who would have me?"

THE AFTERNOON PASSED in a blur of household duties and whispered conversations. My mother cornered me by the olive press, extolling Nadab's virtues and the comfort his riches would bring. When I went out to beat the dust from our carpets, the young girls from our street giggled and asked if I was excited to become a bride and have my own house. They were so young—how could they understand the knot of dread that tightened my stomach with each passing hour?

As the sun began its descent, Father found me sitting beneath the date palms growing outside our city gates. He sat beside me, bracing his hands on his knees, and I wondered if he had already chosen a man to be my husband. The evening breeze stirred the fronds above us, creating shifting patterns of light and shadow across his face.

"The time has come," he said, his tone leaving no room for argument. "Have you chosen a man to marry, or would you like me to choose for you?"

I looked into his eyes, searching for some sign that I might be allowed to refuse them all, that I could wait for . . . for what? For whom?

"Father, I—" As my voice faltered, my gaze drifted to the road that led away from the men awaiting my father's message. That road led southward, eventually to the lands of Canaan and Egypt. What would it be like to travel that road, to leave Haran behind and seek a new life elsewhere?

But I was not Sarah, and that was not my path. I was the daughter of Bethuel, granddaughter of Nahor, great-granddaughter of Terah. My place was here, and my future lay with a man from Haran.

I drew a trembling breath. "Father, I have prayed—"

A disturbance on the road distracted me. A man on a donkey came riding toward us, waving with one hand as he guided his mount with the other. "Who is that?" I asked, grateful for the interruption.

Father squinted. "Is that one of our neighbors?"

Soon the stranger was close enough for me to recognize him as a trader from our market. He recognized my father and began to wave more vigorously.

"Bethuel!" He smiled when he finally reached us. "I am glad to see you. A caravan of many camels approaches, and the leader asked for you by name."

Father stood, his brow furrowed. "Is the caravan from Damascus?"

"I do not know. But the men plan to visit your house."

Father glanced at me, his expression unreadable. "It seems your decision must wait a bit longer, Rebekah. Come, we must go tell your mother to prepare for visitors."

As we walked home, my heart pounded with an odd mixture of fear and hope. Travelers from the south coming to our home on this day of all days. Was this coincidence, or could it be an answer to my prayer?

Once we reached the house, Father went immediately to search for my mother. Visitors had to be shown hospitality, so she would have to prepare food and arrange accommodation for our guests. I took advantage of Father's distraction to grab my water jar and slip away from the house. Father would be irritated to find me gone, but I wanted to see the visitors for myself.

At this late hour, the world beyond the city walls seemed to pulse with a slower rhythm. The air, imbued with the smells of sun-warmed earth and wild herbs, wrapped around me like a soft blanket. I placed my water jar on my head and made my way toward the ancient spring, my troubled thoughts erased by this welcome intrusion into our routine.

In the distance, I spotted a dust cloud. The trader was correct, for a caravan had appeared on the shimmering road. I lowered my water jug and hid myself among the fronds of a palm to watch its approach, my heart beating in gratitude with every step of the camels. By the time the rhythmic thump of their hooves reached my ears, details had come into focus: I counted ten camels carrying loaded baskets, a camel singer yowling on the lead beast, and an old man riding behind the singer.

Overcome by sudden shyness, I leaned against the palm tree and waited while the caravan stopped at the spring. The camel singer commanded the beasts to kneel, which they did, tipping forward and then back, nearly unseating the men who rode behind their humps. The old man dismounted carefully, pressing a hand to his lower back as he straightened.

I had never seen anyone like this elderly man. While the other servants called to each other and strode toward the water, the man closed his eyes and lifted his face to the heavens. Was he praying? He had not unpacked any idols, so to which God was he addressing his prayer?

A flicker of hope ignited within me. The old man's peaceful attitude suggested a connection to a powerful God. One who did not need to be represented by a carved image. Could this man be a worshiper of ADONAI? The thought stirred me. Had I not been praying to my kinsmen's God?

I stood transfixed among the palm fronds. The murmur of the servants, the beating of my heart, and the persistent whisper of the wind converged, sharpening my senses and heightening my inner tumult.

I had been praying to Adonai, and here were people from the south. Though I did not know who they were or why they had come, they had asked for my father so they might stay a few days. Perhaps, if Adonai had heard my prayers, they could suggest a different life for me, something unlike the fate awaiting me in Haran. I could be a servant in my great-uncle's camp, I could be a lady's handmaid, or I could weave for them or care for their sheep.

In my hiding place, my heart dared to wonder if this old man, with his face lifted in sincere devotion, might be a harbinger of a life wherein I walked a different path. Perhaps this caravan and its enigmatic leader might allow me to be shaped by more than my parents' desire for me to be offered wealth and stability.

I closed my eyes, desperately hoping for Adonai to answer my prayers.

Chapter

— 4 —

WHEN ELIEZER REACHED the well, the first hints of evening had begun to paint the sky in soft oranges and deep purples. The ancient spring, part of which had been fortified with a stone wall, was surrounded by patches of scrubby grass and bleached palm trees. Eliezer's lips were parched, his throat dry from the day's journey. As he dismounted his camel, his heart stirred with expectant hope.

Once his aged bones had adjusted to standing erect, Eliezer lifted his eyes to heaven and offered a desperate plea. "ADONAI," he prayed, "God of Abraham, please make something happen before me today, and show loyalty to Abraham, my master. Look, I am standing by the spring, and the daughters of the men of the city are going out to draw water. Now let it be that the young woman to whom I say, 'Please tip your jar so that I may drink,' and she will say, 'Drink, and I will also water your camels'—let her be the one you have appointed for your servant Isaac. So by this I will know that you have shown graciousness to my master."

With each breath he felt the responsibility of his master's trust. His fingers, rough and trembling, clutched at his robe as he finished speaking . . . and waited.

A young woman appeared.

Eliezer blinked, not certain if she was real or a figment of his imagination. Her skin was the color of rich honey, her dark eyes bright and alert. She gave him a glancing smile, then went down to the spring and filled her water jar.

Eliezer walked toward her on legs that seemed to have a will of their own. He cleared his throat and heard himself speaking: "I am Eliezer, from Canaan. Please let me sip a little water from your jar."

She could have refused. She would have been excused, even praised, for retreating from a strange man.

Instead, she smiled and said, "Drink, my lord," and she tipped her water jar so he could quench his thirst.

Never had any water tasted sweeter. Eliezer drank his fill, then straightened, wiped the wetness from his mouth, and drew a breath to thank her.

But she spoke first. "I will also draw water for your camels until they have finished drinking." Her voice was clear and kind, not the hesitant murmur of a shy girl, but the confident tone of a woman accustomed to direct speech. While Eliezer watched in amazement, she poured the contents of her jar into a trough, then hurried back to the spring.

The effort of watering ten camels would be no small task, for each camel could drink an entire trough dry after a long journey. This maiden's arms would burn with the effort, her muscles straining as she lifted the heavy jar again and again. Sweat would pearl on her forehead, her breath coming in measured rhythms as she worked.

Yet Eliezer sat and watched as she fulfilled her offer, showing no sign of complaint or even a hint of reluctance. His eyes misted as he watched her work. The kindness she demonstrated went beyond routine hospitality; it sprang from genuine compassion, a caring not unlike the tender mercies of ADONAI. His heart filled with gratitude and wonder.

When the last camel had begun to drink, Eliezer went to his beast and removed the silver chest Abraham had given him. From it he withdrew the gold nose ring and matching bracelets that had been fashioned from gold shekels.

The precious gifts caught the last rays of sunlight as he walked over to her. "Whose daughter are you?" he asked, his voice trembling. "Please tell me. Is there room in your father's house for us to spend the night?"

The young woman flushed. "I am Rebekah, daughter of Bethuel, son of Milcah and Nahor," she answered. "We have straw and plenty of feed in our house, as well as room for you and your companions to spend the night."

Eliezer nodded, then presented her with the nose ring and bracelets. As she stared, mouth agape, he bowed himself to the earth. "Blessed be ADONAI, the God of my master Abraham, who has not forsaken His loyalty and His truth toward my master. As for me, ADONAI has guided me in the way to the house of my master's brothers."

The young woman looked at him, her eyes wide with wonder, and then she hurried away, leaving her jar behind. Eliezer smiled, knowing she had gone to share the news of their arrival.

Her home would soon be alive with the sounds of conversation, the aroma of roasting meat, and the warmth of unexpected guests. The young woman would tell her story, and Eliezer would tell his. Until then, he would pray that ADONAI would continue to work His will.

His smile deepened. In this moment, at this spring, the threads of ADONAI's promise were being woven into a glorious tapestry.

MY HEART RACED as I ran home, my arm—now heavy with gold bracelets—pressed against my chest. I burst through the doorway, my breath coming in gasps.

"Father!" I called, my voice shrill. "Eliezer—a servant of Abraham—is at the well and asks if he and his men can stay with us."

Mother looked up from her cut vegetables, and Father turned from the hearth where he had been peering at the evening meal. Though the rich aroma of roasting lamb and fresh-baked bread filled the air, dinner was momentarily forgotten as every eye turned toward me.

Laban pointed to the gold on my arms. "What is that?" he asked, his voice sharp.

The story spilled from my lips—how the old man had been praying at the well, how I had offered water to him and his camels, how he had given me magnificent gifts. With each word, amazement widened my parents' eyes.

"He said he had been sent by Abraham and asked if he could stay with us tonight."

My father listened intently, stroking his beard, exchanging a meaningful glance with my mother. "You were wise to add meat to the stew. Apparently, we will have many guests."

"Where is this stranger now?" Laban demanded.

"At the spring," I replied. "He is waiting for Father's answer."

No sooner had the words left my mouth than Laban rushed out, his excitement apparently matching my own. Deborah poured fresh water into a shallow bowl to set by the front door, ready to wash the dust from the travelers' feet. Mother added lentils to the stew and sprinkled it with additional seasonings.

"I do not know what sort of foods they are accustomed to," she said, her brow furrowed. "Abraham is rich beyond measure."

"I do not think you need to worry," I told her. "Anything you can provide for those hungry men will be appreciated."

When Laban returned with Eliezer and the other servants, our house rang with the happy sounds of hospitality. Our servants tended to the camels, and Deborah supplied water for washing hands and feet. Father replaced Eliezer's dusty travel garments with a clean tunic, then asked him to sit at the head of the table, while Mother set out a meal of bread, meat, olives, and wine.

But Eliezer had more than food on his mind. "I will not eat," he declared, "until I have told you the purpose of my journey."

Father sat across from him and folded his arms. "Then speak."

Eliezer spoke in a measured voice, explaining his mission with a gravity that silenced our entire household. He spoke of Abraham, of Isaac, and of the oath he had sworn. He described how he had prayed at the well, and how Adonai had answered his prayer through me.

As he spoke, I watched my family members. Father's face shifted from curiosity to wonder. Mother wore an expression of delight from the beginning to the end of Eliezer's speech. Laban's expression shifted from wonder to skepticism, then to wonder again as he studied the jewelry on my arm. The gold bracelets glowed in the lamplight, a testament to the extraordinary situation that had unfolded in our household.

"If you are willing to demonstrate loyalty and truth to my master," Eliezer concluded, "tell me at once. If not, I will turn to the right or to the left."

Laban and my father exchanged glances that spoke volumes. Their eyes sparked with calculation, and I could see how they appreciated Abraham's wealth, the honor of the connection with our kinsman, and the potential blessing that might come to our family. They had also heard the unspoken ultimatum in Eliezer's words—if they refused him, he would take his leave and continue the search for a bride for Abraham's son.

Eliezer's words lingered in the atmosphere as the oil lamps flickered, casting dancing shadows across the walls. I held my breath, awaiting the outcome of my prayers.

"This thing comes from the Lord," my father finally said, his voice trembling. "We cannot speak ill or good."

Laban, never one to hesitate in the face of profit, responded more fully. "The matter is from the Lord," he agreed. "Here is Rebekah. Take her and go. Let her be the wife of your master's son, as the Lord has spoken."

The room seemed to spin around me. I would soon leave everything I knew—my family, my home, my city—to marry a man I had never met, following a path that seemed ordained by a God I knew by name only.

While I sat in silent amazement, Abraham's servants brought out more gifts for my dowry: beautiful garments, silver and gold coins, and jewelry. The gifts were not only for me; my mother and Laban were also presented with expensive garments and coins.

As everyone focused on the waiting dinner, I took my new garments to my chamber. Deborah caught and embraced me, her tears mixing with her smile. "My precious pet," she whispered, her voice catching, "may you become the mother of thousands of ten thousands."

Before retiring for the night, Eliezer bowed before my father, his weathered face displaying a mixture of gratitude and relief. "Our long journey and my prayers have been answered," he said, nodding at my parents. "Thank you for your hospitality, and may Adonai bless you." Then he turned his smile upon me. "And may Adonai bless the bride."

THE NEXT MORNING, Laban and my parents were in the midst of planning a betrothal feast when Eliezer entered the room and stated his intention to return to Canaan immediately.

Laban and Mother raised a fuss. "Let her stay with us a few more days," Mother said.

"Ten days," Laban added, probably thinking of the gifts our family would receive. "Afterward, she may go."

But Eliezer would not be swayed. "Do not delay me," he said, meeting Laban's eyes. "Since Adonai has made my way successful, send me off so I can return to my master."

After several weak protestations, my family turned to me. Father looked at me with sadness in his eyes as he asked, "Daughter, will you go with this man?"

The choice, ultimately, was mine. I swallowed hard, remembering that only the day before, I had not wanted to marry anyone.

"Will you go?" my father repeated.

Memories played before my eyes—the stranger at the well, his earnest prayer, and my aching arms and legs. Yet I had kept filling my water jug, knowing that to stop would be undeniably *wrong*.

Adonai, the God of Abraham, seemed to be weaving something extraordinary for my life.

But this extraordinary plan would come at great cost. I would have to leave my home, my parents, and my brother. I would have to leave a civilized city and live in a primitive land of rocks and sand beneath a blistering sun. From what I had heard, Abraham and his family did not live in a house, but in tents. Could I live that way?

And of his son—what if this Isaac was less appealing than the five men who had sat at Father's dinner table? What if he was cruel or crude or cranky? What if I married him and regretted my decision three months later? I would have no way back to my old life.

I closed my eyes. Had I not prayed to Adonai? How could I ask Him to provide me with a husband and then question His answer?

I met Father's eye. "I will go."

Those three words sparked a flurry of activity in our household. Deborah gathered my most precious belongings: lovingly woven garments, family keepsakes, and treasures accumulated over the years. Father moved with purposeful energy, selecting the finest provisions for our journey, negotiating last-minute details with Eliezer. Mother pulled pita bread and dried meat from the pantry, packing baskets so Deborah and I would not starve on the journey to Abraham's camp.

As the sun climbed to its highest point, my heart pounded with both excitement and deep sadness. I would be leaving everything I had ever known to live in a place I had never visited.

Deborah's hands trembled as she braided my hair. "My pet," she said, her voice thick, "you are the heart of your family. We will miss you terribly."

I turned to face her. "You will not." Her eyes widened with hurt, but I caught her hands and smiled. "Surely you know that you must come with me. Father would not send me to a strange land alone."

Her eyes filled as she nodded. "Of course I will come. My place is at your side."

Chapter 5

WHEN THE PREPARATIONS were complete, the camels loaded, and our bellies filled, my father offered a simple prayer that seemed to reach beyond our small courtyard and connect us to something larger and more mysterious: "May the gods of our fathers and the God of Abraham preserve our daughter and bless her in her new life."

Laban approached me one last time. "Take care, my sister," he said, his customary tone softened by affection. He pressed a wooden carving into my hand. It was a rudimentary image of our house, something to remind me of my family.

Then my parents and our servants crowded around me to bestow a blessing: "Our sister, may you become thousands of ten thousands, and may your seed possess the gate of those who hate them."

I embraced my family and walked toward the camel that had been reserved for me and Deborah.

The journey would be arduous, crossing landscapes I had only heard about in stories. Deborah and I wore lightweight traveling clothes, plain and practical, but I could not resist wearing my new bracelets. "Keep your arms hidden inside your cloak," Deborah told me. "The sun shining on that gold might attract a thief, so do not let anyone else see it."

As the camels rocked upward from their kneeling positions, I clung to our animal's hump and looked back at my childhood home. The familiar courtyard, kitchen hearth, the palm trees that had witnessed countless family stories—all of it would soon become a memory.

My brother and father and servants walked with us to the city gate and cheered as we departed, a cluster of familiar faces that grew smaller as the singer yowled and the camels loped away.

I did not know what ADONAI would do with my life, but I knew what awaited me in Canaan: a husband I had never met, a land I had never seen, and a destiny that seemed to have chosen me even as I yearned for it.

While Deborah clung to me—the poor woman was terrified of falling from the camel—a sense of peace filled my soul. I knew, without doubt, that the God who had answered Eliezer's prayer and arranged this journey would be with me.

THE THREE-DAY JOURNEY from Haran to Beersheba led us through an endless vista of sand and sky. Each day the sun beat down on us, transforming the dunes into glowing golden waves. And each night, Deborah and I slept in a makeshift tent surrounded by Abraham's servants, the cold breath of the sunless desert making us shiver beneath our cloaks.

When we stopped on that first night, the servants erected a cluster of tents beneath a tapestry of stars. As they set up our shelters, Deborah and I found Eliezer sitting by a low-burning fire. Illuminated by the flickering flames, his face shone like a beacon amid the bustle of activity.

"Please," I begged, my voice trembling, "will you tell me of the man I am to marry? I have heard only whispers of Isaac's history, and I long to know as much as you can share."

Eliezer's eyes, deep and knowing, regarded me for a moment, and then he gestured for us to join him by the fire.

Deborah and I sat as Eliezer cleared his throat. "My master's son is a man of quiet faith and deep contemplation. He walks the fields at evening to pray and seek ADONAI's wisdom." The steward's voice grew tender. "He is gentle in spirit but strong in his convictions."

"Does he ever laugh?" I asked, surprising myself with my bluntness.

A shadow passed over Eliezer's face. "His name means laughter, but my young master does not laugh as often as he once did. The death of his mother three years ago left a wound that has not fully healed. Sarah was everything to him—his guide, counselor, and teacher. Since her passing, a melancholy mood has hovered over him."

My fingers twisted the edge of my cloak. "And his father? How does Abraham fare with his grief?"

"My master Abraham loves his son beyond measure." Eliezer glanced at me as if hesitant to continue, but then his words increased their speed. "After Sarah's death, my master longed for companionship, so a woman called Keturah now lives with him. Isaac stands somewhat aloof, tending the flocks and diligently managing his father's holdings, but loneliness dwells in him. A yearning that calls out for completion."

The fire crackled before us, sending a stream of sparks into the darkness. Watching them, I thought of Laban, of how my parents loved him visibly and completely while my own worth seemed to be measured by the tasks I could perform. That inequity had hollowed my chest and filled me with unhappiness. I, too, longed for completion.

"Has Abraham other wives?" I asked, already knowing part of the answer. "Any other children?"

"His firstborn was Ishmael, son of Hagar," Eliezer said. "But Hagar was a concubine, so Ishmael and his mother were sent away when Isaac was a small child. Keturah is also a concubine and not a legal wife. If she has children, they will not inherit from my master."

I nodded as understanding bloomed. Favorites and cast-asides—both had been found in families since the beginning of time.

I held my hands closer to the fire, letting its warmth caress my fingers as I made a decision: my family would not be like others. ADONAI had chosen me for Isaac, so our union would be unique. We would not be prone to the problems that plagued other families.

Straightening my spine, I announced my declaration not only to Deborah and Eliezer but to the listening heavens. "I will be a wife to Isaac in every way that matters," I vowed, my voice gaining strength with each word. "I will comfort him in his grief, becoming the joy his heart has lost. I will fill his home with the laughter of children, giving him the family for which he yearns." My hand moved to my belly, as if I were already cradling the promise of future generations. "I make this vow before all who hear me now," I continued. "I will never love one child more than another. Each child will know the fullness of a mother's heart without preference or partiality. No child of mine will bear the wound of being less favored, less cherished, or less seen."

Deborah caught my hand, her fingers enclosing mine with surprising strength. "A righteous vow," she said, "but one that might be tested."

"Then let it be." The desert wind caught my words and carried them upward. "Because I have known the sting of second place, I will never inflict that pain on one of my children."

A log toppled in the fire, sending another flurry of sparks into the night. I watched them rise as the desert wind merged with the burgeoning hope in my heart. In that instant, the ancient stories and the miracle of my calling intertwined, and I knew my every hardship, tear, and prayer had led me to this moment.

Soon I would look upon the face of my husband. I would begin to fulfill the promises I had just made . . . promises born from the wounds of my past and the hope for our shared future.

Chapter 6

ISAAC WALKED THROUGH the endless desert, each step stirring up fine, scorching sand. The steady sun hammered him, baking his lips and throat. He had come from Beer-lahai-roi—*Well of the Living One Who Sees Me*—the place Hagar named after her encounter with ADONAI. Isaac had camped by that place for several days, yet despite his longing for the same experience, ADONAI had not revealed himself.

The silence of the desert mirrored the silence in Isaac's heart.

For two years after his mother's death, he had sat at the feet of Noah's descendants Shem and Eber, absorbing the ancient wisdom of the Lord, filling his mind with the lore and laws that promised a blessed destiny. But that knowledge did little to ease the void left by his beloved mother, now gone for three long years. All that remained of her was the memory of a soft voice, a tender touch, and a conviction that no one would ever love him like she did.

As he trudged across the sunlit dunes, Isaac's thoughts turned inward. With unwavering certainty his parents had believed that he was the chosen heir, destined to bear sons and continue a legacy of divine favor. Yet every step he took deepened his doubts. How could he be chosen when the God who had appeared so often to his father had yet to appear to him? He looked for signs of ADONAI's presence everywhere—in the fields, in his tent, beneath the stars—but the Lord seemed indifferent to his pleas for confirmation.

As he neared his father's camp, movement in the landscape caught his eye: a caravan emerging from the undulating heat waves. He saw camels laden with supplies, servants clothed like desert-dwellers, and an old man whose quiet demeanor distinguished him even from a distance.

Isaac watched as the caravan grew closer. Then the ram's horn sounded from the lookout at his father's camp. The camels, seeking food and water, increased their pace as the caravan proceeded toward Isaac's home.

Who were these people? Isaac studied the lead rider, whose head was swathed in cloth for protection against the sun. Whoever he was, he appeared to be asleep or engrossed in prayer.

Isaac increased his own stride, drawn forward by curiosity about the visitors. Had they come solely to honor the renowned Abraham? If so, what, if anything, did their presence portend for him, a mere shadow in the light of his father's reputation?

FROM MY PERCH atop the camel, the encampment that sprawled before us appeared to be a city of goatskin and rope, of bleating sheep and cattle. A lookout signaled our approach, and the sound of the ram's horn stirred something in my soul.

Had I finally reached my new home?

Eliezer waved to the lookout, who shouted a response. The camels must have known they were close to food, water, and rest because they lengthened their strides. But as they charged ahead, movement from the camp's periphery caught my attention. A man carrying a staff and spear was striding toward us with an air of quiet determination.

I raised my hand to shade my eyes. The man appeared strong and well-formed, with a dark beard and a striking face. The wind tousled his long, dark hair, and my heart quickened at the sight of him.

I lowered my eyes at once. I could not allow myself to be distracted by a handsome shepherd, not when I had agreed to marry Abraham's son.

I turned in the saddle, intending to say something to Deborah, but my movement was too abrupt and the camel's trot too uneven. Before I could steady myself, the world tilted and I tumbled from the saddle, landing facedown in a powdery cloud of sand. Despite my embarrassment, or perhaps because of it, laughter bubbled up from within me as I brushed the gritty particles from my cheeks and neck.

"Rebekah!" Deborah's voice rang with concern and rebuke. "You should be more careful, pet. Are you injured?"

I smiled, shaking off my embarrassment as I scrambled to my feet. "Please," I called, running to catch up, "we are close, and so will you drop my veil?"

I could not meet my future groom or father-in-law looking like the sort of woman who followed caravans. After Deborah lowered the veil I had shed in the heat, I draped it over my shoulders.

Eliezer must have heard our shouts because he halted the camels outside the gate and issued a command to kneel. The camels balked, their long-lashed, soulful eyes betraying a longing for the water and food that waited inside the walls.

As I stood on the sand, waiting for direction, my thoughts turned to the shepherd I had seen outside the camp. I strode past the other riders and met Eliezer, who stood at the front of the caravan as if waiting . . . for what?

"Eliezer," I called, lifting my voice to be heard above the wind, "who is that?" I gestured to the man approaching from the west.

Eliezer's gaze followed mine, then a smile touched the corners of his chapped lips. "He is my master."

That could not be Abraham. The man was far too young, so perhaps this was the old man's idea of a jest. I lifted a brow. "Who is he truly?"

"If ADONAI wills," he whispered, his smile broadening, "you will soon meet him."

I glanced at the shepherd again as he drew nearer. If the man was not Abraham, he had to be my future husband.

After an instant of shock, I whipped my veil from my shoulders and draped it over my head. I could not meet Isaac without maintaining at least a modicum of respectability.

Suitably clothed, I studied the man coming our way. My heart stuttered, caught between the shock of revelation and the stirring of something for which I had no words.

In that moment, the vastness of the desert, the moaning of the wind, and the tinkle of camel bells merged into a singular realization: the desert, the wind, the bells, and the man were about to become the essence of my life.

"Come," Eliezer said, gesturing to the gate. "Let me introduce you to Abraham."

DEBORAH AND I followed Eliezer through the draped fabrics and shadowed chambers of a large tent where the scents of cedar and incense combined with the soft aroma of baked bread. The cool interior offered a welcome reprieve from the relentless sun, and I could almost hear the whispered stories of previous occupants in the soft rustle of the woven curtains.

At the center of the dwelling, an old man with hair as white as the sands sat surrounded by a mountain of plush cushions. He rose to greet me, his movements slow and deliberate, his eyes reflecting a lifetime of wisdom. I lowered myself and bowed before him, grateful for the soft carpet under my knees.

"Blessed be ADONAI," Eliezer said, his voice filling the space between the goatskin walls. "Rebekah, daughter of Bethuel, has agreed to be Isaac's wife. She is accompanied by her nurse, Deborah."

The words fell upon my ears like a sacred decree, and a sense of destiny settled in my heart. Before I could fully gather my thoughts, my great-uncle—the renowned Abraham—stepped forward. "Rise, daughter." I lifted my head and saw that his eyes were sparking with joy.

Then another goatskin portal opened, and the man I had spotted outside entered the space. His dark eyes fixed on the veil that partially concealed my face. Isaac.

Since we had not yet been introduced, I kept my focus on Abraham, as was proper. With a quavering voice, I addressed him, promising to obey him as master of the household and as a father.

His eyes shone as he answered, "I am well pleased to accept you into our home, Rebekah. I only wish Sarah could have met you. She would have loved you." His assuring words wrapped around me like a warm embrace.

Then, in a solemn and clear tone, he asked the all-important question. "Will you agree to marry my son Isaac and become part of our family? To worship Adonai, the Lord God, with us?" His voice gentled. "If you need time to consider . . ."

"I have considered already," I answered in the firmest voice I could manage. "Yes, I will marry your son and live with you. I will worship Adonai with you, for I have seen how He works miracles for those who call on Him."

Isaac, who had stood in silence during this exchange, folded his hands. I marveled at his calm demeanor. He must have known that Abraham had sent Eliezer in search of a bride, but he could not have known we would arrive today, and he could not have known who his bride would be. Was he always so compliant?

Abraham turned. "My son, will you take Rebekah, daughter of our kinsman Bethuel, to be your wife? To live with her, protect her, and love her?"

Isaac's eyes probed my veil, and for an instant I feared he would refuse.

Instead, he nodded. "Father, I will."

"Then you may claim your bride," Abraham declared.

Isaac stepped forward. His hands, warm and steady, reached out and squeezed mine. He then removed my veil, exposing every aspect of my face to his gaze. He gave me a gentle, affirming kiss that sealed his commitment.

Abraham's voice, rich with authority and affection, broke the silence. "Sarah's tent now belongs to the two of you. Rebekah, I will have the servants place your belongings inside. Go in peace, daughter, and welcome to our family."

My heart leapt as Isaac took my elbow and led me out of his father's dwelling. Our wedding had been simple and quick, composed of shared promises and faith. Yet Abraham, Eliezer, and we ourselves had borne witness to the beginning of a life with two strangers promising to become one.

How that would happen, I had no idea.

NIGHT HAD FALLEN by the time all my belongings were delivered, so I dismissed the servants with a nod. Deborah was the last to go. "If you should need me—"

"I will call for you," I said, feigning a confidence I did not feel. "Go, find a place to sleep. I will be fine."

I soon stood alone in Sarah's tent, surrounded by baskets laden with garments and keepsakes from home, the quiet punctuated only by the soft rustling of curtains. I inhaled the subtle fragrance of desert flowers someone had scattered upon the richly adorned bed. The cushions were plush beneath my hand, the petals a delicate reminder of how quickly beauty could fade in this harsh land.

Wanting to be useful, I lit the clay lamps scattered throughout the dwelling. Had Sarah done this when she expected her husband to visit? Or had she left that task for the servants while she pinched her cheeks and combed her hair so she would look beautiful when Abraham entered?

My husband had disappeared when the servants arrived with my things, but finally he returned. Feeling inexplicably exposed without my veil, I greeted him and found myself suspended in the awkward silence between a man and a woman newly joined in marriage.

Isaac's dark eyes met mine, earnest and searching. He took my hand and led me to a carved bench at the foot of the bed, then gestured for me to sit. When he spoke, his voice was soft and reverent. "You are a gift, Rebekah. Thank you for coming."

I mustered a small smile. "I was meant to come," I replied, recalling the moment I realized I had to return with Eliezer.

"You displayed great courage in coming here."

I waved the compliment away. "Thank you, but I think it would have taken more courage to remain in Haran and live a life that did not suit me."

Isaac chuckled. "Are you certain that life in the desert will suit you?"

"I have always been curious about Adonai," I said, my voice softening. "We have heard so much about the exploits of Abraham and Sarah and all that Adonai did for them. We even heard about your miraculous birth." I paused as a blush burned my cheeks. "My mother still marvels that Sarah was able to nurse you at such an advanced age."

When I lifted my head, Isaac was studying my form, his gaze raking me from head to foot. My cheeks heated further as Isaac stood and removed his outer robe, revealing a linen loincloth beneath it. My breath caught at the sight of his bare chest—broad and bronzed by the desert sun, marked with the subtle ridges of a man who had known physical labor despite his father's wealth. I lowered my eyes again, my heart racing.

"Rebekah," he said, his voice gentle. I forced myself to look up despite the heat searing my face. I was no stranger to the full meaning of marriage, yet the reality of this moment—of sitting before a man of forty years—left me feeling as bashful as a child.

He traced my cheek with his hand, his touch featherlight. "Like my mother, you are beautiful," he said. "But you are young still."

A mixture of emotions washed over me: pride that he found me attractive, fear of what lay ahead, and a yearning I scarcely recognized. Mother had prepared me for my duties as a wife, and although I was willing, I could not hide the tremor in my hands.

Isaac noticed. His eyes, warm in the lamplight, softened further. He gestured toward the bed with a gentle nod. "I know you are tired from your journey. You should rest now."

"But—"

"I will not force you," he continued, his voice dropping to a whisper. "I will wait for you to grow comfortable, to know me as your husband in your heart as well as in name."

Relief flooded through me, followed by a confusing sense of disappointment. "For how long?" I asked, my voice barely audible to my own ears. Would he wait months? Years?

A smile touched his lips—not the smile of a man amused, but of one who understood, perhaps even better than I did. "You will tell me when you are ready."

With those words, a burden lifted from my shoulders, one I had not known I carried. I watched, mesmerized, as he lifted the bed's finely woven covering, inviting me to rest beneath its protective embrace. I obeyed his unspoken command, the cool fabric a stark contrast to my heated skin.

To my surprise, Isaac settled beside me, maintaining a respectful distance. He lay flat on his back, his hands folded across his chest, his breathing steady and deep. I stared at his profile in the lamplight—the strong line of his jaw, his lashes against his cheek—and felt a bewildering emotion stir within me. Not purely desire, but something deeper—respect perhaps, gratitude, and the first tender shoots of what might grow into love.

I longed to reach out to touch his arm in silent thanks, but my courage failed. Instead, I let the gentle rhythm of his breathing relax me, my eyelids growing heavy as the tension of the day melted away.

One thought kept drifting through my mind. Perhaps this marriage, arranged though it was, could become something we would have chosen on our own.

When all the lamps save one had guttered and died, I was still staring at the ceiling and listening to the bewildering symphony of the night. In my father's house, nights had been quiet. The solid walls kept out all but the occasional call of a night watchman or the distant bark of a dog. But here in Abraham's camp, the darkness seethed with sound.

Sheep bleated to one another. Cattle lowed. Something—a jackal?—howled in the distance and was answered by another of its kind. Wind hooted through the soot-stained vent in the ceiling, causing the tent to billow and snap. Beneath those noises was the constant churr of insects, a sound so persistent it seemed to vibrate my bones.

How could anyone sleep through such a cacophony? Yet Isaac slumbered peacefully beside me, his breathing deep and even.

I envied him. These sounds had to be as familiar to him as the bustle of the market had been to me. I turned onto my side, drawing the blanket higher, and closed my eyes, willing sleep to come.

"They are only noises," I whispered. "They cannot harm you."

Eventually, exhaustion overcame my alertness. I drifted into a fitful sleep, filled with dreams of strange beasts stalking their prey in tall grasses, eyes gleaming amid the darkness.

I do not know how long I slept before a new sound pierced my consciousness. A high, keening wail—almost human, but not quite. My eyes flew open as my heart slammed against my ribs.

"It is a dream," I murmured, closing my eyes again. "Only a dream."

But the sound came again, louder this time, a strangled cry that lifted the hair on my arms. I was not dreaming. I was hearing a sound of pain, of terror, an undeniably human cry.

"Isaac." I nudged him, but he did not stir. I shook his shoulder. "Isaac!"

He grunted and turned toward me, blinking. "What?"

"Listen!"

As if on cue, the scream echoed again, louder and more frantic than before. I clutched Isaac's arm. "Someone is being murdered!"

To my astonishment, Isaac let his head fall back to his pillow. "No one is being murdered."

"But the screaming—"

"Is probably Zillah, one of the nanny goats. She is due to deliver any day. That sound means her time is near."

I stared at him. "That sound is from a *goat*?"

The cry came again, this time trailing off into a series of urgent bleats. It *did* sound less human now that I was fully awake, but the memory of it still pebbled my skin.

"Did you not have goats in Haran?" Isaac asked.

"In livestock pens outside the city," I said, "not outside my window." I sat up. "Should you not help her? She has to be suffering."

Isaac pulled me back down. "The shepherds will check on her. Zillah has birthed many kids."

"She sounds as if she is dying."

"She is strong. By morning she will be nursing her babies."

I lowered my head and tried to calm my racing heart. But the goat's cries continued, rising and falling in the night.

I sat up. "How can you sleep through all that?"

Isaac rolled toward me and propped his head on his hand. "I have heard such things all my life." Even in the dim light of the lamp, I saw a smile curve his mouth. "The night is full of voices—

the flocks, the wind, the big cats that hunt at night. They are the music of the wilderness."

"In the city, such sounds would mean danger."

"Here, silence means danger. If the flocks go quiet, a predator is nearby."

I blinked. "So all this noise is good?"

"Noise means all is well in the camp," Isaac confirmed, lowering his head. "When you have been here a while, you will learn to read the night sounds as easily as you read patterns on a loom." He lifted his head again. "You *do* weave, do you not?"

"Of course." Another scream from Zillah made me wince. "I'm not sure I want to become familiar with the sound of goat birthing."

Isaac laughed, a lovely sound. "Perhaps not, but you may want to see the kids in the morning. New life is always a miracle."

I slid closer to him, his warmth a welcome shield against the scary night sounds. "I was certain someone was being attacked."

"You have good instincts," he said. "They will serve you well."

"If I run to the rescue of a laboring goat, my instincts will make me look foolish."

A smile warmed his voice when he spoke again. "The shepherds would have appreciated your concern, even if they did not need your help."

Zillah's cries changed, becoming shorter and more rhythmic. Isaac noted the difference. "It will not be long now," he murmured. "Listen closely."

I did, and despite my earlier fear, I found myself caught up in the unfolding drama outside our tent. This was my husband's world, a place of birth and death, seasons and herds, night sounds and predators. A world I had only begun to understand.

"Tomorrow," I said, settling the blanket across my chest, "you must introduce me to Zillah and her babies."

"You will be the first," he promised, "after the shepherds."

As if celebrating our agreement, Zillah let out one final,

triumphant bleat, followed by a new sound—the thin, wavering cry of a newborn kid.

"There," Isaac said, satisfaction in his voice. "New life has arrived. If God is willing, there will be another kid soon."

I closed my eyes and discovered that the night sounds were no longer frightening. What had been alien and alarming now told a story I could understand: a tale of life, of a camp safe under the stars, of creatures that belonged to this place in a way I did not—at least not yet.

Sleep came more easily then, my dreams filling not with monsters but with newborn goats taking their first wobbly steps in the morning light.

Chapter 7

THE MORNING AFTER my wedding night, Deborah entered my tent with fresh garments and a smile that faded to a look of confusion when she saw me already dressed and combing my hair.

"You are up early," she said, setting down her basket. Her eyes searched the tent, noting the smooth linens on Isaac's side of the bed. "Did all go well for you?"

I ran the wooden comb through my long hair, grateful for a task that gave me something to do. "He was kind," I said.

Deborah's brows drew together as she took the comb from my hand. "Let me," she said, her deft fingers working through the remaining tangles. After a moment of silence, she softened her tone. "Did he not share your bed, pet?"

"He did." Heat flushed my cheeks. "He lay down next to me and slept."

Deborah's hands stilled. "Did he not find you attractive?"

The question struck with unexpected force. "I-I am not certain. He said I was beautiful, but perhaps he merely sought to please me." I swallowed hard, recalling his words. "He said I was young, so he would wait."

"Wait? For how long?"

"He did not say. When I asked, he said I would tell him when I was ready."

Deborah sighed and began to braid my hair. "I expect you will," she said, a knowing smile on her lips. "Some men are able to practice restraint. Your Isaac must be one of those men, and that is a good thing."

"He was kind when I woke him in the night."

"Why did you do that?"

"I heard screaming."

She gasped. "What?"

"I awoke terrified, but Isaac said I was only hearing a goat in labor."

"He was not angry because you woke him?"

I shook my head. "As I said, he was gentle. He said I should look for the kids this morning."

"Your Isaac will be a good husband." Deborah tied a string around the base of my braid, then came around to face me. She ran her sharp eyes over my tunic, a simple one I had pulled from a trunk. "This garment will do for now, but you must wear something more elegant tonight. You have a week of wedding banquets ahead."

I bit my lip. I was not sure what Abraham's family traditions entailed, but I was glad to know our wedding would be celebrated by more than the five people who witnessed the event.

THE NEXT SEVEN DAYS unfolded in a blur of activity. Each morning, Deborah braided my hair in an elaborate style, lined my eyes with kohl, and brightened my cheeks with ochre. Eliezer planned the elaborate wedding banquets—who would feast in which tent and who would sit in places of honor near the bride and groom.

A tall woman who appeared to be in her mid-thirties oversaw the cooking. She carried herself with authority, and though she was probably fifteen years older than me, I thought her too young to be married to Eliezer.

Since Deborah had been busy learning all about the camp, I asked her about the tall woman. "That," Deborah said, wagging a warning finger, "is Keturah, Abraham's concubine, so treat her with respect."

"Oh." Eliezer had mentioned Keturah, but I had been so preoccupied that I had almost forgotten about her.

Deborah patted my shoulder. "Do not be anxious on her account. Apparently, she oversees the female servants and takes care of Abraham, who often needs help due to his advanced age. But"—Deborah's brows arched—"Abraham is not as frail as one might think. They say Keturah is expecting a child."

"Truly!"

"That is what the servants say, and they seem to know everything."

The next time I saw Keturah I cast a quick glance at her belly but could see no sign of a bulge. Perhaps Deborah's news was a rumor only.

Our wedding week brought visitors from throughout Canaan, and each guest was eager to meet Isaac's bride, deliver gifts, and feast with the family that had become famous for hospitality. A special tent was erected to hold wedding gifts, including a tiger pelt, beautiful garments, jewelry, and a lion cub.

On the second day, I found myself the center of attention. The wives of visiting chieftains circled me like curious birds, touching my hair and remarking on my complexion.

"Such lovely eyes," commented an older woman, her fingers heavy with gold rings. "They shine like the stars Abraham's God promised him."

"And her hair," said another, "thick and lustrous as a young mare's mane."

I did not understand everything they said, for they spoke a different dialect, but one of the servants translated for me. Though their compliments pleased me, my face flamed with embarrassment beneath their attention. In Haran I had been but one of many beautiful girls. In Abraham's household, I felt like a prized lamb at the market.

But at least I had not been sold to the highest bidder.

When the afternoon grew too warm and the visitors retired to the tents provided for guests, I seized the opportunity to escape with Deborah. "Walk me through the camp," I begged her. "I must learn my way around."

Deborah, who had spent hours exploring, led me through the encampment, pointing out who lived where. Many of the tents were occupied by families, she said, because many of Abraham's married servants had been blessed with children.

We passed a group of women grinding grain, their hands moving over the querns in synchronized rhythm. We observed the shepherds returning with their flocks, the metalworkers hammering copper into vessels, and the weavers working at their looms.

"This place is nearly as large as Haran," I remarked, struggling to commit each detail to memory. "No wonder they speak of Abraham as a prince."

"He has been abundantly blessed," Deborah replied. "I am told his wealth grows with each season."

As we walked near the place where the livestock were penned, I caught my first glimpse of Isaac since that morning. "Is that my husband?" I whispered, although I had recognized him instantly.

He stood among the shepherds, his back to me, directing the separation of lambs from their mothers. Even from a distance, I could see authority in his posture and respect in the faces of the men who obeyed him.

Deborah pulled me away. "Let us explore another area. We should not disturb men at work."

But I lingered, watching as Isaac bent to lift a full-grown ewe that had become caught in a bush. He hoisted the animal, his sleeveless tunic revealing his muscular arms, then turned and set the ewe on her feet with a reassuring pat.

I caught my breath as my stomach tightened in a strange sensation.

Deborah chuckled beside me. "He *is* a handsome man," she said, pulling at my sleeve. "Come, let us prepare you for tonight's feast. Perhaps you will capture more than your husband's eyes."

THAT EVENING, dressed in one of my finest garments and adorned with jewelry from Abraham, I entered the banquet area and searched the crowd for Isaac. The feasting had begun at sundown, on low tables spread under the stars. Our guests had dined on roasted lamb, fresh bread, assorted vegetables, spiced fruits, and wine that flowed freely. As musicians played, some of the younger men formed a circle and began to dance.

I spotted my husband across the gathering, deep in conversation with his father. In the glow of the torchlight, Isaac's strong profile radiated strength and dignity, and his smile revealed his deep affection for his father. His hair, thick and curly, caught the torchlight as he moved, and I found myself wondering how it would feel between my fingers.

As if sensing my gaze, he turned, his eyes finding mine in the crowd. For a moment, neither of us moved. Then, slowly, he inclined his head in acknowledgment before resuming his conversation.

I could not explain what passed between us in that moment, but something had changed. When the music stopped and our guests began to depart, I quickly said my farewells and then disappeared into our tent. Deborah helped me remove my festive garment and then pulled a linen tunic over my head and combed my hair until it flowed over my back like a river. She then slipped away.

I resolved to stay awake until Isaac came in, but weariness overcame my intentions. The next morning, his side of the bed was rumpled, but as before, he had risen and departed before I awoke.

The third and fourth days brought more visitors, more gifts, and more feasting, and yet it also brought a new adventure. Isaac and I indulged in a game that involved glances exchanged across crowded spaces, of paths that nearly crossed but did not quite meet. I looked for him throughout the day, watching from a distance as he performed his duties, admiring the steady, thoughtful way he handled conflicts among the servants, the gentle touch he used with animals, the respectful way he addressed his honored guests.

He was not like the men I had known in Haran, quick to anger and even quicker to boast. My husband seemed to move through his world with a quiet confidence that required no validation. When he spoke, people listened, not because he demanded their attention but because his words carried weight. Did that weight come from his position as Abraham's son, or had he earned it on his own? I did not know.

"He is not what I expected," I confessed to Deborah as she helped me prepare for bed on the fifth night.

"What did you expect?" she asked.

I shrugged. "Someone louder. More like my brother, always competing, always trying to prove himself." I sighed, remembering a moment from that afternoon. A child had fallen amid some rocks, and Isaac had knelt beside him and carefully cleaned the boy's scraped knee with the same hands that had lifted a full-grown sheep. "He is gentle, but not weak."

Deborah smiled. "Strength shows itself in many ways."

By the sixth day, our little game of observation had evolved. I would catch sight of Isaac watching me as I spoke with visitors, his eyes following my movements with unmistakable interest. I would turn away, pretending not to notice, only to deliberately pass him later, close enough to catch his scent—sandalwood and sun-warmed skin—but not close enough to speak.

Or I would catch his eye, laugh softly, and turn away, leaving him to wonder what had amused me.

"You are teasing the poor man," Deborah scolded, though her eyes danced with humor.

"He started it," I replied, my cheeks heating. "He could have claimed his rights on our wedding night. Instead, he has made me curious."

"The man is wiser than he looks," Deborah quipped. "And he looks wiser than most."

The feast of the seventh night was the grandest of all. Abraham spared no expense, slaughtering the fattest calves and serving the finest wines. As the honored bride, I sat beside Isaac at the main table, acutely aware of the heat from his body and the way his arm occasionally brushed mine as he reached for his cup.

As the evening progressed and the guests grew noisier, Isaac leaned toward me, positioning his lips next to my ear. "You have been watching me."

My cheeks warmed, but I did not look at him. "I thought you were watching *me*."

A smile filled his voice. "What have you learned, daughter of Bethuel, from all your watching?"

I spoke slowly, considering my answer. "I have learned that you are a man who thinks before he speaks. That you care for those in your charge. That you honor your father." I paused, reinforcing my courage. "Most of all, I have learned that you are patient."

His eyes darkened at my last comment. "What do you think I have learned about *you* these past few days?"

"I cannot read your mind, so I cannot say."

Finally, I met his gaze. He studied me, his eyes traveling over my face as if memorizing each feature. "In you I have seen courage. Intelligence. Kindness." His voice dropped lower. "Beauty that goes beyond what the eye can see, although any man would find beauty enough to satisfy in your lips alone."

Around us, the celebration continued—guests laughing, dancing, helping themselves to more food and wine. In the midst of the noise and movement, Isaac's hand found mine. Without a word, he stood, drawing me up with him.

No one noticed as we slipped away from the feast, moving through the shadows between the tents as we made our way toward our own. My heart knocked against my ribs, not with fear, but anticipation. When we reached the entrance to our dwelling, Isaac hesitated, his eyes questioning.

"Why have you avoided me?" I asked, unable to remain silent. "I was beginning to think you found me repellent."

Isaac barked a laugh. "Rebekah, you are a balm to my soul, not bitterness. I kept my distance, for had I not—"

"What then?"

"I might have acted in haste. And I would not dishonor you, not for all the riches beneath the heavens, though—"

"What?"

"Though my desire for you burns as fire shut up in my bones."

I searched his face, and in his eyes I saw frustration. Until then, I had not understood that it might have been difficult for him to keep his distance. I would not let him suffer a moment longer.

I took his hands and placed them on my waist, then raised my hands to frame his face. His skin was flushed beneath my palms, his beard soft against my fingertips.

"I am not a child," I told him, my voice steady despite the trembling that had begun deep within me. "I am a wife who is eager to please her husband."

Something flared in his eyes—desire, relief, joy?—I could not name it precisely. His arms encircled me, pulling me against the solid wall of his chest, and his mouth found mine.

And as he carried me to our bed, with sudden clarity I realized what Deborah had meant. I had indeed told him when I was ready.

Chapter 8

I AWOKE TO the soft gray hush before dawn, when the air inside the tent still retained the night's chill. Outside, the murmurs of servants drifted by, mingling with the distant bleating of sheep and the grunts of camels waking in their enclosures. I stretched beneath the embrace of a warm blanket, then rose, wrapping a shawl around my shoulders.

Deborah, I noticed at once, had already entered our tent.

"I came as soon as I saw your husband leave," she said, advancing toward my dressing table. "Let me prepare you for the day."

She led me to the washbasin, where she poured water over my hands and feet, then wiped them with a clean cloth. I shivered, the water brisk against my skin. Deborah dropped an under tunic over my head so I would not take a chill. I sat on a stool as she combed and oiled my hair, twisting it into long, dark braids that she coiled atop my head. She dressed me in a clean outer tunic, girded my waist with a woven belt, and draped a light veil over my shoulders.

"Lovely," Deborah said, stepping back to appraise her efforts. "Your family would be pleased to see you looking like a proper married woman."

"A happy married woman," I said, pressing my hand to my belly. "If God is good, Isaac's son now rests within my womb."

Deborah lifted her hands and pretended to be surprised, but I waggled a finger at her. "I know you know everything that happens in this tent."

"It is my duty to know," she said, grinning. "And to serve you in any way I can. So go, my pet, and let the camp see your newfound happiness."

By the time I stepped outside, the sun had splashed the eastern sky with a blaze of red and gold, and the camp had sprung to life. Yawning women stirred clay pots over smoldering fires while young girls carried water jars to the well, their chatter light and bright. Men led sheep and goats out of protective pens toward the grazing areas, their staffs tapping against the hard-packed earth.

I went directly to the women's area, where the daily work awaited. I was the highest-ranking woman in camp, but I did not want to threaten Keturah. While she was but a concubine, she had arrived before me, and Abraham was still the head of this household.

So I joined the women at the grindstones and took my place in the line, kneeling to turn the stones as I had in my mother's kitchen. The scent of crushed wheat filled the air, warm and earthy.

"Lady, you should not be doing such work," one of the women chided, pausing to wipe sweat from her brow.

"I am accustomed to grinding." I poured another handful of grain into the opening in the upper stone. "And I want to help with the work."

"Perhaps," the woman said, "but one day you will carry your husband's child, and then your work must stop. All that matters is that you safely deliver your master's son."

I smiled, but her words struck with an unexpected pang. What if I could not deliver Isaac's son? What if I presented him with a girl? Even worse, what if I could not conceive?

I shook the thought out of my head. Sarah might have been

barren for years, but I had married young, and Sarah had been an older bride. I was surrounded by strong and fertile women, many of whom carried babies on their backs as they worked. ADONAI had blessed Abraham; even the goats gave birth in multiples.

By midday, the heat pressed upon us with its heavy hand. We stopped grinding to pack food into baskets and leather pouches—flatbreads, dried figs, and handfuls of roasted nuts. I joined a group that walked out to the fields where the men watched over the grazing flocks. The land stretched before us, vast and golden, interrupted only by the occasional acacia tree. In the distance, I spotted a grove with tamarisks and date palms, hardy enough to survive in the arid landscape. Once we had delivered food to the herdsmen, we strolled through the fields, delighted to have time to stretch our legs. Some of the women walked to the grove and gathered fruit, their laughter ringing across the sands as they filled their baskets to overflowing.

I looked for Isaac among the shepherds and was both disappointed and relieved that I did not see him. If he had been there, I would have gone to him and would have been embarrassed if he wanted to focus on his work. But I was unhappy *not* to see him because I wanted to hold him and feel his arms around me.

When the sun dipped toward the horizon, we women returned to camp. Keturah went to her tent, and this surprised me. Had she withdrawn because she was sick, or had Abraham told her to surrender her leadership? I would ask Isaac later when we were alone.

With Keturah gone, I directed the servants in preparation for the evening meal. After watching for a week, I was able to tell them which meat to roast, how many bowls of lentils to soak, and how many loaves to bake. I told them to bake an extra loaf of honey bread because I had noticed that Isaac liked it. Other servants came to me with their questions, seeking my direction on what work should be done. When I did not know how to answer, I looked at Deborah, who guided my choices. "Do not worry, pet," she said once the preparations had been arranged. "Soon you will know exactly how to run this household."

At dusk the men gathered to eat, sitting or reclining on cushions in the largest tent. The pleasing aromas of roasted lamb and garlic filled the air, mingling with the sweetness of honeyed dates and bread. We women served the meal, offering platters with practiced efficiency. Only when the men had finished did we take our own portions, eating as we cleaned.

By the time the sky had filled with stars, I returned to our dwelling, where Isaac had lit the iron brazier. The fire cast flickering patterns against the goatskin walls, warming the space with its glow.

My husband pulled me close, his hands tracing the curve of my back. In the hush of the night, we found each other. And as he kissed my temple, I closed my eyes and whispered the prayer I had prayed once before: "Let this be the night, ADONAI. Let life quicken within me."

Outside, the desert wind whistled, carrying my plea into the vast and endless dark.

I HAD NOTICED it from our first days together, the way the animals responded to Isaac. They approached him without fear, sometimes even seeking him out, allowing him to touch them in ways they would never permit with others. Even the wildest creatures seemed to find peace in his presence.

I had grown up around livestock, of course, but the goats and cattle that came back to their pens at Haran were domesticated animals, accustomed to human handling. Isaac's gift seemed deeper and more mysterious. It stirred my curiosity and made me more determined to understand the man I had married.

One afternoon, when I spotted Isaac walking alone toward the fields, I gathered my courage and followed him. The land stretched before me, golden under the afternoon sun, the air shimmering with heat haze. My sandals crunched against desiccated weeds as I hastened to catch up to my husband.

"Isaac," I called, trying to keep my voice steady despite my breathlessness.

He turned, his brows lifting when he saw me. His smile still made my heart stutter, even after four months of marriage.

"I have been watching you," I said, then flushed at the realization of how silly I sounded. "With the animals. They come to you so easily, and I have never seen anyone else with that gift. What is your secret?"

Instead of answering, Isaac gestured toward a bull grazing on the next hill. My steps faltered. The creature was massive, its shoulders broad and muscular, its horns curved and sharp.

"Come," he said. "Watch."

"Are you sure?" I swallowed hard. "I do not think he wants company."

Isaac gestured for me to follow.

I trailed behind him, careful to keep distance between myself and the bull. Isaac approached the beast with unhurried steps and stopped only a few paces away. He made a clicking noise with his tongue, a sound I had heard before but never understood.

The bull's ears twitched. It raised its head, regarding Isaac with what looked like recognition.

Then, after only a moment of hesitation, the bull strolled toward my husband and stretched its enormous head. The animal nudged Isaac's hand with its nose. With gentle movements, Isaac stroked the soft flesh of its muzzle, his fingers moving with practiced ease across its head, finally resting between the ears.

"The sons of Noah taught me about animals," he said. "After the great flood, ADONAI instilled fear and terror of man into every wild animal, every bird, and everything that crawls on the ground—even the fish of the sea."

I took a cautious step, mesmerized by the scene before me. "If they are afraid," I asked, "why do they come to you?"

Isaac's eyes remained on the bull, his hand moving slowly across its forehead. "I allow them to approach me first. I never reach for them, never chase them, never startle them, but wait until they come to me. Sometimes it takes hours, sometimes weeks. But an animal will come once it knows you can be trusted."

The simplicity of his answer took my breath away. I smiled. Had he not handled me in the same way? With patience and gentleness, he had waited for me to approach him. Surely he possessed wisdom from ADONAI.

"Would the bull allow me to touch it?"

Isaac gave me a lopsided smile. "Why not come and see?"

My heart began to race as I approached. The bull was even more intimidating up close, its breath warm and moist. I lifted my hand, thinking I would stroke its side, but as I stepped forward, the animal stepped away, maintaining the distance between us.

I sighed. "It does not like me."

"You must let *him* touch you," Isaac said, "and then you can touch him."

A nervous laugh escaped my lips. "What if I do not know how?"

"He will show you."

We stood—man, woman, and bull—in a triangle of silence. The sun warmed my shoulders as I waited, and my hands began to tremble. I tried to calm myself and behave naturally, as Isaac did.

Time stretched and slowed. The distant sounds of the camp faded, and the world compressed into the space between the three of us. I watched the bull's chest expand with each breath; I saw powerful muscles ripple beneath its hide and sensed the intelligence in its dark eyes.

Finally, the bull swung its massive head in my direction. I held my breath, willing myself to stand perfectly still. The animal took a tentative step toward me, then another. Its nostrils flared, and its hot breath moistened my hand.

Then, like a miracle, the bull pressed its nose against my palm.

A surge of wonder moved through me. My hand curved around

the bull's nose, and I exhaled, amazed at the softness of its skin and the solidity of its bones. My fingers trembled as the animal leaned into my touch, showing me exactly where it wished to be caressed.

Tears sprang to my eyes. Never had I felt so connected to something that could destroy me with a single movement, yet here it stood, choosing to accept my attention.

"I love animals," Isaac said, his eyes sweeping across the cattle in the field. His voice held a reverence he usually reserved for speaking of Adonai. "*This* is what the world was like before the great flood. The animals had no fear of us, and we could walk with lions."

His words reminded me of the lion cub we had received as a wedding gift. It had been kept in a cage, its golden-brown eyes warily following every movement. I had avoided it, frightened by its claws and the frantic anxiety in its eyes.

"What became of the cub?" I asked, still stroking the bull's face. "The wedding gift?"

Isaac's smile broadened. "Once I knew it would be able to feed itself, I released it." His voice softened with what sounded like affection. "He was a good hunter, so he had not been held captive long. He will thrive in the wilderness."

My stomach tightened. "I hope he does not plan a return visit."

"He will not. I told him to go south where the game is more plentiful."

The casual way he spoke of directing a wild lion sent another wave of awe through me. Who was this man I had married? Eliezer had spoken of Isaac's quiet strength, his obedience to his father, and his devotion to his mother, but no one had mentioned this almost mystical connection to the living world around us.

As the bull returned to its grazing with unhurried dignity, I studied my husband's profile. The setting sun cast his features in bronze light, highlighting the strong line of his jaw and the gentle curve of his lips. I considered the life he had lived—the lonely years as a child without siblings, the loss of his mother, his studies with

Shem and Eber—and wondered if those situations had opened him to this understanding of life and death, fear and trust.

"Will you teach me?" I asked, my voice barely above a whisper. "I wish to be as patient as you are."

Isaac turned, and the expression in his eyes made my breath catch. "I will," he said, taking my hand. "But you must be as patient with yourself as you are with others. And whether you seek to tame people or animals, you must believe that they feel, and that they can sense your heart."

I nodded, eager to learn this silent language. How differently I might move through the world if I approached people with Isaac's patience and gentleness.

As we walked back to the camp, hand in hand, I felt I had been given a glimpse into the world that existed when ADONAI walked with man and all creation lived in harmony.

"Tomorrow," I whispered, leaning my head against Isaac's shoulder, "I will begin to learn."

THE EVENING BREEZE carried the scent of roasting meat through the camp as Isaac watched Rebekah walk toward their tent. Her slender form moved with purpose, her steps confident as she disappeared behind the woven curtain. She was so unlike other women. Most of the female servants in the camp were quiet and watched for weeks without speaking, while Rebekah had dared to come into his world, and her zest for life amazed him. She had been his wife only a few months, yet already she had transformed his existence in ways he was only beginning to understand.

Isaac lingered by the goat pen, his fingers absently stroking the coarse hair of a young kid that leaned against the fence. The animal bleated softly, seeking attention. How simple an animal's needs, how uncomplicated his desires.

His thoughts drifted to Sarah, his mother. Her love had been the most obvious thing in his life, a constant presence that shaped him from his first breath. She had protected him fiercely, made his decisions with unwavering certainty, and spoiled him with an affection that bordered on reverence. After all, he was the miracle child, the fulfillment of ADONAI's promise to Abraham. His mother had never let him forget his significance.

In the first months after her death, Isaac had found himself paralyzed by indecision. The simplest choices—what food to eat, which path to walk, what garment to wear on feast days—loomed like mountains he could not climb. He sought refuge in the fields, among creatures who demanded nothing from him. The sheep watched with impassive eyes as he screamed his grief into the wind, wept until his throat was raw, and railed against ADONAI for taking her. The animals neither judged nor advised him; they had simply been present, witnesses to his unraveling.

Yet Rebekah, young as she was, possessed a certainty that eluded him. She had easily adjusted to the rhythms of their camp, entering willingly into the women's work, establishing her place among them with quiet authority. She set out his garments on feast days and trimmed his hair when it grew too long, her fingers gentle against his scalp. In these ways, she offered the same comfort his mother once had.

But Rebekah was so much more.

As they lay together in the darkness of their tent, Isaac felt a completeness he had never known. He could cling to her, feel her hands in his hair, and know that he was not alone in the vast, uncertain world. Her tender touch soothed something broken within him, and her embrace made him believe he might someday be whole again.

Without doubt, ADONAI had brought her to him. Abraham had sent his servant to find him a wife, but ADONAI, not Eliezer, had sent Rebekah to the well where Eliezer and his thirsty camels waited. ADONAI had placed kindness in her heart and given her the courage to journey to a distant land to marry a stranger.

He had no regrets about his marriage. None. If anything, he feared the arrangement was uneven—and Rebekah had been shorted in their pairing. She deserved a man of vigor and conviction, not one who trembled at the significance of his own name. She deserved a man worthy of being called the son of Abraham, not one who felt himself of little value in the eyes of God or men.

Isaac leaned on the fence railing, remembering the years he had spent learning from Shem and Eber, descendants of Noah who had been entrusted with the stories of the beginning. They had taught him of the first man and first woman, who lived in the garden where all began.

"Adam, being a man, was incomplete," Shem had said, *"and so* A*DONAI* *created Eve to be his completer."*

At the time, Isaac listened with the dutiful attention his mother instilled in him, but he had not truly understood. Now, with Rebekah in his life, the wisdom of those words unfolded like a night flower opening to the stars. Rebekah completed him in ways he had never imagined possible. She made it easier to live in a world without his mother—not by replacing Sarah, but by helping him become a man who could stand on his own, who could make choices and find his way forward.

Where once he had known grief and uncertainty, Rebekah brought purpose. Where he had known silence, she brought conversation and laughter. Where he had felt emptiness, she brought fullness.

A movement caught his eye, and he turned to see his wife standing at the entrance of their tent. She raised her hand in silent beckoning, her smile visible even in the gathering dusk. Isaac's heart quickened. When she looked at him that way, he could almost believe he would one day become the man ADONAI destined him to be.

He gave the young goat a final pat, then walked toward Rebekah and home.

IN HARAN, no one had ever asked me to milk a goat. In my father's house, such tasks fell to the servants, and the daughter of Bethuel had been spared such labor. But in Abraham's household, all women, regardless of their station, shared in the daily work.

When Netta, one of the older women, casually mentioned that on the morrow I would be expected to help make cheese, my smile froze. How could I admit I had never drawn milk from a goat? The thought of fumbling before the women who constantly watched me made my stomach twist.

That evening I confessed my inexperience to Isaac.

His brows arched. "You have never milked a goat?"

"My father's servants tended the animals," I said, heat burning my cheeks. "I know how to weave and plan a feast, but the animals . . ."

Isaac stared at me, a smile creasing his face. "Come." He extended his hand. "The moon is bright enough. I will teach you."

"Now?" I glanced toward the tent opening. "But what if someone sees us?"

He gave me a smile that made my heart flutter. "Better I witness your first attempts than the women."

The night air was cool against my skin as we crept to the goat pen. The animals stirred at our unexpected approach, bleating with timid voices. Isaac murmured to them, then moved toward a small white goat with golden eyes.

"This is Levanah," he said, tying her to a fence post. "She is patient, and her milk flows easily."

The goat regarded me with suspicion. I hung back, watching as Isaac positioned a lidded clay bowl beneath her. From a pouch at his waist, he pulled out two small cloths.

"First, we clean her," he explained, handing me one of the fabric squares. "One for each teat. It keeps the milk pure and prevents sickness."

I took the cloth hesitantly, observing as Isaac bent to wipe one of the teats with slow, careful motions. The goat shifted but remained calm under his touch. Of course she did, for she was with Isaac.

"Now you clean the other one."

My fingers trembled as I knelt and mimicked his movements. Despite the cool evening, the animal's flesh felt warm beneath the cloth.

He patted the ground beside him. "Sit. I will now show you how the milking is done."

I knelt awkwardly on the dirt, my tunic bunching about me. Isaac removed the lid from the clay bowl and placed the bowl beneath the goat. He knelt, his hands gripping its teats with practiced ease.

"You act like you have been doing this for years," I said.

He chuckled. "Mothers teach their children when they are small. They never know when they will need milk for a baby. Now." He opened his hands, showing me his grip. "You must be gentle but firm," he said, demonstrating the motion. "Keep the teat between your thumb and fingers. Pull down, do not squeeze, and aim for the bowl."

I watched, mesmerized, as his hands worked in a steady rhythm, switching between the goat's two teats. First one, then the other. Thin streams of milk struck the bowl with a rhythmic sound.

"See how I alternate?" he said. "Like a dance between your hands. Left, right, left, right. The rhythm soothes the goat and keeps the milk flowing. Now—you do it."

When he guided my hands to the goat's udder, I recoiled from the unexpectedly soft texture. "I cannot."

"You must," Isaac said. "You can do it."

I positioned my fingers as he had demonstrated and managed a tentative pull. Nothing happened.

"Harder," Isaac said. "She will not break."

I squeezed and pulled with more force, and suddenly a stream of milk squirted out—directly into Isaac's face. He blinked, milk dripping from his lashes onto his beard.

I gasped. "Forgive me!"

Isaac released a deep, rumbling laugh that warmed me even as I covered my face in embarrassment.

He chuckled, then wiped his face with the back of his hand. "Perhaps I should have chosen a less vulnerable position."

Without thinking, I leaned forward and kissed the milk from his beard. The sweet taste blended with the earthy scent of him, and I heard his breath catch.

"That was not part of the lesson."

"Was it not?" I gave him an innocent smile. "I think it will help me remember your instructions."

Isaac cleared his throat. "Again," he said, his voice thicker than before. "Try again, but this time aim for the bowl."

I positioned my hands and concentrated on the downward motion. This time a stream of milk hit the side of the bowl with only a few drops splashing onto Isaac's arm.

"Better," he said. "Try alternating like I showed you. Right, then left."

I shifted my hands, trying to establish a rhythm. The first few attempts produced only erratic spurts, but finally I fell into a halting cadence.

"Better," he said. "Now continue."

The task was harder than it looked. My fingers cramped, and sometimes the milk refused to flow. Other times it sprayed in unexpected directions. Each time I made a mistake, I stole a kiss—from my husband's cheek, his forehead, the corner of his mouth—until Isaac's breathing grew uneven.

He smiled. "You are not taking this seriously."

"I am. See how much milk is in the bowl?"

Indeed, we had collected enough to fill a small cup.

The goat stamped her foot. "Levanah thinks you are very slow," Isaac said.

"Levanah should be more grateful for my effort." I reached

again for the udder and managed a continuous stream before my fingers cramped.

"Enough." Isaac caught my hands. "You can now milk a goat."

"One more time, please. I do not want to falter tomorrow."

After more practice—and more kisses—I filled half the bowl. My hands ached, but my heart warmed with pleasure.

"Don't forget to leave some for her babies," Isaac reminded me.

"Babies?"

"Levanah has two kids in a different pen. They will be hungry tomorrow."

"Of course."

"If you take the milk to the cooking tent, the other women will show you how to make butter and cheese." Isaac untied Levanah, who trotted away with what looked like relief.

I stood on tiptoe to brush my lips against his ear. "Do you not like being my teacher?"

Isaac's arms encircled my waist, pulling me against him. "If I teach you all the skills of the camp in this manner," he murmured, "I will never complete a day's work."

I leaned into his embrace. "Perhaps we should save some lessons for our private time."

As we walked back to our dwelling, the bowl of milk in my hands, I brimmed with newfound confidence. Tomorrow I would face the women's scrutiny without feeling like a complete fool. And tomorrow night, perhaps Isaac could teach me how to shear a sheep, a task that would certainly require many more kisses to master.

Chapter 9

BY THE TIME several months had passed, I felt secure in my position as the chief woman in Abraham's household. Keturah, everyone understood, served as Abraham's concubine and companion. Now obviously pregnant, she worked when and where she could, but she also spent a lot of time tending to Abraham, who, Isaac pointedly reminded me, had lived one hundred forty years.

One afternoon, as the sun cast long shadows across Abraham's camp, I donned my veil and followed a path the other women had created over the years. I balanced a heavy clay pitcher, filled with honey water and sweetened with mint, on my hip—my excuse to linger in the grove Abraham had planted to attract visitors.

The gathering today was especially large. Several merchants who followed the eastern trade routes had stopped to rest, drawn by Abraham's legendary hospitality. They also came for my father-in-law's stories of ADONAI, tales that had been spread by travelers from Egypt to Babylon.

I poured honey water into a merchant's cup, careful not to spill it as I focused on Abraham's resonant voice. Despite his advanced years, his words carried through the gathering with remarkable clarity.

"You ask how I know ADONAI is the one true God," Abraham was telling a trader, whose clothing marked him as a man from Tyre. "Let me tell you of the time when I lived in Ur of the Chaldeans . . ."

The story of Abram's trial in the fiery furnace was not new to me, yet I never tired of hearing it. Like his uncle, my father had also acknowledged ADONAI, yet he kept a collection of household gods as insurance against misfortune. Abraham's loyalty was indivisible. ADONAI was not merely the highest god; He was the only God Abraham worshiped.

"And when Pharaoh took Sarai into his household," Abraham was saying, his eyes alight, "ADONAI struck his house with plagues until he returned her to me untouched."

Murmurs of appreciation rippled through the gathering. I refilled cups and offered dried figs from a platter, absorbing Abraham's words as the parched earth drinks rain.

"My Sarah was an extraordinarily beautiful woman," Abraham said, his voice softening. His gnarled fingers stroked his beard. "Even when aged, her beauty outshone that of other women. And when she gave birth to Isaac at age ninety and was able to nurse him from her own breast, all of Canaan wondered at the power of our God."

At the mention of my husband's name, I glanced toward the entrance to the grove. Isaac would soon be returning from the fields. Unlike me, he rarely attended his father's teaching sessions. When I first noticed his absence, I assumed he was busy with practical matters of managing his father's vast holdings. But after several months of marriage, I was beginning to wonder if he had another reason for avoiding his father's talks. Had he learned all he wanted to know about ADONAI?

As the sun began its descent, Abraham cleared his throat and gestured for Eliezer to help him stand. "May the Lord bless and keep you," he said, lifting his hand toward those who had come to listen. "And may ADONAI give you peace."

Eliezer helped his master return to the camp while I helped the servants clear away the cups and platters, my mind still swirling with Abraham's testimony of divine intervention and covenant promises.

Later, as twilight painted the sky in deepening shades of blue, I found my husband returning from the fields. He looked weary but satisfied, and his eyes lit when he saw me waiting outside our tent.

"The southern well has been cleared," he said, washing his hands in the bowl I offered. "The shepherds will be able to water the flocks there tomorrow."

I handed him a linen towel and helped him remove his dusty cloak. "Your father had many guests today," I said. "Merchants from Tyre and beyond, all of them eager to hear about ADONAI."

Isaac gave me a smile that did not quite reach his eyes. "The honey of persuasion has flowed from Father's lips since his youth."

I led him inside, then poured wine into a cup and offered it. As he drank, I gathered my courage. "Husband, may I ask you something?"

He lowered his cup and sank onto a cushion on the carpet. "Of course."

I drew a deep breath. "Your father speaks of ADONAI as one who has walked and talked with Him," I began, sitting across from him. "Yet you rarely speak of ADONAI. Do you not share your father's faith?"

Isaac's face remained calm, but his shoulders tensed. He took a long drink before lowering his cup again. "I honor my father's God," he finally said. "I observe the rituals and the sacrifices. I know He exists. But . . ." He stared into his cup.

"But?"

"ADONAI speaks to my father," Isaac said, his voice so low that I strained to hear. "The voice of God has guided Abraham's every step since before I was born. But the Lord has never spoken to me."

The admission hovered in the silence between us. The quiet

resignation in his tone broke my heart. "You have never heard His voice?"

Isaac shook his head. "I have prayed. I have listened. I have even visited the place where Hagar saw ADONAI-in-flesh. But all I hear from ADONAI is silence." He stared into space, his fingers tightening around the cup. "My father hears divine instructions. He receives visits from heavenly messengers. He negotiates with God as one might bargain with a trader in the marketplace. But for me . . ." He shrugged. "Nothing."

I took his hand and rubbed my thumb over the calluses on his palm. "Perhaps ADONAI speaks differently to different people," I suggested. "Your father hears a voice, but perhaps you—"

"My father was instructed to sacrifice me on Mount Moriah," Isaac interrupted, his words as sharp and sudden as a knife thrust. "And he would have obeyed, too."

I froze, my breath catching. Abraham had never shared this story with visitors, nor had anyone shared it with me.

"My father bound my hands and feet," Isaac continued, his voice distant, "after I had prepared the wood and the fire. He bade me lie on the altar, and I obeyed. Then he stood over me with a knife, weeping, ready to plunge it into my heart because ADONAI had commanded it." He looked at me, his eyes shining like stars. "Only then did the Angel of the Lord call out to stop him."

I shivered despite the warmth in the air. "I-I did not know."

"Few do," said Isaac. "It is not a tale my father shares with guests and travelers." He paused. "How does one speak to a God who would ask such a thing? How does one trust such a voice?"

I sat in silence, absorbing the implications of his story. The husband I had come to know—gentle, devoted to his family and flocks—had revealed a new aspect of himself. His reticence about faith had not sprung from indifference or doubt, but from a wound that had not healed.

"Yet you still honor ADONAI," I observed. "You honored Him when you laid yourself on the altar."

"I had been taught to obey ADONAI without question, so I did. ADONAI is my father's God, and if the covenant is true, He will be the God of my descendants as well. As for me, I follow Him from a distance. Cautiously." He looked at me. "Just as you followed that bull in the field."

My thoughts turned to my own journey, how in Haran I had yearned to know more about ADONAI and how I had accepted the call to marry a stranger because I believed it to be ADONAI's will. Now I sat with my husband, discovering that his relationship with God was not at all what I had imagined.

"Perhaps," I said, carefully choosing my words, "ADONAI brought me here not only as your wife, but as a companion in seeking Him." I squeezed his hand. "I have had no grand visions, nor have I heard a divine voice, but I believe He is with us even now."

Isaac did not respond, but the tension in his shoulders eased somewhat.

"Will you join me tomorrow?" I asked. "When your father teaches, we could listen together."

An apologetic smile touched Isaac's lips. "I have heard all my father's stories. The only voice that can ease my doubts is ADONAI's."

I forced a smile. I had no power to command the Lord of lords, so I could do nothing to help my husband. All I could do was love him. And wait.

Isaac muttered something about speaking to Eliezer, so I watched him go before stepping outside into the darkening night. Stars appeared across the velvet canopy of sky. I wrapped my arms around myself and thought of Abraham's stories, of covenant promises and divine protection, and of Isaac's revelation of the altar and sacrifice. Between those two, there had to be a path where my husband could walk with his father's God.

As for me, I would not be dissuaded from seeking ADONAI. Perhaps, through my seeking, Isaac might find his way back to the God who had spared his life on that distant mountaintop.

Chapter 10

I FOUND TALA the midwife grinding herbs beneath the fabric awning of her tent. The scent of crushed anise and bitter fenugreek swirled in the air, mixing with the ever-present aroma of sunbaked earth. My heart pounded as I approached. I had dreaded this visit, yet I could wait no longer.

Tala was old—she had delivered Isaac—with silvered hair in a thick braid and skin weathered by many years under the sun. Her hands, though gnarled, mixed her herbs with precision and skill.

Her dark eyes peered up at me. "My lady." She wiped her hands on her tunic and gestured for me to sit on a woven mat. "What brings you to me?"

I hesitated, though I had rehearsed the words I would say to her. "I need your wisdom."

She lifted a brow.

"I have been Isaac's wife more than a year," I began, "yet my womb remains empty. I have prayed to Adonai. I have offered sacrifices. I have waited. But still I have not conceived." My voice broke. "What if I am barren? W-what if I am like Sarah?"

"You would be blessed if you are like Sarah," the midwife said, her expression unreadable. "She conceived, did she not?"

"Yes, but only after years of suffering." I clenched my hands. "I do not want to wait as long as she did. I will do anything. Anything you tell me, I will do."

"So you want the promise," she said, her tone suggesting that she was speaking to a fool, "but you are not willing to endure the suffering." She tilted her head. "Do you not know that suffering is part of motherhood?"

"If you say so." I inhaled a trembling breath. I had always considered myself strong, but this waiting and uncertainty made me feel helpless.

The midwife studied me for a long moment, then reached into a basket and pulled out a bundle of dried herbs. "There are things we can try," she said, her voice steady. "The womb must be strong and warm—open. Some women drink a brew of fenugreek and date syrup each morning to prepare the body. Others eat pomegranate seeds because the seeds are full of life."

"I will do whatever you say."

She gave me a slow nod. "At night, before you lie with your husband, warm a cloth over the brazier and lay it across your belly. The warmth will stir your blood."

I clung to every word. "What else?"

Tala's wrinkled fingers traced the rim of her bowl. "There is a root—mandrake. Some say it carries the breath of life itself."

Mandrake. I had heard the name whispered among the women. A plant said to be touched by the gods, to stir the womb and awaken desire. "Where do I find it?"

She gave me a knowing smile. "It is rare but not impossible to find. When the time is right, it will find you."

I bit my lip, frustrated by her enigmatic answer. "Is there anything else I can do?"

The midwife's eyes softened. "Walk barefoot on the earth. Speak to your womb as though it were listening. Tell it to open, to welcome life." She reached for my hands, her grip surprisingly firm. "Do not let despair take root in you. It is a poison worse than barrenness."

I nodded, my chest tight.

She pressed the bundle of fenugreek into my hands. "Drink this in a tea every morning. And have faith in ADONAI."

I clutched the bundle to my chest. "Thank you."

As I walked away, Tala's voice followed me. "One day you will carry sons, my lady. And when you do, you will understand why ADONAI made you wait."

Her words sank into me like seeds planted in fertile soil, giving me hope for the future.

MONTHS FELL AWAY, like the leaves of a terebinth tree in the dry season. I did not conceive. Yet at an extravagant banquet several months later, Abraham stood and lifted his cup. Silence fell over the gathering, and all of us women stopped to listen.

"May ADONAI bless you," he said, looking around. "You know that last year Keturah gave me a son, Zimran." Heads nodded, faces smiling—we were all happy for Abraham to have a son in his old age.

I looked for Keturah, but she had remained in her tent with the baby. Zimran was not yet weaned, though I had heard he had been placed with a wet nurse. Perhaps she was not feeling well.

"I must thank ADONAI," Abraham continued, pausing to stroke his beard, "because Keturah will have another child this year. ADONAI has blessed me again."

A ripple of wonder filled the tent, and then the listeners raised their cups and the air filled with shouts of congratulations. I smiled but found it difficult to rejoice. I liked Keturah and loved my father-in-law, but why was ADONAI blessing Abraham—an old man who had more children than he needed—while I remained childless?

I had done everything Tala suggested. I drank tasteless tea, talked to my belly, warmed my womb, and sent Deborah out to search for the tiny purple flowers of the mandrake. When she finally found one, I ate the berries as Tala instructed, but nothing had happened.

Why, I asked Adonai, was I destined to suffer the bitter state of barrenness? But I received no answers from heaven, nor did Adonai appear to me as He had to Hagar.

Though Isaac had advised me to be patient and trust, waiting on Adonai and His blessing of a child was proving harder with each day that passed.

Years piled upon years, like the layers of the garbage dump outside our camp, and yet I did not conceive. I moved through the camp, my face frozen in a smile while my heart continued to ache.

To my great disappointment, Abraham's happy announcement of another son repeated itself several times. While I remained barren, Keturah's womb produced life after life. Every nine or ten months, a new cry from the concubine's tent heralded the arrival of another baby. Soon there were so many that Keturah could not sleep, and so a special tent was erected for the infants and their wet nurses. Each time I passed that place, the toddlers' tiny voices and the infants' cries seeped through the walls and tore at my heart.

One night, as Isaac reached for me in bed, I sat up and confronted him. "Why have I not conceived?" I pounded the mattress beneath us. "I have prayed day and night. I have done my best to please Adonai by following His ways. I know He has promised to make Abraham a great nation through you, so why do I not have a child growing within me?"

Something that looked like bitterness entered Isaac's expression.

"I have no answers for you. And I have my own questions for ADONAI."

"I know what has happened." I crossed my arms. "I think ADONAI has sent babies, but somehow they nested in Keturah's womb instead of mine."

"Now you are being foolish."

"Am I?" A sudden rush of tears cracked my voice. "Then why am I not with child?"

Isaac pulled me into his arms and held me while I cried. I wanted to beat on his chest, but he was right—he had no answers, only questions of his own.

ONE COOL NIGHT, as we walked under a sky brushed with deep violet and sprinkled with stars, I could no longer restrain my protestations. I turned to Isaac, whose eyes seemed to mirror the storm inside me. "Husband," I asked, my voice trembling, "why would your father choose to take a concubine?"

He looked at me as if I had drunk too much wine. "Rebekah"—he slipped his arm around my shoulders—"Father needed a companion."

"But he is old!"

"He is not dead."

I clenched my fists. "If he wanted a woman, why did he not marry a woman past the age of childbearing?"

"Because," Isaac answered, "Father believes ADONAI's promise—his seed will be as countless as the sand by the sea."

"But *you* are the child of promise!" I countered, my words heavy with despair. "And you have no children, yet the cries of Keturah's babies fill our camp. How can you be the chosen heir when my womb remains empty?"

Isaac pressed his lips together, and after a long silence, he spoke of Ishmael, Hagar's son, whose descendants were already as numerous as the sheep in Abraham's flock. "They say Ishmael's sons have sons, but his offspring have nothing to do with ADONAI's promise to Abraham and Sarah."

A bitter laugh escaped me. "Is this what it means to be chosen? To be left barren while others multiply like rabbits? Sarah was barren, and now it seems I am doomed to share her fate."

With those words, so hastily spoken, a chasm opened between us. I sensed Isaac's withdrawal—not physically, for he had not moved more than a step away—but his countenance fell, and the light in his eyes dimmed.

Tears sprang to my eyes. I could have remained silent and waited with perfect trust like Abraham. Instead, I had turned my frustration into a rant against ADONAI himself. If only I could be like Sarah! ADONAI had blessed her with a miraculous birth and an amazing son, whom I loved dearly.

But I did not want to wait as long as she did.

I reached for Isaac. "My lord, I am—"

"I do not know what to tell you," he interrupted. "I do not have the power to make you conceive, and ADONAI does not speak to me. I am sorry your new life has been such a disappointment."

With that, he stood and walked toward the fields. I wanted to go after him, but instead I hurried to our tent, where I fell onto the bed and watered my pillow with tears.

Chapter
— 11 —

MY PESTLE GROUND against the mortar with a harsh grating sound that matched my mood. Sweat beaded on my forehead as I crushed the bitter herbs the old woman from a neighboring camp had sworn would "open my womb." The pungent aroma filled our tent—earthy, sharp, and tinged with desperation.

Time had flowed like the Euphrates, steady and relentless, carving its path through the seasons. After seven years of marriage, my belly remained flat, my monthly bleeding as regular as the phases of the moon. Seven years I had listened as Keturah's tent grew noisier with children's laughter while mine echoed with silence and unspoken disappointment.

I added a splash of water to the crushed herbs, turning them into a paste that looked as unappetizing as camel dung. The concoction would join the long list of remedies I had already tried—teas made from mandrake berries, prayers chanted beneath the night sky, special postures after Isaac and I coupled, ritual baths, and countless other suggestions from well-meaning women.

Nothing had worked.

And Isaac? Now we came together only to try another approach, nothing more. I could not remember the last time he reached for me out of love.

"What are you making?"

His voice startled me. I covered the mortar with a cloth, but not before he caught the scent. "Nothing," I said, my voice sharp. "It is something for . . . women's troubles."

He accepted my vague explanation without question. This had become our pattern. My monthly disappointment, his silent distance, the chasm between us that widened with each new moon.

"I will be in the eastern fields today," he said, turning to leave. "The shepherds have reported a problem with the well there."

"Of course." I gentled my voice. What had happened to me? None of this was his fault. "I will have dinner ready when you return."

After he departed, I stared at the covered mortar, then shoved it away. The old woman had promised results but so had all the others. What could they do when Adonai had closed my womb?

From outside came the high-pitched squeals of children at play. Keturah had produced five sons, and I could not produce even one.

I moved to the tent opening and peered out, watching as two small boys chased each other around a fire while a toddler wobbled after them on unsteady legs. Keturah sat nearby, her belly swollen with yet another pregnancy, her fingers working a spindle while she supervised her offspring.

Envy, hot and unwelcome, twisted in my gut. I dropped the tent flap, shutting out the scene.

The bitter herb mixture sat waiting. I sighed, uncovered it, and grimaced as I choked it down. It tasted of disappointment and false hope, but I swallowed every last bit.

Days passed. My bleeding came again, right on time, bringing with it a fresh wave of pain that left me curled on my sleeping mat, my arms wrapped around my treacherous belly.

"Perhaps it is not meant to be," Isaac said that night, his voice gentle in the darkness. "My father now has many sons through Keturah. Perhaps the lineage will continue through them."

"No," I said, more fiercely than I intended. "The promise was to *you*, not to them. You are Sarah's son; you are the son of the covenant."

I regretted my sharp tone when Isaac did not respond. He had been trying to ease my burden, to close the gap between us, but I had insisted on keeping us apart.

Another month. Another failure. And the other women were whispering.

I saw their subtle head tilts and noticed the conversations that halted whenever I approached. Even Deborah, the most loyal person I knew, had suggested that perhaps Isaac should take a concubine.

The thought made my stomach clench. I would not repeat Sarah's mistake. She had placed another woman in her husband's bed, but I would die first.

In that moment I made a decision. If remedies, patience, and prayers would not solve our problem, I would seek guidance from one who knew ADONAI's ways more intimately than anyone else in our camp.

Though it was unseemly for a woman to speak to her father-in-law of such things, I was desperate.

I would go to Abraham.

I WAITED UNTIL the next day, until the hour when my father-in-law sat in the doorway of his tent to say his morning prayers. With a basket of fresh bread as a pretense, I smiled and walked toward him.

What I intended went against convention—a young woman did not seek a private audience with her elderly father-in-law, especially to discuss matters of the marriage bed. The women of the camp would be aghast if they knew. But desperation had eroded my sense of propriety.

I heard his crackling voice before I saw him. "May the glory of the Lord endure for all time," he was saying, "let the Lord rejoice in His word. Blessed be the name of the Lord from now until forever. From the rising of the sun to its setting, the Lord's name is to be praised."

I stood silently, just out of his line of vision, until he had finished his prayer. Then I stepped forward. "Father? I have brought fresh bread for you."

A smile shone through his snowy beard. "Rebekah, daughter of my heart." His eyes crinkled at the corners. "You honor me with your visit"—he gestured for me to sit on the mat across from him—"and with such fine bread. The aroma alone is a blessing."

I placed the basket between us and folded my hands. Now that I sat before him, my carefully prepared words scattered like chaff in the wind.

"Does something trouble you?" he asked, peering at me. "You carry a burden. I can see it in your eyes."

The affection in his voice nearly undid me. I swallowed against a sudden tightness in my throat and drew a breath. "Father," I began, barely managing a whisper, "I come to you not only as the wife of your son, but as one who seeks the wisdom of Adonai."

His eyes, still sharp despite his years, continued to study me. "Speak freely, daughter. What wisdom do you seek?"

The words tumbled out, a torrent of frustration and fear. "Why am I not with child? Seven years I have been Isaac's wife, yet my womb remains closed. I have tried every remedy the other women suggest. I have prayed. I have done everything a wife should do to please her husband. Yet Keturah's tent overflows with sons, while mine echoes with emptiness."

I had not meant to mention Keturah, and I felt ashamed of the jealousy evident in my voice. Yet Abraham did not seem shocked or disapproving. Rather, a small understanding smile crossed his wizened face.

"Ah, Rebekah, how your words bring back memories." He shifted, adjusting his position, no doubt to ease his aging joints. He stared over my shoulder, and I knew he was looking across a vast expanse of years. "Sarah walked the same path, and her journey was far longer than yours. For decades her arms ached to hold a child. She, too, tried potions and prayers. She, too, watched as other women's tents filled with children while hers remained silent."

I had heard about Sarah, of course, but I had not expected Abraham to be so honest about the woman he had loved.

"She even gave me her handmaid." Regret tinged Abraham's voice. "That path *did* result in a son, but for Sarah it only brought heartache."

He reached across the space between us and took my hand. His skin felt like parchment, though his grip was surprisingly strong.

"God's promise cannot fail," he continued, conviction resonating in every word. "He has promised that my seed will be like the stars in the sky and the sand on the shore. Isaac is the son of promise, the only son of Sarah, and you are his wife. So that multitude of descendants must come from you. It *will* come from you."

Hope flickered in my heart, as fragile as a newly kindled flame. "Then why the delay? What am I doing wrong?"

Abraham chuckled. "Do you think you can force the hand of Adonai? Can your herbs and potions alter divine timing? Sarah was ninety when Isaac was born. *She* did not open her womb, Adonai did. He alone has the power, and He alone knows when the time will be right. Your only duty, my daughter, is to trust Adonai . . . and wait."

His words washed over me like cool water, both soothing and shocking in their clarity. All my frantic efforts, my bitter herbs and desperate remedies—had they been an attempt to wrest control from the God who had arranged my marriage in the first place?

I lowered my gaze, embarrassed and ashamed. What must ADONAI think of me? What must Abraham be thinking?

As if he had heard my thoughts, Abraham added, "ADONAI chose you for my beloved Isaac. So when ADONAI wills it, you will give birth to sons. Those sons will father nations, just as the Lord has promised. Again, the timing will be His."

The aroma of the bread, the heat of the morning, the distant bleating of sheep—all of it combined with my father-in-law's wisdom and made an indelible impression on my heart.

"Am I to do nothing, then?" I asked. "I have only to wait?"

"Wait, yes," he said, nodding, "but not in idleness or despair. Wait with confidence and purpose. Prepare your heart to be a mother of nations. Learn about ADONAI so you can teach your sons. And pray—not with the frantic passion of a woman who believes she must convince God to act, but with *shalom*, the peace that comes from knowing that His promises are as sure as the sunrise."

As he spoke, something within me unknotted—a tension I had carried so long that I had forgotten how to be free. My shoulders relaxed; I breathed more easily. All my striving, all my desperate attempts to control what lay beyond my power—none of it had brought me closer to my heart's desire.

"How will I know when it is time?"

Abraham's smile deepened. "You will not know until it happens. That is the nature of faith. Though the path be veiled in shadow, we walk by faith, for the Lord appoints the hour of light."

I nodded, absorbing his words. The morning sun had shifted during our conversation, casting new patterns on the mat beneath us. Time was passing even now, moving us forward on a path we could not see.

And every day that passed was one less day I would have to wait.

"Thank you, Father." I bowed before him. "I came seeking answers, yet you have given me something far more valuable."

"And that is?"

"Permission to surrender." I smiled. "To stop striving so I can trust in the God who brought me to my beloved husband."

"Come closer, daughter." When I leaned toward him, he placed a kiss on my forehead. "May ADONAI bless you, daughter of my heart."

I left my father-in-law, my steps lighter than they had been in years. The happy sounds of Keturah's rollicking children no longer needled me. Instead, I listened with new ears. Those sounds were not reproaches to my womanhood, but foretastes of the promise ADONAI would one day fulfill in my life.

My womb would open when ADONAI willed it and not a moment before. And when it did, the son I bore would be worth every moment of waiting, every tear of disappointment, every night of longing.

Until then, I would wait. But now, before I did anything else, I would run to Isaac, share what I had learned, and apologize for my reckless disregard for his feelings.

I would appreciate the husband God had given me.

LIKE VINES THICKENING with each harvest, the years twined around us. Three years after my talk with Abraham, I sat on a mat under an awning and laughed as Keturah's unruly children played in an open area near our tent. The six wild boys, a never-ending riot of squeals and shouts, spun about like whirlwinds of energy. They tumbled and raced, their small, bare feet kicking up puffs of dust as they chased lizards—or snakes, or each other—in a chaotic, unrelenting horde.

Keturah had been part of our camp for ten years, but she had not given birth in the last four. Unless ADONAI intervened, I did not believe she would have another child. Surely it was time for ADONAI to turn His thoughts toward me.

I regretted the thought almost instantly and silently assured the Lord that I would wait on Him. But though I had resolved to be patient, I could not help but wonder what would happen to my child when the miracle finally occurred. Would my little one have to compete with Keturah's sons for every affectionate glance? Would the cries of my baby be drowned out by the raucous clamor of these wild, joyful boys?

I watched as Abraham walked out and greeted them with a fond, albeit distant smile. His age did not allow him to wrestle playfully with them, but he often welcomed them into his dwelling to applaud their victories: a successful lizard hunt or the triumphant capture of an aggressive rooster. In those moments, his eyes shone with a pride that both warmed and pained me.

The rest of the household did not find it easy to live with such constant, spirited chaos. The boys' energy, though infectious, left little room for quiet reflection, so I often left the camp in search of silence. With no one else around, I would visit the cattle in the field, stand a safe distance from the huge bull, and wait patiently for him to greet me.

He never did.

But one evening, as the sky blazed with hues of purple and gold, Isaac joined me in the field, and the bull came over to sniff us. After giving him my hand and scratching his head, I turned to Isaac. "Will Keturah's children always be underfoot?" I asked, trying not to sound resentful. "Will our little one be in danger of being run over by one of them?"

Isaac's eyes shifted to meet mine. "I cannot say. You should ask my father."

I pressed further, feeling as though he was distancing himself from a truth he did not want to face. "Is it not *your* place to ask?"

Because he spent most of his time in the fields, Isaac did not have to endure the persistent din of Keturah's sons and the frustration of trying to work with wild children underfoot.

"When my time comes," I said, speaking to the bull to avoid pressuring my husband, "I hope our baby will not be lost in a thunder of voices. I want him to know he is not one of a horde, but a unique child of promise."

"He will know." Isaac slipped his arm around my shoulder. "Because he will have you as his mother, and I do not know anyone more loving."

A sob tightened my chest, and for a moment I dared not look at Isaac. He had always said his mother was the most loving person in the world, the most amazing, the most perfect, so this was high praise indeed.

I put my arms around his neck and pressed my lips to his. "Thank you," I whispered when we pulled apart. "Every day I thank ADONAI for leading me to you."

AGAIN I FOUND myself outside Abraham's tent, smoothing my tunic with damp hands. Though I spoke with my father-in-law every day, only once before had I sought a private meeting with him. But here I was again, my heart burdened by concerns about my promised child.

At last I stepped inside. The air was heavy with the scents of burning incense, warm oil, and dried animal skins. A brass lamp flickered in the space, casting long shadows across the richly woven carpets. Abraham reclined on cushions, a sheepskin draped over his thin shoulders. His beard tumbled over his chest, and when he looked up, his eyes crinkled with warmth.

"Rebekah," he said, lifting his hand in welcome. "Come, sit."

I obeyed, lowering myself onto the cushions before him, my heart racing. I bowed my head. "Father Abraham, I hope I am not disturbing your afternoon rest."

"Never," he said, sitting up. He adjusted a pillow behind his back, then smiled at me. "What is on your heart, daughter?"

I drew a deep breath. "Father, since my arrival in this camp, I hope I have pleased you."

His expression softened. "You have," he assured me. "And I can see that my son is more than pleased with you. You have mended his broken heart and restored joy to his life."

"I am glad," I said, struggling to speak over the lump in my throat. "And I am patiently waiting for the Lord God to fulfill His promise and give us children." I hesitated, then forced the all-important question to my lips. "But, Father, I must ask—will our child be raised with the sons of Keturah?"

Abraham lifted a brow, peering at me as if he would discern the motivation behind my question.

"The sons of Keturah will not be my heirs," he said, his voice even. "I will send them away before your child is born. I will grant them gifts and send them far from this household." A melancholy smile curved his lips. "It seems a lifetime ago, but I have learned that it is not good for the heir to live with the child who will not inherit. Life is better for all if the other child lives apart."

He was thinking of Ishmael, of course. I had heard the stories—how Sarah had grown jealous, how strife filled the camp, and how Sarah had been terrified that Ishmael might harm young Isaac.

"So you will send Keturah and her sons away," I said, "just as you sent Ishmael and Hagar?"

Abraham's eyes flickered. "When the time is right, yes."

"Forgive me for being impertinent, but how will you know when the time is right?"

He looked past me, through the opening, to Keturah's dwelling, which vibrated with the antics of her sons. "ADONAI will tell me. And I will obey Him."

A chill ran up my spine. I did not know what he meant, but one thing was clear—the sons of Keturah would not stay. This camp, this household, this future would belong to Isaac's children alone.

Once the Lord allowed me to bear them.

I leaned toward him, pressing my forehead to my clasped hands. "Thank you, Father."

"Go in peace, daughter."

I rose on shaky legs and left the tent. A scream shattered the afternoon stillness—one of Keturah's sons had undoubtedly smacked one of the others—but I ignored the noise and walked on, my hands shielding my empty womb.

Chapter 12

THE FAITHFUL MOON waxed and waned, weaving our nights into years. One by one, Keturah's sons were circumcised, one by one they reached adolescence. And each night, as I fell asleep with an empty womb, I consoled myself with the knowledge that I had one less day to wait for the fulfillment of God's promise.

Isaac, however, seemed to struggle with his father, and I could not discern the reason for it. Because my husband oversaw the business of the household—the livestock and our trade with traveling merchants—he spent little time with Abraham, a situation that only reinforced the distance between them. Though Isaac had never expressed resentment toward Keturah's sons, I wondered if the sight of them embittered him as it had once evoked jealousy in me. The camaraderie I had once noted between Isaac and his father had evaporated, but I was not sure my husband realized how much things had changed.

One night I walked through the camp and deliberately tried to view the situation with my husband's eyes. I nodded with approval at the herders who brought in the flocks; I complimented the women on their cooking and expressed pleasure at the sight of so many beautiful blankets and mats in the tent reserved for weaving.

But then I approached Abraham's dwelling, and a glance inside revealed my father-in-law laughing with sons he had never been asked to sacrifice to ADONAI. The youngest boys were leaning against his shoulders, and the older ones were displaying the foxes they had caught that day. "They will no longer eat our chickens!" the oldest child proclaimed, a dead fox in one hand and his bow in the other.

I lowered my gaze and stepped away. If Isaac had witnessed such a sight—and I was sure he had—no wonder he no longer wanted to be close to his father. How could he not feel displaced when Abraham so richly showered affection on his concubine's children? Though Abraham had not rejected Isaac—he never would—that knowledge surely did little to ease the feeling of being set aside when, like goats at the watering trough, other sons jostled and bleated for space.

The balance of our family had shifted profoundly, but I was not sure if Eliezer—who saw everything—had mentioned it to his master. I kept my concern hidden, and I dared not voice it myself. But in quiet moments, when the camp hushed and the desert night deepened, my mind replayed scenes of joy and laughter that no longer included Isaac.

I had told Isaac that his father had promised to one day send the sons of Keturah away. But year after year passed, and they remained with us. Did Isaac wonder if his father would keep his word?

Sometimes I would catch my husband staring into the distance with a vacant expression, his brow furrowed. Was he feeling isolated? His once vibrant spirit had grown silent, and he seemed a shadow of the confident man I had married. I wondered how long these other sons would continue to crowd our camp, eclipsing the covenant promise Abraham had received so long ago.

One night, as Isaac and I enjoyed the breeze in the doorway of our tent, a smile crossed his face. Feeling that the moment might be right, I leaned against him. "Something amuses you, husband?"

"Oh." He lowered his head and grinned. "Today one of the young herders tried to ride a cow. He was convinced he could train the cattle to carry a man."

I slipped my arm through his. "What happened?"

Isaac shook his head. "The fool leapt onto a cow's back, and the cow let out a bellow that would scare the sandals off a Philistine. Then she ran for the wadi and stopped at the bank, so the herder was thrown into the water." Isaac caught my eye. "Fortunately, the fool was not hurt."

"And the cow?"

"Affronted, but uninjured."

I laughed. "Your father would appreciate that story. Have you told him?"

Isaac's smile faded. "No."

"Why not go to him? He is probably still awake."

Isaac shook his head. "I am almost ready for bed myself. Will you come?"

When he put out his hand, I knew the subject was closed.

I followed my husband, silently praying that ADONAI would somehow restore balance to our camp and guide Isaac back to his father.

TIME PASSED, the years burning away like the olive oil in our clay lamps. One morning I awoke to a gentle hush, a quiet so thick I almost forgot about the impending celebration, a day that would be marked by jubilation and farewell.

I sat upright in bed and nudged Isaac's shoulder. "Wake! You have overslept."

Isaac squinted at me, then realization filled his eyes. "Oh!" He rolled out of bed and threw on his tunic. "I must check on the butchering."

"Go, then." I gave him a quick kiss and sent him on his way.

Today Abraham's household would celebrate the thirteenth birthday of Keturah's youngest son. After the celebration, Abraham would bid farewell to his concubine and all six of her offspring.

I dressed in one of my finest tunics and nodded when Deborah entered, flushed and perspiring. "I am sorry I am late," she said, "but I promised to help hang the banners."

"No need to apologize." I smiled from an overflow of goodwill. "This is a happy day."

By the time I stepped outside, the camp had been transformed. Vibrant banners of richly dyed cloth fluttered in the breeze, and the aroma of roasted beef swirled with the sweet smell of baking dates and figs. I walked among the preparations, enjoying the pulse of excitement. Servants hustled about, setting long tables with gleaming vessels and heaping platters of food. The low, rhythmic beat of drums and the cheerful laughter of the servants' children signaled a festive, bustling day ahead.

I stopped to help a shorter woman hang a banner from a suspended rope, then went to the cooking area to check on the meal. Everything had been prepared, and no one would be able to say that Abraham had not provided his best for Keturah's sons.

At midmorning, we gathered under a large, open pavilion for the celebratory banquet. Abraham stood in the center of the gathering, his eyes reflecting wisdom and wistful melancholy. "With joy and sorrow, I must say farewell to my youngest sons." His eyes searched the listeners, then focused on Isaac. "I knew from the beginning that I would have Keturah's sons with me for only a brief time. If I have seemed to neglect any of you while they lived among us, know this—I love all my children, but these sons will live apart from me, and I had to give them time while they were here."

I glanced at Isaac's face and saw that his eyes were wet.

One by one, Abraham called the sons of Keturah forward and presented them with gifts.

"To Zimran, the firstborn of Keturah," he announced, "I am giving two tents; three sets of fine garments, complete with shoes; two iron pots; ten goats, two male and eight female; ten sheep, two male and eight female; five camels, one male and four female; and eight donkeys, two male and six female."

As the entire household watched, he placed garments of brilliant hues over the young man's shoulders. Abraham embraced twenty-year-old Zimran and bestowed a blessing.

As he presented gifts to Jokshan, Medan, Midian, Ishbak, and Shuah, the youngest at thirteen, I could not help being impressed by my father-in-law's generosity. A niggling voice inside me whispered that he seemed to be giving away a great deal of the estate that would one day pass to Isaac, yet Abraham had amassed his fortune through the blessing of ADONAI, and I had no claim to it.

I stood at the edge of the gathering, watching as Abraham gave his affectionate farewells. The warmth of his embrace and the firmness in his blessing displayed both love and finality. The young men smiled at the presentation of such generous gifts, and more than one wept when they realized that they would soon be on their way to lands in the east.

After the gifts and the blessings, the celebration continued as the servants loaded pack animals and divided the flocks. When the sun was three-quarters of the way across the sky, Abraham announced that the time of departure had come.

Keturah and her sons walked outside the camp, where a line of loaded pack animals waited, followed by herdsmen and the promised livestock. As the clink of iron pots and the chuffing of animals filled the poignant silence, Abraham walked toward them, embracing Keturah and each young man one final time. Then, in an act of authority, he struck the lead animal's flank, sending it eastward.

A surge of conflicting emotions filled me as Keturah and her sons headed toward the eastern horizon. I was relieved to know that their incessant clamor and untamed energy would leave our camp, but the place would seem silent, even dead, without them.

One look at Abraham's face when he came back assured me that he had cherished Keturah's sons. He had held sincere affection for the stalwart woman who had been his companion and helper in his old age. While he would miss them, he had sent them away for a purpose.

Abraham had made room for Isaac's children. He had kept his promise.

Now we would wait for ADONAI to keep His.

Book Two

BEERSHEBA

Isaac prayed to ADONAI on behalf of his wife because she was barren. ADONAI answered his plea and his wife Rebekah became pregnant.

Genesis 25:21

Chapter 13

TWO WEEKS AFTER Keturah and her sons left our household, I made a decision. When the camp filled with the hush of twilight, and the heat of the day faded into a cool, starlit night, I approached Isaac with a smile, my heart pounding with desperate hope.

With great reverence, I knelt and made my request: "My lord, Deborah tells me that your mother, Sarah, was barren until Abraham prayed for her, then she conceived. Now, please, I must ask you to pray to ADONAI. He will hear your prayer and remember us."

Isaac's eyes, sharp and searching, met mine. "My father has already prayed for me to multiply his seed," he replied, his tone edged with stubborn sorrow. "So this barrenness must come to us from you."

His words ripped at my heart, but I could not allow despair to take root. I was well acquainted with my husband's estrangement from ADONAI. For years, he felt as though the Lord had ignored him, and nothing had changed. So why would his feelings change now?

But Adonai, Abraham assured me, did not change. And to find Him, we had to approach Him.

Fortifying my soul with all the resolve I had developed in our nineteen-year marriage, I urged Isaac again: "Get up and pray, so the Lord will hear your prayer and grant me children."

He did not answer, and we went to bed without speaking. Knowing that I had alienated my husband with my insistent request, I did not sleep for a long while.

But the next morning, Isaac rose, dressed, and shot me an expectant look. "Will you come with me?"

"Where are we going?"

"If I must offer this prayer for you, I will do it from a place where my father once built an altar—a mountain near Beth-El."

I did not know Beth-El, but I would have agreed to go to the other side of the Great Sea, if necessary. I did not know why Isaac had changed his mind, but clearly he had been thinking about his relationship with Adonai.

I dressed quickly, asked Deborah to pack a basket with enough food and water to last a week, and joined Isaac at the stable.

The road from Beersheba to Beth-El was long and barren, but my heart soared to know that Isaac was finally ready to speak to the Lord. It would not be a quick prayer murmured by the sheep pen. Isaac was willing to invest a journey, his labor and sweat, to make this prayer a reality.

We traveled under the blistering sun and stopped to sleep beneath jutting rock formations each night. As I lay next to my husband, the dark sky—an endless tapestry of shimmering stars—seemed to shine with promises of mercy.

On the third day, when we reached Beth-El, we stopped for water and purchased a yearling lamb for a sacrifice. Then we kept moving until we reached the mountain where Abraham had built an altar. The stones were still there but had since been scattered and covered by sand.

Holding the lamb, I sat in the shadow of a tall rock as Isaac reformed the altar. After offering the lamb as a sacrifice, he lifted his face to heaven. I listened, my heart thundering, as his voice broke the silence.

"O Lord God of heaven and earth, whose goodness and mercies fill the earth, you took my father from his birthplace and brought him to this land. You said to him, 'To your seed will I give this land.' You promised and declared that you would multiply his seed as the stars of heaven and as the sand of the sea. Now verify the words you spoke to my father. For you are the Lord our God, and our eyes look to you to give us children, just as you promised. Our eyes are directed to you alone."

Each word reverberated in the desert air, heavy with the ancient promise and personal longing. Standing behind him, I wrapped my arms around my barren womb and hoped my husband's prayer would be answered.

When Isaac finished, a profound silence settled over the place. Yet our destiny still seemed as unsettled as the whispering wind. Adonai did not appear or answer.

But Isaac had surrendered . . . because he truly loved me. For my sake, and on my behalf, he had set aside his questions and resentment to address the Lord of heaven and earth.

As we hobbled the camels and prepared to sleep, I clung to the belief that Adonai had heard Isaac's plea. My heart trembled with anticipation as I prayed for the fulfillment of His promise that would bring the child who would not only heal our battered hearts but mend the fabric of our family.

Chapter 14

I WAS SITTING on a woven mat in our tent when Deborah came to me, her face wreathed with concern. Her eyes searched mine as if seeking information I might not yet be ready to share.

"My lady," she began, "when did you last have your monthly bleeding?"

Her words struck like a chisel. I blinked, suddenly aware that it had been over two months.

Deborah's gaze remained steady. "Are your breasts tender? And have you been sick or uneasy, perhaps in the mornings?"

"I-I am not sure."

A flush of warmth crept over me as I recalled subtle sensations: the ache in my chest; the queasy stirrings I had brushed aside in the bustle of my daily labor. I looked at Deborah, every nerve humming with new awareness.

She knelt to take my hand, her touch a comfort in the confusion of this unexpected vulnerability. "You are with child, my pet," she said, her mouth curving in a broad smile. "Adonai has answered your husband's prayer."

The warm air of the morning, the soft flapping of the tent,

even the cattle's distant lowing faded as the truth entered my consciousness. *With child*. Isaac had approached ADONAI, and I was now with child!

If I had been standing, I would surely have fallen. A flood of emotions overwhelmed me—joy intertwined with fear, hope mingled with uncertainty, gratitude mixed with relief. I closed my eyes, enjoying the quiet beat of my happy heart. Every silent prayer and every secret tear had culminated in this miraculous moment. I was with child. The fulfillment of ADONAI's promise filled me with gratitude for the Lord's great mercy and faithfulness.

"Praise ADONAI," I whispered, bowing myself to the ground. "Bless ADONAI for His goodness and love. He has indeed honored His promise to Abraham and Isaac and has not forgotten His daughter Rebekah. May His name be exalted forever in all the earth."

Deborah bowed next to me. "Amen and amen."

MOMENTS AFTER DEBORAH'S revelation settled in my heart, I obeyed an urge to flee the camp. My feet carried me past the view of the sentinels, past the bleating livestock. I walked around rocks, climbed a hill, and finally found myself in unfamiliar terrain, a spot where I could express my overwhelming joy without being observed.

I kicked off my sandals and whirled in the sunshine, my arms outstretched like wings taking flight. The veil that normally shrouded my face from strangers now streamed behind me, caught by the desert wind. My feet, bare against the hot sand, moved of their own accord, finding rhythms I had never danced before. Twenty years of sorrow fell away with each step.

I spun faster, my heart pounding like a drum. The world blurred around me—the endless sky, the distant mountains, and the scattered rocks became a tapestry of color and light. I laughed, the sound bursting unbidden from my throat, wild and free as it echoed across the wilderness. When had I last laughed like this? Had I ever?

I cupped my hands over my belly, still flat beneath my robes, yet housing the miracle I had longed for through countless lunar cycles. A child. My child. Isaac's child. The promise fulfilled at last.

"You are there," I whispered, twirling again, feeling sweat bead upon my forehead and neck. "You are truly there."

Tears streamed down my face, mixing with dust and sweat, but I did not care. I leapt higher, my feet leaving footprints that the wind would soon erase. My hair came loose from its careful braids, flowing around my shoulders like water. I was a new woman—no longer the despairing, hopeless creature whose monthly disappointments had become as regular as the tides.

The sun bore down, but its heat matched the fire inside me, the burning joy that threatened to consume me. I danced until my lungs burned and my legs trembled, until the rocks and sand ripped at my feet, but I felt only elation.

I threw back my head and released a wordless cry of joy, a shout of thanksgiving that sprang from the deepest place within me. The place that had been empty for years had been filled to overflowing.

My dance slowed as exhaustion finally claimed me. My chest heaved with each breath, and my skin glistened with perspiration. But I could not stop celebrating this victory. I clapped, marking time with the beating of my heart, the rhythm of life itself. My fingers traced patterns in the air, writing the story of this miracle in invisible script on the vast blue canvas above.

"God of Abraham, God of Isaac," I sang, the words and tune filling my head, "He has remembered me, His lowly handmaid. The womb He opened, the promise He kept; the stars and the sand cry, 'Faithful is He!'"

I fell to my knees on the rocky soil, the earth grounding me as tears spilled freely over my cheeks. "ADONAI," I called, my voice trembling, "you saw me. You heard me. You remembered me."

My hands cradled my still-flat stomach, a tender caress for the fragile life within. "I am not barren," I whispered, each word a blessed pardon. "I will not cause your promise to fail. You have planted life within me, and I will bear a son to continue the lineage of Abraham. Isaac will be a father, and I a joyous mother."

A rush of wind stirred a patch of nearby grass as though creation itself had leaned in to listen.

"Blessed are you, ADONAI, Creator of life, Keeper of promises," I cried, lifting my face to the sky. "Let the rocks sing of your faithfulness! Let the grasses dance in praise! Let the trees lift their branches to honor you! Let every beast of the field and every bird of the air magnify your holy name!"

The wind wrapped me in a whirlwind of joy, as though ADONAI's holy attendants were dancing around me. My heart, once burdened with longing, soared with gratitude.

When I fell, breathless and spent, I lay on the earth and considered the new direction my path had taken. Why had God answered my prayers now rather than years before? I did not know, and in that moment I did not care. All that mattered was that He had worked in His time, and I could trust His providence.

I sat among the rocks until I could breathe without panting. As I rested, my heart soared with the memory of when I petted Isaac's bull and the beast looked into my eyes. On that day, I had felt awe at the connection to something that could easily destroy me, but that hour paled in significance compared to this one.

ADONAI had chosen me to be Isaac's wife and planted life within my womb. I was connected to a God who could destroy the world with a single word, yet He chose instead to accept my worship. My devotion. My humble life.

I flattened myself on the earth, overcome by the knowledge and responsibility I had been granted. And when the rocks cooled and the sun began to slide behind the hills, I rose and walked back to camp and to Isaac, my lips murmuring praises with every step.

ISAAC SAT IN the shadowed coolness of his tent, studying the scrolls his father had entrusted to him. The afternoon heat pressed against the goatskin walls, but inside, the air remained still and bearable. His eyes traced the familiar patterns of script, yet his mind wandered. Rebekah had slipped away hours before, something she never did without explanation.

A flurry of movement at the tent's entrance drew his attention. Someone pushed the heavy flap aside, allowing sunlight to spill across the rugs. He shielded his eyes, at first seeing only a silhouette framed in blinding light.

He set aside the scroll. "Rebekah?"

He nearly did not recognize his wife, and her appearance startled him into silence. Her long dark hair, usually braided and covered in public, cascaded down her shoulders in wild disarray. Sand clung to her damp forehead. Her veil—the modest covering she had worn since before their wedding day—was conspicuously absent.

Yet it was her eyes that rendered him speechless. They shone with an intensity he had not witnessed in years, perhaps ever. The dark pools that had been increasingly shadowed with disappointment now gleamed with unmistakable joy. A light seemed to illuminate her face, transforming her dishevelment into a sight that stole his breath.

"Where is your veil?" he said, the words sounding foolish even as they left his lips. Of all the questions flooding his mind, that was hardly the most pressing.

A smile spread across Rebekah's face—not the polite, measured expression she typically offered servants and guests, but a smile wild and unrestrained. She looked younger, unburdened in a way that made his chest tighten.

"I have been with the Lord," she said.

She moved toward him with a light step, seeming to float rather than walk across the carpet. Despite her rumpled clothing, she carried herself with the dignity of a queen, her shoulders straight, her head held high. Whatever had transpired outside the gates had transformed his dutiful wife into someone radiantly alive.

"You have been gone for hours." He stood. "I was beginning to worry."

"I needed to be alone," she replied, her gaze steady. A secret knowledge danced behind her eyes.

Isaac reached out to brush a strand of hair from her face, noting the warmth of her skin beneath his fingertips. She leaned into his touch, her smile deepening, and took his hand.

"Yes," she whispered. "Something has happened."

Isaac gazed at his wife, waiting.

"I wanted to be alone," Rebekah continued, "because I wanted to thank the Lord with my entire heart, body, and soul." She drew a deep breath. "My lord, ADONAI has answered our prayer."

Isaac stared. "Do you mean—?"

Rebekah's smile widened as she pressed his hand against her belly. "I am with child. We will have a baby in"—she averted her gaze as she counted—"about seven months."

Isaac stared at his hand, resting snugly against the fabric of her tunic, against the flesh that would soon swell with new life. He tried to speak, but no words would come.

"A son?" he finally managed to say, his voice scarcely above a whisper.

"Or a daughter." Tears of joy gathered in her eyes. "You prayed, and ADONAI remembered us."

Isaac felt his legs weaken. He sank onto his cushion, pulling Rebekah down beside him. A child after twenty years of barrenness. After watching Keturah's sons fill the camp while his own tent remained silent. After the whispers among the servants, the pitying glances from visitors, the growing frustration in Rebekah's eyes.

But knowledge even more profound had shaken him to his core.

"My prayer," he said, realization dawning like a sunrise. "ADONAI heard my prayer . . ."

For sixty years he had lived in the shadow of his father: Abraham, the friend of God, the man with whom Adonai had made an everlasting covenant. He had always believed himself the mere inheritor of his father's blessing, but though Abraham had prayed fervently for Isaac and Rebekah to conceive, no child had come.

Until now. Until he, Isaac, journeyed to Beth-El, fell on his face, and begged Adonai to remember his wife.

"He heard me," Isaac repeated, looking at Rebekah. "He heard *my* prayer."

Her hand covered his. "Yes, my lord. Adonai heard you."

Something broke open within Isaac's chest, a dam that had held a lifetime of uncertainty. Tears spilled down his cheeks and into his beard. He was not merely a son of Abraham, the passive recipient of a covenant Adonai made with his father. He was known by Adonai and heard by Adonai.

"All these years," he said, his voice trembling, "I believed He spoke only to my father. That I was—" he struggled to find words—"was *insignificant* in His sight. The promised child, yes, but not one worthy of direct attention."

Rebekah touched his face, wiping away a tear. "He sees you, Isaac. He has always seen you."

Isaac closed his eyes, overwhelmed. The God who had spared his life on Mount Moriah, the God who had brought Rebekah to him, had bent down to hear his desperate plea. Not because he was Abraham's son, but because he was Isaac.

"A son." He opened his eyes to gaze at his radiant wife. "We will have a son."

He drew Rebekah into his arms and felt her tears dampen his neck. As she trembled against him, he silently addressed the One who had created this miracle. *You heard me, Adonai. You who created the stars and set them in their courses heard me.*

The God of heaven was also the God who listened to the cries of individual hearts. For the first time, Isaac felt worthy of the covenant that had been passed to him, not merely as Abraham's heir but as a man standing alone before God.

And in seven months, if ADONAI was willing, he would have a child of his own.

Chapter 15

NO ONE COULD deny that my exceptionally round and firm belly contained new life. Isaac, his joy radiant and warm, often sat by my side, his hand resting on the swell of my stomach while he encouraged our son to grow strong and tall. Each time the baby responded to my voice with a kick or movement, my heart fluttered with delight. Each time Isaac spoke to my belly, the child would stop moving, as if he were drinking in this assurance of his father's love.

As for Abraham, his eyes sparkled with pride whenever he looked at me. "Did I not tell you?" he would say. "ADONAI works His will when the time is right."

But as I entered the sixth month, I sensed a strange stirring within. My belly, once a serene cradle, rippled and churned beneath my garments as if a storm raged within its walls. I could see the movements—waves of flesh that startled me—and often my belly moved erratically as though the baby wrestled with unseen forces. Could someone have placed a curse on my child?

Alarmed and mystified, I turned to Deborah for advice, but she only furrowed her brow. I consulted Tala the midwife, who was likewise mystified by my belly's odd contortions.

Determined to find answers, I resolved to seek ADONAI. When I shared my intent with Abraham and Isaac, my husband's eyes clouded with anxiety. But Abraham, ever wise and reassuring, embraced my resolve. "Shem and Eber," he said, "have established a house of study, a yeshiva, in the land of Moriah. Consult the Lord there. Seek Him so your soul can be at peace." Though he could not accompany me, he promised to ensure my safety by sending Minos, Eliezer's chief assistant, as well as servants to accompany me on the journey.

Isaac could not accompany me either, as it was lambing time and he had to oversee the births. I wondered why he could not find someone else to handle his responsibilities, but he insisted on staying behind. At first I thought he might be queasy about childbirth, but then I remembered—Mount Moriah held unpleasant memories for him.

"I will pray for your safety," he said, holding me the night before I was to depart, "and my heart will go with you. Always."

Sighing in resignation, I rested in my husband's arms and tried to sleep.

BECAUSE I WAS great with child, we did not take camels to the land of Moriah but instead traveled on foot—at least the others did. I was told to ride in the supply wagon, though at times I thought I would have been more comfortable walking. Every bump and jolt of the wagon wheels sent waves of discomfort through my swollen body, and the thin cushions Minos had provided did little to soften the journey.

Each morning, my attendants helped me climb onto the wagon bed, their strong hands steadying me as my balance shifted with the weight of my unborn child. The leather straps that held the planks together creaked with every step of the donkey's hooves, a constant accompaniment to our slow progress northward. By midday the sun would beat ruthlessly on us, and despite the canopy of woven reeds over my head, rivulets of sweat trickled between my shoulder blades and gathered at the small of my back.

When the discomfort became almost too much to bear, I forced myself to focus on the landscape. The limestone in this area had been formed in shades of orange, brown, and ivory, a lovely change from the white limestone of Beersheba. Rocky pillars stood like silent sentinels against the azure sky, and the scents of wild herbs wafted on the breeze whenever we passed through valleys. Small lizards scurried across our path, their bodies glinting in the sunlight before disappearing into subterranean spaces.

Just before dusk, the departing sun tinted the land with its long rays and turned the landscape gold. In those moments, even my discomfort seemed tolerable as I watched local shepherds guide their flocks to nighttime enclosures, their silhouettes black against the flaming horizon. The evening air would cool rapidly, bringing welcome relief as my attendants prepared our simple camp. I would clamber out of the wagon, one hand pressed to the small of my aching back as the aroma of lentil stew mixed with the sweet scent of the bread and date honey Minos insisted I eat to maintain my strength.

After four long days, Minos said we had entered the land of Moriah. "You have been patient, my lady," he told me, "and we are very nearly at the place we seek." My back was aching fiercely by then, and my ankles had swollen to twice their normal size, stretching the leather of my sandals until the straps bit into my flesh.

After stopping to ask how to find the yeshiva, we halted the donkeys at a pebbled path that led to a small house atop a hill. Minos helped me from the cart, his hands strong under my arms as I struggled to find my balance. My legs trembled after the long ride, and the weight of my belly pulled me forward.

I adjusted my veil, the rough linen scratching my sand-crusted skin. I took a moment to arrange my tunic over my bulky belly, the fabric darkened with patches of perspiration, and began to walk the path. The bitter taste of fear coated my tongue as I imagined falling in such a place. I took extra time, terrified that I might trip over a jagged rock or turn my ankle on a loose stone. The stones shifted beneath my feet with each step, and dust rose to coat the hem of my garment.

My breath came in shallow bursts as I clutched my aching belly, exhausted by the restless gyrations of the child within. Yet the wind whispered through the sparse trees, tugging at my robes and urging me forward. The scent of cypress hung in the air, reminding me of the incense in our tent. I thought of Isaac, of the burden he had carried on his long-ago journey to a mountain near this place. Had he felt betrayed when his father told him to climb onto the altar? How could he not have been terrified?

With relief, I approached Shem and Eber's house, a humble structure nestled between two rocky outcroppings. The stone building blended with the hillside, its walls the same dusty brown as the surrounding earth. A thin plume of smoke spiraled from a small opening in the flat roof, carrying the faint aroma of roasted barley.

Noah's son and grandson stood in the doorway filled with the slanting sunlight. They greeted us with curious nods, their faces as weather-beaten as the landscape. Their eyes lit when Minos introduced me as Abraham's daughter-in-law.

After murmuring a welcome, Shem's gaze focused on my belly. Eber brought a wooden stool and gestured for me to sit. I lowered myself awkwardly, grateful for the support as my knees threatened to buckle. The stool creaked under my weight.

"Tell me, daughter of Abraham," Shem said, his voice cracking with age, "why have you come to us?"

"Please," I began, "I have never birthed a child, but the midwives say they have never seen anything like my condition. It is as if my baby is troubled in my womb. Why is this happening to me?"

Shem's brow lifted in unspoken question, so I pulled my tunic tight over my belly, the linen fabric stretching across the mound. I pressed two fingers into my abdomen, encountering the firm resistance of a tiny back or perhaps a head. In response, my belly contorted—half rolling one way, half another—and I grimaced at the sharp jab of what must have been an elbow or foot against my ribs. The movements were visible through the fabric, a rippling wave that seemed impossible for a helpless infant.

Shem and Eber studied me, their expressions intent as they watched the bizarre spectacle. Then they looked at each other, some silent communication passing between them as their brows furrowed with concern.

They gestured that I should go into the small hut, out of the weather. The wind had picked up, sending columns of dust spinning across the open area, and the afternoon light had taken on the golden quality that preceded sunset.

Minos took my arm and helped me stand, his callused hand steady against my elbow. He led me into the hut and gestured to a narrow cot against the far wall. The straw mattress crackled beneath me as I lay down, grateful to be horizontal. "Rest, my lady," he said, covering me with a wool blanket that smelled of sheep and woodsmoke. "I will wait outside."

I closed my eyes, inhaling the scents of wood and ash from the hearth in the corner. The earthen walls seemed to breathe with the wind outside, and somewhere water dripped steadily into a clay vessel, marking time like a heartbeat. And then, as distinct as the blast of the ram's horn, I heard the voice of ADONAI.

Two nations are in your womb.

My eyes flew open as His voice resonated through my bones, not in my ears but somehow inside me, filling every hollow space.

Two peoples from your body will be separated. One people will be stronger than the other, and the older will serve the younger.

I gripped the blanket as a flood of gooseflesh rippled up each arm and collided at the base of my neck. Two babies? Two nations? The midwives had suggested the possibility of twins, but never had they heard of any woman experiencing such turmoil between children in the womb.

And of those two nations, the older would serve the younger. I shook my head, unable to make sense of the words. But by the time my babies had become two nations, I would no longer be living, so should I worry about the future? ADONAI would do what He wanted to do.

I rested my hands on my belly, eager to differentiate between the two babies. Yes, I could sense them—the energetic one, the instigator, lay beneath my right palm, kicking and pushing as if demanding to be first in all things; the quieter one lay under my left hand, responding only when pressed upon, yielding yet present. The contrast was as clear as day and night.

My sons would produce two nations. ADONAI had spoken and His words had carved themselves into my soul.

"Be it unto me and my sons as you have said," I whispered, tears blurring my vision as I struggled to sit up. "Thank you, ADONAI."

Shem and Eber came through the doorway, their eyes alight with the same fire I felt within me. The last rays of sunlight slanted through the small window, illuminating the dust motes dancing in the air. "We have heard from the Lord," Shem said. "Two nations are in your womb, and two peoples from your body will be separated."

I smiled as Eber continued, his voice stronger than his great-grandfather's but with the same cadence. "One people will be more powerful than the other, and the older will serve the younger."

An otherworldly peace settled over me. "Praise be to ADONAI," I said, "who not only speaks but gives assurances according to His word."

Shem lifted a brow, his sparse white hair gleaming in the fading light. "You knew this?"

"ADONAI spoke the same words to me." I placed both hands over my womb, grateful that the babies had apparently paused to listen. "Now He must give me strength to birth the babes, who have nearly torn my womb apart, and the wisdom to raise them properly."

A smile gathered up the wrinkles by Shem's ancient mouth. "He will provide the strength you need, daughter of Abraham. You have but to ask."

ISAAC STOOD AT the entrance of his tent, watching Rebekah as she approached, the weariness from the journey evident in her posture. She moved slowly, one hand pressed to her back, but a smile lit her eyes. Had she found the answers she sought?

When she reached him, she caught his hands, her face a mixture of awe and exhaustion. Isaac's pulse quickened. "Did you learn anything?"

Rebekah nodded. "Adonai spoke to me," she said, her voice tinged with reverence. "I heard His voice as clearly as I hear yours."

Adonai spoke to her? His gaze sharpened, searching his wife's face as he waited for a clarification. "What did He say?"

Rebekah released his hands and caressed her stomach. Her eyes went soft with memory, but her voice remained firm. "The Lord said I am carrying two nations. He said one would be stronger than the other, and the older would serve the younger."

Isaac's heart stuttered. "*Two* sons?"

Rebekah smiled. "Yes, they are sons."

Isaac's breath caught, his chest tightening. He had seen the odd way the babies moved inside her, but would his sons not dwell together in unity? Would they not share the promise given to Abraham?

His hands trembled. "They will be born at the same time," he said, thinking aloud. "How could one be stronger than the other? How could the older serve the younger?" He shook his head, trying to make sense of the words.

Rebekah's gaze softened. "ADONAI spoke of nations, not children, and He cannot be wrong. We may not understand how He will work, but He will."

"You must have misunderstood," Isaac murmured, but when her gaze met his again, he wished he had held his tongue.

Confident trust burned in her eyes. "I heard exactly what ADONAI meant for me to hear, and I could not wait to give you the news." She reached for his hand. "Years ago, husband, I vowed to raise my children without favoritism, loving each child equally. That is what I will do. And ADONAI will do what He will do." She sighed. "We need not understand what will happen with generations to come, but we will walk this path together no matter what comes our way."

Isaac inhaled a deep breath, allowing the comfort of her words to wash over him. "If it is ADONAI's will," he said, nodding, "then so it shall be."

OUTSIDE THE CAMP, Isaac walked until the heat stung his eyes and the distant landscape blurred into a wavering mirage. The desert stretched before him, vast and indifferent, much like the silence he had carried within him all these years.

When Rebekah told him of her encounter—how the Lord had spoken to her about their unborn sons—something disintegrated inside him. A dam of quiet acceptance crumbled, so he found himself stumbling toward the entrance of the camp, away from her glowing face, away from the evidence of divine favor that seemed to touch everyone but him.

Yes, the Lord answered his prayer. That news, combined with the knowledge that he would soon be a father, had lifted his spirits for days.

But what if ADONAI had answered Rebekah's prayer? The Lord God had just spoken directly to her, although He had never uttered a word to Isaac.

The sun burned the back of his neck as he climbed a rocky ridge. His throat burned with thirst, but he welcomed the discomfort. It matched the wasteland of his spirit.

He sank to the ground and felt the strength of limestone beneath the windblown sand.

"Why not me?" he asked, his voice reduced to nothing by the roaring wind. "My father walks with you. He heard you command him to leave his homeland. To circumcise the men of our household. To take me, his only son, to Mount Moriah."

He closed his eyes against the memory: the wood heavy across his shoulders, the difficult climb, his father's trembling fingers binding his hands and feet. The knife. The ram. The supernatural voice that to Isaac had sounded like thunder.

"Now you speak to Rebekah?" He dug his fingers into the hot sand, letting it heat his skin. "My wife carries my sons in her womb. You tell her their fate, but say nothing to me?"

He blinked as a scorpion scuttled past his foot. He watched it go, remembering how his father had described God's voice—yes, like thunder, but sometimes like a whisper, and always like certainty itself. To his knowledge, his mother had never heard from ADONAI, but she had Abraham to listen for her. And he had been given to them as a miracle, the fulfillment of an illogical promise.

Was that all he was meant to be? A bridge between promise and fulfillment? A lamb meant for sacrifice?

He lifted his gaze to the wide blue bowl of sky. "Am I flawed? Is there some darkness in me you cannot abide? Some reason I am unworthy of hearing your voice or feeling your presence?"

The wind stirred, sending a spray of sand into his face, but he did not flinch. The sting felt like an answer—the only one he might receive.

He thought of the wealth he had accumulated for his father, the wells he had dug, the peace he had diplomatically maintained with their neighbors. He had been obedient. He had been faithful. He had never questioned ADONAI.

Until now.

"I am weary of being the silent one," he said, lifting his voice to the rocks. "The one who inherits faith instead of forging it. The one who waits while others hear and act."

He stood, his legs unsteady beneath him. The sun had begun its descent, streaking the desert with hues of amber and gold. When he turned, he could see the dark silhouette of their camp, where Rebekah sheltered the future within her.

Two nations. Two peoples. One stronger than the other, the older serving the younger.

He believed it. Just as he believed in the promise given to Abraham, the covenant that guaranteed countless descendants and this land for an eternal inheritance.

He had witnessed too many miracles to turn away from his father's God.

Isaac pressed his hand against his chest, where his heart pounded like a blacksmith's hammer. Perhaps he would never hear ADONAI's voice as his father had. Perhaps he would never know why the Lord God did not speak directly to him.

But he was more than Abraham's son, more than Sarah's beloved boy and Rebekah's husband. He was Isaac, the one who laughs, though laughter had felt foreign to him for a long time.

"I may not hear your voice," he said, watching a raptor pinwheel across the darkening sky, "but I will continue to seek you. I will find a way to know you."

As he turned to walk back to camp, the cooling air felt almost like a caress against his skin. Not an answer perhaps, but a presence. And for now, that would be enough.

Chapter
16

WITH NOT EVEN a scrap of dignity remaining, I squatted on the woven mat in our tent, every muscle trembling as I struggled to bring forth life. Around me, Deborah and Tala—the steadfast midwife whose seasoned hands had guided my husband into the world—murmured soothing words and coached me through each contraction. The sound of Abraham's rumbling prayers came from outside the tent, his voice a steady accompaniment to my birth pangs. His fervent supplications had kept me going throughout those agonizing hours.

I did not know where Isaac was. Deborah asked about him, but I shook my head. "He is probably out with the livestock. Someplace where he can be in control."

Sweat trickled down my temples, mixing with tears of agony and anticipation. My heart beat unsteadily as I labored, and Tala's soft encouragement shifted to a tone of command. "Child, grip Deborah's hands. The first is coming now."

I obeyed, gripping Deborah's hands with all my strength as I bore down. The first cry split the air. I snatched a breath, hoping to relax, but renewed pressure reminded me that my labor had not ended. I clasped Deborah's hands again and strained, sweat dripping from my forehead. Then a smaller cry, soft but insistent, accompanied the squalling firstborn.

Tala's eyes gleamed with humor. "Look," she said, elbowing Deborah, "he holds on to his brother's heel."

I looked down. "What?"

Deborah pushed the wet hair from my face and helped me lie down. "Tala lay the first child between your legs. The second grasped his brother's foot as soon as he could."

Exhaustion wrapped around me like the desert night, yet a fierce, abiding joy thrummed beneath my fatigue. My struggles had birthed two lives. Two sons, just as ADONAI had promised.

Tala held up my firstborn, a small but solid baby with a mat of red curls on his head and a reddish coating on his body. I gasped, never having seen a baby with such red hair.

"And here is your second son." Deborah held up the second born, an even smaller infant whose head was as smooth as an egg. This child lay curled in Deborah's embrace, hands fisted and eyes closed, while the firstborn thrashed in Tala's arms, eyes wide and searching.

"I think he is hungry," Tala said, observing the eldest. "I hope you can find a wet nurse, for this one will have quite the appetite."

When Isaac returned, his eyes shone at the sight of our sons. Father Abraham visited, exclaimed over both boys, and offered prayers of praise to ADONAI.

Isaac settled on the bed beside me. "What shall we name them?" he asked, slipping his arm around my shoulders.

"We do not have to decide right away," I reminded him. "We could wait until their circumcisions."

"The first one came out of the womb covered in hair," Tala said, her eyes twinkling. "You should call him Esau because it sounds like the Canaanite word for *hairy*."

"Esau." I smiled at the baby in the crook of my right arm. "It fits."

"Since the second caught hold of his brother," Tala said, "we have another word that will suit: *jacob*. It means *to take by the heel*."

I looked at Isaac. "What do you think?"

Isaac studied the babies in my arms. "Those names will suit very well."

I sighed, relieved to have those questions answered.

I wanted to lie beside Isaac and study our babies for hours—their fingers and toes, the delicate crevices in their ears, the way tiny hairs swirled on their foreheads—but a profound yet peaceful weariness settled over me like a heavy blanket. I rested my head against Isaac's shoulder, knowing beyond a doubt that our future had been sculpted by the hands of ADONAI.

Isaac kissed my forehead. "Sleep now. I will watch over you."

FIVE DAYS AFTER the birth of our babies, I sat in the quiet of our tent, my body still weak from childbirth and the unending demands of nursing. My heart ached as I tried to nurse both my precious sons, but Esau, the firstborn, proved insatiable. His greedy mouth clung to me, biting my tender breast, eliciting pain that raced through me like wildfire. Every time I attempted to soothe him, his hunger and roughness overwhelmed me, leaving me physically exhausted and emotionally torn.

In contrast, Jacob was a gentle soul. His soft, delicate hands patted me lightly as he latched on, and his calm presence was a balm to my frayed nerves. Yet even his sweetness could not counteract the exhaustion that kept me in bed.

I realized then that Tala was right—I could not nurse both of them. With a heavy heart, I asked the midwife to find a suitable wet nurse, and within a day she had found Shira, who was planning to soon wean her daughter.

Tala brought Shira to my tent, where the nurse bowed before me. "I am happy to be of service, my lady."

"I would be grateful for your help," I told her. "Thank you."

She looked from one baby to the other. "Which of your sons shall I take?"

ADONAI's words came rushing back on a wave of memory. *The elder would serve the younger.* Yet I would not play favorites as my parents had; my choice was a simple matter of not being able to handle the more demanding infant. "Take Esau," I said, gesturing to him, "and I will nurse Jacob."

Bittersweet relief washed over me as Shira lifted Esau into her arms. "I will bring him to see you every day," she said, rubbing his back as the baby began to fuss. "But it sounds as though this little boy is already hungry."

"He is *always* hungry," I murmured. I thanked her, then watched as Shira carried him away, the sound of his cries fading into the distance.

"What have I done?" I asked Deborah. "I feel as if part of me has just vanished."

"Nonsense," she said, tucking the blanket around my waist. "You cannot feed both of the babies, and you need your strength. Nursing Jacob will give you time to recover from a difficult pregnancy."

She was right, of course. I was not playing favorites but had to choose what was best for all.

When Isaac returned to our tent, he was surprised to discover that Esau was not in his basket. "Where is Little Red?" he asked, sitting beside me.

I nestled into the space beneath his arm. "I have arranged for him to be fed by a wet nurse. It is the best way to be sure both boys are well nourished. If you wish to see him, you may fetch him—if he is not asleep or nursing."

Isaac leaned forward as if he would leave, then hesitated. "He is probably asleep," he said, settling back next to me. He nodded at Jacob, who was sleeping in my arms. "That is what all babies seem to do."

I snuggled closer to my husband. "They are not even a week old, yet already we feel the pain of parting from Esau. What will we do when they are old enough to take wives?"

"Why should they part from us?" Isaac lifted a brow. "Why can they not remain with us? They can raise their families here, so we can enjoy our grandchildren."

"But ADONAI said they will be two nations," I reminded him. "Have you ever heard of two nations occupying the same land in peace?"

Isaac's brow furrowed. "They are not two nations yet," he said, lowering his head to his pillow.

ISAAC STOOD AT the center of the tent, pride and anxiety rioting in his heart. The gathering hummed with excitement and anticipation as Rebekah and Deborah held his sons, their tiny forms barely discernible beneath loose blankets. Today marked their eighth day, so Isaac would obey the Lord's command and circumcise his sons to mark their entrance into ADONAI's covenant.

Abraham's entire household had gathered in a wide circle to celebrate the event. Abraham stood at the center of the assembly, his eyes shining with joyful reverence.

Terrified by the heaviness of his responsibility, Isaac's finger brushed the cool metal of the knife. He hoped the blade was sharp enough to cut swiftly and cleanly. He attempted to steady himself, but the rate of his breathing increased nonetheless. Each part of this ceremony was a sacred act, each gesture a reflection of the promises made to his father so many years before.

Despite his anxiety, pride welled in Isaac's chest, fierce and uncontainable. He had finally become a father, with two sons who filled his heart with joy and awe. And though his own father had sired many sons, Abraham had never fathered twins.

Abraham lifted his hands to begin the ceremony with prayer. "Blessed are you, Lord our God, King of the universe, who has commanded us concerning circumcision."

As his father prayed, Isaac's eyes roved over the faces of those gathered to witness the sacred rite. The sun, heavy in the sky, cast long shadows outside the tent, yet Isaac felt as if time itself had stopped to witness this moment.

His fingers clenched the hilt of the blade, and his thoughts focused on his sons.

When Abraham turned toward Isaac, he announced that his firstborn would be called Esau. Rebekah stepped forward and unwrapped the baby as Isaac dipped his hands in a bowl of water, then dried them with a clean towel. Rebekah held the baby in her left arm while Isaac drew a swift breath and made the cut. The baby wailed, and Isaac felt his stomach turn over. Tala covered the wound with a poultice, then Rebekah handed the baby to Deborah.

When it came time for the younger child, Isaac announced his name, "Jacob, to follow." He gazed upon his second born, whose small hands grasped at the air as Rebekah unwrapped him. Again, Isaac made the cut, the baby screamed, and Tala applied a poultice.

As Rebekah comforted her son, Abraham stepped forward. "Just as these children have entered the covenant, so may they enter marriage and righteousness." He lifted his hands. "Blessed and praised, glorified and exalted, extolled and honored, adored and lauded be the name of the Holy One, blessed be He, who is far above all blessings and hymns and praises and consolations which are spoken in the world, and say amen."

The assembled household repeated, "Amen."

Isaac stepped back, his heart bursting with pride for his sons and relief that he had not injured either infant. Rebekah gave him a sympathetic smile. When they were first married, she had been horrified by the knowledge that the males of Abraham's household circumcised their babies. Now she understood that it was a visible symbol of their relationship with ADONAI, though she had gone pale when he made the cuts.

With the ceremony finished, Isaac could now relax. He met his father's joyful eyes and felt a profound peace. The covenant had been fulfilled. The promise would continue for another generation.

Chapter 17

OUR SONS GREW so quickly that I could hardly keep up. Every day they seemed to change before our eyes, growing taller, stronger, and more independent. One day they were tiny infants, the next they were walking, their small feet pattering around our tent in an almost constant rhythm.

Esau, though only a moment older, seemed to dominate our world. Shira, the wet nurse who would be part of his life until he was weaned at three years old, brought him to my tent every morning. I would watch as my firstborn bounded in, his robust body bursting with energy. His red hair remained thick and dark, and his movements reminded me of a rabid dog—unpredictable, wild, and contrary. His frame was bigger than Jacob's, as was his voice, which could upset the cattle from a hundred paces away.

Jacob, in contrast, was smaller, thinner, quieter. He had always been delicate with an almost feminine beauty. His ivory skin gleamed in the sunlight, and his dark eyes seemed to brim with deep thoughts even as a baby.

When the boys played together, everyone noted the stark differences between them. Esau, loud and brash, barreled through every activity, ripping through baskets and blankets and the reed mats we spread over the sand.

Jacob watched. Like a mountain cat eyeing its prey, he parsed the world around him. He studied Esau's movements, his brows knitting, appearing to weigh and analyze. Esau might act first, but Jacob learned from Esau's victories and mistakes.

Isaac loved both of our boys, but he adored Esau. He would take the twins into the fields, their little hands gripping his strong fingers as they strolled together through the tall grasses. But when Isaac needed to ride, Esau always rode in front, his legs bouncing against the donkey, while Jacob rode with Minos or one of the other servants. Isaac never seemed to realize how he favored our firstborn, but Esau's size and energy appealed to Isaac's heart.

As I watched my sons, I found myself wondering what their futures would hold. Esau moved with the force of a whirlwind, but Jacob was no less powerful. Quiet, observant, and perceptive, intelligence shone in his eyes, along with a spark of calculation. He reminded me of the silent, swift leopards I had seen racing over rocky crags, calculating before they pounced on unwary prey. Esau acted before thinking, charging into any situation with bravado and enthusiasm, while Jacob pondered before making a decision.

One day, Deborah and I took the boys for a walk outside the camp. The crisp air was invigorating, and the earthy scent of the desert wrapped around us as we strolled through the landscape. The boys ran with the unpredictable rhythms of lambs let loose at springtime. I watched them, joy warming my chest as they bounded over the grass, their laughter like music. In their faces I could see glimpses of the men they would become.

We came upon a crevice in the rocks, an opening between two large boulders. Before Deborah could stop him, Esau, ever curious and bold, darted forward and thrust his hand into the gap. A moment later, he brought out a honeycomb, dripping with golden sweetness.

Jacob's eyes fixed on the honeycomb with longing. I feared he would follow his brother's reckless example, but before Jacob could act, a deep buzzing broke the silence, and the air filled with the wrath of a thousand angry wings. Deborah gasped, scooped up Esau, and ran. The swarm followed, and Deborah cried out as the bees stung her arms. Esau howled in pain.

And Jacob? He did not scream or panic but walked over, picked up the honeycomb Esau had dropped, and took a big bite of it.

I could hardly breathe when I caught up to Deborah and Esau. Both of them were trembling from stings that had raised welts on their arms and faces. But Jacob had outwitted the swarm.

I carried Esau, who whimpered in pain, and Jacob—still eating the honeycomb—followed Deborah back to camp. We visited the midwife, who gave us an ointment that helped to ease the stings.

Later, when the four of us rested in my tent, I could not help considering how my sons' different personalities would shape their paths. The older would serve the younger, Adonai had said. Perhaps in ways I could not yet comprehend.

But their futures were being revealed in afternoons like this.

THE BOYS WERE in their third year when Isaac held a great feast to celebrate their weaning. My husband invited all the leaders and dignitaries from nearby cities—wealthy men and their well-dressed wives, whose carefree laughter mingled with the scents of spring. The day was warm, bringing a gentle breeze that pushed through the tents and carried the aromas of roasting meat, fresh bread, and honey cakes.

I felt as though only a moment had passed since I cradled my sons as infants, yet there they were: my twins, so different from each other, yet mine to love equally. I watched them during the celebration, trying to divide my attention between them. One of the women at the banquet—a merchant's wife I barely knew—leaned close and said with a knowing smirk, "You must have looked at a red cow when you were carrying Esau. He is as bright as fire."

I smiled, though her remark made me uncomfortable. Remarks highlighting the boys' differences always unsettled me. All too well I remembered my own childhood, how Laban had been the favorite and how my parents' partiality had shaped me. I had vowed that I would never allow such favoritism to affect my own children.

Yet as the feast continued, I found my attention drawn more often to Jacob, who sat quietly by my side while Esau entertained the guests. Jacob's gentle calm resonated with something deep within me. When he looked at me with his long-lashed eyes, my heart filled with a tenderness I could not deny. He was so much like Isaac in his thoughtfulness, the Isaac I had come to love, not the Isaac who beamed at Esau's boisterous movements.

After their weaning, I began to teach my children. I taught them how to dress themselves, how to clean their teeth, how to use the privy and the chamber pot. As they grew older, I gave each a stick and went with them to an area with moist sand, the perfect place to teach them how to scratch out the symbols that would one day enable them to send messages.

I was not their only teacher. Abraham often took the boys to teach them about ADONAI and the history of his ancestors. I lingered at the side of the tent because I wanted to hear the stories, too. Jacob always sat still, his eyes wide with wonder, while Esau fidgeted and wriggled as if the significance of the lessons was too much for him. In those moments, I fought against my natural inclination to praise one son and scold the other.

As I listened to Abraham explain the covenant—how ADONAI had promised descendants as numerous as the stars—a question formed in my heart. Whoever said the blessing could fall to only one son? Could both boys not carry ADONAI's promise? Could Esau *and* Jacob not bring forth descendants like the stars in the sky? The question both comforted and fascinated me. If ADONAI's blessing was truly as boundless as the heavens, surely there was favor enough for both my sons.

That evening, as the servants cleaned up after the feast, I sat with Deborah and confessed my struggle. "I try to love the boys equally," I told her, "but it becomes more difficult each day. Isaac clearly favors Esau, and I find myself drawn to Jacob."

Deborah looked at me, her eyes soft and understanding. "Do you favor Jacob because you pity him?" she asked.

The question pierced me. Was I subconsciously trying to balance Isaac's favoritism, or did I have another reason?

"Jacob needs me in a way Esau does not," I admitted. "He is gentler and more vulnerable. Perhaps I am drawn to his need, but I also see in him a steadiness that reminds me of Isaac."

"And in Esau, Isaac sees a bold courage that reminds him of you," Deborah added.

I waved her comment away, but after a moment, I voiced the deeper question. "Why can ADONAI's covenant not extend to both our sons? Why must only one be chosen? Cannot ADONAI's promise of descendants be fulfilled through Jacob *and* Esau?"

Deborah folded her hands. "The ways of ADONAI are certainly mysterious," she said at last. "Perhaps it is not about who is worthy, but who He sets on His path."

"Could He not set both boys on the path of blessing?"

Deborah shrugged. "I suppose. But I do not know much about these things."

I pressed my lips together, frustrated by my own lack of knowledge.

Later that night, as I watched my sleeping boys—Esau sprawled across his mat, Jacob curled neatly on his side—I renewed my vow to love them equally, each for his own self. They were both mine and both precious. If I leaned naturally toward Jacob, I would work harder to connect with Esau.

But in the depths of my heart, I could not silence the voice that had spoken to me years before.

As the younger son, Jacob was destined to become the father of a powerful nation. And though I would fight against favoritism every day of my life, I feared that at some point I might be forced to correct their paths.

Chapter 18

THE DAYS UNFURLED like the turning of a potter's wheel, each moment shaping the next. My sons learned to converse and question; they sat at Abraham's feet and learned of Adonai. They also spent days in the field with their father, managing the flocks and overseeing the breeding of our goats, cattle, and donkeys. Tutors from neighboring cities came to our camp to teach my sons how to keep records, read, and write upon clay tablets, but Esau had no patience for reading or writing. Jacob excelled at both tasks.

My sons studied the phases of the moon and how the stars move through the heavens. They learned the history of the world, about the great flood, and stories of the kings who ruled in diverse lands. Jacob enjoyed his studies, but Esau found it difficult to complete any task for which he needed to sit still.

Time passed with the changing of the seasons and the inevitable births of new cattle, goats, camels, and babies. Our household continued to grow, each day adding its own new responsibilities. The fields flourished, the herds multiplied, and the air seemed to hum with motion and routine. Our lives were full. Abraham's wealth, once incomprehensible to me, now seemed almost ordinary.

Abraham had more servants than I could count, and his flocks—his cattle, sheep, camels, and goats—stretched across the horizon. People came from miles around to buy his camels and barter for cheese, soap, oil, and other goods that sprang from his holdings. The grove he had planted still attracted travelers, who rested in its shade and filled their bellies with its fruit.

As my father-in-law grew older, I noticed a change in him. Though his strength remained formidable, I sensed a new urgency in his actions, a renewed determination to teach Esau and Jacob about Adonai. Every morning, the boys would go to his tent, where he would sit propped up on pillows and tell them the stories of his youth. He shared everything he had learned from Noah and Shem—of how Adonai created a beautiful world with one man and one woman, Adam and Eve. He told them about how this beautiful world became so sinful that God destroyed it with a flood, and how only Noah and his family survived. He spoke of how Adonai saved him in Ur and of the dangers he faced in Egypt and in the land of the Philistines. He spoke of the promises made to him and how Adonai had told him that his descendants would outnumber the stars in the sky and the sands of the desert.

"You are my descendants," Abraham told the boys, his voice vibrant. "Adonai will make nations out of you."

Jacob would always sit close to his grandfather, his eyes wide, hanging on each syllable. The words of the Lord stirred something in him, and he often came away from his grandfather's tent with a preoccupied expression.

But Esau never lingered a moment longer than necessary. He would fidget, look longingly at the doorway, or invent an excuse to leave. He would say he needed to tend to the animals or complain of hunger or weariness. Each time Esau left Abraham's side, I saw disappointment in the old man's eyes, yet I did not want to interfere. Once I asked him if I should force Esau to stay and listen.

Abraham looked at me, his gaze heavy with resignation. "You cannot force someone to love ADONAI," he said, his voice full of conviction. "That desire must spring from the heart and the will. You cannot make it grow."

I took his words to heart, even as I watched Esau slip away again and again. Perhaps he would be a different kind of man. A different kind of son.

AFTER ONE MORNING visit, when both boys had gone, I turned to my father-in-law, his frail form reclining against the colorful cushions that supported him.

"Honored Father," I said, my sandals whispering against the carpet as I approached, "if you are not too weary, may I ask a question?"

His eyes, always bright, sparkled with curiosity. Deep wrinkles framed his face, each a testament to his advanced age. "What do you want to know, daughter?"

I sank to the carpet at his feet, the rough wool pressing against my skin. "I heard you tell the boys that ADONAI would make nations of them. Does that mean that both of them will carry the covenant blessing? That both will inherit the land of Canaan?"

I expected a quick answer because I had already convinced myself that ADONAI would be unfair to bless one son and not the other.

I was not prepared for his reply.

My father-in-law closed his eyes, his chest rising and falling as he drew a breath that seemed to come from the depths of the earth. The tent filled with a silence so thick I could hear the distant bleating of sheep and the soft rustle of the palm fronds outside the tent.

When he spoke, his voice had changed, resonating not just in my ears but in my bones.

"I know why you ask this." He spoke slowly, as if weighing his words like precious stones. "I know your mother's heart. And yes, ADONAI will give each of your sons descendants and land. But the covenant is about more than those things. It is also about blessing and salvation."

The latter word hung in the air, almost visible in the shaft of golden light that entered through the vent in the ceiling. I faltered in the presence of a truth both vast and incomprehensible. This was something I had never heard, something Abraham had never taught my sons.

I shook my head. "I do not understand."

His eyes found mine, and in them I saw not just the wisdom of his years but something ancient and eternal. "I do not have the knowledge of ADONAI," he said, his bony hands resting on his knees. "But do you remember the story of Adam and Eve in the garden?"

I nodded. He had shared the familiar tale on countless occasions.

"Good." He drew another breath, and I heard a slight rattle in his chest, a reminder of his mortality. "When ADONAI confronted the first man and woman, He cursed the serpent who had tempted them and said, 'I will put animosity between you and the woman—between your seed and her seed. He will crush your head, and you will crush His heel.'"

The words seemed to vibrate the air, like the trembling of a bell. I shivered with a sudden chill. "I still do not understand."

Abraham's gaze had become distant, as though he could see beyond the confines of the goatskin walls. "When ADONAI appeared to me, He said, 'I will bless those who bless you and curse those who curse you; and all the families of the earth will be blessed through you.'" He leaned forward, his eyes probing mine with an intensity that held me in thrall. "One will come," he said, his voice dropping to a whisper that filled the entire room. "One who will crush the serpent's head. This One will bless the entire earth. Do you not see?"

My heart quickened as something stirred within me, like water moving beneath desert sand.

"When I stood ready to sacrifice my only son," Abraham continued, a quaver in his voice, "the Lord supplied a ram for our sacrifice, and ADONAI promised that all the nations of the earth would be blessed in my seed."

Abraham leaned back, as though sharing the secret had exhausted him. Beads of sweat glistened on his brow, catching the light like tiny jewels. "I do not have the knowledge of ADONAI," he said again, his hands trembling, "and I have not yet shared this with Isaac because he is not ready to receive it. But the Deliverer who brings salvation will come from my lineage."

One Deliverer would eventually come from a branch of Abraham's family. It could not be otherwise.

Realization came, not as an obvious revelation but as a tiny speck of light. Slowly it grew, connecting with all I had learned through the years, illuminating dark corners in my understanding.

"All the sons of Abraham will be blessed," I said, watching him nod, the movement causing a lock of white hair to fall across his forehead. "Even the sons of Ishmael and Keturah."

"Yes."

"And Esau and Jacob will be blessed with a nation of descendants, but only one can carry the promise of the Deliverer." My fingers dug into the carpet, anchoring me even as the magnitude of the revelation threatened to undo me.

"The covenant promise is about land, descendants, and deliverance," Abraham said, and the words seemed to echo in the tent, bouncing off the walls and returning with greater significance each time. "But only one of Isaac's descendants will crush the head of the serpent."

Abraham lowered his head, and in that moment he seemed both ancient and ageless. "I do not know when the Deliverer will come, or how, but I do know *why*," he said, each word falling like stones into still water. "He comes to defeat the tempter who brought death into the world."

I sat for a long moment, the only sound my heartbeat in my ears. Abraham's family—and I was now part of it—would play a role in ADONAI's ancient plan. The serpent who had deceived Eve would be crushed, and death would be defeated.

I pressed a hand to my cheek, as if the weight of it might steady the storm inside my head. A chill passed through me, though the day was warm.

Tears welled, unbidden. I blinked hard, but they spilled over my cheeks.

This revelation cast me low in trembling awe. The knowledge was too glorious to bear.

When I could speak again, I leaned forward, caught Abraham's hand, and kissed it. "Thank you," I whispered, my voice thick. "You have opened my eyes to the future."

As I rose to leave, light from the chimney vent caught dust motes swirling in the air, transforming them into particles of gold. Outside, life continued—servants calling, animals braying, children laughing—but within me, *everything* had changed.

THE WHEEL OF YEARS turned like a millstone, pressing one month into the next. Though my sons had been planted in the same soil and were raised by the same gardeners, they continued to be opposite in temperament. "Jacob is like a spring rain," Deborah told me one afternoon. "Esau is a thunderstorm."

Like Isaac, Jacob enjoyed working with the herds because the work allowed him time for contemplation. Esau did not enjoy tending the livestock. He preferred instead the excitement of the hunt and became an excellent archer. Isaac gave him permission to hunt instead of working elsewhere, and nearly every day Esau brought home something for our kettle: a deer, a mountain goat, even a leopard.

Abraham refused to allow the leopard to be prepared as food. "An ox is chased by a lion; a sheep is chased by a wolf; a goat is chased by a leopard," he told Esau. "Therefore, the Lord God says, 'Do not bring me an offering from the pursuers, but from the pursued.' So we will not eat animals that pursue others, but only those who are pursued."

When Isaac saw that Esau's countenance had fallen, he took our son aside. "We will not eat the leopard," he said, "but you have killed a predator that might have taken many of our sheep and goats. You have done well, my son."

In the twins' fifteenth year, on a summer afternoon, I received word that my father-in-law wished to see me. Abraham had grown frail over the past few seasons, and his once-commanding frame was now bent. When the servant came to our tent with his summons, I knew instinctively that this was no ordinary request.

"He asks for you and the master," the servant said, his eyes downcast.

I checked the pouch of medicinal spices at my waist—in case Abraham was in pain—and adjusted my veil before striding toward his dwelling. The dust of the camp swirled around my ankles as I walked, and the familiar scent of roasting meat filled my nostrils.

The flap to Abraham's tent had been pulled open when I arrived. Inside, oil lamps cast dancing shadows against the goatskin walls. Abraham was leaning against strategically placed cushions, his beard luminous in the dim light. His eyes, now clouded with age, still held the spark of purpose I had always found both comforting and unnerving.

"You sent for me, Father?" I asked.

"Rebekah." He lifted his head. "Come, sit before me."

I lowered myself onto the carpet, my heart quickening.

"My days grow short," he said, waving a trembling hand. "And certain matters should be settled."

I kept my head bowed out of respect, but my chest tightened. What matters required my presence with Isaac? My husband had been out hunting with Esau since dawn, and I did not know if he would return before dark.

"Look at me, daughter," Abraham commanded.

I lifted my gaze and was startled by the intensity in his expression. When he leaned forward, I heard wheezing in his chest.

"One of Isaac's sons will be a blessing to humanity," Abraham said, his gnarled fingers curling in his lap. "He will be the glory among all the descendants of Shem. From him the Lord will establish His people, a people more enduring than any who are on the earth. And in his seed, through one of his descendants, all the nations of the earth will be blessed."

He exhaled sharply and fell back to the cushions. When he remained silent, I wondered if he was waiting for me to respond.

"Isaac loves Esau best," I said, admitting to the division that had become evident in our household.

Abraham nodded, his eyes dark with knowing. "My son Isaac does favor Esau. But you have favored Jacob."

"I have tried to love them equally," I said, a note of defensiveness entering my voice. "But they are so different."

Abraham smiled. "I have many sons, but Isaac is dearer to me than the others because he is Sarah's son, the promised child of our old age. He will be blessed forever, and his seed will fill the earth." My father-in-law sighed as peace settled over his features. "You, daughter, will understand what ADONAI intends," he said, closing his eyes. "When the time comes, you will know what to do."

Would I? *Please, ADONAI, let it be so.*

I turned as the tent flap rose, and Isaac entered, his face flushed.

"Come," Abraham said, his lined cheeks lifting as he smiled. "Kneel, my son, so that I may bless you."

Isaac shot me a look of confusion, but he knelt before his father. Tears flowed over my cheeks as Abraham pressed his hands to Isaac's head. "May all the blessings with which the Lord has blessed me be given to your seed," Abraham declared. "May my name and the names of my ancestors—Shem, Noah, Enoch, Malaleel, Enosh, Seth, and Adam—find blessing through you. And may the world find blessing through your descendants, and deliverance through the One who was promised."

As the ancient names fell from Abraham's lips, I could almost sense the presence of those fathers, stretching back to the beginning of all things. Isaac and I would not be alone in this charge; we stood in a line of chosen vessels, tasked with preserving the divine promise of salvation.

Overcome with joy and dread, I rose to my knees and placed my hand over Abraham's. "I will guard my sons," I vowed, my voice steady in spite of my surging emotions. "I will ensure ADONAI's blessing rests upon them."

"Now," Abraham said, wheezing, "send my sons Esau and Jacob to me separately, so that I may bless them."

ABRAHAM'S TENT smelled of incense and myrrh when I returned with Jacob. My beloved father-in-law remained on the mound of cushions, his frame frail but his spirit undiminished.

Again I sat on the carpet in front of him. Jacob sat next to me, folding his hands and remaining silent. I had told him that his grandfather wanted to see him, nothing more.

Abraham looked at me. "And Esau?"

"I am sorry, Father. I told him you wanted to see him, but he picked up his bow and went into the desert."

"So be it." Abraham closed his eyes and nodded. "Jacob, come closer."

With a quick glance at me, Jacob rose and knelt before his grandfather.

Abraham reached for him, his hands trembling as they rested on Jacob's head. "My son," he said, his voice thin but steady, "ADONAI has blessed you."

Jacob's breath hitched.

"My son Jacob," Abraham murmured, "the one my soul loves." He leaned forward and kissed Jacob's brow, lingering as if he were imparting an intangible gift. My son inhaled, absorbing his grandfather's affection like the desert sand drawing in the sun's warmth.

My breath caught in my throat. The tenderness in Abraham's voice, the unwavering certainty in his blessing—this moment would shape Jacob's future forever. My son was beloved, not only by me but by this man who had walked with kings and bargained with the Almighty.

Abraham lifted trembling hands. "May the God of my fathers, the One who called me from the land of my birth, bless you from above the firmament." Though his voice had been weakened by time, his words carried the force of the sacred covenant. "May all the blessings bestowed upon Adam, Enoch, Noah, and Shem be upon you and your descendants forever."

Jacob shuddered. I leaned forward and saw no dread in his eyes, only an overwhelming awareness that he had received something sacred. He was only fifteen—how could he fully understand the impact of the blessing?

I had never shared with Jacob what ADONAI told me before he and Esau were born. I did not want to burden him with knowledge that could affect his feelings for his brother, but Abraham had just reinforced the Lord's words.

Abraham dropped his hand to Jacob's shoulder. "May the Lord himself be your Father." His fingers tightened upon Jacob, as if ensuring that his words would take hold.

A hush settled upon us, as thick as the carpet beneath my knees. The silence was broken only by the flapping of the awning as the evening breeze murmured outside.

Abraham's lips parted once more, his words a gentle reminder: "ADONAI blessed our father Noah, our ancestor Shem, and my own father, Terah. But he called me out from Ur, away from my father's house, to make of me a great nation. He promised me land, descendants as numerous as the stars, and a covenant that will never be broken."

Jacob's gaze flicked to me. I nodded, wanting him to understand the gravity behind his grandfather's words.

"Your father is part of that covenant, and so are you. Through you, ADONAI's promise will continue."

I studied my son, the way his fingers curled against his tunic and the slight furrow of his brow. Though he was uncomfortable, understanding shone in his eyes.

I stood and placed my hand over my father-in-law's, aware of the many years he had carried this promise. "You will walk in the way of ADONAI," I told Jacob. "You will be the father of nations."

Jacob's lips parted, but he only bowed his head, humbly accepting the blessing that would shape his destiny.

Abraham released a long, peaceful breath. The promise had been passed.

Jacob had stepped into the story ADONAI had written for him.

As for Esau, only ADONAI knew how the promise would be fulfilled in his life.

SEVERAL DAYS LATER, I stood outside Abraham's dwelling and watched as Isaac paced in an anxious rhythm. The tent that had sheltered generations bore the marks of countless repairs—patches upon patches, a testament to Abraham's long life. Now that life was drawing to its close.

"He asked for all of us," Isaac murmured, his eyes fixed on the ground. "All his sons."

My throat tightened. The esteemed patriarch was slipping away from us. The man who had welcomed me when I arrived as a young bride, who had blessed our union with his gnarled hands, now lay on his deathbed in the place where all his sons had been conceived.

Messengers had been dispatched days ago—east to where

Keturah's sons had settled, south to the lands where Ishmael and his twelve sons lived. Would they arrive in time? Would they come at all? The relationships between Abraham's sons bore scars from old wounds and unspoken grievances.

I placed a hand on Isaac's arm. "They will come," I said, though I was not sure they would. "A father's blessing is not easily refused."

As the words left my lips, the ram's horn sounded from the lookout post. "Riders from the east," the man called.

Isaac's forearm tensed. "The sons of Keturah."

I lifted my chin. Would they even recognize us? I was now forty-nine, and my dark hair had gone gray. Isaac was seventy-five, far older than any of Keturah's sons.

They arrived first—Zimran, Jokshan, Medan, Midian, Ishbak, and Shuah—adorned in the colorful garb of eastern lands. Their garments dripped with embroidery, their fingers were weighted with rings. Behind them came *their* sons, ten young men with curious eyes and cautious gestures. I watched as they dismounted from their camels.

Jokshan approached us first, embracing Isaac with formal affection. "How is our father?" he asked, his voice heavy with concern.

"Waiting," Isaac replied. "He will not leave us until all have gathered."

I escorted them to Abraham's tent. Inside, the air was thick with the aroma of herbs intended to mask the odor of death. Abraham lay on a bed of woven rugs and cushions, his breathing shallow but steady. His eyes, once sharp and commanding, now seemed distant, as if he were already studying the world beyond.

"Father," Zimran called, kneeling beside the dying man. "We have come."

Abraham's lips moved, forming words too faint to hear. Keturah's sons leaned in, their faces solemn. I stood back, allowing them a private moment with their father.

A commotion outside drew my attention. The ram's horn

sounded again, then loud voices combined with the braying of donkeys. I slipped away in time to see a second group approaching from the south. These men were wilder in appearance, their clothing loose and their skin darkened by years under the desert sun. The leader had to be Ishmael, who rode with a straight back despite his eighty-nine years.

Isaac stood as if frozen to the spot as he watched his half brother approach. The two men had not seen each other in decades, their lives having taken different paths after Sarah expelled Hagar and her son from the camp.

"Brother," Ishmael called, his voice crossing the distance between them. The word seemed to release something in Isaac, who strode forward to meet him.

I watched as they embraced, awkwardly at first, then with increasing warmth and affectionate slaps on the back. Behind Ishmael stood his twelve sons—Nebaioth, Kedar, Adbeel, Mibsam, Mishma, Dumah, Massa, Hadad, Tema, Jetur, Naphish, and Kedemah—princes of their tribes, men who carried themselves with the confidence of those who knew their place in the world.

"Father calls for us," Isaac said, gesturing toward the tent. He beckoned to Jacob and Esau, who waited beneath an awning. "Come. He wishes to bless all his sons and grandsons before he joins his ancestors."

I stepped forward, wondering if I should ask Ishmael to wait until the sons of Keturah had taken their leave, but the saving grace of second thought kept me silent. Abraham only had so much strength; he might not be able to recite three separate blessings. Let them listen to their father as one group. Let them all be blessed together.

Ishmael removed his headgear and entered the tent, his sons following behind. I hesitated, uncertain of my place in this gathering, but Isaac reached for my hand. "Come," he said. "You are his daughter."

Inside, the tent seemed to have shrunk. The presence of thirty-two men filled the space, and all of them were blood of Abraham's blood.

I slipped quietly through the gathering, helping to arrange them around the dying man's bed. The old man's eyes had opened wide, drinking in the sight of his sons and grandsons with wonder.

"My sons," Abraham whispered, "you have come."

"We are here, Father." Ishmael knelt on one side of the bed while Isaac knelt on the other.

Abraham's hands—once strong enough to bind the promised son for sacrifice, now thin and trembling—reached out to touch Ishmael's and Isaac's faces. "God promised me descendants as numerous as the stars," he said. "And here you are, the beginning of that promise."

Tears welled in my eyes as I watched my beloved father-in-law prepare to leave this world. The tent that had sheltered him through the conception of his sons, the laughter and tears of his wife and concubines, and countless prayers and sacrifices now witnessed this final gathering.

One by one, Abraham called his sons to him. To Ishmael, the firstborn, he spoke of the wilderness and the twelve princes that would spring from his line. To each of Keturah's six sons, he uttered words of guidance and prosperity. And with Isaac, he reaffirmed ADONAI's promise of land and descendants.

"Promise me, Isaac," he said, gasping, "promise that you will keep the Lord's commandments . . . that you will turn neither to the left nor the right . . . all the days of your life."

Isaac clung to Abraham's hand. "Father, I promise."

The blessing continued as day faded into evening. Deborah and I lit lamps, the golden light casting long shadows across the goatskin walls. Brothers who had not spoken to each other in years exchanged forgiving smiles.

These men, born of different mothers, would part ways after Abraham's burial. Their lives would follow separate paths; their tribes would grow into nations. But for this moment, they were one family, gathered around their dying father.

As Abraham's voice grew fainter, my thoughts drifted to the women who had borne these sons—Sarah, Hagar, and Keturah. Women were equally responsible for producing these strong men. Even I would have a place in this story because I had birthed sons who would carry the covenant forward.

When Abraham had finished blessing all thirty-two of his descendants, he closed his eyes, his chest rising and falling in the uneven rhythm of the dying. The sons of Abraham fell silent, watching and waiting, until he exhaled his last breath.

Then Isaac stepped forward and ran his hand over the aged face, closing his father's eyes. "He has gone to his ancestors," he announced, his voice a rough whisper. "Our women will prepare him for burial in the cave at Machpelah. You are welcome to stay with us for as long as you like. We will provide tents, food, and drink. If you need anything, you have only to ask for it."

The mention of food spurred me into action. The servants had been cooking for hours, and several tables had been filled with meat, olives, cheese, dates, and bread. These men had spent hours maintaining their vigil, so they had to be starving.

But before I moved to the cooking area, I stopped to look up at the dark sky, lit by countless points of light. "As numerous as the stars," I whispered. In the tent behind me, thirty-two men proved the validity of that promise. How many would there be in generations to come? In the future, would Abraham's descendants be found throughout the entire world?

I did not know the answer, but standing under that sparkling canopy, I could not help but be amazed that I, a simple girl from Haran, had been divinely chosen to be part of a story that would continue long after all of us had returned to dust.

Chapter 19

THE FUNERAL PROCESSION was a solemn affair, but no one in the area was surprised to hear of Abraham's death. He had lived 175 years, an uncommonly long time, and he had died in peace.

When the inhabitants of Canaan heard that Abraham had died, they came with their kings and princes and all their important men to bury him. "There has been not a man who feared God like Abraham," they said, "for he feared God from his youth and served the Lord, from all the days of his life, from his childhood to the day of his death. And he brought all the children of the earth to the service of God, and taught them the ways of the Lord, and caused them to know the Lord."

The children of the land wept on account of Abraham, for he had been kind to them and had been honest with both God and men. The news traveled as far as Haran, and the important men of that city came to mourn Abraham, for he had lived among them for a time and had taught them of ADONAI. All the visitors who entered Canaan comforted Isaac, Ishmael, and the sons of Keturah.

My father and brother were among the group who arrived from Haran. I barely recognized my father, who had lost his hair and gained a sizable belly, but I knew my brother at first sight. At fifty-two, Laban looked very much like my father at that age, but in other ways he had not changed.

I also met Laban's wife, Adinah, a quiet woman with large eyes and a subdued demeanor. When I asked if she needed extra bedding for her children, she replied with a firm shake of her head. "We have no children. The gods have not blessed us in that way."

I reached out, wanting to comfort her, but she stared at my arms as if they were snakes. So I quietly withdrew and went in search of my brother. I found him on a lookout tower, where he seemed to be counting the livestock in the field.

"I cannot believe my little sister lives with such wealth," Laban said after joining me by the gate. "I have always heard that Abraham was rich, but look at all this! How did he keep track of his possessions?"

"He relied on his steward, Eliezer," I said. "Surely you remember him. He came to Haran to find me."

"Ah." Laban smiled. "How many servants have you? How many cattle?"

"I have no idea." Eager to hear news from home, I waved the subject away. "I met your wife, and she is lovely. Do you still live in Father's house?"

Laban nodded. "We have no children. My wife makes daily sacrifices, but the gods have not yet acted on her behalf."

I wanted to tell him that I waited twenty years for the arrival of my sons, but Laban was clearly not interested in women's matters. He was too busy scanning the camp, apparently calculating the value of Abraham's—now Isaac's—household.

"Do you remember this?" I pulled out the small wooden carving he had given me when I left Haran. "I look at this whenever I miss home."

"I am sure you have not missed much," Laban said, only glancing at the carving. "Why would you when you have so much here?"

"How is our mother?" I asked, resisting the urge to wave my hand before his wandering eyes. "Why is she not with you?"

"Someone had to stay behind to guard our house." Laban smiled, probably intending his words as a joke, but I did not find it funny.

His preoccupation with wealth, I told myself, was probably the difference between people who lived in a busy city and people who lived in simple tents.

But it was not the only difference.

Book Three

Gerar

After Abraham's death, God blessed Isaac his son, and Isaac lived near Beer-lahai-roi. Now there was a famine in the land. . . . So Isaac went to King Abimelech of the Philistines, to Gerar.

Genesis 25:11; 26:1

Chapter 20

WE FORMED A funeral procession and traveled north to Hebron. Our caravan moved in hushed reverence as sand coated our sandals and the hems of our garments. Isaac told me the history of our destination while we traveled, his voice occasionally breaking as he spoke. Mamre was where Abraham had camped and built an altar when he first entered Canaan, and Sarah had run to that sacred place when she thought Abraham was about to kill Isaac.

"But Father and I were not at Mamre," he said, his eyes distant with memory. "We were on Mount Moriah. So my mother died there, and when my father arrived, he purchased the cave of Machpelah from a man of Hebron."

The day after our arrival at Mamre, we buried Abraham in that cave next to his beloved wife. A lump formed in my throat when I thought of the many years they had shared and the bond they had formed in faith and love. My eyes burned with tears when Isaac's shoulders trembled as he stood at the mouth of the cave, his head bowed in grief.

After saying farewell to those who had traveled to attend the funeral—clasping hands and exchanging tearful embraces beneath the ancient oaks—we packed our tents and traveled back to Beersheba. On the journey, Isaac announced that he wanted to move our camp from Beersheba to Beer-lahai-roi, which I remembered as the place where Hagar had met Adonai.

I stared at him in surprise. "Move? But we have lived so long in Beersheba—"

"Beersheba was my father's home," Isaac interrupted, his eyes focused on the road ahead. "Now that he sleeps beside my mother, I want to live elsewhere. After we have completed our days of mourning, we will move the camp to Beer-lahai-roi."

The name awakened another memory. He had been returning from that place when I saw him for the first time. He had gone there in hopes of hearing the voice of Adonai, only to be disappointed. Was that why he wanted to move? Did he long for assurance that he was walking in the right path? I saw longing in his eyes as he searched the southern sky. Was he waiting for Adonai to call his name?

We mourned for forty days, then Isaac gathered our household and announced that we would move to Beer-lahai-roi. I was not the only one who marveled at his reasoning. I overheard the servants whispering that the area was parched land that could not even grow barley, the hardiest of grains. Yes, the area had a well, but could it water our people and our herds? If he intended to raise livestock, what would the cattle eat?

Regardless, we packed our tents, loaded the donkeys and camels, and hauled our belongings into wagons. My back ached from the near-constant bending and lifting. Sweat trickled between my shoulder blades as I directed the servants. The herders counted the animals and filled leather bags with food and water for the journey. Moving a camp as large as ours would not be easy, yet Isaac was determined to do it.

We made slow progress, leaving land that had been worn into ruts by our feet and our cattle, caves that housed our dead, and underground caches of our refuse. Each step away from Beersheba felt like severing a tie to the past. We woke each morning before dawn and set out, stopping to erect a temporary camp when the sun reached its zenith. We rested in the afternoon, ate quick meals of bread and cheese, and packed in the cool of the evening. We slept beneath wagons and hastily erected awnings, then set out before sunrise to take advantage of the cool air.

Finally, we arrived at Beer-lahai-roi, a way station between Kadesh and Bered. I went to the well to splash dust from my eyes and lips. The well had attracted travelers for decades, so a well-worn path led to the place.

"Here." Isaac stretched his arm toward an open, flat space. "We will set up camp here."

As we moved to unpack our belongings, I noted that although the land offered little vegetation other than scrubby trees and bald hills, the area teemed with wildlife. On the journey, we had seen deer, ibex, gazelle, wild boar, rabbits, and rock badgers. The constant scurrying of small creatures among the rocks offered a strange comfort in the barren landscape.

Isaac smiled at me as we directed the servants, his hand warm on my shoulder. "We will never be hungry here. There is plenty of game, and plenty of land for our herds."

Of course—this land suited Esau.

"Once the rains come, perhaps," I said, despairing of the sandy fields. "If it does not rain, the sheep will have to eat dirt." I bit my lip, immediately regretting the sharpness in my tone.

"It will rain," Isaac promised, his eyes bright with hope. "ADONAI would not desert us now."

I bit my tongue and watched Isaac help Jacob and Esau set up the tent poles. My husband had promised to keep the Lord's commandments, to turn neither to the left nor the right, but he had not yet heard the voice of ADONAI, so how did he know which way to go? My heart ached for him as I watched him direct our household, his slender frame carrying the weight of new responsibility.

Once the camp was established, we tried to resume our usual routines, but the herdsmen struggled to find grass for the animals, and predators killed several of our lambs and kids. Would Isaac's bringing us to this wilderness destroy everything his father had built?

I found it hard to relax in the new place. My nighttime dreams—filled with images of skinny cattle and empty waterskins—woke me from sleep, leaving me alert and anxious. Without Abraham, who had guided us with goodness and wisdom, I felt unanchored. Adding to that sense of unease was this strange land, a place much drier, more desolate, and less livable than Beersheba.

After being awakened by yet another bad dream, I sat up in the dark and listened to Isaac's deep breathing. He was worn out by the work of building new pens and feeding the livestock. Eliezer had helped arrange the layout of the tents, but Eliezer was an old man, and the move had exhausted him.

I stared into the dark and prayed for a sign that we had done the right thing. What did Adonai have in store for us here? Would He speak to Isaac as He spoke to Abraham? Would He continue to bless us even in this place? I pressed my palm against my chest, trying to calm the flutter of my anxious heart.

We could only wait, the taste of dust on our tongues and the memory of Abraham's faith fading like footprints in the sand.

A WEEK AFTER his arrival in Beer-lahai-roi, Isaac stood motionless by Eliezer's bedside, his mind struggling to grasp the reality of another death. The man who had been as constant as the stars themselves, who had walked beside his father through fire and war, whose stories had filled Isaac's childhood with wonder, now lay silent. The familiar face, which had sought his bride and creased with joy at Isaac's wedding, was now slack, its owner at rest.

Tightness seized Isaac's chest as memories flooded his thoughts: Eliezer's strong hands guiding him through the intricacies of managing the flocks, his resonant voice mediating disputes among the servants, his quiet presence during evening prayers. He had been more than a servant; he was a living witness to Abraham's earliest trials, a keeper of their family's sacred history.

"It is as if his work was done," Isaac said, his voice breaking. "He did not stay to help me."

"He lived to serve your father," Rebekah answered, her voice gentle, "and now you must find another man to stand by your side." She took his hand. "Minos has always been at Eliezer's right hand. He would be honored to serve you."

Her words only emphasized the sudden, crushing solitude. Without Eliezer, without his father, the mantle of leadership lay heavily upon Isaac's shoulders. Some part of him had believed that Eliezer would always stand guard over his family.

Rebekah's robe rustled as she turned to fetch servants to tend to the body. But before leaving, she looked at him, her eyes gleaming with compassion. "I am not afraid of hard work," she said, "and until you find a man you can trust, you may rely on me just as you relied on him."

In her voice, he heard echoes of Eliezer's faithfulness, the same unwavering devotion that had led Abraham's servant across the desert to find her. This, too, was part of the man's legacy. He had brought Isaac a partner to help shoulder the responsibility of his inheritance.

Chapter 21

THEY DID NOT stay long at Beer-lahai-roi. Two months after their arrival, Isaac realized that spring had come, but the attendant rains did not arrive. The land lay desiccated under a pitiless sun, its cracked earth a testament to months without rain.

He ordered his servants to pack their belongings. They would move again, but eastward this time, to the Philistine capital of Gerar. Abraham had once camped outside Gerar, and the city's king had befriended his father.

After setting up in the same area his father had inhabited, Isaac sat on a low mound outside the gate of his compound, his eyes fixed on the hazy horizon. Gerar was close to the shore, where clouds often rolled in from the sea to water the earth. But since their arrival, he had seen no clouds and no rain. The once fertile pastures lay barren, and the threat of continued drought concerned him. The grass would not grow without rain, and without grass, his cattle, sheep, and goats would surely starve. Wild game would feed his family and servants, but the livestock, even the camels, would perish.

Should he go to Egypt? His father had gone down to Egypt during a famine, and the Nile's annual flood had ensured the survival of Abraham's flocks. The dread of moving again—to Egypt—filled Isaac's mind and troubled his thoughts.

As he wrestled with the decision, the air around him seemed to still, as though nature itself held its breath. Then a man appeared from out of nowhere, a man unlike any Isaac had ever seen. His skin glowed with an unearthly light, and his commanding voice spoke directly to Isaac's soul.

"Isaac," the Lord said, for this could only be ADONAI-in-flesh, "do not go down to Egypt. Stay in Gerar, for I am with you. I reaffirm the covenant I made with your father, Abraham."

Each word was as bracing as cold water on hot skin. Isaac had never heard the Lord's voice, nor had he witnessed such an unmistakable sign of divine favor. Even the dust of the air glistened with His glory and vibrated with His voice.

Each beat of Isaac's heart was like a blow to his chest. A tremor of fear and anticipation shot through him. Why had his father never told him that the Lord's voice was terrifying? And the sight of the Lord was overwhelming, enough to send panic rioting through a man.

ADONAI's voice then softened to a more reassuring tone: "Live as an outsider in this land, and I will be with you and bless you—for to you and to your seed I give all these lands—and I will confirm my pledge that I swore to Abraham your father. I will multiply your seed like the stars of the sky, and I will give your seed all these lands. And in your seed all the nations of the earth will continually be blessed, because Abraham listened to My voice and kept My charge, my *mitzvot*, my decrees, and my instructions."

Overwhelmed with awe, Isaac bowed his head. His anxieties vanished as the words of ADONAI took root within him. His fear of famine and his dread of Egypt—all his concerns melted away in the certainty of the covenant.

The Lord was with him. Knowing that made all the difference.

When Isaac lifted his head again, the world had returned to

the way it was. The earth was still dusty and the sun still hot, but Isaac's turmoil had been replaced by resolve.

He would remain in Gerar, trusting fully in ADONAI's promise, confident that his future would be secured under the Lord's watchful care.

WITH AN IRRESISTIBLE smile and a fair amount of wheedling, Isaac pulled me away from the camp, treating me to a walk through the busy streets of Gerar. The day was warm but not suffocating, and the city air carried the earthy scent of sweat and the faint perfume of flowers for sale in the marketplace. Bustling with organized chaos, the ancient Philistine city provided a delicious change from the camp, and walking its streets lifted my spirits.

My husband's hand brushed mine as we strolled, and for a moment, my worries, duties, and the constant pull of my responsibilities faded. Isaac's eyes snapped with purpose, and I wondered what had animated him. Surely not anything that had happened in the camp. Earlier that morning, his face had been lined with worry.

"What has happened?" I caught his hand and turned to face him. "You have a secret."

"I do," Isaac said, his voice brimming with an emotion I could not define. He lowered his head until his lips brushed my ear. "When I went out this morning . . . ADONAI appeared before me. He spoke to me just as He spoke to my father."

Ripples of shock spread from the center of my chest, tingling my head and numbing my feet. "You *saw* Him? What did He say to you?"

Isaac hesitated, clearly struggling for words. "He reaffirmed the covenant with my father," Isaac continued, his tone echoing with wonder. "The Lord said He is with me and He will bless me, and my descendants will inherit this land. All of this—this legacy, this land—has been given to me and to us."

I sighed, overjoyed to know that the Lord had finally provided the assurance my husband needed. "Oh, beloved." I grasped his hands. "This is wonderful. The promises of Adonai never failed your father. And now you know He will never fail you."

Isaac's eyes watered as he nodded. "I was not a mere part of His plan to test my father. Now He is guiding me."

With hearts giddy with wonder, we walked on and entered the city. The sights and sounds of the market brought our thoughts back to reality. I was about to ask Isaac if we should buy barley seed when a crude voice shattered our peace. "Hey, sister! Will you allow me to have my way with you?"

The voice came from a group of men near the city stable, their laughter pouring like a foul river into the otherwise peaceful afternoon. From their rude gestures, I knew they were addressing me.

I turned away, my face heating with embarrassment. "Impudent fools. Have they no respect for a married woman?"

Isaac did not look at or address the men, whose lewd remarks had spoiled our afternoon. Instead, he guided me away until we were hidden behind a row of booths, where he refused to meet my gaze.

"Isaac? Will you do nothing?"

Sighing, he gave me a look of mingled regret and apology. "The people of Gerar do not know we are married," he said, his voice dripping with guilt. "When we arrived, I let it be known that you are my sister."

I pulled away as a sense of betrayal pricked the back of my neck. "Your *sister*?" My voice trembled. "Isaac . . ." But I could not finish my thought. How could he lie about who I was, who I had been for decades?

Isaac's face remained impassive, though his stance softened as he met my eyes. "My father did the same thing when he first visited Gerar," he added, as if that justified this falsehood. "He thought it would be safer. The people here are ruthless, Rebekah. It is better for you to be safe than risk something worse."

"Safer for me or you?" A rush of humiliation heated my skin. "Why would you allow your own sister to be subjected to such rude talk?" My hand trembled as I gestured toward the stable, the men's comments still ringing in my ears.

Isaac stepped closer, as if he could shield me from the sound of their ribald laughter. "Better to sully your ears than have you become a widow. They would kill me to get to you."

"Did ADONAI not say He would be with you?"

Isaac blinked, then stammered out a reply. "I made the claim before ADONAI appeared to me."

"Then go forward now and confess the truth. Tell everyone in the market that I am your wife and the mother of your sons."

When Isaac looked away, spurning my advice, my heart sank. Our encounter with those men—an encounter that proved the Philistines not to be followers of ADONAI—had revealed the fear still tucked deep within my husband's heart.

I drew a deep breath, my thoughts roiling in irritation and confusion. One thing was clear: while Isaac appreciated ADONAI's promise to guide and bless us, the Lord's assurance had made no difference in this moment.

Would it make a difference in our future?

I DID NOT SPEAK on our walk back to camp. After arriving, I went immediately to Deborah's tent and told her what had happened. She listened, her face crinkling in sympathy, as I voiced my concerns and pounded the air in frustration.

"I do not understand," I concluded. "The blessings of Abraham are now Isaac's. The God who created the universe walks with him and blesses his endeavors, yet Isaac chooses to live like a timid mouse. Why can he not act with more confidence? Why can he not be more like Abraham?"

Deborah waited until I had finished, then crossed her arms on her bent knees. "You say he saw ADONAI this morning?"

I nodded.

Deborah smiled. "So you want your husband to be more courageous."

"Of course! Especially since he now knows ADONAI is with him."

"He knows," Deborah said, "but courage is not foolhardiness. He would have been foolish to challenge those men in the public square, especially since you were with him. He did not want to endanger you, my pet, so he remained silent."

I gaped at her—this was not what I wanted to hear.

"Your husband," she continued, "has been the head of this camp for only a few months. He is still learning his role, learning how to lead. Before his father's death, Isaac was allowed to be in the background. Now you must give him time to discover the sort of leader he will be. Once he has determined which things are the most precious to him, he will find his courage."

I shook my head, not fully understanding. "I thought he cared about me."

"He does," she said, smiling. "But perhaps he does not realize how much."

WHILE MY HUSBAND was attempting to find his courage, I decided I would live like his sister and sleep in Deborah's tent. Whenever he suggested that I return to his bed, I feigned a headache or pleaded exhaustion. I have spent all day in the fields, I would say, and I am weary of counting sheep and lambs. I do not have your gift for making them stand still.

One morning, Deborah attempted to convince me that I had gone too far. "Do you want your husband to take a concubine?" she asked. "No, you do not. Look at the trouble Abraham's concubine caused in his family. If you want your husband to be faithful, you cannot keep turning him away."

I crossed my arms. "But he lied to the people of Gerar. Every time I take goods to market, I am subject to the comments of the men and the whispers of the women. Why? Because my husband's words do not match his actions. He says he follows the Lord, but he does not."

"Have you lived in perfect obedience to the teachings of ADONAI?" Deborah asked, her voice sharp. "Have you always acted in perfect faith? Displayed perfect courage? Never had a doubt?"

I snapped my mouth shut. Deborah was well acquainted with my imperfections.

"Stop thinking of your wounded pride and instead think of Isaac," Deborah continued. "Allow ADONAI to correct your husband after you return to his bed. Dress in your best today, perfume your neck, and give your husband a warm embrace instead of a chilly reply."

I did not want to listen, but I did. I resisted only a moment more before surrendering, knowing she was right. Though she had never been free to marry, Deborah possessed wisdom I could not ignore.

SHE DRESSED ME in my finest robe, perfumed my neck and arms, and brushed my hair until it shone, braiding and piling it atop my head to reveal my neck.

"Your husband plans to go to the city today," she said. "Go to him and tell him you have missed his company."

I blew out a breath. "What if he does not believe me?"

"*Make* him believe you." She arched a brow. "You can do that, pet."

I found Isaac near the stable, loading a donkey with cheese and grain. "My lord," I said, gentling my voice. "I have missed you. May I go with you into the city?"

His brows rose. "Do you want something from the market?"

I forced a smile. "I want only your company."

Isaac finished loading the donkey and then we set out. The walk was pleasant. The dry, rocky path wound through hills dotted with olive trees and patches of wildflowers. The sun warmed the earth beneath our sandals, and a faint breeze carried the salty scent of the sea. Despite my residual anger, my heart warmed toward the handsome man at my side.

Once at the market, we sold our wares to an enterprising merchant, then wandered through a collection of bustling booths. We tasted warm breads, sampled spiced wines, and examined golden wheat from Egypt. Isaac's hand rested gently on my back, a warmth I had missed.

In a deserted alley, my husband pulled me into his arms. "I have missed you," he whispered, nuzzling my neck. "I have missed reaching for you in the night." His hand moved from my neck down to my waist as my pulse quickened.

But as I lifted my gaze, I spotted a disapproving face in an upstairs window.

"My lord," I murmured, pushing his hands away, "we are not alone."

THE THRONE ROOM of Abimelech's palace loomed around us, its towering stone columns carved with images of lions, olive branches, and winged gods. Braziers of incense filled the air with a smoky sweetness, mingling with the aroma of oiled wood. Bronze shields gleamed from high on the wall. Rich tapestries fell like a crimson waterfall behind the large iron throne, embroidered with gold threads that flickered in the wavering torchlight.

I shivered. Not from cold, but from dread. This room had been designed to intimidate, and it had accomplished its purpose. I did not know what Isaac was feeling because I was afraid to look at him.

The guards who had stopped us on the street said the king demanded to see us. "Why?" Isaac asked. "We have done nothing wrong."

"Ask the king," the largest guard said, taking Isaac's arm. The second guard did not touch me because I willingly followed my husband.

Now my fingers gripped my shawl as my sandals slapped the king's polished stone floor. I looked around, realizing that Sarah had once stood in this same chamber, her heart no doubt pounding as fiercely as mine. She had been taken into the king's harem and was spared only by the hand of ADONAI. Surely He would spare me and Isaac as well—or would He?

The king, Abimelech, grandson of the ruler who had known Abraham, sat upright on his throne, his kohl-lined eyes sharp with fury. His golden crown, adorned with precious stones, glinted as he leaned forward.

"This woman is your *wife*," he spat, glaring at Isaac. "No man kisses his sister as you kissed her."

Isaac's throat bobbed as he swallowed, but in a clear, strong voice he declared the truth. "I was afraid I might die because of her beauty," he admitted. "I thought men would desire her . . . and kill me to have her."

Abimelech snorted. "Of course they would. What is this, then, you have done to us? Thinking her your sister, one of my men could have ravished her, and you would have brought guilt upon us!"

A drop of perspiration traced the length of my spine. I cast a quick glance at Isaac, who wore a faint look of self-reproach. I struggled to maintain a blank expression, as a supportive wife should, though I thought my heart might burst from the effort.

As the king stared at us, a corner of his mouth quirked. "I have read the chronicles and know what your father did during my grandfather's reign. He lied as you did, and my grandfather paid dearly for your kinsman's mistake. But my grandfather also saw the power of your God, and our forefathers signed a treaty of cooperation. For the sake of my people, I shall extend the same treaty and cooperation to you."

Isaac bowed his head before the king. "We are grateful, O king."

The king stood, gripping his scepter. "Let it be known that this man and his wife are under my protection; anyone who touches them shall surely die!"

Isaac bowed deeply, his face to the floor, and I followed his example, my breath steadying as relief washed through me.

As we left the throne room, I knew ADONAI had demonstrated His protection once again. The falsehood that had separated us had been erased, not by my doing, but by the Lord's. Isaac had not denied his lie but had freely confessed it. And in the court of a king, that was an act of courage.

I reached for my husband's hand and felt peace.

Chapter 22

THOUGH I HATED to admit it, Abraham's generosity had concerned me when he sent the sons of Keturah away with such an abundance of gifts. I wondered if his kindness would leave us vulnerable, but even though the fields appeared depleted for a few years, ADONAI's favor rested upon my husband as it had on Abraham. Within a few months of our arrival in Gerar, Isaac's fields produced far more than they had at Mamre. He sowed, and ADONAI blessed one hundredfold.

I ran my hand through fields of golden grain, their heavy heads bowing under the blessing of abundance. Our flocks multiplied. The ewes often birthed twins, even triplets, and our cattle grew fat on the verdant pastures. Servants came to our camp, drawn by our prosperity, and I found myself overseeing a vast and thriving household.

Yet every silver lining has a cloud, and Isaac's success stirred envy in the hearts of the Philistines. I first noticed it in the whispers I overheard when I carried our goods to the market at Gerar. I then spotted furtive glances and the occasional merchant that refused to accept our goods. When I tried to buy supplies, other merchants would not barter with me.

Then came the defilement of our wells. Abraham's servants had dug several wells in his day, and the Philistines enjoyed the use of those wells for years afterward. Yet when we went to water our livestock with water from Abraham's wells, we found them filled with earth and rocks. Such mischief was common and spiteful, but the consequences were severe. Water meant life for our livestock, and the Philistine herders sought to choke our supply of it.

Isaac sent word to the king, and Abimelech responded by coming to our camp. He stood before Isaac, his expression grave, eyes dark with resentment. I was certain he had been experiencing pressure from the chiefs among his people.

"You have become too powerful among us," he said, crossing his arms. "You must go from here."

What could we do but obey him?

We packed our tents and drove our flocks eastward, our servants transporting what they could to our new camp in another valley. My husband's men dug again, and when they uncovered a wellspring, I celebrated with them. But our joy was short-lived. Herdsmen from Gerar soon approached with their faces hard and their staffs gripped like weapons.

"This is our water," they declared. "It belongs to us."

I gritted my teeth, but Isaac, ever the peacemaker, named the well *Esek*—Quarrel—and kept the peace. Again, we moved. Again, we dug. Again, we found water. And again, the Philistines came.

Their claims were unjust, but they were many, so we yielded once again. Isaac named that well *Sitnah*—Accusation.

At that point, I wondered if he had been too quick to surrender. My husband was not a man of war. Life had taught him that adversity was not something to be fought but endured, like a passing storm.

We moved farther east until we found a place where no one

disputed our right to exist in the land. When our servants dug and found water, Isaac named the well *Rehoboth*—Wide Spaces—saying, "Because now ADONAI has created wide spaces for us. We will be fruitful in the land."

And we were . . . until restlessness stirred in our hearts.

YEARS MOVED THROUGH our lives like a caravan crossing the desert, leaving faint tracks on our aging faces. Our sons grew, our servants multiplied, and we lived in shalom.

But one day Isaac said we were going to move again.

"Where?" I asked.

"Beersheba."

My restlessness departed. After more than five years of wandering, we returned to the place where we had started. Our worn footpaths had disappeared, as had the trails worn by our cattle. Even the packed earth of our former camp had softened and was covered with grass.

As I helped the servants set up our tents, a sense of homecoming warmed my spirit. Isaac rebuilt his father's altar, and my heart filled with certainty. For us, Beersheba was holy ground.

On that first night, as the camp settled into stillness, ADONAI spoke to Isaac again. My husband came into our tent, his face shining with peace and assurance.

"'I am the God of your father Abraham,'" he whispered as he sat on the bed and took my hands. "That is what ADONAI said to me just now. 'Do not be afraid, for I am with you. I will bless you and multiply your offspring for my servant Abraham's sake.'"

Relief flooded my soul. We would not be defenseless in this land. ADONAI had led us back here, and He would establish us here. Isaac and I went to the rebuilt altar, where he sacrificed a lamb. As the smoke billowed into the starlit heavens, my soul filled with gratitude.

We had just broken our fast the next morning when a group of servants came running into the camp. "We have found water!" they cried.

I laughed and lifted my hands to heaven. Yes, Adonai had led us to this place. He had provided once again.

Chapter 23

ISAAC STOOD AT the edge of his encampment, the sun casting golden streaks across the dry earth. The heat of the day still hung in the air, though the evening breeze had begun to stir the dust at his feet. He wiped his brow with the back of his hand, his fingers coated with soil from the day's work. The past weeks had been exhausting—searching for new wells, moving his flocks, and striving for peace while his family members and servants adjusted to their new home.

Now, as he watched riders approach from the west, his stomach tightened. He recognized Abimelech's standard at once. Was his household not safe even here? The Philistine king did not control all of Canaan.

The king himself finally came into view, his royal robes billowing behind him. With him came Ahuzzath, his chief advisor, and Phicol, the commander of his army. Isaac set his jaw. He had not forgotten the way these men had cast him out, fearing his prosperity, driving him from their midst like a wild dog. Yet here they were in Beersheba.

His herdsmen muttered and shifted uneasily. He held up his hand, warning them to remain silent.

The Philistines dismounted, their dusty faces solemn. Abimelech took a step forward and inclined his head toward Isaac in a gesture of respect.

Isaac was in no mood to reciprocate. "Why have you come here," he asked, folding his arms, "since you hate me and sent me away from you?"

Abimelech's expression softened. "We have plainly seen that ADONAI is with you." His words, though measured, carried an undertone of apology. "So we said, 'Let there be a sworn pact between you and us. Let us make a covenant with you, that you will do us no harm, just as we have not touched you and have done you nothing but good, sending you away in peace.'"

Isaac pressed his lips together. How had they given him peace? He had been expelled from two locations, his wells stopped up, his land claimed. But he had seen ADONAI's hand in his expulsion. Every hardship he encountered had been met with an abundance of provision. Every well the Philistines stole was replaced by another. For every pasture he abandoned, ADONAI had led him to a more productive field.

Still, Abimelech's words weighed on his heart. He did not seek conflict. If their offer of peace was sincere, he would not reject it. Exhaling a slow breath, Isaac nodded. "Very well. We will make a feast, and in the morning, we will swear this covenant before the Lord."

Abimelech inclined his head in a regal nod. "This my grandfather did with your father years ago. They swore an oath, and your father called this place 'Beer-Sheba,' meaning the *Well of Seven*."

"Seven?"

Abimelech smiled. "He gave my grandfather seven young ewes to bear witness to our treaty."

That night, Isaac's servants prepared a festive meal beneath the open sky. The scents of roasted beef and lamb swirled with the sweetness of figs and the aroma of baked bread. Laughter and conversation floated through the air, though Isaac himself remained watchful. Even as he ate, he studied the faces of Abimelech and his men, searching for any sign of deception.

At dawn they made their oath, sealing their peace with solemn words before Adonai. And as Abimelech and his men departed, disappearing into the shimmering heat haze, Isaac felt contentment settle in his heart.

Later that same day, as the sun blazed overhead, his servants came running, their faces alight with triumph. "My lord," one of them cried, "we have found another spring!"

Isaac walked with them to the new well. The ground gushed with crystal-clear water, spilling over the earth like a blessing from heaven. He knelt, cupped the cool liquid in his hands, and let it ripple over his fingers.

"*Shivah*," he murmured, his voice thick with emotion. "We will call this well *Pledge*." He lifted his gaze to the sky, his heart swelling with shalom. At long last, he would have peace.

I found Isaac in the wheat fields, his figure silhouetted against the golden afternoon light. His hands were stained with soil, his back bent from the work of overseeing the harvest. The sun had turned his skin darker than it had been in our early days, and gray strands threaded his beard.

Yet after nearly forty years of marriage, my heart still beat faster at even a glimpse of him.

"My lord," I called, gathering my robes as I stepped carefully into the rows of grain.

He straightened, shielding his eyes against the sun. A smile touched his lips when he saw me, though it did not entirely reach his eyes. Perhaps he sensed what I had come to discuss.

"Rebekah." He wiped his hands on his tunic. "What brings you to the fields? Is something wrong?"

"No," I said, reaching him. The familiar smells of earth and sweat clung to his garments. "I only wished to speak with you."

The workers kept their distance, pretending not to watch as the master conversed with his wife. A warm breeze stirred the stalks as I took a deep breath and gathered my courage.

"I saw you leave with Esau early this morning. Another hunting trip?" I kept my voice light, though the words felt thick on my tongue.

Isaac's shoulders tensed. "The lad has a gift. You should have seen how he tracked the gazelle. His instincts are remarkable."

"And Jacob?" The question escaped before I could soften it.

"What of him?"

"You never invite him to join you."

Isaac pushed hair away from his forehead. "Jacob does not like to hunt. You know this."

"Have you ever asked him?"

A flash of irritation crossed Isaac's face. "Why would I ask what I already know? Jacob prefers to stay in the tent with his writings and scrolls and his—" he waved in a vague gesture—"his *thinking*."

"Thinking is not a fault, my lord. His mind is quick and deep."

"I did not say it was a fault." His voice hardened. "But you speak as if my spending time with Esau is wrong."

"I did not mean—"

"And what of you?" His eyes met mine, alive with challenge. "When was the last time you sat with Esau as you do with Jacob? You sit with him for hours, telling him stories, answering his every question."

My cheeks burned. "Is that wrong?"

"Why do you never sit with Esau?"

"Esau never *wants* to sit and talk. He barely acknowledges my presence when he returns from his hunts. He takes his food and goes."

"And Jacob barely speaks when I try to teach him about tracking game or managing servants. He looks at me as if I am speaking a foreign tongue."

We stood there, the wheat whispering around us, each defending our position and wounded by the truth in the other's words. For a moment, neither of us spoke.

Then I thought of my parents and how they had favored Laban. But parents always favored male children because they were the family's future. Females were destined to be bartered away.

"When I was a girl," I said, my voice wavering, "I vowed I would never love one child more than another." I blinked against the moisture welling in my eyes. "I *do* love both my sons. But I do not know how to show love to a child who does not want to receive it."

"Esau wants it, but he does not know how to ask for it."

Isaac's expression changed as sympathy softened his eyes. He reached out and touched my cheek, catching a runaway tear.

"It is the same with me," he admitted. "I love Jacob, I do. He is my flesh. But I do not know how to answer his probing questions. How can I know the mind of ADONAI? Jacob does not talk to me the way he talks to you."

I reached for his hand, feeling his calluses against my palm. His fingers closed around mine, warm and strong. "We must do better," I said, my words both a confession and a promise, "to show our sons that we love them. Surely we can do that while respecting their differences."

Isaac nodded. "Agreed. We will do better."

He pulled me closer, his arms encircling me as they had countless times before. I rested my head against his chest and listened to the steady beat of his heart. His scent—earth and sweat and the faint trace of the cedar oil he used in his beard—filled my senses.

Around us, the golden wheat stretched toward the horizon. Above, birds wheeled in a sky so blue it hurt to look at it. And within me, something knotted began to unravel—not completely, but enough to let me breathe more deeply than I had in months.

We stood together, husband and wife, parents of sons as different as the sun and moon, knowing the work ahead would not be easy. But in that moment, with Isaac's arms around me, I was certain we would find our way.

I WAS STITCHING a piece of embroidery when Deborah burst into my tent, her face flushed and her eyes bright.

"Rebekah," she said, brushing a wayward lock of hair from her face. "You will not believe what has happened."

I raised a brow. "What?"

"Jacob." She lowered her voice. "He is working in the fields, and this morning I took him lentils, onions, and spices for stew. We were talking when Esau came toward us, his bow over his shoulder. He had been hunting, but apparently he was unsuccessful." She paused, as if debating how much to tell me.

"Yes?" I pressed. "Esau came upon you . . ."

She nodded. "He was hungry, as always, and the stew did smell wonderful—" She bit her lip.

I sighed. Would I have to pry this story from her? "And?"

Finally, the words tumbled out of her. "Esau asked for a bowl of stew. Jacob smiled and said he would give him some if Esau sold his birthright in exchange. I thought he was jesting, but Esau agreed."

I stared at her, not certain if I had heard clearly. "Esau sold his birthright to Jacob?"

Deborah bobbed her head. "For bread and lentil stew. He was so hungry, he cared about nothing but filling his belly. I could not believe he would trade something so significant for a single meal, but he did."

I leaned back, my thoughts whirling in disbelief. Esau had been careless with his birthright. Isaac was strong and healthy, so Esau was not thinking about his inheritance. The young never thought about death until it was upon them, yet the birthright, a double portion of the inheritance, was no small thing. It guaranteed the firstborn wealth, position, and responsibility, especially when the deceased was as prosperous as Isaac.

I breathed deeply and felt a stab of memory, a sharp recollection of a tiny hut on a remote mountain. I had sought wisdom from Adonai about my pregnancy, and Adonai had given me an answer. The matter had been ordained before my sons were born.

I resolved to remain calm. Esau's impetuousness was not surprising, but never had his decisions held such significance. I gave Deborah a measured nod. "Esau has made his choice," I said. "But we shall say nothing more about it to my sons. For now."

ISAAC RECLINED on his bed, the tenseness in his muscles easing as he stretched out. The air still smelled of spiced wine and baked bread, lingering remnants of the meal he had almost been too tired to eat.

The flap lifted, and Rebekah entered. Her face was composed, but her eyes shone with an intensity that made him sit up. She moved with deliberate steps and sat beside him.

"You look troubled." Isaac turned. "What weighs on your mind?"

She folded her hands in her lap. "Something happened between our sons today, and you should know of it." Her voice remained steady. "Jacob made a stew, and Esau was hungry, so ravenous that—" she paused, as if choosing her words carefully—"he traded his birthright to Jacob for the stew."

The words lingered in the air, odd and unexpected. Isaac remained calm at first; he knew the impulsiveness of his eldest all too well. But as the significance of Rebekah's words registered, he shook his head in disbelief. "He traded away his birthright?"

"Yes. Esau returned from hunting, and he was famished," Rebekah repeated. "He asked Jacob for some of the stew. Jacob asked for the birthright in exchange." For the first time, she met Isaac's gaze. "Esau agreed."

Isaac rose and moved toward the glowing embers of the brazier. The crackle and hiss of burning wood mirrored his turmoil as he processed the news. "What foolishness." His voice grew louder. "How could Esau be so shortsighted?" He turned to face his wife. "The birthright is not a trinket to be exchanged for food."

Rebekah remained seated, her posture straight. "You are correct, of course, but this must be part of ADONAI's plan. Remember what I was told when the twins struggled within me? The Lord said the older would serve the younger."

Her eyes held no triumph, only certainty, but Isaac frowned as suspicion reared its head. Rebekah had always held a special affection for Jacob; her eyes always softened when she spoke his name.

He shot her a sharp glance. "Did you have something to do with this? Jacob is clever, but this seems too cunning even for him." He stepped closer. "Did you suggest that he lay this trap for Esau?"

A flicker of hurt crossed her face. She stood, her dignity intact despite the accusation. "I did not. I think Jacob might have made the suggestion in jest." She met his eyes without flinching. "Only you and I know what the Lord said to me when I sought Him. I was as surprised as you when I heard what happened."

Isaac examined her steady gaze and the delicate lines of the face he had known and loved for years. She had never lied to him, not in all their time together. She was a righteous woman, devoted to ADONAI and their family.

His suspicion melted away. "Forgive me. I should not have doubted you."

Rebekah nodded, wordlessly accepting his apology.

"How could Esau be so reckless?" Isaac continued, speaking more to himself than to his wife. "A bowl of stew for his birthright?" He pressed his hands against his temples. "I have tried to teach him to think beyond momentary hunger and desire. And yet . . ."

Rebekah walked toward him, slipped her arms around his waist, and met his gaze. "Our sons are who they are, my lord. Esau is a man of impulsive action. Jacob is thoughtful and disciplined. Each path carries its own consequences."

"What consequences will this bring upon our household? When Esau realizes what he has done, when he understands what he has traded . . ." Isaac shook his head again.

"That will be between him and ADONAI." Rebekah placed her hand against his cheek. "We cannot undo what has been done."

Sighing, Isaac wrapped his arms around his wife. If Esau would trade something as significant as a birthright for a bowl of stew, what other rash decisions might prove to be his undoing?

"I have tried," he whispered near Rebekah's ear. "I have tried to teach him the difference between wisdom and foolishness. I have tried to lead by example, but—"

Rebekah pressed her fingertips to his lips. "Our sons are men full grown," she said, silently reminding him that the twins had reached the age of twenty. "They are responsible for their own decisions, foolish and wise."

Isaac nodded, but that realization did little to lessen the regret that burdened his heart.

Chapter
—24—

YEARS FELL AWAY like the leaves of an oak in the spring. In Beersheba, the land stretched before us, golden in the late-afternoon light. The fields flourished under ADONAI's blessing as our flocks filled the hillsides, their coats thick and their numbers increasing. The rich scents of fertile earth, of ripened grain and sun-warmed herbs, filled the air as I walked through our camp and watched day after day, season after season, fade into evening.

ADONAI had firmly established us in the land, but even as I considered our prosperity, a shadow haunted my heart. My sons had reached the age of forty, and yet neither had taken a wife. Abraham had been even older when he married Sarah, and Isaac was forty when we met, so when would my sons create families of their own?

The subject of marriage was not broached during our meals or casual conversations, yet it hung between us like a woven blanket never cut from the loom. When our servants married, we celebrated their weddings with joyous feasts. Our neighbors and acquaintances married, and we journeyed to celebrate their weddings, even returning to Gerar to celebrate the wedding of

Abimelech's son. But our sons did not seem inclined to consider the importance of family, or if they did, they never spoke of it.

I saw Esau returning from the fields, sweat-stained and likely smelling of blood after a successful hunt. I studied Jacob at the hearth, his hands cradling an orphaned lamb, his mind focused on the care of his flock. The two men were mature, yet neither of them had asked Isaac to arrange a marriage. Neither had even expressed an interest.

I turned my face toward my tent, where Isaac sat beneath the awning of our doorway, his face serene in the glow of the setting sun. He did not seem troubled. He had not spoken of our sons' marital future. Did the matter not concern him? Abraham had arranged *our* marriage—should he not give thought to the marriages of our sons, or did he expect ADONAI to do it for him?

My fingers tightened around the folds of my robe. Time was passing too quickly. Our sons were no longer young men, and the future would soon press upon us. A mother knew when the balance of a household was shifting, and I felt as though we were about to experience an earthquake. My husband was one hundred years old; he would not live forever.

If Isaac would not act, perhaps I should. I turned from the fields, my heart stirring with resolve. The time for waiting had passed.

That night, after serving dinner to the men of my family, I slipped into our tent and found Isaac asleep. I bent and kissed him, my lips brushing his forehead before I settled beside him.

His eyes fluttered and opened.

"Have you thought about our sons?" I propped my head on my hand. "Have you never longed for grandchildren?"

Isaac blinked, his eyes widening. He exhaled slowly, as if turning the thought over in his mind.

"You were the same age as our sons when we married," I reminded him. "And though the Lord did not bless us with children until later, He might bless our sons with little ones right away."

Isaac cleared his throat. "I will mention the matter to them."

"What will you say?" I pressed. "Perhaps you should send Minos to Haran. He could inquire about eligible maidens among our kinsmen."

Isaac shrugged as a smile tugged at the corners of his lips. "You do not startle prey in its den. For now, it is enough that our sons should begin to think about marriage."

ACCEPTING ISAAC'S STATEMENT as tacit permission, the next morning I made my way to Jacob's dwelling. The air was cool, the sky heavy with clouds, and the roosters energetically announced the new day.

I found Jacob inside, the light from an oil lamp painting his complexion with a golden glow as he busied himself sharpening a blade, his hands steady.

He looked up as I entered and set the blade aside. "Mother." He stood, his dark eyes searching mine. "What brings you out so early?"

I lowered myself onto a cushion. "I wanted to speak with you," I said, smoothing the folds of my tunic. "Have you given much thought to marriage?"

His throat bobbed in a convulsive swallow. "Sometimes I think about it," he admitted. "But I am in no rush." His eyes flicked to the entrance of the tent, where the wind stirred the open flap. "Among all the women of this land, I have not yet found one who stirs my heart or who worships ADONAI."

My own heart ached at his words, for I knew the truth of them. The daughters of Canaan followed foreign gods, not the Lord God. And Jacob would not turn from the Lord, nor could he bind himself to one who did not share his beliefs.

I took his hand. "ADONAI will guide you," I assured him. "When you are ready, let me know. I will speak to your father about a journey to Haran."

Jacob smiled and said, "I will."

A sense of peace settled over me as I stood. Though I could not know our future, I knew ADONAI's hand was upon my son. Abraham had known it, too. And in that assurance, I could rest.

THE NEXT MORNING, I caught Isaac in the fields. "My lord, did you speak to Esau about marriage?"

Isaac, who had been studying a bull in the distance, turned toward me. "I did."

"What did you tell him?"

"I told him"—he returned his attention to the bull—"that marriage was a good thing, and he was old enough to consider it."

"Is that all?"

Isaac looked at me again. "What else would you have me say? When he wants to marry, I will talk to him again."

I sighed. "Did you tell him we could send someone to Haran to find a woman whose family worships ADONAI?"

Isaac's brow wrinkled. "Your family did not worship ADONAI."

Unable to deny this, I folded my arms and sighed.

WHEN ESAU DISAPPEARED for several weeks, Isaac and I thought nothing of it. He often roamed in his hunting, his restless nature pulling him far beyond the hills and valleys around our camp. But one morning, as I sat to knead the dough for the evening meal, the blast of the lookout's horn commanded my attention. A caravan was approaching.

Our servants stopped what they were doing to look toward the gate. Even Isaac emerged from our tent, shading his eyes against the sun. Together, we watched as a line of donkeys meandered toward us. When they got closer, we saw a man in colorful finery at the head of the procession.

"How odd," Isaac said, standing beside me. "He walks like Esau."

I squinted at the caravan. "Indeed, he does, but . . ."

My words died on my tongue. The caravan had come close enough for me to see that the leader *was* our firstborn, and he led two donkeys, each bearing a woman dressed in scarlet, gold, and indigo. Their robes shimmered with elaborate embroidery, their arms gleaming with copper bracelets. Their faces were unveiled, their eyes wide and assessing as they approached our gate.

"Who?" I asked, my heart in my throat.

Isaac shook his head. "Let us hope Esau is helping travelers who have lost their way. We will feed them, let them rest, then send them on to their destination."

Something in me hoped Isaac was right, yet my heart knew better. Esau was bringing women home. *His* women.

The women were beautiful, I admitted, if one liked brazen, garish females who held their heads high, their smiles curling with insolent confidence. They were like the women of Gerar, the ones who worked outside the pagan shrines.

Esau stopped at the gate and shouted for all to hear: "Father! Mother! See what I have brought!" He gestured to the women beside him; his bare chest puffed with pride. "These are my wives: Judith, daughter of Be-eri the Hittite, and Basemath, daughter of Elon, another Hittite chieftain."

Isaac and I stood like those who watched the earth split beneath their feet—unable to move, unable to find solid ground.

The Hittites worshiped Tarhun, the storm god, and their men were raised to be warriors, quick to shed blood and skilled in shaping bronze into deadly weapons. My heart pounded beneath my ribs. How could our son bring these women into our home? Would they bend toward our ways or break us?

I looked at Isaac, whose face remained unreadable. He nodded slowly. "Welcome," he said, his voice strained. Then he turned and gestured for Esau's guests to enter the camp.

Esau, oblivious to our dismay, laughed as he led his brides toward his tent. I remained frozen in place, struggling to catch my breath. Without guidance from Isaac or Adonai, our son had made his choice.

What would this mean for us?

TWO WIVES. Two *Hittite* wives.

I stood in the doorway of my tent, watching Esau stride across the camp, his latest kill slung over his shoulders. My heart cracked like pottery dropped on rock.

"Judith and Basemath . . ." I whispered their names to the evening air, tasting the foreign syllables on my tongue. They felt sharp, unfamiliar, nothing like the names of our people.

I pressed my palms against the rough wall of the tent and let my head fall forward. The coarse fibers scratched my forehead, but the physical discomfort was nothing compared to the ache in my chest. Where had I failed? How had my firstborn wandered so far that he sought wives among people who carved images of their gods from wood and stone?

"Rebekah." Deborah's hand touched my shoulder.

When I turned, the tears I had been holding back spilled over. "It's my fault, Deborah. All of it." My voice broke. "I should have spent more time with Esau. I should have made sure he understood what it means to be part of a family chosen by Adonai. I assumed Isaac would counsel him to seek a wife from those who know the true God."

The words tumbled out of me like water from a broken cistern. I wiped my face with the back of my hand, tasting salt. "If I had been a better mother, if I had paid more attention instead of always . . ."

I stopped before I could say it: *instead of favoring Jacob*. The guilt of that truth sat heavy in my stomach.

Deborah's dark eyes crinkled at the corners. "And Esau loves ADONAI so much that he would listen to you?"

The question struck like a slap. I opened my mouth to protest, then closed it again. My shoulders sagged as the truth mocked me. Esau—my wild, impulsive, passionate son. When had I ever seen him bow his head in prayer? When had I ever found him seeking solitude to commune with the Almighty? I shook my head. "You are right."

Both my sons loved the solitude of the wilderness, but they loved it in different ways. Jacob would disappear for hours, returning with dirt on his knees and peace in his eyes, speaking of dreams and visions. Esau came back with blood under his fingernails, his eyes bright with the thrill of the chase, the satisfaction of the hunt.

"Jacob spends his days in prayer and study," I said, more to myself than to Deborah. "But Esau . . . all he wants to do is chase and kill."

Deborah nodded, her eyes kind but unflinching. "You cannot make a wild lion into a sheep, my pet. No matter how much you love it."

I sank onto the pile of cushions where I did my embroidery, suddenly exhausted. The familiar scents of our tent—wool and herbs and the lingering smoke from our lamp—usually comforted me, but in that moment they felt stifling. Through the tent flap, I could see Esau's wives moving within their new dwelling. Judith with her elaborate braids and jingling ornaments; Basemath, younger and quieter, with the same foreign grace in her movements.

They were beautiful, I had to admit, and seemed happy about this marriage. In the days since their arrival, I had seen their faces light up when he returned from hunting and noted the way they rushed to tend to his needs. Perhaps that was enough for Esau.

"I should make an effort," I said, "to know Judith and Basemath. They are now part of our family whether I approve or not."

Deborah nodded. "That would be wise, pet."

I stood and smoothed my tunic, squaring my shoulders. Through the tent opening I could see Judith grinding grain, efficient and practiced. Basemath tended the fire in the brazier, her head bent in concentration. They were trying to fit in, to belong. For the first time since Esau's return, a flutter of hope stirred in my chest. "Perhaps we will become good friends." I lowered the flap of the tent and turned to Deborah. "Will you arrange my hair? I do not wish to look like a wild woman when I visit them."

"Certainly," Deborah said.

I sat, and she began combing my hair.

The evening breeze stirred the tent walls, carrying with it the scent of roasting meat and fresh bread. Somewhere in the distance, Esau's deep laugh mingled with his wives' higher voices. The sound no longer felt like a knife in my heart. Change was inevitable, and I should accept Esau's wives as graciously as Abraham had accepted me.

I would learn to love what my son loved, not because I understood his choices, but because love requires opening your arms wider than you ever imagined.

I RAN MY FINGERS over my freshly combed hair, checking the smooth strands Deborah had so carefully arranged. My best earrings swayed against my neck as I walked, and I wore my finest tunic of deep blue. I wanted to welcome my daughters-in-law properly.

The short walk to Esau's tent felt longer than usual. As my sandals crunched on scattered pebbles, I could hear voices from within—Esau's familiar rumble mixing with the lighter, musical tones of Judith and Basemath. Taking a deep breath, I called out, "May I enter?"

"Mother!" Esau's voice boomed with genuine pleasure, and

he swept aside the tent flap before I could even lift my hand. Esau stood before me, his face bright with the infectious grin that had charmed everyone since he was a boy. "Come, enter! Judith, Basemath—my mother is here."

I stepped inside, blinking as my eyes adjusted to the dimmer light. The tent smelled different from ours, scented by spices I did not recognize and something that made me think of distant gardens. The women rose from where they had been sitting, their movements as fluid as dancers.

Judith was the taller of the two, with elaborately braided hair that caught the lamplight. Her eyes were lined in a way that made them look enormous, and when she smiled, her teeth gleamed like polished bone. Basemath was smaller and more delicate, wearing rings that chimed softly when she moved. Both wore robes of fine linen in shades I had never seen—deep purple and the green of new leaves in springtime.

"Welcome." I opened my arms in what I hoped was a motherly gesture. "Welcome to our family and to our home. I am happy you are here."

Judith tilted her head, her brow furrowing in a way that suggested she had caught most of my words but not all. She spoke, her voice melodic but the words strange.

I looked to Esau, who had learned many different dialects in his travels. He laughed, a sound that filled the tent like warm honey. "She says thank you, Mother, and she is honored to meet the woman who gave birth to such a mighty hunter."

Heat rose in my cheeks, whether from pleasure at the compliment or embarrassment at needing translation in my own family, I could not tell. "Tell her I am honored to meet the woman who has captured my son's heart."

As they chattered, I looked around the tent. The dwelling had been divided into sections with curtains, probably to allow Esau privacy with each wife—a problem I had never encountered. Brightly colored cushions filled the open area where we stood.

One of these women knew the art of dyeing fabrics. A low wooden table stood in the center of the space, and a wooden box sat away from everything else in a secluded place of honor. Someone had carved the box with figures similar to those I had seen in Haran, where such images decorated the walls of pagan temples, painted around niches designed to shelter idols in family homes.

A shiver crept up the ladder of my spine. I forced a smile. Surely Esau knew better than to allow his wives to bring idols into our camp.

I looked up as the women finished another exchange in their lilting language, and this time both women giggled. Basemath spoke, gesturing with her ring-adorned hands, and I caught a few words that sounded almost like our tongue but not quite.

"She wants you to try her honey cakes," Esau translated, his eyes twinkling. "She is also asking if you are sure because I told them you are particular about food."

"Esau!" I swatted at his arm but smiled despite myself. "You should not have said such a thing."

"I may have mentioned your strong opinions about proper seasoning," he said with mock solemnity, then burst into laughter when his wives nodded and began what might have been an animated discussion about spices.

Judith disappeared behind a curtain and returned with a plate of golden cakes that glistened with honey. The scent was wonderful—sweet and rich with hints of something I could not identify. I took one, keenly aware that three pairs of eyes watched me intently.

The cake melted on my tongue, flooding my mouth with flavors both familiar and foreign. Honey, yes, but also nuts I did not recognize, and a spice that left a pleasant warmth in my throat. "Wonderful," I said, and their faces lit up with such pleasure that I took another.

"Judith's grandmother taught all the village girls how to cook," Esau said. "She says the secret is in the grinding of the . . ." He turned abruptly and spoke to them, then shrugged. "I do not think we have a word for that spice. It comes from a purple flower near their home."

"Tell me about your home," I said, settling on the cushions they offered.

A lengthy conversation followed, with Esau serving as interpreter for increasingly animated descriptions. Their home, it seemed, was a place of wonders: cities with walls of white stone, gardens where fruit trees grew in neat rows, temples with columns that reached toward the sky. Judith's father was a merchant who traded in precious metals, while the women of Basemath's family were skilled weavers whose work was prized throughout the region.

"The summers there are not like this," Basemath said through Esau, fanning herself and making an expression of such dramatic distress that I could not help but laugh. "She says the heat here makes her feel like bread in an oven."

"And the sand!" Judith added, apparently catching enough of our conversation to join in. She gestured around the tent, then at her carefully arranged hair, and said something that made Esau grin.

"She says the sand here gets into everything—her hair, her food, her dreams. She is convinced it follows her even when she sleeps."

I laughed, remembering my own struggles with the endless sand when I first arrived as Isaac's bride. "Tell her it takes time to adjust. Tell her that eventually she will stop noticing it."

But as Esau translated, something flickered across both women's faces, a kind of polite resignation. They smiled and nodded, but their eyes grew distant, as if they were again seeing those white-walled cities and green gardens of their homeland.

The conversation continued, touching on everything from cooking methods to weaving techniques to the proper way to arrange a woman's hair. Both women were gracious, even charming, but I began to notice something that made my heart sink.

Every story they told circled back to home. Every comparison favored their homeland. When I asked about their families, their faces grew soft with longing. When I mentioned the beauty of our hills at sunrise, they spoke of mountains that touched the clouds. When I praised the sweet water of our wells, they described rivers that ran like liquid silver.

And through it all, their attention kept drifting to Esau. When he spoke, they leaned forward like flowers turning toward the sun. When he laughed, they laughed as if his joy was their own. When he moved, their eyes followed. But when I spoke—even when I was asking them direct questions—their gazes slid past me to rest on my son.

I was a duty to be endured, I realized. A requirement of their new life, like learning to tolerate the sand and heat. They were polite enough, but they were not truly interested in knowing me. I was simply Esau's mother, an appendage to their husband, not a significant person.

That understanding settled over me like a cold wind. I finished another honey cake, complimented their hospitality, and made the appropriate noises about how good it was to meet them. But the warmth I had felt earlier had faded, replaced by a hollow ache.

When I finally rose to leave, both women stood as well, their movements perfectly courteous. They smiled, said what I assumed were the proper farewell words in their language, and even embraced me. But I could feel their eagerness for me to leave, their desire to have Esau to themselves.

"Thank you for visiting," Esau said, walking me to the tent entrance. His voice was warm, genuinely pleased; he had not noticed the undercurrents I felt. To him, the visit had been a success.

I forced another smile. "They are pleasant women."

"I knew you would like them."

I kissed his cheek, breathing in the familiar scents of Esau: leather and sunshine and something wild that had always been uniquely his. Then I walked back to my tent, my steps growing ever heavier.

I had tried, but my effort felt insufficient. The breeze picked up, carrying with it the sound of laughter from Esau's tent—laughter that had begun the moment I left. They were speaking their own language now, no doubt relieved to be free of the need for translation, free to speak of home without having to pretend they were happy in Canaan.

I pulled my shawl closer around my shoulders and tried not to remember how their eyes had looked past me as though I were already gone.

Chapter 25

THREE MONTHS AFTER the arrival of Esau's wives, Isaac and I stepped out of our tent. My husband's frame had grown frail and his hair stark white. He leaned on my arm as we walked, my steps steady and sure, his slower and more uncertain. Though I was seventy-four, I remained strong, while Isaac's age and a sleepless night weighed heavily on him.

The previous evening had been filled with the noise of revelry from Esau's tent. Instead of the usual night noises, the sound of his wives' shrieks and laughter carried across the camp.

I felt the strain in my bones. "You should ask Esau to move his tent away from the camp," I said, tightening my grip on Isaac's arm. "He might prefer to have greater privacy."

Isaac shook his head. "The situation is only temporary. Remember how lively we were when we first married? Soon they will settle down."

I opened my mouth to reply, then halted. My breath caught when I spotted an obstacle in our path.

Isaac, who could no longer see clearly, frowned. "What is it?"

I could not answer. A chill ran down my spine as I stared at the object in the dust. Our household was deteriorating, and I could smell the decay.

Before me, in the center of the path, lay a heap of stones. Atop the stones lay a headless chicken, its feathers matted with dried blood. Two wooden statues, crudely carved, stood on either side of the bird, their eyes vacant. I knew what this was. I had seen similar sacrifices to pagan idols in Haran. The Hittite women had brought the idols into our camp, and I had sensed their malignant presence. I did not know what gods these were, but they had no place among us.

Isaac sensed the tension in my stillness. "Speak, Rebekah, and tell me what is wrong."

"Idols," I said, my voice sharp with disgust. "And a dead chicken in the middle of our camp. This could only have come from—"

"Say no more," Isaac interrupted. "Call someone to take the abomination away at once. I will speak to Esau."

He released my arm and shuffled off, leaning on his staff, the anger fading from his features as he struggled to find his way without my guidance. I watched him go, discouraged by his weakness. My husband was responsible for our camp, but I would have to deal with the noise, the disrespect, and the defilement of our home.

I moved forward, kicking the pile of stones, scattering the idols and the blood-soaked feathers. I spotted a servant and asked him to clean up the mess and burn anything that remained.

As I strode back to our dwelling, my breath quickened at the sound of Esau's laughter, loud and ribald even at this early hour. How could he bring this evil into our camp? How could he so recklessly dishonor our God?

I slipped into the cool darkness of our tent, my heart thudding in my chest, but I had to be strong. The time for tolerance had passed.

THE COOL AIR of dusk, heavy with the perfume of blooming jasmine, clung to my skin as I motioned for Jacob to join me beneath the date palms. My body ached from the day's labor, but important matters pressed upon my heart.

Above us, stars had begun to emerge, pinpricks of silver against the deepening purple sky, and in their light I could see my son's face—a mixture of strength and gentleness, like his father's.

"Come, sit with me," I said, patting a space on my bench. The rough wood against my palm reminded me of the many meals we had shared in this spot. We had talked endlessly about herds and harvests, but never about anything as significant as the topic I needed to broach tonight.

Jacob's eyes, dark and subdued, met mine as he sat. He was forty years old, yet at times I could still see the sweet boy who had clung to my tunic. The silver threads in his beard caught the light of the lamp I carried, casting shadows across the hollows of his cheeks.

A lamb bleated in the distance, and somewhere behind us Esau's boisterous laughter blended with the giggles of his Canaanite wives. I lowered my lamp and steeled myself against the sounds, not wanting to grimace in front of Jacob.

I wrapped my hand around his wrist, his pulse steady beneath my fingertips. "My son, you must not marry any of the Canaanite women. You must not even touch them."

Jacob's brows rose, and a slow smile spread across his face. "Mother, I have not known or touched any woman, nor have I betrothed myself to anyone." He turned his hand to grip mine. "I have not even thought about taking a wife from the daughters of Canaan."

The tension in my shoulders eased, but I remained silent and waited for him to continue.

"I remember what Grandfather told me." Jacob's voice dropped to a respectful tone. "He commanded me not to take a Canaanite woman, but to take my wife from among my father's relatives."

I sighed, my heart swelling with relief. The taste of sweet date wine from dinner still lingered on my tongue, but it was not nearly as sweet as hearing those words.

"I have heard," Jacob said, releasing my hand, "that my uncle Laban now has daughters." His dark eyes searched my face. "I have set my heart upon choosing one of them to be my wife."

I had heard the same news.

"For this reason," Jacob continued, "I have guarded myself against being corrupted with regard to lust and fornication." A flush crept up his neck. "Grandfather gave me explicit advice about such things," he added, his gaze dropping to the sand at our feet. "Esau has urged me to take a sister of his wives as my own, but I will not do what he has done."

The night insects began their chorus, a rhythmic chirring that pulsed with my heartbeat. I raised my face to the heavens, where countless stars glittered like scattered jewels on a deep blue cloth. The night air caressed my upturned face as I extended my hands, palms open to acknowledge the gratitude welling within me.

"Blessed be the Lord God," I whispered, my voice breaking with thanksgiving that threatened to spill into tears, "and may His holy name be blessed forever, for he has given me Jacob as a pure son and a holy seed." The words poured from my lips like honey. "For he is yours, O Lord, and yours will his seed be throughout generations to come."

I closed my eyes as the jasmine-scented breeze caressed my eyelids. "Bless him, Adonai. Place words of righteousness in my mouth, so that I may bless him."

The bench creaked as I stood and placed my hands on Jacob's head. Words I had not known were within me streamed into the silence: "Blessed are you, O Lord of righteousness and God of the ages. And may He bless you, Jacob, beyond all the generations of men."

Jacob's eyes closed, his lips moving in silent prayer as I continued. "May He give you, my son, the path of righteousness, and reveal righteousness to your descendants. May He give you many sons. And may they arise according to the number of the months of the year."

A tear slipped over Jacob's cheek, glistening in the lamplight.

"May their sons multiply beyond the stars of heaven, and their numbers be more than the sand of the sea. And may He give Jacob's descendants this goodly land, as He said He would give it to Abraham and to his descendants after him. And may they hold it as a possession forever."

Jacob's body trembled beneath my touch, and my own heart quivered with the significance of the words God had given me.

"And may I see born to you, my son, blessed children during my lifetime." The image of Jacob's children filled my mind, eliciting a fresh surge of emotion. "And may all your descendants be a blessed and holy seed."

I took Jacob's face between my hands. "Blessed be he that blesses you," I whispered, "and anyone who curses you falsely, may they be cursed." I leaned forward and pressed my lips to his forehead. "May the Lord of the world love you," I murmured, "as the heart of your mother rejoices in you."

I pulled away in a sudden silence; the insects and livestock had gone quiet, as if all creation had paused to witness this moment. Jacob's eyes gleamed with unshed tears, and in them I saw the future unfurl like a scroll—generations upon generations, countless as the stars watching over us in the vast desert sky.

AS HEAD OF THE FAMILY, Isaac talked to Esau, who promised us that his wives would no longer sacrifice to their gods within the camp. They would offer their sacrifices outside the walls, far from our tents, where they would disturb no one.

But I felt a sharp pang of frustration as I listened to Esau's promises. "They should not be worshiping idols at all!"

Esau, ever defiant, only shrugged. "Can a thornbush bear figs?" he said. The words made no sense, but he did not seem to care.

As Isaac and I watched, Esau strolled back to his waiting wives.

"At least we will have some measure of peace." Isaac rubbed a weary hand over his face. "But for how long, I wonder?"

Peace did reign for a time, but the problem with Esau's wives involved more than idols. The difficulty stemmed from the women themselves, who had never heard of ADONAI before Esau brought them to our camp. They had no natural modesty, no sense of devotion or reverence. They walked with their unveiled heads held high. Once they began to learn our language, in loud voices they used crude words, adorning themselves, even in the camp, with gold jewelry and expensive fabrics. They did not offer to help with any work and would have fattened their bellies on our food alone if Esau had not commanded them to prepare the game he had killed.

Worst of all, the adoration they initially felt for Esau wore thin, and they began to mock him at every opportunity. They obeyed only when he raised his voice and screamed at them, and throughout the camp we heard their brawling voices as Esau roared his orders.

In short, I saw no softness or reverence in them—only the cruel edge of Hittite ways. Despair over my firstborn's marriages burdened me, chafing every time I saw or heard one of his women, but he had made his choice. What could I do?

One evening, as the sun dipped toward the western sky, I found Esau sitting outside while Judith attempted to cook venison on a brazier. The air was thick with tension, and the acrid scent of burning meat mixed with the woman's agitated voice. Anger boiled beneath the surface of Esau's face, barely contained as Judith placed her hands on her hips. "I have already cooked," she said, pointing to the brazier. "Your dinner is there!"

"My dinner is burnt!" he snapped. "Cut another piece of venison."

Instead of obeying, the woman stalked away. I glanced at Esau and caught his gaze. "I cannot believe your wife behaves like that."

When his eyes flashed a warning, I knew I should not have spoken.

"This is the only way they know," he said, standing. "It is how they were raised. Hittite women respect strength. Gentle words accomplish nothing with them."

My heart broke for him as he stomped after her. Was our household destined to be plagued by continual brawling and disrespect? Would Jacob and our servants learn to accept this behavior as normal?

I lifted my eyes and begged ADONAI to prevent Jacob from following Esau's path.

Chapter 26

TIME SIFTED THROUGH my fingers like fine desert sand. About a year after Esau brought his two wives into the camp, Jacob told us he wanted to return to Moriah to study with Shem and Eber. Isaac and I looked at each other in surprise, but how could we object? From Noah's son and great-grandson, he would learn more about the ways of ADONAI and the history of the world—far more than Isaac or I could teach him.

And perhaps, we realized, Jacob wanted to escape the strife in our household.

So we gave him our blessing and sent him off with a servant to keep him company. While Jacob was away, Minos, who had stepped into Eliezer's shoes after the steward's death, took on even more responsibility, easing the burden on Isaac as he oversaw the care of the livestock, the rotation of our crops, and the management of our servants.

ADONAI continued to bless us, and we remained at peace with all our neighbors, including the Philistines. Indeed, the only strife in our lives came from Esau's tent. On several occasions I wanted to intervene in an argument between our son and his wives, or between the two women, but Isaac always stopped me. "They are adults," he reminded me. "You must allow them to learn their own lessons."

For the next several years, Jacob studied at the yeshiva. I missed him terribly, but occasionally we received messages through travelers who had come through the land of Moriah. Jacob always wrote that he was well and learning a great deal. He wrote that he loved and missed us, and he prayed that ADONAI would keep us well.

I read his letters with tears in my eyes, then I read them to Isaac, who wept as well. I offered to read them to Esau, but he had no interest in Jacob's studies or learning of ADONAI's deeds.

And then, as the autumn rains prepared us for the cooler days of winter, the lookout blew his ram's horn. I stopped weaving and walked toward the gate, then broke into a run. Two figures were approaching with a donkey, and one of them looked like Jacob.

My son and his servant had come home!

I hurried toward the gate, my heart racing faster than my aging legs could carry me. Jacob—my Jacob—had returned after fourteen long years. Even from a distance, I could see that he had grown broader in the shoulders and sturdier in his frame. The midday sun caught highlights in his beard, which was far longer than when he had departed. My son was now a man of fifty-five, his countenance lined by more than a decade of study, prayer, and contemplation.

"Mother!"

I threw my arms around him and inhaled a mixture of dust from the road, the herbs he favored, and something new, something that spoke of years poring over scrolls in a dimly lit room. I pulled back, my fingers tracing the new lines around his eyes.

"Let me look at you." I held him at arm's length, tears blurring my vision. My hands trembled as they patted the face I had dreamed of seeing for so many years.

Isaac approached more slowly, his steps careful, his sight now so diminished that a servant had to lead him by the hand. But when he heard Jacob's voice, his face transformed, years falling away from his features.

"Father!" Jacob broke from my embrace and rushed to Isaac's side. He took his father's hands and pressed them to his face.

"My son." Isaac's fingers traced Jacob's features and lingered on the furrow that had formed between our son's brows. "You have changed."

"Yet I am still your son," Jacob replied, his voice thick.

As they embraced, I wiped away tears with the corner of my veil. The hollow ache that had existed beneath my ribs for more than a decade finally eased.

I turned to the servants, who had gathered at the gate. "Prepare a feast! Our son has returned!"

As the camp erupted in activity, I watched Jacob tenderly guide his father toward our tent, their heads bent in conversation. Jacob's movements were more deliberate now; he walked like a man of knowledge and responsibility. The man I sent away from our camp had returned with depths of knowledge in his eyes.

Tonight, we would feast. Tonight, our family would be whole again. And tomorrow I would sit with my son and learn what knowledge, wisdom, and dreams he had brought with him from the land of Moriah.

I HAD HOPED to hear details of what Jacob learned during his years of study, but though he was quick to tell stories about Adonai's creation of the universe and the world before the great flood, most of my questions were answered with a quizzical look. "I cannot recite a list of exactly *what* I learned," he finally told me. "Most of my time was spent studying Him."

I made a face. "I do not understand."

"Adonai. I spent most of my time learning who He is as

revealed through His creation and His deeds. Yet even now, I wish I knew Him better."

The answer made my mouth go dry. I worshiped Adonai, I believed in Him, and I trusted Him. But to study Him for years . . . the thought astonished me.

After that, I did not ask Jacob any more questions.

Jacob had been home only a few months when we received word that Shem, Noah's son, had died after living six hundred years. Jacob mourned the old man, who had been wise and righteous.

Months passed. Jacob went back to the fields to care for the livestock, and Esau continued to hunt in the wilderness. Both sons provided meat for our table, but neither had much to do with the other.

Esau's wives, however, made us grandparents. Judith bore Esau a son called Eliphaz, and Basemath bore him a son called Reuel. Both boys were small versions of Esau. As soon as they could ride a donkey, they went with him into the wilderness and learned to hunt.

I watched them, marveling that though they had come from different mothers, they were so like their father. What, I wondered, would Jacob's sons be like? And when would Jacob decide to seek a bride?

Laban's daughters, I reckoned, had to be nearing maturity. They would be ready for marriage soon.

The winter shifted to spring, and with it came the rains—gentle at first, then insistent, until the wadis filled and the earth smelled of life once more. Isaac and I both fell ill, as did many in our camp. A wet cough settled in our chests, and though the sun soon warmed the tents, the catarrh clung stubbornly to my husband.

Deborah helped me brew tea from hyssop and thyme, crushed herbs into poultices, and boiled fig syrup to soothe his throat. I sat by his side, placing cool cloths on his brow, listening to the rasp in his lungs, and praying to the God who gave him to me. Yet in the quiet hours, doubt crept like a shadow. Isaac's years were numbered at one hundred twenty. Few men of our generation had seen as many. And now, it seemed, he had begun to feel the weight of them.

He grew quieter by the day. He stopped asking after the herds. He no longer rose to sit beneath the shade of the awning. He stared—not at me, but beyond me—as though watching something only he could see.

At night, when his breathing turned ragged, I would lie beside him, my hand resting lightly on his. I remembered the day I first saw him in the field, walking toward me like a promise fulfilled. Now I feared I was watching that promise slip away.

He often spoke of Abraham—of the ram in the thicket, of the altar and the voice of ADONAI. I knew what these stories meant. Isaac was measuring his days. Preparing, perhaps, to meet the One who had called his father from Ur.

Then one afternoon, his mood shifted. The wind was hot and dry again, and the tents flapped against their poles. Isaac called for pillows and sat up with effort. His hands trembled, but his voice—when he found it—was sure.

"Send for Esau," he said to the servant waiting at the doorway of our tent. "Let him hunt for me and prepare the game I love."

When Esau arrived, windblown and ruddy from the sun, I followed but stopped short of the doorway, curiosity pulling me like a thread. The afternoon heat warmed my skin as I pretended to sort the dried herbs hanging nearby. My fingers moved over bundles of hyssop and mint, but my ears were tuned to the voices within.

Isaac's voice, once strong and commanding, now trembled like a dry leaf. He could no longer see more than vague shadows, and his steps were no longer steady.

My stomach tightened. I had seen this day coming. Isaac was preparing to give the blessing that would shape our sons' future. I stepped closer to the goatskin wall of the tent, its surface brushing my shoulder.

Isaac's voice grew clearer: "My son, I am old, and I do not know the day of my death. Take your weapons, your quiver and bow, and go out to the field and hunt game for me. Then prepare me a delicious meal, such as I love, and bring it to me so that I may eat, and my soul may bless you before I die."

Esau strode from the tent, his eyes fixed on the horizon. I bit my lower lip. What should I do?

Inside, Isaac was coughing, wheezing, struggling for breath. No wonder he believed death was near.

My hands trembled. The smell of the herbs around me—thyme, coriander, garlic—nearly overwhelmed my senses. *"Prepare me a delicious meal,"* Isaac had said. I knew the meal he meant. How many times had I made it, teaching the servants the exact way to season the meat so it would be tender and savory?

Perhaps I should stand aside and let Esau obey his father. But what of ADONAI's words? What of that day when I sought the Lord and the Holy One spoke to me?

What of Esau's carelessness, trading his birthright for a bowl of stew? Did Isaac not remember that day? Or had he chosen to forget, favoring the son who brought him wild game over the one who loved ADONAI, tended the flocks, and honored the ways of our people?

I took two steps toward the cooking tent, then halted. What was my duty as a wife? The question hovered in the air, shimmering like the distant horizon. Should I remain silent and watch Isaac bestow the blessing meant for Jacob upon Esau?

Which was greater, obedience to my husband or obedience to ADONAI?

I closed my eyes and pressed a clenched fist to my forehead. The herbs in my hands released their sharp scents. I turned toward Esau's tent and tilted my head to listen. From within came the swish of Esau's mantle, the creak of his bow, the rattle of arrows in his quiver.

Being a skilled hunter, Esau would return within hours. Should a loyal wife let her husband make such a grave mistake? Should a loving mother stand by while the birthright passed to the one who had rashly squandered it?

No. She should not. Isaac might choose to ignore ADONAI's word, but I could not. I drew a deep breath to steady myself, knitting the raveled threads of my courage. "Jacob!" I called, striding toward his tent. "Come to me, son."

As I waited for him, the plan took shape. We had young goats in the flock, tender kids. I knew how to make them taste like wild game. I knew the spices needed as well as the method. I knew how to ensure Jacob received what ADONAI intended for him.

When Jacob appeared, his eyes searching mine, I did not hesitate.

"My son," I said, "I heard your father speak to your brother, saying, 'Bring me game and prepare a delicious meal that I may eat and bless you in ADONAI's presence before my death.'"

Jacob frowned, confusion crossing his face, but I would not be dissuaded.

I slipped my arm around his shoulders. "Listen to me and do what I command you. Go to the flock and bring me two choice young goats, and I will prepare them as a meal your father loves. Then you will take it to him, and he will bless you."

Jacob hesitated. "Mother, my brother Esau is a hairy man, and I am smooth. What if my father touches me? He will think I am mocking him. He will bring a curse on me instead of a blessing."

I straightened, my resolve hardening like clay in the sun. "Let your curse fall on me, only obey my voice. Go now. Bring me the goats."

As soon as he had gone, I lifted my voice. "Deborah! I need you!"

THE METALLIC SMELL of fresh blood mixed with woodsmoke as Deborah and I worked over the slaughtered kids.

Her weathered hands moved with practiced efficiency, her fingers separating skin from flesh while I gathered the herbs that would make the goat taste like game. The late-afternoon sun cast long shadows across our work area. Sweat trickled down my back despite the shade of the cooking tent.

"Carefully," I warned as Deborah cut strips of the goat's skin. She nodded, gray hair escaping from beneath her headscarf as she laid each piece over the smoldering fire. The skin needed to dry quickly; we did not have time to cure it.

A pot of water simmered over the fire, thick with garlic and wild onions. I added handfuls of herbs: hyssop for brightness, coriander for sweetness, cumin for the gamy taste Isaac loved. The mingled aromas filled the air, familiar yet strange in this context of deception. My legs trembled as I stirred the pot and watched the meat become tender in the fragrant broth.

Jacob sat nearby, his shoulders tense, his ear cocked toward the lookout tower. Every few moments he would start at some sound—a dove's wings, a child's cry, the bleating of sheep—thinking it might be the lookout announcing his brother's return. His anxiety fed my own, but I forced my hands to remain steady.

"Mother," he said, his voice low, "are you certain?"

"Yes," I said, more sharply than I'd intended. Then, in a calmer voice, "Trust in ADONAI, my son."

Memories filled my mind as I worked. Isaac's face on our wedding day, full of joy and wonder. The years we spent building our relationship, his gentleness and uncertainty about ADONAI's purpose for his life. Our love had deepened with time, which made this moment particularly painful. But was it not loving to prevent a husband from making a grave mistake?

I added more wood to the fire. Like the leaping flames, my resolve grew stronger with each passing moment. How could Isaac not see the obvious? Esau did not deserve the blessing of the firstborn. He was far too quick to anger and too willing to cast aside ADONAI's precepts. I remembered the day he brought home his

Hittite wives, how they had sacrificed to an idol in the midst of our camp. The memory still made my stomach tighten.

Deborah touched my arm, drawing me back to our task. "The skin is nearly ready," she murmured, her eyes dark with understanding. She had been with me since childhood; she had helped me birth my babies and knew what sort of men they had become. And she was helping me do what was right.

I glanced at Jacob. He sat with his hands clasped, his lips moving in silent prayer. *This* was the son ADONAI wanted to inherit, the one who kept the laws, honored the covenant, and understood Abraham's legacy. Not Esau, who had traded his birthright for a bowl of stew and chosen to marry pagan wives.

The meat was tender, falling away from the bone. I added the last of the spices, the secret blend that was so dear to Isaac's heart. Oh, my beloved and blind husband! Could he not see past Esau's physical strength to recognize Jacob's spiritual maturity? Did he not understand that leadership required more than skill with a bow and spear?

"The meat is ready," I said, my voice steady despite the raging storm in my heart. "Come, Jacob. We must work quickly."

As I lifted the pot from the fire, I sent up a silent prayer. *ADONAI, forgive this deception. You know my heart. You know I do this not for myself, but because of your promise. "The elder shall serve the younger." You spoke those words to me. Give me the strength to see this through . . .*

The sun was perched on the western horizon, about to set. Soon we would know if ADONAI's will would prevail.

THE GLOOM THAT had become Isaac's constant companion pressed upon him as he waited, leaning back against the cushions that held him upright. The air carried the scents of goatskin, wool, and the lingering aroma of breakfast. His hands rested on his thighs as he listened for his son's return.

When footsteps approached, Isaac lifted his head. "Who is there?"

"Father." The voice was soft, measured. "It is Esau, your first-born. I have done as you told me. Please, eat, that you may bless me."

A whisper of doubt stirred Isaac's confidence. The voice seemed off, but then he inhaled the familiar aroma of the perfectly seasoned meat that always made his mouth water. He took another breath, savoring it. "How is it that you found game so quickly, my son?"

"ADONAI your God granted me success."

Isaac tilted his head. Esau rarely spoke of the Lord, and never had his voice resonated with such reverence. He straightened and extended his arms. "Come near so that I may know whether you are really my son Esau."

As the footsteps came closer, Isaac's hands trembled. His fingers met warm skin, rough with hair, exactly as Esau's should be. Yet something felt different—the texture was not quite right. He ran his hands over the arms and neck, front and back, finding coarseness in every area he touched. He parsed the scent of the wilderness—Esau always smelled of earth and herbs and fresh air—but beneath that smell was something he could not identify. Confusion clouded his thoughts. The hands that served the meat were Esau's. The voice held Jacob's gentleness, but the smell evoked Esau's strength.

Isaac squinted through his weakened eyes. "Are you *really* my son Esau?"

"I am."

Still uncertain, Isaac tasted the meat, which flooded his mouth with memories of countless meals Esau had prepared for him. The wine, too, was rich and sweet on his tongue. As he finished, contentment overrode his doubts. "Come nearer and kiss me, my son."

As his son leaned forward, Isaac pressed his face into the woven garment, which smelled of the open field and wild places. As his remaining doubts melted away, the blessing sprang to his lips.

"See, the smell of my son is like the smell of a field the Lord has blessed. May God give you—from the dew of the sky and from the fatness of the land—an abundance of grain and new wine. May peoples serve you, and may nations bow down to you. Be master over your brothers. May your mother's sons bow down to you. May those who curse you be cursed, and may those who bless you be blessed."

"Thank you, my father. And now I must go."

Isaac frowned. "So soon?"

"I hear commotion and must seek the cause of it."

Isaac felt a breeze from the tent flap rising and falling, then from another opening a different set of footsteps padded over the carpet—heavy, familiar steps that made Isaac's heart stop. The smell of fresh game and sweat filled the tent.

"My father! Get up and eat of your son's wild game that your soul may bless me."

The voice—Esau's unmistakably—cut through Isaac like a blade. He trembled as comprehension crashed over him. "Who are you?" he whispered, though he already knew the answer.

"I am your firstborn, Esau."

"Then who was it that hunted game and brought it to me? I ate it all before you came, and I have blessed him. And yes, he will be blessed."

After a moment of silence, Esau's anguished cry pierced the air, tearing at Isaac's heart. "Bless me, even me also, O my father!"

Isaac shook his head, his voice breaking. "Your brother came deceitfully and stole your blessing."

Esau's rage filled the tent. "Is he not rightly named *Jacob*?" he shouted, his tone as bitter as wormwood. "For he has cheated me twice. He took my birthright, and now he has taken my blessing."

Isaac's useless eyes burned with tears. His hands, which had bestowed the irrevocable blessing, trembled in his lap. The darkness around him deepened as Esau's pleas continued, becoming more desperate with each breath.

"Have you not reserved a blessing for me, Father? Surely there is something you can give me."

Esau's words were like thistles, stinging Isaac's heart. "I have made your brother master over you," he said, "and all his brothers I have given to him as servants. I have provided him with grain and new wine. What then can I do for you, my son?"

Isaac's heart broke as the sound of Esau's weeping filled the tent. Finally, he spoke again. "Behold, away from the fatness of the earth shall your dwelling be, away from the dew of the sky above. By your sword you shall live, and you shall serve your brother; but when you tear yourself loose, you will tear his yoke off your neck."

A deep silence enveloped the tent, broken only by the slap of the goatskin awning over the door.

And Isaac knew he was alone.

He sat motionless in his darkness, the taste of the meal still on his tongue, the smell of the field still in his nostrils, and the sound of his sons' shattered relationship in his ears. He had been deceived by every sense he trusted. Now he could only bear the consequences of what could not be undone.

MY HANDS SHOOK as I stumbled away from the tent, my feet carrying me instinctively to Deborah. She would know what to do.

"Deborah!" My voice cracked as I entered the supply tent, empty but for my nurse. "A servant overheard Esau, who said he will kill Jacob once the days of mourning for Isaac are completed."

Deborah frowned. "Surely he jests."

"He does not." I began pacing in the narrow space. "What am I to do? Esau could easily kill Jacob out in the fields—no one would even know what happened. An arrow, a hasty grave, and my younger son would be gone forever."

"Then Jacob must leave at once. You must send him to a safe place."

I bobbed my head frantically. "Yes! We will prepare a mount for him. We will pack bread, dried figs, cheese, waterskins . . ." My words tumbled over each other as I helped Deborah gather supplies and wrap wheels of cheese.

Jacob appeared in the doorway, his face shadowed with concern. "Mother? Why are you in here?"

I grabbed his hands. "You must leave us," I said, lowering my voice. "We are preparing supplies for you."

His dark eyes searched my face, confusion written across his features. "Where am I going?"

"Haran. My brother will take you in there and keep you safe."

"But why must I—?"

"My son, we do not have time for questions!" When Jacob flinched, I forced myself to calm, glancing toward the open space beyond the tent. "Your brother's anger burns as hot as a desert wind. He plans to kill you, but I will not let him."

Deborah worked silently behind me, packing supplies with swift efficiency.

"I will get a camel, and Deborah will load your supplies."

"I cannot run." Jacob's jaw jutted forward. "Father will consider me a coward if I do."

"Is that what you think? Let us go to him, and we will see what he says."

Behind me, Deborah cleared her throat, reminding me that time was slipping away. "I will get the camel," she said, "while you take Jacob to see the master."

I pulled Jacob close, my second-born by a moment, my gentle son. Tears burned my eyes as I pressed kisses to his cheeks.

"I do not believe Father is close to death," Jacob said, "though I *am* certain of Esau's anger."

"I do not think your father will die, either." I smoothed his hair as I had when he was small. "Stay with Laban until your brother's fury subsides. In a few days, your father will be better, and Esau will forget what has happened." I tried to sound confident, yet my voice quavered with uncertainty. "I will then send for you and bring you home. And if you find a bride in my brother's house, is that not a good thing?"

I cupped his face, studying his handsome features as if for the last time. "If you do not go, your brother will surely kill you. And the one who sheds human blood must have his blood shed by another. Is that not the law of ADONAI?"

Jacob nodded, and I tightened my grip on him. "Losing either of you would break my heart, but losing both of you would destroy me."

Jacob's eyes shone with tears, but he did not weep. No doubt he was trying to be strong for my sake.

I released him and swallowed the sob in my throat. Outside, Deborah was preparing baskets for the camel harness, the leather straps creaking in the silence of dusk.

"Now," I said, drawing a deep breath, "we must face your father. I will explain what I have done and then you must go. He would never forgive me if I let you depart without saying farewell to him."

Chapter 27

I STOOD IN the shadows of our tent as Isaac blessed Jacob again. Lamplight illuminated my husband's lined face as he placed his hands on our son's neck. This time he did not doubt who stood before him.

When I first entered, I found Isaac sitting with his head bent, his shoulders shaking. I whispered his name, and he lifted his head, cheeks wet with tears.

"You were right," he said, his voice breaking. "I knew ADONAI's choice, yet I would have countered the Lord's will." He shook his head. "How foolish I was to think such a thing would be possible."

I knelt by his side and took his hands in mine. "Esau is angry and has said he will kill Jacob . . ." I swallowed the rest of my thought. "Jacob must go away for a while. Bless him, dear husband, so that he may travel safely to my family in Haran. Let us pray that he finds a bride in my brother's house."

Isaac nodded. "Send for Jacob."

I went out and called for Jacob, who came at once.

I quickly reentered the tent. "My lord, Jacob is here."

Isaac squared his shoulders. Visibly trembling, he extended his hands and waited for Jacob to kneel beside his father's bed. I guided Isaac's hands to Jacob's head.

"May El Shaddai bless you, make you fruitful and multiply you." Isaac's voice grew stronger with each word. "And may He give the blessing of Abraham to you and to your seed, that you may take possession of the land of your sojourn, which God gave to Abraham. May it be your will, ADONAI, that you should lead Jacob and direct his steps in peace. Save him from every enemy and ambush, from robbers and wild beasts, and from all punishments that come to the world. May you confer blessing upon the work of his hands and grant him grace and mercy in your eyes and in the eyes of all who see him. Lead him to a bride who will bless and honor him. Blessed are you, O Lord our God, who hearkens to our prayers."

I blinked back tears as Jacob caught his father's hands and kissed them. This was how it should have been from the beginning—a blessing freely given, not taken through guile.

Isaac called for Minos, who entered the tent carrying a rectangular wooden box. "Take this," Isaac said, waving in Minos's direction. "I would not send you off without a bride price. Take these gifts, along with gold and silver, so as not to approach your uncle with empty hands."

Jacob embraced his father, and I turned away, a sob rising in my chest.

Outside, Deborah waited with the camel, now loaded with provisions and treasure. The evening air cooled my skin as I followed Jacob out of the tent, my sandals whispering against the packed earth. Around us, the camp was preparing for sleep. Everyone was abed, save for myself, Jacob, and Deborah, who waited beside the kneeling camel.

When we reached the beast, Jacob turned to me, his eyes glinting in the torchlight. I stroked his hair and traced the line of his beard.

"My son, be careful in Haran. Your uncle . . ." I hesitated, remembering my brother's nature. "He is a good man, but he is shrewd. Watch and learn from him but guard your heart. And do not forget what you learned from Shem and Eber."

Jacob nodded. "I will not forget, Mother."

I stepped back. "And when you choose a wife—" my voice caught, but I pressed on—"do not choose carelessly, as some young men do. Choose someone who will love you, who will strengthen your faith in Adonai, not weaken it."

The evening breeze stirred his dark curls, just as it had stirred mine when I traveled from Haran to meet Isaac. How strange to think that Jacob would follow the same road. Would the journey bring him love, as it had me?

"Look for a woman of understanding," I continued, smoothing his cloak over his shoulders, "a true partner who will stand beside you in times of trouble, who will love Adonai and teach your children to love Him, too."

Tears blurred my vision as I embraced my son one final time. "May Adonai keep and protect you," I murmured into his ear. "May He guide your steps and bring you safely to your destination."

Jacob's arms tightened around me before he stepped back. "I will remember," he promised.

I caught Deborah's hand as my son mounted the camel. The rising moon illuminated his profile, and for a moment I glimpsed the gentle boy he had once been. My heart swelled even as it ached at the thought of separation.

Jacob uttered a command, and we stepped back as the camel stood. I blinked away tears and lifted my hand in a silent farewell, as did Deborah. We knew the best way to keep Jacob safe was to put distance between him and Esau. The long road to Haran would protect both of my sons until Esau's anger dissipated.

As the camel walked away, Deborah and I remained by the gate of the camp until Jacob disappeared behind a moonlit hill. "Adonai, watch over my son," I prayed. "Guide him to the wife you have chosen for him. Then bring him home again."

I SPENT THAT NIGHT in Deborah's tent, wrapped in blankets that smelled of herbs. Sleep eluded me as I replayed the day's events in my mind: Jacob's trembling as I helped him dress into Esau's clothes; Isaac's confusion and questions; and Esau's fury. Though my heart felt sick, I knew I had done the right thing.

The morning sun had barely touched the hilltops when I rose to prepare Isaac's breakfast. My hands moved through the motions—breaking off hunks of bread and mixing honey with fresh goat's milk—yet my stomach was too knotted to eat anything myself. The simple act of preparation steadied my nerves as I moved to face my husband.

Isaac was awake when I entered our tent, but his shoulders were bent as though burdened with unspoken thoughts. He sat on his bed, his unseeing eyes veering toward the soft sound of my footsteps. The morning light caught the silver in his beard, and my heart squeezed at the sight of his pale face. He had not slept well, either.

"So," he said, his voice rough, "you chose to deceive me."

I set the platter on the mattress. "Yes," I answered firmly. "And last night you admitted that I made the right choice."

"But why did you not come to me first?"

"Because you gave me no time." My face heated as the words tumbled out of me. "You had clearly decided to bless Esau with the rights of the firstborn. You did not consult me about the blessing. What was I to do?" My anger faltered when a tear rolled over Isaac's cheek, catching in his beard. The sight pierced my heart.

"I love my sons," he said, his voice tattered. "And I pity Esau. He is a lion who does not know how to curb his strength. Yes, I remember what ADONAI said, but how can I turn my back on my firstborn? Jacob will be blessed, but Esau should not be forgotten."

I stepped forward to join my husband. I pulled him into my arms, embracing the familiar shape of his shoulders. "Esau will not be forgotten," I murmured, running my hand along his arm. "You blessed him as well, but he is not yet of a mind to appreciate it." I gripped his shoulder. "Esau wants to kill Jacob, and so he had to leave our camp."

"For how long will he be away?"

"That will depend on Esau." I kissed my husband's head. "And you have not lost either of your sons. As soon as Esau's temper cools, we will send servants to bring Jacob home."

Isaac sighed, his body relaxing, his fingers intertwining with mine. We sat together, silence stretching between us, broken only by the sounds of the awakening camp—women calling to their children, sheep bleating, servants laughing as they went about their work.

As we listened, my own words ran through my head: *he is not yet of a mind to appreciate it*. Despite my vow never to favor one child over the other, I had to admit, at times I had not been of a mind to appreciate Esau. I loved Jacob's gentle nature, perhaps because he reminded me so much of Isaac.

"Now," I said, "how is your cough this morning? Did it keep you awake last night?"

He shook his head. "I did not sleep much, but not because of the cough."

I smiled. "That is good. You are getting better."

"I suppose so."

I pressed my cheek against his silver hair, remembering the dark curls of his younger years. We had weathered so much: drought, famine, conflicts with our neighbors, our sons' near-constant rivalry. We would weather this storm, too, with ADONAI's help. And surely, in time, our family would be stronger for it.

Book Four

MAMRE

So Isaac called for Jacob, blessed him, commanded him and said to him, "Do not take a wife from the daughters of Canaan. Get up, go to Paddan-aram, to the house of Bethuel, your mother's father, and take for yourself a wife from there, from the daughters of Laban, your mother's brother. Now may El Shaddai bless you, and make you fruitful and multiply you, so that you will become an assembly of peoples."

Genesis 28:1–3

Chapter
— 28 —

In those first days after Jacob left, the camp felt like an empty tomb. I moved through it like a sleepwalker, my heart aching at every reminder of my absent son. The sight of his empty tent, the untended sheep, the iron pot where he prepared his morning porridge—each glimpse was like a splinter pricking my flesh.

He had left us before, of course. But he had *chosen* to spend years learning from Shem and Eber. That absence was not forced upon him.

Isaac spent long hours in our tent, his grief evident in the way he barely touched the food I urged him to eat. At night he murmured our sons' names in his sleep. His cough improved, but still he mourned. Deborah continued to administer herbs and potions to improve his health, yet I could not tell if his melancholy was due to illness or grief.

While Isaac and I mourned, Esau's anger filled the camp like a storm cloud. For a week, he turned away whenever I approached, his broad shoulders rigid with rejection. The other women in camp whispered behind their hands when I passed, their eyes following me with either sympathy or judgment. Only Deborah stood with me, her quiet presence a testimony to my intentions.

One night, as I ground grain for the next day's bread, Esau's shadow darkened the entrance of the cooking tent. My shoulders tensed, but I forced my arms to continue their steady movements as I looked up. "Can I help you, son?"

"Do you hate me?" His voice was as rough as the stones beneath my hands.

My heart contracted at the pain in his voice. "Of course not. But I have to do what is right."

His jaw tightened. "Why was it right to cheat me of my birthright?"

"You sold your birthright," I reminded him, taking pains to gentle my voice. "Years ago, when you deemed lentil stew more important than your rights as the firstborn. You made your choice; and allowing you to take the firstborn's blessing would not have been fair to Jacob."

I searched his face, hoping to see a glimmer of understanding, but his eyes dazzled with fury. He stormed out of the tent, his cloak flapping in his wake.

Aware that the servants were watching, I went back to the quern and turned it through tears.

For the rest of the month, Esau remained away from camp. His wives said he had gone hunting, though I suspected he was nursing his wounds in some desolate place. I spent those days in an odd limbo, my heart divided between missing Jacob and fretting about Esau, between nursing Isaac and convincing my husband that we had done the right thing.

Esau finally returned, and nothing could have prepared us for his surprise. He did not come home alone, but with another wife: Mahalath, one of Ishmael's granddaughters, walked beside him.

Once we recovered from the shock of discovering that Esau had married again, my heart twisted when I realized why. By choosing a wife from Abraham's lineage, our wayward son had wordlessly demonstrated that he wanted to please us.

The realization tore at my heart. Years before, I had vowed to love my children equally, but my sons had not proved equally lovable. Yet here was Esau, being true to what he was, yet striving to please us with a well-intentioned gesture.

Would he commit to worshiping ADONAI as well?

We welcomed Mahalath to our household, and then Isaac pulled Esau aside and asked the question uppermost in our minds. Now that he had taken a wife who worshiped ADONAI, would he set aside his idol-worshiping women?

"No!" Esau's face flushed. "Why would I do that?"

Isaac and I remained silent, realizing that his gesture had been halfhearted. If he was not willing to sever his relationship with idol-worshipers, then he was not willing to worship ADONAI alone. He could marry every female descendant in Abraham's line, but his heart would remain unchanged.

Later, in the privacy of our tent, I leaned against Isaac's shoulder. "Do you remember the black cat who kept bringing me dead mice?" I asked. "Esau is the same. He will always be wild, but he wants to please. That is why he has brought home a daughter of Ishmael."

"Our son is like a feral cat?"

"At times, yes. But Mahalath should know about ADONAI. She might help cool Esau's rage."

"Perhaps," Isaac said. "Unless the other wives convince her to worship their gods."

After that, I watched the three women as they worked and argued and fought together. I could not imagine sharing a man with other women, but Esau had made his choices.

Now he had to live with them.

AS THE WEEKS PASSED, life settled into a familiar rhythm. The summer heat gave way to autumn breezes. The flocks grew fat on grass from the rains. Esau spent more time in camp, though he spoke to me only when necessary. I watched him teach his new wife about our routines, and sometimes I caught glimpses of the son I remembered—the one who once sought my approval as eagerly as his father's.

Three months after Jacob's departure, I woke one morning to find the air had changed. The northern wind was cooler than usual, and I knew, as surely as I knew my own name, that the time had come.

As I walked to Deborah's tent to arrange the journey to Haran, I whispered a fervent prayer. "ADONAI, let Esau's heart be truly at peace. Let him remember that he is not only my firstborn, but he is also Jacob's brother. When Jacob returns, let there be peace between my sons at last."

I CREPT INTO OUR TENT, my footsteps soft against the carpet. The cool morning had given way to a hot afternoon, but our dwelling still retained a trace of cooler air.

My husband lay on his cushions, his chest rising and falling in the steady rhythm of sleep. He had been sleeping more these past weeks—due to his advanced years and due to his grief. His body had healed from the catarrh, but from experience I knew how grief could sap a person's strength.

Esau visited his father daily, but his presence—which had always comforted Isaac in the past—brought little joy now. In light of Esau's decreased inheritance, his wives had grown even more insolent since Jacob's departure. In years past, Isaac would have rebuked them, but not now.

I placed my hand on his shoulder. His eyes opened, and when I whispered his name, he seemed to find my face. "My lord, I wish to send Deborah, Minos, and three guards to bring Jacob home. Deborah will represent me to my brother, and the men will keep her safe."

Isaac's forehead creased as he considered my words, then nodded. "I miss my quiet son," he said, his voice breaking.

I pressed my lips to his forehead, holding him close as his shoulders trembled. He wanted Jacob home for other reasons, too. We needed a man with resolve enough to speak against the wayward wives and model a life based on ADONAI's principles. Isaac had the desire to lead, but he no longer had the strength. Esau had strength but lacked the desire to live a godly life.

"I miss him, too," I whispered. Pulling back, I met Isaac's clouded eyes. "Have no fear, my lord, for Deborah will bring our son back to us."

ONCE ISAAC GAVE his consent, I did not waste a moment. I stepped out into the afternoon heat and summoned the steward and three of our most capable guards to Deborah's tent. Minos, our steward, stood before me with quiet confidence, his copper-toned skin catching the light as it filtered through the tamarisk branches. As Eliezer once journeyed with me to Haran, so would Minos now guide Deborah on her way.

"Take six camels," I instructed him. "You must depart at once for Haran and the household of my brother, Laban. There you will find Jacob." I paused, drawing a breath that caught somewhere between memory and joy. "Tell him he can safely return home. If he has taken a wife, she may ride the extra camel."

My heart tightened as I turned to Deborah, my beloved nurse. The woman who had held me as an infant, who had nursed me and delivered my sons.

I reached for her strong, familiar hands and held them fast. "Dearest lady," I said, "I ask you to care for my son—and for the woman he may have chosen—with the same tenderness you have always shown me. You are the keeper of my trust, Deborah. My prayers will follow you like a shadow on the road. I am sending my heart with you."

Her eyes glistened as she embraced me, cradling my grief and my hope.

"I will serve them both with all that I am," she promised. "And I will pray for you until we are all gathered again."

When the camels were packed and ready, I stepped outside. The sun, now lowering in the west, poured gold over the hills. Shadows stretched long behind the caravan as they prepared to depart. Minos nodded to me in farewell, and Deborah lifted her hand in a quiet blessing.

They would not get far today, but they would make a start. Then they would bring Jacob home.

I watched until they vanished into the northern horizon, the dust of their leaving curling into the sky. I did not weep, not this time.

Instead, I pressed a hand to my chest, where joy had begun to stir once again. Soon my son would return home.

LIKE LIQUID DRIPPING from a waterskin, the days passed, one after the other. On the tenth day, I found myself pacing the area just inside the gate, scanning the northern landscape until my eyes watered. I paced on the eleventh day, the twelfth, the thirteenth and fourteenth.

"Something must have happened," I told Isaac, "or they would have returned by this time. The journey to and from Haran would take six days, and if Laban insisted on a wedding, the feast might last for seven days. Fourteen days would have been more than enough time for travel, meeting, marrying, and returning."

"Do not be impatient," Isaac said, idly stroking his beard. "Perhaps the woman wants time to say a proper farewell. You should give them a month to return. At least a month."

He was likely right, yet my stomach still clenched each time I thought of Deborah being detained in Haran. She was strong, but age had begun to slow her step and increase her aches and pains. I did not want Laban to keep her a moment longer than necessary. Though Minos was skilled, bandits prowled the trade routes. I had arranged for only three guards; should I have sent more? Anxiety gnawed at my peace as a desert jackal gnaws a bone.

Twenty days after Deborah's departure, I finally spotted riders in the north. I ran to the gate, my heart leaping at the thought of greeting Jacob and his bride, but after a moment my joy deflated. In the approaching party I counted six camels, two without riders. There should have been seven. I counted again, shielding my eyes against the blinding sun. Where was Jacob's mount? His camel should have been in the caravan . . . unless he never arrived. The thought struck like a serpent, sending cold fear through my veins.

By the time the caravan entered our camp, my hands trembled so badly I had to clasp them together. I examined the riders' dusty faces, spotting Minos and the three guards, but no Deborah, no Jacob, and no daughter-in-law.

"What happened?" I demanded, my voice rasping as I ran toward our steward. "Where is my son? Where is Deborah?"

After commanding his camel to kneel, Minos dismounted, his face calm. He bowed. "Your son is well, my lady. He has found love with Rachel, the younger of your brother's twin daughters. In exchange for her, he has agreed to serve your brother for seven years."

I blinked, astounded and horrified. *Seven years?* Did Laban think my son a slave that he should submit to a period of indentured service? My father had not dared suggest that Isaac work for me; I had been surrendered to him in exchange for the gifts Abraham sent. My father had respected Abraham's wealth and position, and he would not have asked Isaac to be his servant.

So what had possessed Laban? Did he not regard Isaac as a

man of importance, or was he simply a greedy fool? Isaac had sent silver, gold, and treasures—did Laban want *more*?

"The bride price was not enough?"

Minos closed his eyes, opened his mouth, then closed it again—a sign he had news he did not want to share.

"Minos? What happened to the bride price?"

He exhaled a sigh, then met my gaze. "Your son met with bandits on the road. They took the treasure. He counts himself grateful to have escaped with his life."

I swayed on my feet as panic prickled my spine. "Is he safe? Is he well?"

Minos dipped his chin in a sober nod. "He praised ADONAI for saving his life. But he arrived in Haran with nothing but his camel and the clothing on his back."

My mind filled with sour thoughts. After hearing about the robbery, Laban should have understood that Isaac would send silver and gold to replace that which had been lost. So why did he not give his daughter to my son? Why had he insisted that Jacob work like a common hireling?

I swallowed my frustration and fear; this was not the time or place to worry about what could or should have happened. "And Deborah, my nurse? What has become of her?"

Minos folded his hands. "She chose to remain in Haran, my lady. She said she had promised to serve Jacob's betrothed, so you would understand why she remained behind."

Yes, she had promised, and I did understand. Relief flooded through me, but in its wake came a crushing wave of despair. Deborah, my constant companion, would be serving my daughter-in-law, but I would lose Deborah for seven years? And Jacob?

I sank onto a stone bench, my mind flooding with information I needed to consider. First, Jacob had been accosted by bandits. I should have sent guards with him; I should never have sent him out alone at night. I would never forgive myself for not thinking more clearly, but ADONAI had kept my son safe. For that I would always be grateful.

And Rachel, my brother's daughter, was she worthy of my son? Was she kind? Beautiful? Strong? I clenched my fists, wishing Deborah had returned, if only to assure me that Rachel would be a good wife for Jacob. But Deborah had seen a need and had stayed behind to fulfill it.

I would have to go tell Isaac that we would not see our son for seven years. I would have to explain about the robbery and add that Laban did not respect Isaac enough to surrender his daughter but had insisted that Jacob pay for his wife with seven years of servitude.

How *could* he?

My shock yielded quickly to fury. I strode into our tent, rummaged in my trunk, and found the small wooden carving Laban had made for me when I left Haran. I carried it outside and hurled it into the nearest cookfire.

Why did Laban think he had the right to treat our son, *his nephew*, like a common herder? And why had Jacob agreed to Laban's ridiculous terms?

I groaned and lowered my head to my hands. If I had known my plan to save Jacob would separate us for so long, would I have sent him away? Everything within me said no, but in the face of Esau's rage, what else could I have done?

I ENTERED OUR TENT with a heavy heart. The smell of savory meat lingered in the air. Earlier, Esau must have brought his father's favorite meal. I found Isaac resting on his cushions, his face turned toward the sounds filtering through the goatskin walls.

"My lord," I said, settling beside him, "I have news of Jacob." I studied his face. "He has been betrothed to Laban's youngest daughter. Because Jacob was robbed on the journey, my brother insists that Jacob work seven years before he can marry the girl."

Isaac remained quiet for a long moment, his sightless eyes directed toward the tent's opening. Outside, I could hear the wild laughter and singing of Esau's wives. The sounds made my skin crawl.

"Jacob will work seven years?" One corner of Isaac's mouth lifted. "He must love the girl more than life."

"I do not know what Laban is thinking. He should have known you would replace the stolen treasure."

"Laban is thinking of himself, as most men do." Isaac cupped his hands around his bent knee. "Jacob could have refused, but he did not. So perhaps this is for the best."

I wanted to argue, but my husband was right. Seven years would be hard for us, but it would give Esau time to forget what had happened with his blessing and birthright. And seven years was a small price to pay to ensure that Jacob did not marry women like those in Esau's tent.

"ADONAI knows what is best," I admitted. "But right now I am disgusted with my life because of these daughters of Heth." The words poured from my soul, years of frustration finally finding an outlet. "If Jacob were to take a wife like those women, what would life be to me?" I shuddered. "Better that he remain in Laban's household. Better that he marry this Rachel."

Isaac turned, his brow furrowed in thought. "What of the elder daughter?" he asked. "If Rachel is Laban's youngest?"

The question startled me. I had not thought about Laban's older daughter, though Isaac would consider such details. "Surely Laban will find her a husband," I replied. "In seven years, someone worthy will come along."

Yet even as I spoke the words, premonition lifted the hair at the back of my neck. I knew my brother, and this latest development had demonstrated his character yet again. Would he allow the elder girl to be courted by a man from Haran? Or would he wait like a cat in tall grass, hoping she might marry Jacob as well? At Abraham's burial, Laban had openly marveled at Isaac's wealth.

I pushed the troubling thought away. Seven years was a long time. Surely all would be well when the time was done.

Outside, the unrestrained laughter of Esau's wives grew louder, and I winced at a particularly sharp shriek.

Yes, better seven years of separation than a lifetime bound to women like those. Better for Jacob to marry Rachel, a stranger to me, than a Canaanite woman who would bring nothing but grief to our household.

Chapter

— 29 —

ISAAC AWOKE WITH A START, his body tensing against the wool-stuffed mattress. Something was wrong. His blind eyes opened to gray gloom, but his ears told him what his eyes could not. Silence coiled around him, as cold and malevolent as a serpent in the dark.

Beside him, Rebekah lay sleeping, her breaths coming slowly in the unearthly quiet.

He lay still, his chest rising and falling beneath his tunic. The morning air felt unusually cool against his thin skin, and he strained to hear the familiar sounds that had greeted him every morning for decades. But he heard no bleating of sheep anxious for pasture. No servants calling to one another as they began the day's work. No laughter or crying from Esau's children. No rhythmic sound of women turning the quern. Nothing but an unnatural quiet, as unyielding as the desert heat at midday.

A knot of unease tightened in Isaac's stomach. He pushed himself upright, his joints protesting with pain that radiated from ankles to hips. More than one hundred twenty years of living had carved furrows into his body, and each movement required deliberate effort. His fingers, as gnarled as ancient olive branches, fumbled for his robe. The soft wool slid against his skin as he wrapped it around his thin frame, the familiar weight comforting amid the irregularity of the morning.

The smells of the tent enveloped him—the lingering fragrance of last night's lamp oil, the scent of the wool carpet underfoot, the mustiness that accompanied age. Missing were the aromas of baking bread and the pungent odor of goat's milk being heated for the morning meal.

Isaac shuffled toward the tent opening, one hand extended, fingers splayed to ward off obstacles. The leather flap felt rough beneath his palm as he pushed it aside. He flinched when sunlight struck his face, warm and sudden. The air carried the scents of dust and wild herbs from the surrounding hills, but none of the usual odors of a busy camp—no cookfires, no animal dung, no unwashed bodies moving purposefully about their tasks.

Isaac firmed his voice: "Is anyone there?" A slight rustle caught his attention. "Who are you?"

"Minos, my lord." The steward's voice was flat, drained of its usual deference and energy.

Isaac took a cautious step forward, small stones pressing through his thin sandals. "What has happened?"

"He took almost everything." Minos's voice was little more than a whisper. "Everything but a handful of servants who refused to abandon you. They are huddled in a tent, awaiting your command."

Isaac's heart thundered in his ears, each beat a painful reminder of his frailty.

"Esau?" The name escaped as a question, though he knew the answer.

"I tried to stop him," Minos said, "but three of his men beat me. I am sorry, my lord. If I could give my life in recompense, I would—"

"I will not take your life." Isaac shook his head, his tongue moving against his dry lips. "Did he say *why*?"

"No." The answer hung in the air between them, stark in its simplicity.

Isaac's heart contracted until he could barely draw breath. "I know why." His firstborn had nursed bitter resentment for years, and today that anger had given birth to thievery.

The knowledge spasmed inside Isaac's chest, causing pain as tangible as the arthritis that plagued his bones. He loved Esau—his hunter with the ruddy skin and the hearty laugh; the son who brought him savory meat and smelled of the fields and open air. But Esau would never be the heir of promise. The prophecy given to Rebekah had marked Jacob as the one to carry God's covenant forward, and Esau could not accept that truth.

Even though Jacob had gone away, Esau could not be content under his father's authority or under ADONAI's. Therefore, he had departed, and he had taken with him . . . what? Isaac lifted his head. "Did he take the livestock?"

"All but a third of the herds and flocks, my lord."

Isaac chuffed a bitter laugh. "At least we have a lamb for dinner."

"It will be a sickly lamb, my lord. He left the weakest animals behind."

How would he explain this to Rebekah?

A tremor started in Isaac's hands and traveled up his arms to his shoulders. Though the sun beat on his uncovered head, his teeth began to chatter. He sank to the ground as his legs went soft and buckled.

His fingers scooped up handfuls of sand, the grains sharp against his palms as he poured the sand over his head. It caught in his beard and hair, ran down his neck and beneath his robe, but Isaac barely noticed the discomfort. His chest swelled with a sob, and his throat convulsed against the grief that threatened to overwhelm him.

"My Esau . . ." he whispered, his voice as tattered as his heart. "My beloved betrayer."

The silent campground offered no reply. Above him, a hawk released a screeching cry, the only sound in the hollow silence of the morning.

I AWOKE WITH A START, my eyes flying open as an eerie awareness settled over me. Light seeped through the tent flap, scattering stray sunbeams across the carpet, but an unnatural silence pressed against my ears as thick as wool. Had I lost my hearing? I lay still, straining for the familiar sounds of morning—the calls of servants, the bleating of goats, children's laughter rising and falling with their play. But I heard only a roaring hush.

I sat up, the woven blanket slipping from my shoulders. I turned toward Isaac's place, my stomach tightening at the sight of the vacant mattress, its surface bearing only the imprint of his body. My fingers flew, fastening my robe, smoothing my hair. Each movement was precise, instinctive, though my pulse pounded in my ears. Something terrible had happened; I could sense it.

I hurried forward and pushed aside the tent flap. Sunlight struck my face, momentarily blinding me. I blinked and lifted a hand to shield my eyes. My breath caught in my throat.

Isaac sat on the ground in front of me, hunched and small, his white beard and hair dusted with sand. Beside him, Minos knelt in silence. The steward's face was swollen and bruised, his lips cracked and bleeding. Yet his appearance did not alarm me as much as the emptiness of our camp.

Our bustling encampment, home to us, our servants, and our livestock—all was nearly deserted. The space that had housed dozens of families now held only a few sagging tents. The animal pens were almost empty, almost all our storage tents had vanished, and the cookfires were dark and cold. My gaze swept the hilly horizon, searching for our flocks, our camels, the cattle that had spread across the hills like a living sea.

But I saw only a few thin cattle, goats, and sheep. Two camels and a dozen donkeys. Inside the camp, the wind stirred sand over the hard-packed earth and the scattering of scrawny chickens.

Near the edge of camp, a man and woman emerged from a tent, their faces twisted with confusion. A few others followed, their hands limp at their sides, looking toward Isaac as if awaiting an answer.

One glance at my husband's face told me he had no answer to give.

I took a step forward, my legs trembling, the earth warming the soles of my bare feet. I willed myself not to weep. Not now. Instead, I closed my eyes against a sudden rush of tears. Yesterday, we had been the wealthiest household in the Negev. Now we had almost nothing.

Without asking, I knew who had done this. Anger surged through me. Had Isaac finally realized what I had known for years? That his favored firstborn, the son he indulged and adored, cared more for himself than for his family. Esau, who had been given so much, had repaid us with devastation.

Sharp words, unbidden, rose to my tongue. *I told you. I warned you. This is why Jacob had to receive the blessing. This is why he had to flee.*

But then I saw Isaac clawing at the dirt as if seeking to anchor himself in a world that had upended. My anger faded as quickly as it had flared. My husband had been broken. What good would sharp words do?

The wind shifted, favoring us with the astringent scent of wild sage. I breathed it in and straightened my shoulders. I had borne twins, survived famine, and secured my son's future by daring and quick thinking. I must not crumble now.

"Minos." My voice cut through the hush.

The steward lifted his bruised face. "Mistress?"

"Did he try to take you?"

Minos looked away. "He ordered me to join him, but I refused."

"Thank you for your loyalty." I studied his bruises, then shook my head. "How many servants remain?"

"Sixty-two by my count."

"Sixty-two men?"

"No—men and women. Some with children."

Sixty-two servants. Of the two hundred who had filled our camp, only these few remained. And of the sixty-two, probably only half were men capable of wielding a sword.

Traders, caravans, and travelers passed our encampment every day. They would look in this direction, expecting to see the well-defended, prosperous home of Isaac, son of Abraham. Instead, they would see the ruins of an abandoned camp, a small gathering of servants, two old people, and a bloodied steward. Esau had plundered us; others would finish us off.

I set my jaw. "We are no longer safe here."

Minos nodded, but Isaac did not move or acknowledge my words. He remained lost in grief, his sightless eyes fixed upon the ground.

Minos was watching me, his posture straight. "About the master—"

"Let him mourn," I said. "Though I would rather he be wounded by a lion than by a thankless son." I glanced around, realizing that we would have to abandon nearly everything that remained. "We must leave," I said, my voice low but firm. "We are weak, and we are exposed."

Isaac lifted his head. His blind eyes sought my face as his mouth curved downward. "Why should we worry?" His voice rasped with despair. "We have nothing left for others to steal."

I stepped toward him, my shadow falling across his face. I knelt before him and took his hands. "We still have you. And you have a wife, sixty-two servants, and a steward who has remained faithful. We cannot let them be taken by slave traders. We will gather what we can and leave this place." I squeezed his hands, pressing my strength into him. "We must act at once."

Isaac's chin fell onto his chest. A gust of wind lifted the fine strands of his beard and scattered the sand on his tunic. "ADONAI has abandoned us," he murmured.

Something fierce and protective surged within me. I reached up, gripped his chin, and held his face. "No. Esau has abandoned you, but ADONAI remains. He will never leave us." I released his chin. "But we must go from this place."

Another breeze stirred, bringing a moment's respite from the heat, filling my head with the essence of the land—dry, ancient, and enduring. A bird called in the distance, sounding like an answer.

"Out there," I said. "Our future lies out there."

Isaac remained silent, his face contorted with grief, doubt, and anger. At last he nodded. "I will seek ADONAI." His voice was stronger, though still ragged with sorrow. "I will pray about where we should go."

His words were simple, but at least he had retreated from the abyss of despair. He was still my husband, still the leader of this household.

I stood and placed my hand in his. An invitation. A promise.

Above us, the sky stretched vast and blue, witness to all we had lost—and to the faith that would carry us forward.

Chapter 30

ISAAC KNELT ALONE at the edge of the empty camp, his knobby knees pressing painfully into the rough earth. The afternoon sun flailed his uncovered head, the heat penetrating the thin hair to scorch his scalp. He had left Rebekah and Minos to prepare for the journey to wherever the Lord would lead them.

His breath caught, then eased out like a sigh too tired to rise. The loss of his wealth—flocks, servants, provisions—brought pain, but Esau's betrayal cut far deeper, a wound that throbbed with each beat of his faltering heart.

"ADONAI . . ." Isaac prayed, his voice catching. The wind muffled the sound of the sacred name, and he wondered if God would hear such a feeble utterance. He lowered his eyelids, shutting out the dim light he could still see. "I have been blind," he continued. "Blind not just with my eyes, but in my heart." His fingers dug into the earth, the soil warm and dry against his palm. "I have been blind to your will in the matter of my sons."

A memory surfaced then: Esau as a child, ruddy and vibrant, returning from the hunt with his first gazelle, pride radiating from every pore. Isaac had shared his joy, reveling in the connection with his son, the recognition of a spirit so different from his own. In Esau, Isaac had tasted the wild aspects of nature and lived vicariously through his son's boldness.

"I loved Esau too much," he confessed. "Too much to rebuke him when he needed guidance. Too much to see his heart turning away from you." A tear carved a hot path down his cheek.

He listened for the voice of Adonai but heard only the sound of Rebekah calling to Minos. Her voice twisted the knife of shame even deeper. She had seen what he had not. She had taken steps to acknowledge God's will, while he, the bearer of the covenant, had been blinded by favoritism.

"I confess my weakness before you," Isaac prayed, his shoulders slumping farther. "My blindness of heart, my stubbornness, and my refusal to see what you declared from the beginning. Guide us," he pleaded, his voice breaking again. He swallowed hard, tasting the salt of his own tears. "Guide us to a place where Rebekah and I can live until it is time to die."

The inevitability of death hovered over him—not as a distant prospect, but as an imminent reality. His joints ached, and the simple act of breathing was more difficult than it had been the year before. At times, when he least expected it, his heart fluttered in his chest like a trapped bird. Even now he could hear death's footsteps moving toward him.

Isaac lifted his face to the sky, taking grim pleasure in the searing heat against his skin. "I am ready," he added, "to join my father Abraham in the cave of Machpelah. But first, show me where we are to go."

The wind shifted, brushing his tear-dampened face. And in that instant, Isaac heard the answer.

Mamre.

The voice seemed to come from everywhere and nowhere, whispering on the wind and resonating in his mind.

Mamre, where Abraham built an altar.

The voice was unmistakably Adonai's, deep and authoritative.

The same voice that had guided his father and rolled like thunder on Mount Moriah. A voice he had not heard in years.

Your mother and father rest in that land.

Isaac's hands trembled as memories flooded his mind: Mamre with its ancient oaks offering shelter from the harsh sun; the small enclosure where Abraham had pitched his first tent, where he built an altar to the Lord; the proximity to Hebron and the cave of Machpelah, purchased as a burial place for Sarah and now holding Abraham's remains as well. One day it would hold his body and, when her time came, Rebekah's.

You will be safe at Mamre, for the people of Hebron know you.

The voice faded as suddenly as it had come, leaving Isaac trembling in its wake. ADONAI had spoken, and with His voice came a profound sense of rightness that soothed Isaac's ravaged spirit.

Isaac then heard the rustling of a garment and knew Rebekah stood behind him. He smelled the fragrant oils she used in her hair and caught the soft exhalation of her breath as she waited for him to finish his prayer.

"I know where we will go," he said with certainty.

"Where, my lord?"

"Mamre." The name was a promise on his lips. "Near Hebron, where my father had friends. Where he built an altar." His voice grew stronger with each word, the decision settling in his bones with the comfort of divine confirmation. "We will return to that place."

The wind gusted, carrying the fresh scent of rain, a blessing in the arid landscape. Isaac lifted his face again as the presence of God wrapped around him like a cloak.

Esau had taken most of his possessions, but he could not take the covenant promise. That remained as unshakable as the mountains that lined the horizon.

"We will return to Mamre," Isaac repeated, his voice carrying across the empty campground. "We will go home."

DAWN BROKE like a cracked egg over the eastern hills, spilling golden light across the barren landscape as we prepared to leave Beersheba. I watched Isaac's hands—once strong and sure, now trembling with age—as he helped Minos tie the last of our transportable belongings to the donkeys' backs. Six strong pack animals, purchased from traveling merchants with the gold bracelets and nose ring Eliezer had given me as a bridal gift. Six beasts to carry what remained of a lifetime.

"Is that the last of it?" I asked our steward.

"Yes, mistress." Minos bowed his head, the silver in his beard catching the morning light. "Everything is ready."

I turned to look at our camp one last time—the place where my sons had been born, where I had watched them grow into men so different they might have sprung from different wombs. Isaac and I had built a life in this place. Now it resembled a battlefield, scarred by fire pits and littered with bowls, water jars, and harnesses for animals we no longer possessed. Two carved trunks, which still held my finest garments, sat on the dusty carpet of our tattered tent, too heavy and bulky to transport. Esau had taken our wagons, carts, everything of practical use.

"Rebekah." Isaac's voice broke into my thoughts. "It is time."

I blinked back tears. Perhaps Isaac's blindness was a blessing, for he could not see these remnants of our past. Yet I could see pain carved into my dear husband's face—pain caused by our firstborn son.

My chest tightened at the thought of how Esau had hurt his father.

"Yes," I said and waved to the herders, who were preparing our remaining livestock for the journey ahead. "Let us go."

THE SUN CLIMBED HIGHER, coating the landscape in honey-gold, as we trudged over the sand. Isaac leaned heavily on his staff, his breathing labored but determined. From the corner of my eye, I watched the man who had frequently carried me into our tent, who had taught our sons to pray, who had blessed the fields and flocks that Esau had taken. My heart ached with each of his faltering steps.

"Do you remember," I said, hoping to distract him from his pain, "when Jacob caught his first fish?"

Isaac's smile broke through his beard. "He was so proud. And so careful not to harm it before putting it back into the water."

"Unlike Esau, who would have speared a dozen just to prove he could do so." The words slipped out before I could catch them, and Isaac's smile faded.

"Both of our sons have gifts, Rebekah." Though his voice was soft, the words were laced with reproach.

"I know." I reached for his hand, finding comfort in the familiar calluses. "But I am not blind to who they are."

We walked in silence for a while, the donkeys plodding beside us, the remaining servants herding livestock around us, and Minos bringing up the rear. Our servants' children seemed to find the journey a grand adventure and called to each other as they ran, their voices echoing among the rock formations.

"The little ones will exhaust themselves," I told Isaac. "I hope we left room on the donkeys for a child or two."

The road stretched ahead, winding through scrub land and stony ground. My legs ached, and dust coated my throat, yet each step took us farther from what we had lost and closer to what remained—the promise, the blessing, and the covenant.

"I used to watch him," Isaac said. "The way Esau moved through the fields, the way he could track a deer for miles without tiring. He was so strong. So sure." He hesitated. "I thought—I truly believed—that such gifts have a divine purpose."

I squeezed his hand. "All gifts come from God. But the one who receives them must be open to ADONAI."

We walked in silence a few moments, and then I looked again

at my husband. "Jacob may not have Esau's strength or speed, but his heart is turned toward heaven. When he studies the stars, he sees God's handiwork. When he tends the herds . . ." I caught myself, wondering if our remaining livestock could even be called a herd. "When he *tended* the herds, he cared for each animal as if it were precious."

"Yet I favored Esau," Isaac said. "I saw only with my eyes, noting Esau's courage, skill, and strength. I was as blind to his heart as I am to the path that lies before us."

I looked away to gather my thoughts. Isaac blamed himself, but had I not been just as blind when it came to Jacob?

"We both made mistakes," I admitted, the words heavy on my tongue. "But our love for each other has been constant."

A smile lifted his lips. "Even when I said you were my sister?"

"Even then, my lord. I was angry because I cared."

One of the donkeys brayed, a harsh sound that startled a covey of quail from a shrub beside the road. The birds burst into flight, wings thrumming in the hot air. I watched them scatter, remembering how Esau had once brought home a dozen of the small birds, proudly displaying his kills. Then Jacob had asked if they had young in their nests that would starve as a result of Esau's hunting.

"So different," I said.

Isaac turned. "What?"

"Our sons. They are so different." I shook my head, feeling my silver earrings against my neck, the only jewelry I still possessed. "Esau sees what he wants and takes it. Jacob considers the cost to others."

"And yet," Isaac said, "Jacob took Esau's blessing."

The air between us stilled, as if even the wind held its breath. Months had passed since the day I clothed Jacob in Esau's garments, yet none of us would ever forget that memorable afternoon.

"I did what God wanted," I said, my voice barely audible over the moan of the wind. "The blessing of the firstborn was meant for Jacob. You know it is true."

"Perhaps that is why Esau has done this cruel thing. Perhaps he is trying to compensate for what was taken from him."

"Or perhaps," I countered, heat rising in my cheeks, "he has always been a man who loves himself above all. Who would sell his birthright to satisfy a fleeting hunger. Who was so determined to have the firstborn's share that he would steal it even before his father died."

"Surely not—"

"That is exactly what he has done. You cannot see it, but I can. I count the servants, the flocks and the herds, and I see that he has taken the firstborn's share and left us with Jacob's portion. He probably thought you were dying, so it was only a matter of time—"

My voice broke on the last word, and to my shame, a sob escaped my chest. I, a woman who had watered camels for Abraham's servant without complaint, who had left my home to marry a man I had never met, who had birthed and raised two sons through famine and plenty . . . I stopped and wept like a child in the middle of the windswept road.

Isaac's arms encircled me, his body still strong enough to support mine. "My beloved," he whispered into my hair.

I clung to him, taking comfort in the beating of his heart. "How could he do this to us? How could our son give so little thought to our welfare? He took for himself the wealth you and your father built over a lifetime."

"He could never take everything," Isaac said, depth returning to his voice. "He has not taken my faith. He has not taken your love. He has not taken God's promise."

I pulled back to search his face, looking beyond the cloudy eyes to the soul beneath. In that moment, Isaac looked so much like Abraham that my breath caught in my lungs. In his eyes, I could finally see the same unwavering faith.

"Yes." I wiped my tears with the edge of my veil. "We still have what matters most."

Isaac smiled, his lined face lifting. "We also have Mamre ahead of us. The place where my father spoke with Adonai."

"And it has a well," I added, thinking of our empty waterskins.

Isaac laughed, a sound I had not heard in weeks. "My Rebekah. Eyes on heaven, feet firmly on earth."

I smiled. "Someone must think about food and water while you commune with God."

We resumed walking, my steps lighter despite the devastating heat. Ahead lay Mamre and Hebron and whatever future God had preserved for us. Behind lay Beersheba and the son who had spurned his parents' love.

Despite my disappointment and anger, Esau was still the boy who had brought me wildflowers in his dirty fist. The boy who had curled against my side and shivered during thunderstorms.

I tugged on Isaac's sleeve. "Do you think Esau will ever return to us? That his heart will change?"

Isaac's smile faded. "All things are possible with God. But to receive, a man must choose to open his fist."

I nodded. Esau had closed his hand around what he wanted, refusing to receive what God offered. Jacob had opened his hands to receive the birthright and the blessing, but now we had little to offer him.

"We will pray for both of our sons," I said, my gaze returning to the hazy road ahead. "We will worship at Mamre's altar and remember who we are and whom we serve."

The road stretched before us, barren and long. But I could almost see the hills of Hebron, rising against the blue horizon. Mamre was waiting there . . . and so was Adonai.

Chapter

— 31 —

The journey to Mamre stretched for six days, which ran together like storm clouds merging with the mountains. On camels they could have covered the distance in two days, but such luxuries belonged now to a previous life.

Yet Isaac did not complain. The slow pace gave him time to recall his father's stories of Mamre and Hebron and to prepare his heart for what lay ahead.

When Rebekah declared that she could at last see the sprawling oaks at Mamre, Abraham's stories flooded Isaac's memory. Two angels and Adonai-in-flesh had visited Abraham at this place. And Sarah had laughed when Adonai spoke promises that seemed impossible . . . until Isaac was born.

"I see two giant trees and a low stone wall around them," Rebekah said, her voice hoarse with weariness. "Is that the place?"

"Yes," Isaac said, forcing words through a suddenly tight throat. "That is where my father sat when the Lord appeared to him."

They soon entered the stone enclosure. After looking around, Rebekah assured him there would be room enough for their tents.

"Lead me to the altar," Isaac said, extending his hands. "I would like to see how many stones remain."

She guided him to a spot near the tree. He sank to his knees and plunged his hands into the sand. The remains of a stone altar were evident, though some of the rocks had been moved. Isaac caressed the remaining stones, his fingertips finding the rough edges his father had once handled. "I will rebuild it," he announced, turning to Rebekah and Minos. "As soon as we have shelter, I will restore the altar."

"First the tent," Rebekah said, a smile in her voice. "Then you rest. The altar will wait for you."

Isaac sighed, accepting her wisdom. "Minos, let us unpack. We will make camp here under the oaks."

He listened as the loyal steward moved away and gave orders to unload the donkeys.

The day had cooled by the time Rebekah took Isaac's hand. "Our tent is ready," she said, helping him up. "We should sleep now."

Isaac wished he could see his new home. "The camp, it is—?"

"It is established," Rebekah finished. "The servants are sharing tents. The children are safe. We are home."

"The animals?"

"Are in the field nearby, and there is plenty of grass. They will not wander far."

Isaac nodded, his heart brimming with an odd mixture of hope and loss. Their new home might be humble, but it stood in a place sanctified by God's presence and His promises to Abraham.

She led him into a shelter and helped him sit. "I have spread a blanket here," she said, placing his hand on the fabric. "This will be our bed tonight."

He snorted. "How strange . . . the humble things we owned yesterday are now precious."

He stretched out, squirming to avoid the root of a tree beneath the blanket. When he was mostly comfortable, he turned his head toward Rebekah. "Do we have another blanket to cover ourselves?"

"Not yet." She settled beside him. "It is enough that we have each other."

He sighed. "Tomorrow, Minos and I will go to Hebron. We will present ourselves to the elders of the city. If they welcome us, perhaps we can barter for a blanket."

"And a decent pot." Fabric swished as she turned toward him. "Are you certain you will be welcome? We spotted a few elders near the city gate today. If they do not know you, they might not welcome you to this area."

"We are no threat to anyone in Hebron. Our livestock will not overgraze their land, and we are not wealthy enough to make them feel small." Isaac reached out, finding the hair that framed her face. "This was my father's home before the young men of Hebron were born. And we have come here in peace."

"Yes," she conceded, but he heard concern in her tone. She had already lost so much; she feared losing him, too. "If you go, will you return before dark?"

"I will," he promised, then pressed his lips to her forehead.

"THE CITY OF HEBRON," Minos said, reporting as he and Isaac walked, "it rises from the land like a stone mountain. It is protected by thick walls."

Though Isaac's parents had spent years in this area, he himself had visited only twice, and he had been in mourning on both occasions. He was welcomed warmly when he came to bury his mother and father, but would the locals welcome him as a permanent resident?

He lifted his eyes toward the south but could see nothing. "Are the elders assembled at the gate?"

"They are."

"Then let us greet them."

Isaac kept walking, leaning more heavily on his staff than he would have liked. He would have preferred to present himself as a strong ally, not as a weak and elderly man.

At least Minos was at his side.

"They are studying us," Minos said. "After we stop, they will wait for you to speak."

Isaac halted when Minos touched his arm. Despite his blindness, he could sense the elders' scrutiny like heat upon his flesh. They were assessing his person, his travel-worn garments, and the solitary servant with him.

"Peace be with you," Isaac began, raising his voice. "Though I have not been here in years, you may know me as Isaac, son of Abraham."

His words sent a ripple of wonder through the group. Isaac heard the snap and creak of aged knees as the elders stood.

"You are the son of Abraham? The prince who dwelt at Mamre?"

"The same," Isaac confirmed, relieved that his father's name still commanded respect.

An elder stepped forward and embraced him, kissing his cheeks in the traditional greeting. "I am Ephron, chief elder of Hebron," the man said. "I was but a boy when your father lived here, but my father spoke often of Abraham's wisdom."

One by one, the other elders embraced and kissed Isaac. Most were too young to have known Abraham, yet they treated Isaac with a deference that soothed his troubled heart. Though he left Beersheba with little, here he might become rich in friendship.

One man introduced himself as Zibeon. "Your father purchased the cave of Machpelah from my grandfather. Your family burial ground is there."

Isaac smiled. "Indeed, it is. Considering my age, I suspect I will be making use of it soon."

Isaac's acknowledging his advanced age drew appreciative

chuckles from the elders. He was comforted to know that in one sense, he had come home.

One of the elders cleared his throat. "Though we are pleased to welcome you, why have you returned? Do you need to bury someone else?"

"Only my wife and I when the time comes," Isaac answered, choosing his words with care. "We have come to live in the land, and we have pitched our shelter near the great oaks where my father once dwelt. We wish to live in peace with the people of Hebron, as my father did." He paused, wondering if he should share more of their circumstances. Pride battled with practicality. He decided that these men would discover the truth soon enough and so continued, "We have come with very little. Our flocks and herds are small. I assure you, we will not compete with Hebron's shepherds for grazing land."

The elders conferred among themselves, their voices a low murmur. Isaac waited, acutely aware of his vulnerability. If they refused to help him, what could he do?

Finally, Ephron spoke again. "You do not have to worry about grazing land; there is plenty for all. But your father established the well at Mamre as a place of hospitality, and the tradition remains. Will you maintain this custom? Will you offer water to thirsty travelers, regardless of their tribe or tongue?"

"I would never deny water to any living creature," said Isaac.

Ephron chuckled. "Then we welcome you, son of Abraham. It is fitting that you should dwell at Mamre."

Zibeon, who had mentioned the burial cave, spoke up. "You should know that Mamre is a regular stop for traders traveling to Egypt. Many caravans pass through the area."

Isaac lifted a brow, recognizing an opportunity. "That is good. We will welcome news from throughout the land."

"Then we are agreed," Ephron said. "Isaac, son of Abraham, is welcome to stay at Mamre and live in peace with Hebron."

Isaac bowed his head in grateful acknowledgment to the people of Hebron and to Adonai. "Thank you."

The elder Ephron embraced him once again. "May the God of Abraham bless your return."

"And may He bless Hebron with peace and prosperity," said Isaac.

As Minos guided him back to Mamre, Isaac lifted his face to the heavens. "Lord God of my father Abraham," he prayed, "I return to this place diminished in the eyes of men but seeking your face. Here where you spoke to my father, speak also to me."

Chapter 32

DESPITE OUR GRIEF at losing our sons, our home, and our livelihood, we still had to eat. I found myself grateful for the daily work of feeding and caring for our reduced household, but nothing could fill the emptiness left by Jacob's absence. I had not understood how deeply I would miss my beloved son, but in Mamre, unlike Beersheba, I did not expect to see him behind every tree or tent.

Though we were poor in comparison to what we had been, we survived. The men who had moved with us went hunting every day, and their women helped me prepare the game they brought to our fire pits. Several of the older children went to work in the fields, driving the goats and leading the sheep to green fields and flowing streams. The well at Mamre provided us with clear, cool drinking water, and the gigantic oaks shaded our work area and kept us from being scorched by the desert sun.

We were not without support. Several women from Hebron began to visit, often bringing goods to trade. We did not have much, but occasionally we were able to exchange venison for woven goods or rabbits for clay pots. Little by little, we were able to equip ourselves with what we needed for life in a new place.

The elders at Hebron were right about the well's popularity. Frequent travelers stopped at Mamre to drink and water their beasts. Like his father before him, Isaac maintained an open tent, offering shade, water, and hospitality to anyone who stopped at our camp. I never knew who I might find conversing with my husband. At times I found him talking to mountain men transporting war horses and mules, traders bringing coral, rubies, and turquoise from Aram, herdsmen driving sheep, cattle, and goats from Arabia, or Egyptians trading linen for wool.

We did not need coral or rubies or horses, but we did occasionally feed travelers in exchange for a ram and ewe or a bull and heifer. The servants erected pens for livestock outside our camp, and we prayed that the animals would reproduce in the spring.

Though I rarely addressed the traders directly—propriety forbade a woman from speaking to strange men without her husband present—I found ways to gather news. Isaac spent most of his time in the shade of our tent, so I counted on Minos to supply me with information about the world beyond our small camp. He would question travelers while they watered their animals or rested beneath our oaks, always seeking word of Jacob in Haran and Esau in Edom.

Many of his inquiries proved disappointing. Some traders bypassed those areas entirely, while others stopped in those regions but never encountered our sons. I sighed with each negative report, though I tried to hide my disappointment behind a polite smile.

But occasionally, blessed be Adonai, Minos would send word that someone knew Laban, who was a trader himself. On those occasions, I would join him, my heart racing like a wild donkey as I sought news of my son. One merchant, his face darkening at being directly addressed by a woman, turned away with barely concealed disdain. I retreated, stung but not surprised.

Later, as the trader took his meal, one of his servants approached me in the cooking tent. Her name was Keshet, and her dark eyes sparkled with kindness as she drew me aside.

"You are Rebekah?"

I nodded.

"My lady"—she lowered her voice—"I can tell you what you wish to know. We stopped to trade with Laban of Haran a few days ago."

My hands trembled as I gripped hers. "You know something about Jacob?"

She smiled. "Your handsome son is well—more than well. He is deeply in love with Rachel, the trader's daughter."

My smile deepened. "I have heard about her. I am thrilled to know she makes him happy."

Keshet chuckled. "They say Jacob sings while he tends the flocks, and his joy is evident for all to see. He says his years of labor will feel like only a few days, so great is his love for Laban's daughter."

My smile faded. "Has Laban told everyone that he is making Jacob work for his bride?"

Keshet shrugged. "The arrangement is not unusual. They say Jacob had nothing else to offer her."

"You are probably right." I swallowed hard, wanting to add that Jacob could have sent word and we would have given him anything to offer as a bride price—when we still had treasures to give. I shook the thought from my head and asked, "What do you know of this person? Is she as beautiful as they say?"

Keshet's smile broadened. "Rachel is one of the most beautiful girls I have ever beheld. She is also more unreserved than her sister. Leah is not unattractive, but she could never compare to Rachel."

I pulled my shawl tighter around my shoulders. An older sister. A girl strikingly less beautiful than her twin. How would Laban find a husband for his elder daughter if she was markedly less attractive than the younger? Was he even trying?

I shook my head. I would trust Adonai to arrange Jacob's

marriage. But I was also concerned about someone else in Haran. "Did you happen to meet a woman called Deborah? She used to be my nurse, but now she cares for Rachel."

"Oh, yes." Keshet dimpled. "The old woman thrives, my lady, and cares for Rachel as if she were her own daughter. Age has not dimmed her spirit."

My heart turned over. "I am happy to hear that."

The woman squeezed my hands. "My master, Te'oma, is from Aram, but he makes this journey every year. I would be happy to bring you news of your loved ones."

Hope bloomed in my chest like a desert flower after rain. I pulled my silver earrings from my ears and pressed them into Keshet's palm. "Please," I said, "bring me news whenever you return to this area. And if you can, tell Jacob that we have moved to Mamre. I want him to know where to find us when he comes home."

She pressed the earrings back into my hand. "You must keep these. It is my honor to serve you, my lady."

As I watched her scurry back to her master's retinue, my heart felt lighter than it had in months. This tenuous connection to Jacob and the promise of regular reports felt like stumbling upon a spring in the desert. It was not enough to substitute for my son's presence but would feed my soul until I saw him again.

I smoothed my tunic and walked toward our tent, eager to share my news with Isaac. But as I walked, a chiding voice rose in my head. *Do you not miss Esau?*

I braced myself in case Isaac asked the same question. But Esau had been a thorn, a splinter in my palm. No one missed a splinter once it was removed.

TIME SLIPPED BY like the wind through the desert palms—always moving, always bringing change. The children in our camp grew another year older; we who were old drew nearer to the grave. But though we knew we had entered the winter of our lives, Adonai was not yet finished with us.

After our first year, I established a tradition to mark our time in that place. I took my sharpest knife and cut a diagonal slash on the side of the oak that faced the altar. I did not know how many slashes I would create, but I prayed I would not make many more before Jacob returned.

As months passed, Isaac's frame grew thinner and weaker but being at Mamre renewed his spirit. The altar he rebuilt stood solid and strong, and every morning and evening he stood before it to offer his prayers, his voice echoing throughout the camp. I often leaned against the oak, wondering if Sarah had stood in the same spot to listen as Abraham prayed. What had been her feelings as she listened? What had been her dreams for her son?

I had only a few dreams remaining—I prayed to see Jacob again. I prayed to meet his Rachel, and if Adonai willed, I prayed to embrace his children and bless them in the Lord's name.

When I thought of Esau—*if* I thought of my older son—I did not know how to pray. The part of my heart that used to love him had turned to stone.

But because I had vowed to treat my children equally, and because I knew Adonai had promised to bless all the sons of Abraham, I prayed that he would find happiness, that he would have many children, and that he would find Adonai somewhere far away from us.

I HAD JUST FINISHED CUTTING the sixth slash in the oak when I spotted a line of pack animals descending the path toward our camp. My pulse quickened as I shaded my eyes against the midday sun, counting five, seven, *ten* heavily laden mules followed by a small herd. The procession moved directly toward us.

"Isaac!" I called. "More traders are approaching. Will you welcome them, or should I send Minos?"

Isaac, who had been resting beneath the oak, straightened, his head swiveling toward the sound of jangling bells and braying mules. "How many?" he asked, leaning on his staff as he stood. His joints troubled him in the cooler months, but this day was warm, the air heavy with the fragrance of spring blossoms.

"At least ten mules, two wagons, and livestock," I replied. "They are coming here."

Minos appeared from the storage tent, where he had been organizing supplies. "Shall I meet them?"

Isaac nodded, then straightened his shoulders and adjusted his garments—threadbare but clean, like everything we possessed. "Let us offer what hospitality we can."

I hurried into our tent, splashed water on my face, and smoothed my hair before covering it with a veil. The past year had etched new lines around my eyes, but the peaceful rhythms of this smaller camp had eased some of the bitterness that had gripped my heart when we first arrived. Still, anxiety fluttered in my chest as I picked up our only jar of sweetened wine—reserved for special occasions—and our last loaf of barley bread.

By the time I emerged, the procession had reached our camp. A man dressed in the garb of cooler climates dismounted from the lead mule and approached Isaac with a respectful bow.

"Peace be upon you," he said.

I lifted my head. His accent marked him as being from the Paddan-aram region, where Laban lived. He might have news of our son.

"I am Jashub," the man continued. "I seek Isaac, son of Abraham, and his wife, Rebekah."

"I am Isaac," my husband replied. He waved in my direction. "And that is my wife."

The messenger bowed again, this time to me.

"I bring greetings and gifts," he announced, "from your son."

My heart started beating at double speed. "Jacob?" My voice cracked on the name I had not spoken in weeks. "You have seen our son?"

"I serve in Laban's household," Jashub confirmed. "Your son has sent me with these goods, provided by his own hand, to provide you with comfort and joy."

Jashub gestured to his companions, who began to unload the carts. I watched, astounded, as bundle after bundle was set in front of us. Two men struggled to carry a cedar chest from a wagon, then placed it before me. One of them grinned as he lifted the lid, revealing garments of fine linen—robes in deep blue and russet, and soft woolen tunics in purple and saffron yellow.

Another servant opened a wooden box and revealed clay bottles sealed with wax. "Aged wine," Jashub said, sweeping his hand over the bounty.

"Master," Minos called, scarcely able to contain his delight. "Here are baskets of dried meats, rounds of cheese, and jars of dried dates."

Isaac blinked. "I hear the lowing of cattle." He turned toward our steward. "Do my ears deceive me?"

Minos stood on a chest to better see the livestock milling outside our camp. "Master, I see a half-dozen sheep and the same number of goats and cattle. All are healthy and strong."

"Yes," Jashub said. "When your son heard that you had moved to Mamre, he thought you might benefit from additional livestock."

I sighed, ruefully accepting the terrible truth: Jacob knew what had happened to us. When Keshet described meeting us in Mamre, she would not have spoken of our large tents and many servants. But she might have mentioned our small camp, our modest herds, and even my patched tunic. Jacob would have realized that our circumstances had been greatly reduced.

He might have even discerned why.

I looked at Isaac, wondering if he had come to the same

conclusion. Apparently, he had because he was listening to Jashub with a distracted look as though his thoughts were elsewhere.

Then his eyes flooded with tears.

For a moment I thought he might break as he had the morning he discovered Esau's treachery, but he lifted his head. "Praise be ADONAI," he cried, his voice breaking. "And blessed be Jacob, who will help us rebuild our household."

I sank to a large chest, overwhelmed by the sudden abundance. Determined to build up our flocks, we had not slaughtered any of our livestock but had been surviving on game and vegetables from our garden, trade with our neighbors and occasional caravans, and the modest payments Isaac received for mediating disputes among the people of Hebron. We had survived because ADONAI had provided, and Jacob's gifts would enable us to thrive in this place.

The scent of the cedar oil Isaac used to massage his stiff joints blended with the smells of livestock and sweet aromas wafting from open baskets. When the servants had finished unloading the mules and wagons, Jashub bowed. "Your son Jacob sends a message with his gifts. He says, 'I will send you goods between plowing and harvest, between autumn and the rainy season, and between winter and spring. I will not forget you.'"

The tears came without warning, hot and sudden, spilling over my cheeks as the meaning of Jacob's promise washed through me. This was not a single delivery; he was promising regular provision throughout the year. Esau had taken the best we had, but Jacob would not let us suffer. Even from afar, he would provide.

I pressed my fingers to my lips, trying to compose myself, yet my sobs would not be contained. Isaac's arm slipped around my shoulders, his body trembling as he held me close.

"Forgive me," I managed to tell Jashub, who seemed to understand my reaction. "These last few years have been difficult."

"Tell us of our son," Isaac said. "How fares Jacob?"

"He is well," Jashub replied, "strong and healthy."

"Has he made plans for his wedding?" I asked. "He has been in Haran nearly seven years."

Jashub gave us a lopsided smile. "When we left, the entire household was busy with preparations."

I gripped Isaac's arm, knowing he would intuit my thoughts. I would give anything to be present at my son's wedding, but the journey to Haran would not be feasible.

"We will send a message in return," I said, facing Laban's servant. "You and your men will sleep here tonight, of course. We will prepare a meal from these gifts."

Jashub bowed in acceptance.

"When you return," I continued, "please carry our love to our son. Tell him we pray for him daily, asking ADONAI to bless him in all things." I paused, swallowing hard. "And tell him that, ADONAI willing, we hope to see him and his wife as soon as God allows."

Isaac's hand found mine. "Tell my son," he added, his voice thick with emotion, "that his father blesses him from Mamre, where ADONAI appeared to Abraham. The blessing continues from generation to generation."

Jashub grinned, accepting the responsibility. "I will deliver your message. But I will write it down first."

As the women and I prepared a meal for our guests, I smiled with a joy I had not known since before we left Beersheba. The ache of missing Jacob remained, as did the wound of Esau's betrayal, but something else had begun to blossom amid the pain: unexpected hope.

THAT NIGHT, as Isaac and I lay in our shelter beneath a new blanket, I whispered into the darkness, "He has not forgotten us."

Isaac's hand found my cheek, his thumb brushing away a tear I did not know I'd shed. "Of course not. He is our son."

We had two sons. One who had carefully carved out and stolen what he presumed to be his; one who gave with open hands.

I voiced the question that had haunted me through the year. "Do you think we will see him again?"

Isaac remained silent for a moment. "The God who brought you to me at the well, who opened your womb after years of barrenness, who led us here when we had nowhere else to go . . . this God can surely bring Jacob back to us before we rest with our fathers."

I nestled closer to him, drawing comfort from his certainty. Outside our tent, I heard the soft sounds of our visitors settling down for the night, the occasional stamp of a mule's hoof, and the wind whipping the ancient oaks' leaves into soft applause. Tomorrow our guests would depart, carrying our message to Jacob.

I would rather have Jacob than his gifts. Nothing could replace the sound of his voice or the sight of his face across the table. But his gifts were a bridge across the distance, a reminder that we had not been forgotten.

THOUGH I HAD MANAGED to convince myself that Jacob would return home after his marriage, Isaac pointed out something I had ignored. "Jacob's message," he reminded me one afternoon, "said he would send provisions between plowing and harvest, autumn and the rainy season, and winter and spring. How can he do that if he plans to return soon?"

I stared at Isaac, my hope collapsing like a tent with a broken center pole. He was right. Perhaps the gifts were Jacob's way of telling us not to expect his imminent return.

I closed my eyes, my heart aching. "I had hoped . . ."

"I know you are disappointed," Isaac said. "But consider how blessed we are. Our son has generously provided for us. He has married the woman he loves, and apparently he is happy to remain in Haran for a while."

I drew a slow breath. "I miss him so."

"As do I, but Esau is also gone. This is the way of children, Rebekah. They grow, they marry, they establish their own households. I suspect that Jacob will not return to Canaan until he is able to support his family. Necessity demands that he remain in Haran while he builds his wealth."

For once, my husband was being more practical than I. "You are right," I said, sighing. "He must know that we can barely support our own household."

"Jacob will want to provide for his wife and children," Isaac said. "Just as I wanted to provide for you."

I took Isaac's hand and squeezed it. "Children! Perhaps Rachel is expecting. He would not want her to travel with a nursing infant. Our Jacob is considerate, and he will wait until the child is weaned."

Isaac chuckled. "Let us hope he does not wait too long. Because Rachel may have another baby, and another, so if Jacob waits until they are all weaned—"

"Bless ADONAI," I said, cutting him off. "I can wait, but I pray we will not have to wait too much longer."

FOR THE NEXT SEVERAL MONTHS, I went about my work with an eye on the northern horizon. My heart bounded upward each time I spotted a caravan, and finally I saw one that might be from Aram.

"ADONAI be praised," I whispered when I recognized the rider on the lead camel. "Te'oma has returned."

I left Minos to deal with the trader while I walked down the line of camels and searched for Keshet. I finally found her in a wagon and had to wait until the overseer released her to go with me.

Knowing the woman had to be hungry, I took her to the cooking tent, prepared a platter for her, then gestured for her to sit on a carpet. "Here," I said, pouring her a cup of honey water. "Welcome to our camp. Have you news from Haran? I am hoping you will tell me of my first grandchild. We have received gifts from Jacob, but the man who brings them is not overly fond of conversation."

If she was offended by my blunt inquiry, she gave no sign. "I have news," she said just before taking a huge bite of bread.

"Surely Jacob is married to his beloved Rachel," I said, giving the woman a moment to chew. "And surely she is with child or he could have come home so we could meet his wife."

Keshet's expression shifted as she swallowed. "I do have news, but probably not the news you expect."

I sank to the carpet as the details spilled from her lips in broken fragments, like shattered pottery reassembled in the wrong shape. She spoke of a wedding feast, a veiled bride, a wedding night, and a deception. Laban, my brother, led Leah, not Rachel, to Jacob's bed in darkness. The morning light revealed the truth. My son raged, and Laban responded with cool indifference: *"Finish the bridal celebration. Agree to work for me another seven years, and you shall have Rachel as well. You may marry her as soon as you finish Leah's bridal week."*

I gripped Keshet's wrist, my breath shallow and quick. "My son agreed?"

"What else could he do? Now he is married to Rachel, and you *do* have a grandson. But the boy is Leah's; she named him Reuben."

Keshet picked up a piece of venison and ate as I sat on the carpet, my mind roiling. I had a grandson. Reuben. A grandson from a daughter-in-law I had not expected.

Jacob had married Leah first. By custom and tradition, the first wife was the primary wife, and higher in status than the second. Jacob's beloved Rachel would be subservient to her elder sister . . . unless she refused to acknowledge her position. That attitude would create tremendous strife in my son's household.

Perhaps as bad as the strife that had divided my own.

A tremor passed through my bones as I pressed trembling fingers against my lips. Laban had done exactly what I had done. He switched the siblings and tricked an unwary victim. But unlike me, he had not acted out of righteousness. His deception had risen from greed, and he had taken no thought for the hearts he would shatter—Jacob's, Rachel's, Leah's . . . and mine. Jacob would not return to us for another seven years.

Would ADONAI allow me to live that long? What about Isaac? He had already seen one hundred twenty-seven summers, and Sarah, his mother, had died at that age.

I lifted my face toward the heavens, tears welling in my eyes. "ADONAI," I whispered, "please let us live to see our son again. In your mercy, grant that we may kiss our grandchildren before we die."

The wind stirred the olive branches above me, and for a long moment I listened, hoping, longing for a sign that my prayer would be heard and answered.

THE NEXT TIME Jashub arrived with gifts from Jacob, I insisted that the man carry a letter to our son. "It is not that I do not trust you to share a verbal message," I said, handing him a sealed papyrus, "but I have many things to say and do not wish to burden your memory. Please have Jacob write us in return, so we may know he is well."

With mixed feelings, I watched Jashub and his companions depart. Nine winters had passed since I last held Jacob in my arms. Nine seasons of planting and harvesting, of dry seasons and wet, of waiting for word from Haran.

Three months later, as the land warmed and flowers appeared, Jashub arrived with more gifts and a letter.

Jacob did not fill the page with many words, but his letter spoke briefly of his life as Laban's servant—of the joy he found in the fields, of how he had come to love solitude, and of how much he loved his wife Rachel. He wrote that Leah was a faithful friend and a wonderful mother to Reuben, and he prayed that all would be well with us until he could return.

My eyes welled when I read about Reuben, the grandson whose face I had never touched, whose laughter I had never heard. My feelings for him shifted from indifference to longing. Was he not Jacob's son? Was he not a descendant of Abraham?

Every day I sat beneath the giant oaks of Mamre, the trees' ancient branches providing shade as I spun wool and imagined details Jacob had not shared. I pictured beautiful Rachel waking in his arms. What did Leah do on those mornings? How often did he visit the elder sister's bed? I knew he would not ignore her. She had given him a son, and Jacob's nature would not allow him to neglect the mother of his child. He referred to her as a friend, so I imagined him sitting beside her on their bed, the baby on his lap, Leah resting her head on his shoulder . . . or was I imagining too much?

Sometimes, in the shimmering heat, I looked up and thought I saw him—my son, returning to me across the fields. But it was always a mirage, a cruel trick of light and longing.

Isaac grew thinner with each passing season. His eyes, which once saw traces of light, now offered nothing but darkness.

When I guided his hands to the gifts Jacob sent—the fine cloth, the aromatic spices, the jars of honey—he smiled and nodded, but I knew he would rather hold our son than these tokens.

"Perhaps next season," I told him every time Jashub departed. "Perhaps next time he will come himself."

The servants of our household enjoyed living at Mamre. Provisioned by Jacob's gifts, we now wanted for nothing. Our flocks multiplied across the hills, our storehouse remained full, and the respect of our neighbors had not diminished.

But our tent held an emptiness that no abundance could fill.

At night, when Isaac's breathing deepened in sleep, I whispered prayers into the darkness. "ADONAI, keeper of promises, protector of your chosen ones, how much longer must I wait? I am no longer young. My hands tremble when I work the loom. My back aches when I stand each morning. Will I live to see my son's face again? Will I hold his children on my lap?"

Sometimes Isaac spoke of Esau, his voice warming at pleasant memories of our firstborn. "He had such strength," he would say, or "Remember how he could track a deer for days?" And though it pained me, I nodded and smiled, for I could not bear to sharpen the edges of Isaac's grief with my bitterness.

How could I tell my husband that I still burned with anger whenever I thought of Esau? That I could not forgive the son who simply took what he wanted and moved away without a backward glance? The son who left without a word of farewell, who had sent no message in all these years? Were we dead to him? Though my anger burned every time I remembered what he had done, I could not—would not—determine to forget him.

He was my son, fruit of my womb, blood of my blood. I could not close my heart to him, not completely.

One night I walked to the gate that led out of our camp. The night breeze carried the scent of ripening figs outside the stone wall. Soon the servants would harvest them, preserving some to send to Jacob with the next caravan. I would send a papyrus with Jashub, asking when—when, my son, will you return to us?

Logic told me that Isaac and I had fewer days ahead of us than behind. Each sunrise was precious, each sunset a reminder that our time was growing short. I tried to trust in ADONAI's timing and in the promise that Jacob would fulfill his destiny. But oh how the waiting consumed me, like a slow fire that never burned out.

I looked up. The stars above Hebron were especially bright that night. I began to count them, remembering the promise that Abraham would have descendants as numerous as these brilliant points of light. Somewhere, under these same stars, Jacob slept with his family. Did he look up and think of us? Did he long for home as we longed for him?

He still sent messages with his gifts, but he wrote of Laban's flocks, his goats, and of hours spent beneath the sun. Other than saying all was well with his household, he did not write of his family, his wives, or his children.

Did he not want to share the intimate details of his family? Or did he fear burdening us with strife we could do nothing about?

We had waited eight long years. But I had endured twenty years of emptiness before the Lord filled my womb with twins. I would endure this separation as well, however long it lasted.

ADONAI, merciful one, do not let it be much longer.

Chapter 33

WHEN YOUR HAIR TURNS WHITE, I discovered, the days turn swift.

Isaac and I stayed busy with the care of our herds and our household, but I kept one eye on the northern horizon, searching for any sign of a traveler who might be Jacob.

Running a household was not as easy as it had been in our younger days. We worked, but our bodies did not cooperate as they once had. My fingers stiffened and ached when I did my embroidery, and Isaac complained that his back hurt after even a few moments of standing. After falling several times, he began to use a staff when he walked. Not only did it help with his balance, it enabled him to discover if any unexpected objects lay in his path.

One spring, after the rains had watered the earth and caused mold to grow on our tents, Isaac's severe cough returned. I set a group of women to scrubbing the tents while I cared for Isaac. At times I regretted sending Deborah away because she had always known exactly what to do.

But Isaac and I had encountered catarrh before, so I made him a tea of ginger and honey and coated his chest with a mustard poultice to draw out the congestion. The poultice, made of flour, mustard powder, and warm water, made Isaac crinkle his nose, but I ignored his protests and dutifully applied the mixture every morning. After two weeks, he finally improved, and I became more careful to make certain our tents stayed free of mold.

Isaac was not alone in his physical suffering. One day I was hurrying to catch a trader when I tripped over a rock. I extended my hand to catch myself, but I fell onto the hard ground. When I rolled over, I discovered that I could not move my arm.

Minos came running, then he helped me up and led me to my tent. Later he appeared with an old woman from Hebron, who examined my arm with the sharp eyes of a healer. "You have broken the bone," she said, lifting a brow. "You are old now—your bones will break easily."

I sucked air through my clenched teeth when she poked the middle of my forearm with a gnarled finger. "I *know* I am old, but I need my arms."

"You shall have them," the healer said, turning to her basket. "But you shall not have the use of them until two moons have passed." She rummaged in her supplies, then pulled out a spool of narrow linen and a thin rectangular stone. While I watched, she placed the stone on my forearm, then placed the end of the linen under my thumb. "Hold," she ordered.

I held the end of the strip as she wrapped it tight around my arm, ignoring my groans and hissed breaths. When she reached my elbow, she tucked the end of the linen beneath the wrapping and put out her hand. "One egg," she said.

I frowned, confused. "Do you want me to eat an egg?"

"I eat it," she said, giving me a toothless smile. "It is soft."

Ah—she wanted an egg as payment. I nodded to Minos, who was watching with an anxious look. "Give her an egg, please. In fact, give her two."

WHEN WE WERE NOT TRYING to navigate a world in which we had become infinitely more fragile, Isaac and I prayed. My husband adopted Abraham's habit of evening, morning, and midday prayers, and I often joined him in front of the altar, our eyes on the heavens, our hearts turned toward ADONAI. But Isaac's customary prayers were not petitions—they were recitations of praise to remind us of who ADONAI was.

"We thank you," he prayed most mornings, "for you, O Lord our God, are our fathers' God for all eternity, our Rock, our Shield that saves through every generation. We thank you and declare your praise for all your tender care. We trust our lives into your loving hand. We are always in your keeping; your wonders and miracles are with us daily, evening, morning, and noon. O you who are all-good, whose mercies never fail us, Compassionate One, whose faithful love never ceases, we ever hope in you."

My husband's prayers never failed to cheer me, because ADONAI had blessed us beyond my imagining. After being devastated by Esau's betrayal, ADONAI had brought us safely to Mamre, where we established a new home. ADONAI replenished us through Jacob's regular gifts, and though our herds were not as numerous as they had been in Beersheba, we did not need as many animals to feed a smaller household.

ADONAI had promised to be a compassionate God, and I saw that His love did not cease.

I joyfully placed all my hope in Him. Hope for a reunion with Jacob. Hope that I would one day hold and bless his children. Hope that he would return to live with us.

And sometimes when I prayed for Jacob, I thought of Esau as well. The devastating wound he had inflicted was no longer fresh—time and ADONAI had healed it. So I prayed for Esau, his wives, and his children, that they would be well.

And someday, I told the Lord, if Esau happened to bring them to Mamre, I would like to see them, too.

THOUGH ADONAI HAD NOT YET brought Jacob home, we did receive regular updates from Keshet, the trader's slave. Each year she brought us news of Jacob's children—more sons, born from Leah, Bilhah, and Zilpah, his wives' handmaids turned concubines. I was astounded to learn that Zilpah, Leah's handmaid, was Keshet's sister.

"We were sold into slavery and purchased by different masters," she said, her cheeks flushing. "I serve Te'oma the trader. She serves your son and daughter-in-law."

My breath caught. "Your sister bore one of my grandchildren?"

"Two of them." She nodded, her face now crimson. "It is why I am grateful to make this journey each year. I can see Zilpah, however briefly, and assure myself that she is well."

"Still . . ." My thoughts returned to the fact that Jacob was sleeping with his wives' handmaids. The sisters were apparently competing with each other, but what could I do about it? Like his grandfather, Jacob had taken concubines to keep his wives happy, and children had been born as a result.

I could only pray that the concubines' children would be happier than Ishmael had been.

Though Keshet gave me regular reports on Jacob's many children, year after year, she sighed and said that Rachel had not yet borne a child. But in the seventh year of Jacob's marriage—fourteen years after he left us—I spotted Keshet from a distance and hurried to meet her, my aging legs protesting with every movement. Something in her walk seemed different.

"Shalom, Keshet," I called. "What news from Haran?"

Her face broke into a wide smile. "Leah has recently borne a daughter."

My breath caught. "I have a granddaughter?" Tears sprang to my eyes. "Tell me of her."

Keshet smiled. "They call her Dinah. They say she has Leah's persistence and Jacob's spirit."

I pictured a small girl with Jacob's curious nature and questioning mind. A girl who might yet sit at my feet so I could teach her to spin wool and bake bread. "Anything else?" I asked.

Keshet dimpled. "I have saved the very best news, my lady. Your daughter-in-law Rachel has finally borne a son."

My hand flew to my heart. "Truly?"

"A healthy boy she named Joseph, for at his birth she said, 'God has taken away my reproach,' and 'May the Lord add another son to me.'"

It was a fitting time for tears, so I hung my head and wept them, remembering the moment I felt life quicken within me after so many years of emptiness—the wonder, gratitude, and overwhelming joy of that miracle.

"I am familiar with Rachel's suffering," I said, wiping my eyes. "I am acquainted with the waiting that stretches into years, the prayers that seem to go unanswered, and the monthly disappointment that wounds like a knife. But I have also felt her joy, and how much sweeter is the gift that takes years to arrive!"

We walked to a hill, where Keshet sat across from me and described the happy event: Rachel, radiant despite her exhaustion, forgetting the pain as she cradled the infant at her breast; Jacob weeping with joy, his face transformed by wonder; the household celebrating the son born after so many years of waiting.

"I could not believe I was fortunate enough to be present," Keshet said, her eyes shining. "Jacob could not stop smiling. He says the child has his eyes."

I exhaled a slow breath, a thrill shivering my senses. If only I had been there!

"And your sister?" I asked, suddenly remembering Zilpah. "How is she handling these changes?"

"She finds her place." Keshet's expression grew thoughtful. "Her sons give her standing. And she says the sisters are now kinder to each other. The children have bound them together, as has Jacob." She smiled. "Zilpah wanted me to tell you that Jacob teaches his sons about their grandmother Rebekah, who remembered Adonai's promise and set him on the path of following the Lord God."

Is that what I had done?

I closed my eyes, trying to imagine my son surrounded by his children, rich in blessings in spite of his trials. And at his side, Leah and Rachel, finally at peace.

Behind Keshet, the setting sun was painting the hills with gold, reminding me that grandchildren were a gift from Adonai. We had met Esau's eldest children, but we had no idea how many his family now included since we had heard nothing from him. We had heard that he was living in Mount Seir, an area south of the Salt Sea.

Through Jacob, Isaac and I had eleven grandsons and a granddaughter we might never see unless Adonai brought them to us. Yet knowing they existed and that Rachel's tears had turned to laughter was more than enough for now.

"Please," I said, strengthening my voice, "tell my son and his wives that Rebekah blesses them and their children. Tell them I praise Adonai for His faithfulness to our family through another generation. And tell your sister that I honor her contribution to our family's legacy."

As Keshet nodded, promising to deliver my message, I placed my hand over my heart and smiled at the promise of tomorrow. Rachel's little Joseph was living proof that God heard the cries of brokenhearted women, and that His timing, though inexplicable, was perfect.

Chapter 34

SQUINTING AGAINST THE SUN'S GLARE, I watched the northern horizon until my eyes burned. The fourteen years of Jacob's service to Laban had been completed. In fourteen years, I had not touched my son's face, put my arms around him, or heard his laughter. Now that his time of servitude was complete, surely he would return to us.

Each morning I rose before dawn and climbed the small rise behind our compound, scanning the northern road for any sign of movement. Each evening I returned to Isaac with a heavy heart and the same empty words: "Not today."

Isaac would nod, his blind eyes staring at nothing. "The Lord will bring him when it is time," he would say, his voice steady with a patience I could no longer muster.

I found one small, unexpected way to console myself while we waited. Not long after word reached me of Joseph's arrival, a woman in our camp gave birth to a son. Little Etan was only a few weeks younger than the son who had finally been born to Rachel, so I watched him with an overflowing heart—part sentry, part grandmother.

His hair was the color of desert sand after rain, and his skin held the same softness I imagined Joseph's would. I offered to tend him while his mother ground grain or carried water. My guardianship began as a favor but soon became a tether. I learned the weight of him, the milk-sweet scent of his breath, the way he reached up with curled fists trying to bat my chin. I was with him when he took his first wobbling steps—arms flung wide, his laughter echoing like chimes—and when he formed his first word, a bubbling sound that meant nothing and everything. I applauded when he grinned up at me, his gums slick and toothless, a drop of drool glistening on his chin like a pearl.

During my years of barrenness, I had kept my distance from the camp's little ones. Their laughter felt like splinters, their presence was a reminder of all I lacked. Later, when I bore my sons, I poured myself into them as a mother should, body and soul. I had no room in my heart for any children but my own.

But when I heard about Joseph, the son of Jacob's beloved wife, something cracked open. I began to yearn not just for news, but for the feel of him, the scent of him, the warmth of his small fingers in mine. I had not been able to anticipate the birth of Jacob's other sons, yet I had prayed earnestly for Rachel's, so I allowed my heart to fasten to Etan. He was only a proxy, an echo of the grandson I had never met. Watching him grow, carrying him on my hip, singing to him at dusk—somehow these things brought Joseph closer.

I yearned for all my grandchildren, of course, but Joseph had something in common with my sons—he had arrived after his mother suffered years of barrenness. He was a special gift from God.

Sometimes, in quiet moments between chores, I imagined I was holding Jacob's youngest son. I would whisper a blessing into Etan's curls and pretend Joseph could hear it, wherever he was.

WHEN KESHET ARRIVED that year, hope surged within me like a flash flood. I rushed to meet her, my sandals kicking up sand, my breath coming in gasps.

"Is he on his way?" I asked before she could even offer a proper greeting. "Has Jacob finally left Haran?"

The compassion in her eyes revealed her answer: "No, my lady. Jacob remains with Laban."

My shoulders slumped as frustration squeezed me, crushing the breath from my lungs. "But *why*? His commitment has been fulfilled. He has his wives, his children—"

"He has struck a new arrangement with Laban," Keshet said, leading me to the shade of the oak tree. "He is to continue his management of Laban's livestock, but certain animals—I forget which—will belong to Jacob. The animals with pure colors will remain Laban's."

I frowned, trying to make sense of her answer. "An agreement about *livestock* keeps him in Haran?"

"Jacob is building his own flocks," she said. "Zilpah says he wants to accumulate enough to sustain his household before he returns to Canaan."

Ah—Jacob did not want to rely on his inheritance from Isaac. Perhaps he had heard that Esau left us with the poorest animals. Or perhaps he simply wanted to make his own way in the world.

Though I understood my son's reasons, I could not hide my disappointment. Later, as I helped the servants prepare the evening meal, Jashub arrived with gifts from Laban, not Jacob—fine woven cloth, jars of honey, an intricately carved wooden box for Isaac.

The messenger bowed, respectfully presenting the gifts. "My master Laban knows he is blessed because of Jacob," he told Isaac as I eavesdropped. "His wife bore only daughters until Jacob arrived, but since then he has fathered three sons. So he is eager for your son to remain with him."

"And Jacob?" Isaac asked. "Is my son eager to stay in Haran?"

The messenger hesitated. "Your son is prospering," he finally said. "He has many herds and many children to feed."

That night, as Isaac slept, I ran my fingers over the wooden box and wondered if any of my grandchildren had touched it. How old would they be now? Reuben, the firstborn, must be around eight. And little Joseph, Rachel's miracle . . . he was still Etan's age, barely crawling.

I closed my eyes and tried to picture them: Reuben with Jacob's height, perhaps, and Leah's thoughtful eyes. Simeon and Levi, perhaps more mischievous, running through Laban's camp with the energy only young boys possessed. Judah, serious and watchful. Dan and Naphtali, Bilhah's sons—would they look like their mother? And Zilpah's boys, Gad and Asher—did they resemble Keshet? Issachar and little Dinah, my only granddaughter, and precious Joseph, with Rachel's beautiful eyes.

Esau's children had nothing to do with their father's actions, so how could I not think about them? Did they look like Esau or their beautiful mothers? Were they as active as Esau had been, or were any of them quiet like their uncle Jacob?

Isaac and I had met little Eliphaz and Reuel, Jeush, Jalam, and Korah, but surely other children had been born to our firstborn. Would I ever know anything about them?

TIME PASSED, one month folding over the last like the mended edges of a shepherd's cloak. Messengers from Haran came and went, gifts were exchanged, news of our growing grandchildren was shared in fragments I pieced together like a tattered garment.

I learned that Joseph had his mother's beauty and his father's mannerisms. That Dinah was headstrong but intelligent. That Reuben always tried to keep the peace among his brothers.

Each tidbit of information only made me hungry for more. I grew restless and impatient. The sound of camel bells brought me rushing from whatever task occupied me to the hill behind our tents.

Isaac always chuckled as I hurried past.

"One day it will be Jacob," he would say. "One day those bells will herald our son's return."

But the bells were never on Jacob's camel. They belonged to traders, messengers, and travelers passing through the land. And year after year Keshet, Jashub, and Jacob's letters repeated that he remained in Haran so he could support his growing family.

The seasons blurred—planting and harvest, dry season and rainy, the cycle of the moon marking months that stretched into years. My hair thinned, and the ache in my knees deepened. Still, I watched the horizon and listened for bells.

Six years after Jacob's agreement with Laban—when Reuben would be thirteen, practically a man, and Joseph around six—Jashub visited again. He brought the usual gifts: fine wool, containers of oil, and spices from the east. A pair of dark lambs and two spotted goats.

As Jashub shared our evening meal, the wine loosened his tongue. "There are certain tensions," he said, lowering his voice, though only the birds and stars could overhear our conversation, "between Jacob and the sons of Laban."

"His sons?" I frowned. "How old are they?"

"Seventeen, eighteen, and nineteen," Jashub replied. "Nearly men."

Isaac's hand reached for mine. "What sort of tensions do you speak of?"

Jashub took another swig from his cup. "Laban's sons accuse Jacob of stealing their father's wealth. But in truth, they are jealous of his success."

"They are jealous of their brother-in-law?"

"See for yourself." Jashub gestured to the pen where we had placed the newly arrived kids and lambs. "Jacob's animals—the spotted ones, the speckled and dark ones—grow stronger each season, healthy lambs and strong kids. Laban's flocks"—he shrugged—"do not thrive in the same way."

Isaac tugged thoughtfully on his beard. "The animals we receive from Jacob are good breeders."

"It is not so with Laban's herd." Jashub shook his head. "They grow weaker while Jacob's animals grow stronger. And when Laban looks at Jacob"—he hiccupped—"his expression is not as genial as it used to be."

Despite the warm night, a chill shivered my bones. I knew all too well how quickly favor could turn to envy and how blessing could breed resentment. Had I not seen it in my sons?

"Is Jacob in danger?" I asked.

Jashub considered the question. "Not yet. But the eyes that watch him are no longer friendly."

Sleep eluded me that night. Wrapped in my shawl, I paced the perimeter of our camp, watching the northern stars as if they might rearrange themselves into a warning for Jacob.

"How much longer, ADONAI?" I whispered. "How many more seasons must pass before you bring him home?"

The stars offered no answer, and the night wind carried only the distant howl of jackals. But I sensed the time of waiting was drawing to a close. Soon the horizon I watched would reveal the shapes of camels, wagons, flocks . . . and my son, coming home at last.

AS THE TWENTIETH YEAR without Jacob arrived, I made yet another slash on the sprawling oak tree and turned toward the northern skyline. My eyes were not as sharp as they had been in my younger years, and Isaac, who had long been blind, was now losing his hearing.

But I thought I saw movement on the horizon—a line of camels that signaled the approach of a caravan. Could it be?

I squinted against the sunlight. My bones ached as I straightened and stretched to my full height, a sharp reminder of how time had burdened me. I pressed my hand against the oak's rough bark, letting it bear some of my weight as I peered into the distance.

"Isaac," I called, my voice more tremulous than it used to be. "I see a caravan."

My husband sat in the shade, his cloudy eyes staring at nothing. His thin beard now fell in wisps across his chest. Without either of our sons to strengthen us, we had both become fragile.

"Who comes?" Isaac asked, his fingers working at the fringe of his robe.

I watched as the dust cloud grew. "I cannot tell."

My fingers played over the slashes on the tree trunk. Nineteen years I had waited by this tree, nineteen times I had chipped away bark, each slash a monument to my prayers that Jacob would come home to us.

As the caravan drew closer, I could see riders on the camels. None of them appeared familiar.

"Mistress Rebekah," one of my servants called. "These riders bear the markings of Laban's household."

My pulse quickened. Could it be Jacob? Laban had no reason to visit us.

I gathered my tunic and hurried toward the gate as quickly as my stiff hips would allow.

Once inside our enclosure, the riders dismounted, bowing low. Their leader, a man I did not recognize, spoke first.

"Peace be upon you, Rebekah, daughter of Bethuel, and upon your husband, Isaac, son of Abraham."

"And upon you," I replied, my voice steady despite the tremor in my hands. "Do you bring news from Haran?"

The man's gaze flicked toward Isaac, then rested on me. "I am called Bashan, and I have come from the house of Laban, your brother. We bring news of Jacob."

My son's name hung in the air like sweet incense, but the man's tone was somber. I pressed my hand to my chest, suddenly unable to breathe. "Tell me my son lives."

"He lives and prospers," Bashan confirmed. "He is traveling to Canaan with his wives, his children, and many possessions. He has left the house of Laban and travels at a slow pace to avoid stressing his little ones."

Tears blurred my vision. Jacob *was* coming home! The keeper of the covenant was returning to us.

"Isaac!" I turned. "Did you hear? Our son is on his way home."

Isaac's head lifted, hope and fear mingling in his expression. "Is all well with him?"

I turned back to Bashan, expecting good news, but the man shook his head. "All is not well. Laban has sent me to tell you of his complaint against your son."

I recoiled from the words. "My brother has a complaint?"

Bashan continued, his words dropping like stones. "He would have me tell you that Jacob did not allow him to kiss his daughters and their children, but led them away like captives, along with all the cattle and property he acquired in Laban's land."

My joy soured even as my temper flared. I knew my brother and was well acquainted with his greed and manipulation. Jacob knew him, too, so if my son fled without a proper farewell, he had good reason to do so.

"There is something else," Bashan added, refusing to meet my eye. "Laban has also sent runners to inform Esau of Jacob's approach."

I blinked as the landscape shifted around me. "He told Esau of Jacob's return?"

The man dipped his chin in a sharp nod. "Laban hired men to tell Esau where to find Jacob on the road. They were instructed to tell your older son to do to Jacob whatever Esau's soul desired."

My knees buckled at the menace in the words. One of my handmaids rushed forward to support me, but I barely noticed her. The world spun as a suppressed cry tightened my throat.

Why would Laban do such an evil thing? Twenty years might not have been enough to dull Esau's rage; did he not demonstrate his anger when he left us? He had sworn to kill Jacob once Isaac died. What would stop him from killing his brother on a lonely road?

"Where?" I whispered, my voice raw. "Where will Esau intercept him?"

Bashan squinted in calculation. "It is impossible to say exactly where, but they should meet near the ford of the river Jabbok. According to my scouts, Esau is now traveling to that place with four hundred men."

Four hundred men? Even with his wives, children, and servants, Jacob would be vastly outnumbered. Was he accompanied by any fighters, or did he travel with a group of nursemaids and shepherds?

I bit the inside of my cheek to keep from wailing.

"Why?" Isaac shouted at Bashan, his features contorting in a mask of accusation as he staggered forward. "Why have you tormented us with this news? Laban clearly wants to punish Jacob, and you work for Laban—"

"Speak softly, sir," Bashan said, his gaze focused on Isaac's face. "I have worked alongside your son and know him to be a righteous man. He does not deserve to be met with his brother's hostility, so I have chosen to warn you."

The man dropped to one knee. "Command me, if you will, and let me be of service."

Isaac drew a breath. "Rebekah"—he squeezed my arm with surprising strength—"we must act swiftly."

I forced my whirling thoughts to steady. Panic would not save my son. Action might. And surely ADONAI would.

I turned and saw Minos standing behind me, his face a study in concentration. "Gather our strongest men," I told him. "Take the most loyal from our household, these men with Bashan, and any willing men from Hebron. They must ride with all haste to intercept Jacob before Esau reaches him."

As our steward hurried to obey, I turned to Bashan. "How far is Jacob from this river? How much time do we have?"

"Three days, perhaps four," he answered.

Three days. My heart ached as I lifted a frantic prayer to ADONAI.

IN MY TENT, I pulled out a piece of papyrus, found a quill and ink, and scratched out a message:

Jacob,

I have heard, my son, that your brother has gone forth against you on the road with four hundred men from the fierce Horites. Hearken to your mother's voice and do as I say. When Esau approaches you, do not speak rashly to him, and offer him a gift from whatever you possess and from what God has favored you. And when he asks about your affairs, conceal nothing from him. Perhaps he may turn from his anger against you, and you will save your soul, as well as the souls of all who belong to you. It is your duty to honor him, for he is your elder brother.

A drumbeat pounded in my rib cage as I folded the letter.

BY NIGHTFALL, seventy-two men stood before me, torchlight casting long shadows across their determined faces. I stepped forward, my resolve firm.

"Ride with the swiftest riders to find my son Jacob," I told Minos, my voice carrying across the silent camp. "When you find Jacob, give him this letter and make sure he reads it. Do not, I beg you, let anything happen to it or to him." My fingers trembled as I pressed the folded papyrus into our steward's palm.

I turned to the others. "When you reach Jacob, warn my son that his brother comes with four hundred men. I am not asking you to risk your life for my son, only to stand with him when his brother approaches. My son's life may depend on your presence."

As the men turned to mount mules and camels, I returned to Isaac's side. He sat motionless, his face lifted toward the stars he could no longer see. "Will our actions follow us to the grave?" he whispered. "Will one son kill the other because of what we did?"

Did he mean what *I* did?

I sat by his side and watched as the riders disappeared into the darkness. The night air chilled my skin, and fear rattled my teeth. I thought of Jacob—the man I had sent away was now ninety-seven—would I recognize him? Would he recognize *me*? The years had not been gentle with me, and grief over my sons had marked my face and my posture. Jacob might not know who I was, but he would remember what I had done.

Would he be angry with me for setting him on this path? Would he understand that my chief concern had always been fulfilling God's promise?

And Esau—my firstborn, whose blessing I had secured for Jacob. His terrible rage had always been his undoing. I could not forget the threats he had made and how he had consoled himself with the thought of Jacob's death.

"What have I done?" I whispered. "What have I set in motion?"

"You did what you thought was right," Isaac said. "While I ignored what I knew to be true."

Isaac's hand found mine, his palm as dry and thin as papyrus. "We have done what we have done. Now we must trust ADONAI to protect what is His."

I leaned against my husband's bony shoulder, his body as frail as mine. We had grown old waiting for Jacob's return. Now he was on his way, but the journey would bring him face-to-face with the danger we feared most.

"Please, ADONAI," I prayed, tears flowing freely, "let Minos reach Jacob in time. Soften Esau's heart. And let me see my son's face once more before I die."

The night stretched before us, filling with our prayers and memories of the twins who had once slept with their arms wrapped around each other. As Isaac and I prayed, all I could do was wait and hope that the God who had spoken to me before Jacob's birth would preserve him in the days to come.

Chapter
— 35 —

I COULD NOT SLEEP. Two days had passed since our men departed with my message to Jacob—two days of torment, of dire imaginings and suppressed fears. I visualized every possible outcome of Jacob and Esau's meeting, but we received no news from either our sons or our servants.

The evening breeze pushed at the tent walls as I paced, my sandals wearing a path in the wool carpet Jacob had sent with his last delivery. I swallowed, my throat parched despite the honey water I had been sipping all day. I paused at the doorway of our tent and stared into the darkness, as if I could see across the miles to the place where my sons would meet.

"He will heed my message," I said, my fingers working at the embroidered edge of my tunic. "Jacob has always listened."

But doubt gnawed at me. Would he heed my words when faced with his brother's wrath? Would he bow as I had instructed, offer the gifts in proper order, speak with humility rather than pride? The Jacob I sent to Haran would, but how had he changed in his years of serving my brother? Had he adopted any of Laban's bad traits?

I closed my eyes and saw them again. My sons who had struggled against each other even while in my womb. Esau leading four hundred fierce Canaanites who lived by the sword. And Jacob with his wives and children, his shepherds and servants—and only seventy-two men to defend him, if necessary. The numbers alone made my heart race.

Behind me, Isaac's labored breathing provided an accompaniment to my thoughts. The stress of the last two days had sapped his strength, so he had spent most of his time abed. When awake, his thoughts were clear and his mind sharp. Sometimes I thought it sharper than in his younger days, as if ADONAI had taken his sight but given him wisdom in exchange.

"You fear too much," he said, startling me.

"How can I not?" I sat on the bed and took his weathered hand in mine. "Esau swore to kill him. He travels with four hundred warriors. You do not bring four hundred warriors to a reunion of brothers."

"Perhaps Esau fears Jacob."

The thought made me snort with derision. "Esau has never had a reason to fear Jacob."

"Perhaps Esau fears ADONAI, who guards Jacob." Isaac lifted a brow. "After all, the same God who rescued Abraham from the vast army of the five kings watches over Jacob—and Esau." His fingers tightened around mine. "Trust Him."

I wanted to scoff. Had he forgotten what Esau vowed after the blessing? Had he forgotten the rage in our firstborn's voice? But then I spotted wetness on Isaac's cheeks, outlining the contours of his face.

"I pray for Jacob," he said, "as you do. But I also pray for Esau."

His words, uttered so simply, pierced my heart.

"Esau has wives," Isaac continued, "and children. He is also our son. Whatever happens, I pray ADONAI spares them both."

I pulled my hand away. "I know he has wives and children, but Esau chose his path. He married pagan women against our wishes.

He seized the inheritance of the firstborn and left us without a word. He—"

"He is still our son," Isaac interrupted. "Do you think ADONAI would have formed him in your womb if he were not significant?" He halted, seized by a fit of coughing, and I waited while he struggled to catch his breath.

Finally, he spoke again. "After my experience on Mount Moriah," he said, his voice weaker than before, "I thought ADONAI formed me only to test my father's faith. Not until after he died did I understand that ADONAI also had a plan for me, but I would have to wait before it became clear. We may not understand what Esau will become, but ADONAI knows. Just as ADONAI knows about Jacob."

I stared at him, blinking, then sank to my knees at the side of the bed, my face in my hands. Images played across the backs of my eyelids: Esau as a small boy, grinning as he returned with his first gazelle, his face glowing as he presented it to his father; Esau lifting me when I slipped off a camel, his arms gentle despite his strength.

"What have I done?" I lifted my head. "If they kill each other—"

"ADONAI will not allow it." Isaac spoke with such certainty I almost believed him.

For two days and two nights, I had imagined almost every possibility, but I had not allowed myself to consider the most frightening prospect—that in the throes of a heated confrontation, I might lose both my sons.

So I prayed not only for Jacob's safety, but for Esau's. "Forgive me," I whispered, and I did not know if I spoke to ADONAI, Isaac, or my absent children.

Isaac's hand crept across the mattress and found mine, his touch unexpectedly tender. "Now we wait," he said, "and trust in the Lord."

Outside, the night wind carried the sound of thunder from distant hills. Somewhere far away, my sons were about to meet for the first time in more than twenty years.

And I, for the first time since Bashan's arrival, surrendered the outcome to hands stronger than my own.

I AWOKE WITH A START, my body aching from another night of fitful sleep. The third day of waiting had dawned bright and clear, the morning air cool as I rose and walked through the camp, checking on the servants and their chores, trying to occupy my restless hands with the daily routine.

Isaac had been praying since dawn. I could hear his voice, low and steady, coming from the altar. The sound both comforted and unsettled me. His faith seemed unwavering while mine trembled like a leaf in the wind. Years ago, when we struggled with my barrenness, I had been the one who did not doubt. But that was before Jacob went away and Esau betrayed us.

I wanted to believe ADONAI would protect our sons. He had always kept His word in the past. But I knew Esau's rage and felt powerless before it.

As the sun began to lower toward the west, the lookout shouted, "A traveler approaches! Alone! On a camel!"

My heart leapt in my chest. Jacob would not be approaching alone, but perhaps it was a messenger.

I dropped the wool I had been carding and looked toward the gate of our encampment. Isaac turned from the alter, his sightless eyes seeking the source of the commotion.

"Who is it?" he called, his voice sharp with urgency.

"A messenger, I hope," I replied.

The camel loped across the sand, bringing the rider closer. Not one of Jacob's men, I thought, for the man had a curled beard, and I could not identify his clothing. But as he drew closer, I recognized him as one of the men who had arrived with Bashan.

"Fetch water and bread," I told a servant, who hurried to obey.

The man guided the camel through our gate, then commanded

the beast to kneel. I waited, scarcely daring to breathe, as the beast rocked to-and-fro, and the man dismounted. Dust and sweat streaked his face, his eyes wet and red.

"My lord," he gasped out, bowing before Isaac. Then he straightened and accepted the water a servant offered. He drank deeply for a moment, then lowered his cup. "I am Resheph, a servant of Bashan," he said. "I bring word of your sons."

Isaac's hands tightened on his staff. "Speak."

I moved to my husband's side, gripping his arm with fingers that had gone cold. "Do our sons live?" I asked, unable to wait for formalities.

Resheph nodded, and I sighed in relief, though the man's expression remained grave. He cleared his throat. "Our party encountered Esau and his warriors on the road."

"And?" Isaac prompted, his voice far steadier than my racing heart.

"Esau knew Jacob was approaching," the man continued. "But . . ." A dubious look crossed his face when he glanced at me.

"Speak freely," I said. "Whatever the news, I would hear it."

Resheph straightened his shoulders. "Bashan greeted Esau, and your elder son responded with pride and contempt. He said, 'I have heard what Jacob has done to Laban, who exalted him and gave him his daughters for wives. As Jacob tricked Laban, so did he trick me, twice supplanting me. So I have come with my men to meet him, and I will do to him what I should have done years ago.'"

I swayed on my feet, and Isaac's arm—the one I had been clutching—strengthened to steady me.

"May Adonai have mercy," I whispered. Twenty years had neither cooled Esau's rage nor softened his memories.

The lines around Isaac's mouth deepened. "What of Jacob? Bashan left this place to find our younger son, to convey our wishes—"

"We found him," Resheph continued. "We left Esau straightaway and rode north in search of your other son. We found Jacob at rest in his camp with his wives and children. Your steward went at once to deliver Rebekah's message."

"And?" The word slipped from my tongue. "Did he read it?"

The old man shook his head. "I do not know. Bashan commanded me to return here before I learned the outcome of our visit. When I departed, Jacob was standing apart in a quiet place, praying to his God."

I covered my mouth and exhaled a slow breath. The news of Jacob's prayer brought some comfort, but not enough. Even if Jacob followed my advice, would his actions assuage Esau's anger?

Yet I was glad to know Jacob had gone to ADONAI instead of relying on my advice alone.

"I *did* hear," Resheph said, lowering his voice to a conspiratorial tone, "that your younger son had sent messengers on the road to Mount Seir, telling his brother of his coming. His men said the message was amiable and pleasant, intended to win his brother's favor."

"Did it?" Isaac answered. "Did Esau respond?"

Resheph blew out a breath. "I spoke to one of the messengers myself. He said Esau replied only with the news that he was coming to meet Jacob with four hundred men. This news disturbed Jacob, so he intends to divide his camp. If Esau attacks one group, the other might escape."

A vivid image filled my mind, one of burning tents, blood soaking into the ground, the bodies of helpless women and children scattered over the desert sand. I turned away, unable to bear the messenger's sympathetic gaze. One of our sons was preparing for confrontation, the other expected to lose at least half his family.

Which of my grandchildren would die? Which of Jacob's wives would be slain? A sob rose in my chest, but I pressed my hand over my mouth to stifle it.

"Thank you for bringing us this report," Isaac said, his voice hollow. "Rest now. Eat. You have journeyed far."

Resheph bowed and followed the servants toward the cooking tent, leaving Isaac and me alone with our fear.

"Did I give Jacob good advice?" I asked, clutching Isaac's robe. "What if he follows my counsel, bows before Esau, and Esau strikes him down? Should I have counseled strength instead of meekness?"

"Your counsel was wise." Isaac reached for me, his hands settling on my shoulders. "ADONAI has planned this meeting for His purpose, not ours."

"But our sons—"

"Will be in His hands." As Isaac pulled me closer, I buried my face against his chest, inhaling the familiar smells of wool and incense. "Come," he said. "We will take comfort in prayer."

I walked with him into our tent, but as he began to call upon ADONAI, I knelt beside him in silent agony. In my mind, I saw Esau, his face set in anger, his body encased in armor, his broad hand wrapped around the hilt of a sword. Jacob would appear as an ant beside him, especially if he followed my advice.

ADONAI, preserve my sons!

Isaac's prayers continued, steady and true, while mine came in broken gasps, the desperate pleas of a mother who might lose both sons in a single day—one to death and one to a crushing guilt he would carry forever.

Outside, the sun began its descent toward evening. Another night of waiting had begun.

I SAT UP IN BED, as awake as if someone had shaken me from sleep. When my eyes adjusted to the dim light seeping through gaps in the goatskin panels, I peered into the darkness and saw nothing.

Why was I awake?

Then I saw my younger self on a camel with Deborah's arms fastened like a vise around my waist. "I make this vow before all who hear me now," I was saying. "I will never, ever love one child more than another. Each child will know the fullness of a mother's heart, without preference or partiality. No child of mine will bear the wound of being less favored, less cherished, or less seen."

"A righteous vow," Deborah said, her breath warming my ear, "but one that might be tested."

"Then let it be," I replied, "because I have known the sting of second place. I will never inflict that pain on one of my children."

The memory, which had been as vivid as my recollection of evening dinner, faded into darkness. Had I been dreaming? I pinched my arm and felt the sharp edge of my fingernail. If this was a dream, I had never had one like it. So why had it happened?

I lifted my gaze to the vent at the top of the tent, half expecting to see a heavenly visitor. I had *heard* ADONAI, but I had never seen Him, so perhaps . . . I waited but saw nothing else.

Disappointed, I lay back on my pillows, but my thoughts would not let me rest. Why had the Lord brought that memory to mind? I had been so young when I traveled to Canaan, so inexperienced and so foolish.

I should never have made a vow I could not keep. As a young woman, what did I know of children, of sons who were different in every way? I could not have known that one son would love me while the other would ignore me. I could not have known that motherhood, which I had desperately desired, would bring me the greatest joy and the greatest pain.

I dashed a tear from my eye. Why was Esau the way he was? Why had he insisted on disappointing us? And why had Isaac turned a blind eye to his foolishness for so many years?

I remembered the day Isaac sent Esau for savory game, intending to grant our eldest the blessing of the firstborn. If I had not acted, ADONAI's will would have been ignored.

I remembered the deception, the stolen blessing, Esau's rage that had driven Jacob from our home. The loneliness of those years without my younger son, and how the constant presence of Esau's pagan wives pressed on me until I could scarcely breathe.

How could that young woman on the camel have been so rash with her vow? But even then, Deborah had known; she had said my vow might be tested, and it was. It was tested, broken, forgotten. Because my firstborn proved to be too much for me. Too much to handle, too much to teach, too much to love.

The harder I tried to ignore the truth, the more it persisted. I had not loved Esau as I should have. I was so consumed with ADONAI's prophecy, with the birthright, with shaping the future that God had promised that I forgot to love my firstborn for who he was. I had failed not by loving Jacob too much, but in loving Esau too little.

And at times, I had hated him.

I turned away from Isaac, lest he wake and sense the storm of emotion in my heart. Oh, how narrow the distance between love and hate! Yes, I loved my firstborn, but at times I had hated him, and why? I closed my eyes, pondering the question, and the answer came: because he hurt me. Even as an infant, his greedy suckling caused me pain, so I found someone else to nurse him. As a youngster, he ran to Isaac for comfort, so I devoted myself to Jacob. When I tried to teach Esau how to write or tell him about ADONAI's ways, he crossed his arms, refusing my instruction, so I focused on Jacob. He married women who mocked me and my God. Finally, he stole most of our livestock, servants, and possessions, leaving us alone and nearly helpless in our old age.

If an enemy had been as cruel, would I not be excused for hating him? But I had suffered those things at the hand of my own son. And I had hated him for it because he broke my heart.

"*Rebekah,*" Deborah had once scolded me after I had fought with Laban, "*do not say you hate your brother because I know you love him. If you did not love him, you would not care enough to be angry.*"

She was right. The opposite of love was indifference, and I could never be indifferent toward Esau. The mention of his name tied my stomach in knots. The thought of never seeing his children made my heart ache. And the knowledge that he had turned from ADONAI was enough to drop me to my knees.

A memory ruffled through my mind like wind on water: Isaac standing with me in a field, the bull nuzzling his hand. I had been terrified, but Isaac had said that the secret to winning an animal's heart was to be patient, to realize that it had feelings and that it could sense my heart.

No wonder I had never been able to tame an animal the way Isaac could. I could not even tame my wild son, probably because I did not consider his feelings or give him time to know my heart.

That thought brought another in its wake, with a chill that struck in the pit of my stomach. Had Esau behaved badly because of how I had treated him?

I gave him to a wet nurse for three years, so no wonder he ran to Isaac as soon as he could walk. Isaac was a constant in his early life, while I was a mere shadow.

Perhaps Esau resisted my teaching sessions because I praised Jacob so highly.

Perhaps Esau married pagan women because he did not want to marry a woman like me.

Perhaps he stole our possessions to claim what I helped Jacob obtain. He must have seen my actions as evidence of my hatred for him, and that realization had deepened his resentment. No wonder he had schemed to take the firstborn's portion.

Yes, the Lord had promised that the elder would serve the younger, but ADONAI did not need me to accomplish His will.

In a flash I could barely comprehend, I realized something else. I would have helped Jacob even if ADONAI had never spoken of my sons' future. I would have done it because *I loved Jacob more*.

The awful knowledge twisted and turned inside me. Had I wronged my elder son? Could his anger, the culmination of a lifetime's resentment, be laid at my feet?

Chapter 36

THE AFTERNOON SUN slanted through the branches of the giant oaks at Mamre, dappling the earth with shifting patches of gold. The wind barely stirred the branches above me, yet my heart thrashed like a goat caught in brambles.

Three nights of fitful sleep had left me exhausted. I stretched out on a blanket beneath the largest oak, my eyes heavy and my body engulfed in a tide of guilt and weariness. Sounds came to me—the soft chatter of women at work, the lowing of cattle in the field, the insistent braying of a protective donkey.

I drifted into a doze in which memories combined with inchoate fragments of fear. At first I heard only a murmur on the edge of silence, a dry rhythm against the earth, like hands brushing grain from the stalk. Then came soft bleating, carried on the breeze like the voices of lost children. Sheep, goats, the jangling bells at their necks, each sound rising, swelling, as if the earth were remembering a summer day long forgotten. I listened to the hush between shuffling hoofbeats, straining past the clamor for a deeper sound.

I then heard the groan of leather straps, the sway and grunt of burdened camels. Beneath those sounds, the faint hum of human voices—Jacob's voice perhaps. I sighed in pleasure. These were not the sounds of approaching strangers. They were the sounds of return.

The lookout's cry shattered my sleep. I sat up, fully awake, and was startled to discover that the sounds were real. A company was approaching from the north.

A tremor shivered my limbs as my heart stirred with hope. I stood and looked toward the north, where dust swirled in the distance. Was this Jacob or Esau?

I ran to the gate, willing the caravan to move more quickly. A few moments later, a bearded figure emerged from the dust, and there he was. His frame was no longer the slender form I remembered, but that of a mature man, his shoulders rounded from age. His eyes, sunk deep into webbing at the corners, found mine. Though he walked with a limp, his pace quickened as he neared the gate.

Finally, my son had come home. "Jacob . . ." I said.

His hands trembled as he reached for me. "Mother." He bowed, his forehead brushing my hands. Then he straightened and kissed them, his lips warm against my knuckles.

"Adonai has answered my prayers." I choked on a suppressed sob. "He has brought you safely home."

Jacob turned to Isaac, who now stood behind me, his blind eyes turned toward the sound of our son's voice. When Jacob took his father's hands and pressed them to his face, Isaac released a shuddering breath.

"My son," he rasped. "My son."

Jacob placed his right hand on my shoulder and his left on Isaac's. "Merciful Adonai," he prayed, "may you bless my father, my teacher; and my mother, my teacher; who have taught me your ways and led me in the path of truth. May we all be blessed as you blessed Abraham and Sarah, Isaac and Rebekah. Then we shall exult in your righteousness. Amen."

When he said *amen*, I studied my son's arresting face. He had grown old, my Jacob, but wisdom shone in his eyes, and the lines in his forehead spoke of patience. But something else had changed in him, a quality I could not name. Had he learned so much working for Laban?

Isaac caught Jacob's arm and held it tight. "Your brother," he said, his voice flat. "You met him in the road?"

Jacob looked from Isaac to me. "I did."

"And what happened?" I asked.

Jacob smiled. "My brother ran to meet me. He hugged me and kissed me, and we wept together. He met my wives and children and accepted my gifts. Later, we departed in peace."

Though I had a feeling Jacob had neglected to tell us everything, I threw my arms around him, then pulled away and lifted my hands in praise. "I would dance with joy," I told him, smiling until I thought my face would break. "But these old bones are too brittle." The same relief and gratitude shone on Isaac's face.

"You must tell us all about it," I said, reaching for his arm. "We will prepare a feast and let your little ones rest. You can stay as long as you like, Jacob, and—"

"I have news," he interrupted, a shy smile lifting the corners of his mouth. "ADONAI has changed my name. I am now called *Israel*."

"Israel." Isaac's brows lifted. "ADONAI has spoken to you?"

Jacob's eyes met his father's, and an unspoken understanding passed between them.

"Yes," Jacob said, his voice restrained. "I have heard Him and wrestled with Him, and I prevailed."

Isaac's eyes widened, but I shook my head. I did not understand how such a thing could be possible, but these men had experienced far more of God than I had.

"ADONAI might have renamed you," I said, "but you will always be Jacob to me."

Isaac wanted to know more about Jacob's encounter, but our son had turned and was beckoning to those who waited behind him. "Come," he said, his eyes sinking into nets of wrinkles as he smiled. "I want you to meet my family."

The sun stood high, casting sharp light across the camp. The stones at my feet radiated warmth; I could feel it through the soles of my sandals. My shortened shadow lingered beside me, trembling faintly in the breeze. I had waited so long for this day that I had stopped imagining how it would come.

A woman stepped forward, her shoulders strong, her wide-eyed gaze steady. "This is Leah," Jacob said. "She has been a good and faithful wife."

She bowed, and when she looked up, I saw kindness and sorrow mingling in her eyes. Was that a remnant of the sisters' rivalry or something else?

I embraced and kissed her, and then I met her offspring: Reuben, Simeon, Levi, Judah, Gad, Asher, and Dinah. I knew their names, and from Keshet I knew which had been birthed by Leah's handmaid. I embraced and kissed each of my grandsons.

"And here are more." Jacob gestured to another group of sons and introduced them as Dan, Naphtali, and the youngest, Joseph.

Joseph . . . I would have known him anywhere.

I had met Jacob's sons one by one—strong-limbed, dark-haired boys with their father's walk and their mothers' features. They had greeted me with respect, even warmth, but I had felt no tremor in my chest.

Joseph stepped forward. He was smaller than the others, with legs like reeds and shoulders just beginning to square. His hair was black as a raven's wing, curling slightly at the edges where the blade had touched it. And his eyes . . . oh, his eyes. They were dark like his father's; large and full of questions like mine.

I could not speak.

He came to me without prodding or glancing back at his brothers, as if he had been waiting, too. "Are you my father's mother?" he asked. His voice was high and soft, like Etan's.

I crouched, slowly lowering myself on aching knees, and let my hands rest on my thighs. "I am. And you are Joseph."

He nodded. "My mother says you are very old."

I laughed. "She is not wrong."

He tilted his head. "But you do not look like a hundred."

"I thank you for that." Then I reached out—not with urgency, but with awe—and cupped his cheek in my hand. His skin was warm, smooth, alive with breath and blood.

For a moment he stood perfectly still, letting me examine him. I traced the curve of his brow, the sweep of his lashes. I had memorized Jacob's face in the awe of early motherhood, and now I beheld that face again, softened by years and influenced by a woman I had not yet met.

"You have your father's eyes," I said.

He leaned into my palm like a lamb into a fold. "So people tell me."

Around us, Jacob's other sons watched, respectfully silent. But in that moment, there was no one else. Just the child I had waited years to hold. I drew him gently into my arms. He fit beneath my chin, light as a dream.

"I have missed you," I whispered, though I had never met him before this day.

Somehow, impossibly, he answered, "I have missed you, too."

And then, with pulse-pounding certainty, I knew I was about to make a mistake. Even though I sensed something special about this child, I could not allow the others to believe I favored him.

With an effort, I released Joseph and smiled around the circle of Jacob's sons. "I am so happy to meet all of you," I said, extending my arms. "You are all precious to me."

Jacob stepped forward and gestured to a woman who stood alone, a little apart from the others. "And this," he said, his voice vibrant with warmth, "is Rachel."

The woman stepped forward. Slowly, almost ceremonially, she removed her veil.

I blinked.

Her beauty was not the attractiveness that fades with age, but the kind that radiates from within, as if a hidden flame warmed her from inside. Her features were delicate: high cheekbones, full lips, eyes the color of obsidian, deep and gentle. Her hair spilled around her shoulders like a dark river.

"Mother Rebekah," she said, and her voice held no trace of fear or formality—only spirit and something that sounded like gratitude. She extended her hands, palms up and open. "I have so longed to meet you."

I caught her hands and pulled her to me. Her fingers were warm and slender, callused in the right places—this was not a slothful woman. A sob, unbidden, rose from my chest. A sound of recognition and release.

"ADONAI is merciful," I said, and though I addressed her, I spoke more to the heavens. "I never expected to see this moment, yet here you are."

I wrapped my arms around her and pressed my cheek against hers. In that moment, time folded in on itself. I was again the girl beside the well, the mother of twins, and the woman who waited and prayed. And this was the answer I had never dared hope for.

"Can you have forgotten *me*?"

Another voice—one dear, familiar, far from forgotten—cut into my thoughts. I released Rachel and turned in time to see Deborah standing behind her mistress. Though her frame was bent and she leaned heavily on a wooden staff, her bright eyes held affection and warmth.

"Deborah!" I threw my arms around her and rubbed her back as I held her tight. "How I have missed you!"

She pulled away and looked into my eyes. "I hope you are not angry that I stayed in Haran."

"I understood why you wanted to stay, and I am glad you did."

Deborah turned and gestured to two women who had been standing apart from the others. "These women are Zilpah and

Bilhah," she said as they bowed to me. "I believe you know who they are."

I smiled, knowing that Keshet would have shared as freely with Deborah as she did with me. "I do."

"I would not have been able to birth Joseph without Deborah's help," Rachel said, smiling at my old nurse. "And I feel as if I already know you, for Deborah speaks of you often. My father speaks of you, too."

I took her hand in mine, then extended my other hand to Deborah. "The Lord has been kind to bring us together at last. Come, let me get to know you better. I have waited so long for this day."

"And Leah," Deborah said. "You must not forget Leah."

"Of course not." I pointedly looked at Leah and the two concubines. "You are all welcome in my tent. Come and be at ease."

THE AFTERNOON SUN hung low over the hills, casting long shadows across the compound as I led Deborah away from the bustle of the tents. My heart still fluttered with the joy of seeing Jacob after so many years. His face had been creased by time and travel, yet he was still my beloved son.

My prayers had been answered. Despite Esau's original intentions, he had accepted Jacob's peace offerings and his brother's respect; then he had welcomed him with an embrace, tears, and a kiss.

Who but ADONAI could have arranged such a change of heart?

After embracing Jacob, Esau had met Jacob's wives and all of his children. Esau offered to leave warriors in order to protect Jacob's family on the journey, but Jacob had insisted on traveling ahead alone.

After hearing the story of their reunion, my heart felt lighter than it had in weeks.

Now the other women were in my tent, napping or resting with their little ones. But I was too excited to relax.

"Let us walk a little, old friend," I said to Deborah, offering my arm. "These aching bones need stretching after sitting all day."

Deborah's face crinkled with the smile that had comforted me since I was a girl. She took my arm, her touch familiar in spite of all the years we had been separated. Her spotted hands were now as gnarled as olive roots, yet they remained strong.

"You lean on me, and I shall lean on you," she said, her voice thin but warm. "That is how it has always been, no?"

We walked beyond the edge of the camp, where the bleating of sheep grew distant and the wind whispered through the tamarisk trees. My sandals scuffed against the dusty earth, each step a quiet reminder of the years that had whittled away at my bones. The air smelled of sage and the coming night, cool after the heat of the day.

"Do you remember," I said, stopping to catch my breath, "our journey to Canaan? When I left my father's house to marry Isaac?"

Deborah nodded, her eyes distant with memory. "As if it were yesterday. You were so young, so full of hope."

"You were afraid you would fall off the camel," I said, patting her hand. "Your arms were so tight around my stomach that I could barely breathe."

"I was not the only fearful one," she countered. "You were also afraid."

"You are right," I admitted. "I reminded you then of how my parents favored my brother." The old pain flickered in my chest, faint but never fully extinguished. "I vowed that if the Lord blessed me with children, I would never love one more than another. I would not inflict that wound on my own flesh."

We settled ourselves beneath a twisted olive tree on a rocky ledge, its ancient trunk wider than both of us together. Deborah eased herself to the earth with a soft grunt and arranged her robe around her ankles.

"I remember something else," I continued, watching a pair of doves flutter in the branches overhead. "You said my vow would be tested."

"I was right." Deborah's voice held no judgment, only the quiet certainty of one who had seen many lives unfold.

"When the twins were born, I renewed that promise," I murmured. "But it *was* tested, and I failed."

Deborah's hand found mine, her skin cool against my palm. "You should not worry about loving your sons equally, my pet," she said, "because love cannot be measured." She looked toward the darkening horizon, wisdom etched into every line of her face. "Just love them. That is all you can do."

The simplicity of her words stung me. I covered my face as tears blurred my vision. "I have done a terrible thing."

She reached up to pull my hand away, just as she had done when I was a child. "What have you done?"

"I have done the thing I vowed never to do. By favoring Jacob, even from infancy, I have driven Esau away. My sons are reconciled only because of ADONAI's mercy and goodness. I could have lost both of them. I *deserved* to lose both of them."

Deborah studied my face with considerable absorption. "I know you," she said. "And I am sure you did your best. I watched as you tried to teach both your sons about ADONAI. You invited Esau to sit with you as well as Jacob, but Esau did not want to sit. You are not responsible for your sons' choices. Each has chosen his own path."

I sat in silence as her words settled in my heart. She was right—I *had* worked to teach and lead both boys. I earnestly desired to be impartial. But at some point along the way, I had lost my patience with Esau.

"Suppose," she said, gesturing to the sandy ground, "someone gave you a young date palm and an olive tree. Would you plant both of them in the same soil? Would you expect them to grow at the same pace and in the same way?"

I gave her a puzzled frown. "They are two different trees," I said, and then understanding dawned. I sighed and patted her hand. "Jacob and Esau are two different men."

"Yes." She chuckled. "I knew you would understand, pet. Your sons grew differently and required different things. You were best suited for Jacob, but Isaac was better suited for Esau. And now each man is following the path Adonai ordained for him."

As always, Deborah helped me understand the truth that had been in front of me for years, but I had been too close to see it.

"Thank you." I leaned over and kissed her cheek. "I understand. But I could have been more patient with Esau. I could have made more of an effort to understand him."

"Which of us has no regrets about the past?" Her mouth curved with tenderness. "I should have taught you how to ride a camel. Then you would not have fallen off on a very important day."

I laughed, remembering the day we finally reached Abraham's camp. What a sight I must have been, lying prone in the sand, my hair askew and my eyes round with curiosity.

We sat in silence for a while, then Deborah squeezed my hand again. "Adonai is merciful and good," she finally said. "He has brought Jacob home to you. Perhaps He will bring Esau back as well."

As the first stars appeared in the deepening sky, I knelt in the sand and confessed my failings. Alone with Deborah and Adonai, I declared how I had favored Jacob and disdained Esau. "You entrusted those children to me," I prayed, remembering my turbulent pregnancy, "and I was not the mother Esau needed. Forgive me, Adonai, and restore a loving heart within me. Help me to see both my sons as worthy of my love and yours, no matter what they do."

After uttering those words, peace flooded my heart. The aroma of cooking meat floated toward us on the breeze, filling me with hunger and a sense of hope I had not felt in years.

"Come," I said, rising slowly. I offered Deborah my hand. "Let us go back. Tomorrow, I will send word to Esau. It is time to heal what has been broken."

Deborah smiled up at me, her eyes as bright as the first star of twilight. "Now you are the wise one, my pet."

We walked toward the wavering lights of the compound, our

shadows stretching behind us, two old women leaning on each other. And for the first time in many years, my mind was set on a purpose that had nothing to do with prophecies or promises of greatness, but everything to do with love.

JACOB AND HIS FAMILY remained with us for several days. We rejoiced in our son's homecoming as the laughter of our grandchildren filled the air. But soon Jacob came to us with regret in his eyes.

"Father, Mother," Jacob said, "we must depart. My herds have grazed as much as the land can bear. We must seek pasture elsewhere."

Isaac sighed, then lowered his chin in a solemn nod. "Go, my son. But before you go, bring your wives and children to me, so that I may bless them."

Jacob summoned his wives, concubines, and children to stand in front of our tent. Isaac placed his hands upon Jacob's head and blessed him:

> "May the covenant of Abraham rest upon you,
> And the oath sworn to our fathers be established in your house.
> May the tents of Rachel and Leah be fruitful,
> And may Bilhah's and Zilpah's children be as olive shoots around your table.
> Let the sons of your loins become a company of nations,
> And your name be mighty in the midst of Israel.
> May the Lord who has chosen you
> Keep you and your seed forever,
> And may you walk in His statutes all your days,
> Who reigns from everlasting to everlasting. Amen."

When Isaac had finished, Jacob's family gathered their belongings, struck their tents, and began to move their flocks. Dinah, Joseph, and Zebulun, the youngest children, clung to my robes, reluctant to part from me. I kissed each of them, my heart aching at the thought of farewell. Would I ever see them again?

Jacob embraced me once more before mounting his camel. "We will come again," he promised.

Would I still be here?

I watched as Jacob's caravan disappeared over the hills, a dust cloud rising in their wake. My heart stirred with mixed emotions, but joy overruled them all.

Adonai had been faithful. He had kept His promise. And I would continue to trust Him.

Six months later, as the sun stood high in the sky, the sharp blast of the ram's horn disturbed the quiet afternoon. The lookout called from the ridge, his voice carrying throughout the camp. "A large company approaches from the southeast!"

I rose swiftly, my heart thundering in my chest. This was either a trader coming to our well or . . .

I called for my handmaid. She hurried to my side, steadying me as I leaned on her arm. My legs trembled, but my heart surged with hope.

I looked at the dust cloud and realized the procession was far too large to be a trade caravan. This was my son, and I would not wait for him to reach the camp. I would meet him outside the gate as an eager mother should.

I hurried forward, my breath coming fast. Esau was coming home.

Isaac joined me at the gate. We stared at the approaching caravan, our certainty fading. We expected to see Esau, but why would he be traveling with herds of livestock?

Then I spotted our eldest son, his red hair now white, his shoulders still broad. He rode forward on a camel and commanded the beast to kneel, then dismounted and fell to his knees, bowing until his forehead touched the sand.

Isaac extended a trembling hand. "Rise, my son."

Esau lifted his head, his eyes dark with sorrow. "I have come," he said, his voice splintering with regret, "to repay you for what I took so long ago. I acted in anger, and I was—I was wrong."

Isaac bent, resting his hand on Esau's shoulder. "Keep your animals, my son. ADONAI has met all our needs."

Esau did not look at me, and why would he? He had been Isaac's favorite, and Jacob had been mine.

But he was my son, too.

I stepped forward, my breathing unsteady. Lines of grief and weariness had been etched into Esau's face, and my heart contracted at the sight of them.

"The Lord has spoken to me," I said, my voice trembling. "You are your father's son, but you are also *mine*. I have not always loved you as a mother should, and I hope you can forgive me for my lack of affection. But from this day forward, hear this: I promise to always love you."

Esau's dark eyes glistened as they met mine. A single tear slipped over his weathered cheek as my heart, so long indifferent toward him, softened and broke. I reached for him and lightly stroked his face. Esau was not Jacob and never would be. But he was a son of Abraham, a son of Isaac, and a son of mine.

And ADONAI had promised to bless him.

"Stay with us a few days," I said, my hands settling on his shoulders. "Send for your sons and daughters and their children, so we can bless them. And when you are ready, return to your home and know that all is well between us."

Esau remained on his knees in the sand, the sun low behind him, setting fire to the earth at his feet. He lowered his head, hiding his face from us. Why?

Long ago I had feared the future like a storm cloud and fought to shape it with my own hands. I thought I would have to choose among five futures, but not one of them led to this place.

Now I saw the truth: I was never meant to be the author of my story.

Adonai was.

Not one moment was wasted, not one wound unseen. What I stole, He restored. What I withheld, He returned. Just as He had brought my wayward son home.

Esau lifted his face to us once more, his expression gentled by mercy, his eyes wet with tears. And in that moment, I no longer feared the future.

I trusted the One who held it.

Epilogue

AND REBEKAH, DAUGHTER OF BETHUEL, wife of Isaac, and mother of Jacob and Esau, waxed old and was full of days. As she weakened, she sent for both her sons, who came to her. With both in her presence, she said to Esau, "I ask that you and Jacob love one another, and you shall love your fellow like yourself."

Esau replied, "Jacob, my brother, I shall love more than all flesh. I swear to you that I will love him."

Then Rebekah said to Jacob, "Will you love your brother Esau?"

"I will," Jacob replied. "I swear it."

Committed to each other, her sons departed.

Content with her sons and her life, Rebekah then breathed her last, and her spirit was gathered unto her people.

And when word reached Jacob that his mother was dead, he rent his garments and wept with great weeping. Esau also came, and together the sons of Rebekah laid her in the cave of Machpelah, in the field which Abraham bought of the children of Heth for a possession of a burying place.

And the years of Rebekah's life were one hundred and thirty and three years.

And they mourned for her many days, for she was beloved of Adonai and steadfast in all His ways.

And her name was remembered in Israel, for she walked with God, and her faith was not forgotten.

Author's Note

I always try to anticipate questions readers might have about how much of a novel is fictional, especially if the story is based on biblical characters. At times a novelist must "fill in" certain details not recorded in history or the biblical record, but in this story I invented surprisingly few events because so much is in fact recorded in other books. I hope the following information is helpful.

Q. Why did you have Rebekah falling off her camel?

A. Because that's what my Bible translation (Tree of Life Version) says in Genesis 24:63–64: "Isaac went out to meditate strolling in the field at dusk. Then he lifted up his eyes and saw, behold, camels were coming. Rebekah also lifted up her eyes and saw Isaac. Then she fell off her camel." If this story were a romcom, we could say they had a "meet cute."

Q. The Bible says that Keturah was Abraham's wife. Why do you call her a concubine?

A. Sarah was Abraham's legal wife, the first wife, the wife whose child would be Abraham's heir. Though Scripture does refer to Keturah as Abraham's wife, in reality she was more like a concubine since her children were never meant to inherit with Isaac. She was Abraham's companion and did bear him six sons, but she did not usurp Sarah's position in Abraham's family.

Q. Did Rebekah really have to ask Isaac to pray for her to have a child?

A. Yes. The Bible tells us so in Genesis 25:21. The Book of Jasher relates Isaac's rather callous reply to Rebekah's first request but then tells us that he traveled to the "land of Moriah" to offer that prayer.

Q. Did Shem and Eber have a house of study (yeshiva) in the land of Moriah?

A. Their "house of study" is not mentioned in Scripture, but the account of Rebekah's visit is found in the Book of Jasher. The land of Moriah was the land surrounding the mountain where God told Abraham to sacrifice Isaac. In 2 Chronicles 3:1, "Mount Moriah" is the location of the threshing floor over which Solomon eventually built the Temple. On a modern map, the land of Moriah would be the land surrounding Jerusalem.

Q. How much did Abraham understand about the coming Messiah?

A. I don't believe anyone can say exactly how much he understood, but he did have knowledge of Eden, and he did know that God had promised that the son of a woman would defeat the serpent. He also knew that through his lineage, the entire world would be blessed. Perhaps the Spirit of God revealed more.

We do know that people before the Messiah's appearance were saved because they had faith He *would* come. We are saved because we have faith that He *did* come. So Abraham certainly had faith that a Messiah was coming and that the covenant's "blessing of the entire world" meant the Messiah would come from his lineage, just as He did.

Q. Were all of Abraham's sons and grandsons present at his death?

A. The Bible tells us that Abraham died at 175 years (Genesis 25:8–10), and that Isaac and Ishmael buried him in the cave of Machpelah with Sarah, his wife. The Book of Jubilees says that Jacob was with his grandfather and fell asleep; when he woke, Abraham had died. So Jacob told Isaac, who sent word to Ishmael and the sons of Keturah. Ishmael and Isaac buried Abraham at Machpelah, but all of his sons, including the sons of Keturah, mourned him for forty days. The Book of Jasher adds that all the people of Canaan, including the little children, mourned Abraham because he had been kind to them.

Q. Does the Bible say that Deborah went to bring Jacob home?

A. Not directly, no. But Deborah, who is serving Rebekah at the beginning of the story, dies on Jacob's journey back to Canaan (Genesis 35:8). And the Bible does tell us that Rebekah told Jacob, "Stay with him [Laban] a few days, until your brother's rage subsides, until your brother's rage turns away from you and he forgets what you have done to him. Then I will send for you and get you back from there" (Genesis 27:44–45). Apparently, Rebekah *did* send a group of servants, including her trusted nurse, Deborah, to fetch Jacob home. Of course, by the time they arrived, he had fallen in love with Rachel and was working for Laban, so I think we can assume he refused to go back, and Deborah stayed behind to serve Rachel.

Q. Were Leah and Rachel actually twins?

A. That idea comes to us from Jewish tradition, so there is no way to know for certain. But twins tend to run in families.

Q. Did Esau really steal his parents' possessions?

A. The Bible does not record this story, but the Book of Jubilees tells us that Esau took all his father's flocks and left the camp, leaving his father effectively destitute and forcing him to move to Mamre/Hebron, where Isaac had friends and allies.

Some believe that Genesis 36:6, where it says that Esau "took his wives, his sons, his daughters and all the people of his household, as well as his livestock, all his cattle, and all his possessions that he had acquired in the land of Canaan, and went to a land away from his brother Jacob" refers to Esau's seizing of Isaac's property. He could have justified this to himself by reasoning that he was the elder brother and would have inherited the goods after his father's death, conveniently ignoring the fact that he had sold his birthright.

Q. Was Jacob able to communicate with his parents from Haran?

A. Egypt pioneered a state-sponsored postal service that dates back to 2400 BC. That system was used by the pharaohs to communicate with their officials, but it is also possible that traders in other lands—especially those that regularly traveled the established trade routes—could have delivered and accepted messages, whether written or verbal.

Q. Did Jacob send gifts to his parents? Would it have been possible for him to send written messages?

A. The account of Jacob's gifts is recorded in the Book of Jubilees. And yes, the Canaanites had developed a script that enabled them to communicate through the written word. It is entirely possible that Jacob, having been tutored, and Rebekah, who might have had a tutor in Haran, were able to communicate through written messages.

Q. How old was Jacob when he married Rachel?

A. Answers vary, but it's safe to say he was elderly by modern standards. But by ancient standards, men were still active and fathering children after they had passed 100 (remember Abraham?), so many Bible scholars believe Jacob was in his seventies when he married Rachel and Leah.

The figure is derived from several Scriptures:

1. We know that Jacob died at age 147 (Genesis 47:28).
2. We know that Jacob went to Egypt (to join Joseph) when he was 130 (Genesis 47:9).
3. When Jacob entered Egypt, Joseph was about 39 because he started working for Pharaoh at age 30. By the time Jacob joined him, they had experienced the seven years of plenty and two years of famine (Genesis 41:46).
4. So Jacob's 130 years minus Joseph's 39 means that Jacob was 91 when Joseph was born.
5. Jacob wanted to leave Haran right after Joseph's birth, but Laban convinced him to stay for another six years (Genesis 30:25–26; 31:41). When Jacob finally left Haran, Joseph was around 6 and Jacob had been in the land 20 years. If Jacob was 91 when Joseph was born, he would have been 97 when he finally left Haran and 77 when he met Rachel.

We might assume that Jacob married at age 40, like Esau, but nothing in Scripture supports that timeline. It's more logical to reason that Isaac, supposing he was near death at age 137 (when Jacob and Esau would have been 77), decided then to give his blessing to his sons, thus setting the stage for Jacob's flight to Haran to escape Esau's rage.

Q. Did Laban send people to tell Esau to ambush Jacob?

A. The details of that story, including the message that Rebekah sent to warn Jacob, comes from the Book of Jasher. The Bible relates part of the story in Genesis 31:22–29, and in that account we see that Laban was furious when Jacob left Haran without telling Laban, which implies that Laban intended harm to Jacob until God appeared to him in a dream. (Laban tells Jacob, "It is in the power of my hand to do evil with you, but yesterday the God of your fathers spoke to me, saying, 'Watch yourself—lest you say anything to Jacob, good or bad.'")

I don't know if the actual story unfolded as portrayed in Jasher, but the Bible confirms that Esau was coming to meet Jacob with four hundred men, and Jacob was alarmed by the news. And the words he told Esau, when they finally met, were in line with what Rebekah urged him to do in the Jasher account.

Jacob, however, remained wary of Esau. When Esau offered to leave some of his people with Jacob's company, Jacob refused and never met up with Esau in Seir as he had said he would. Jacob went instead to Sukkot and built a house for himself (Genesis 33:17). He lived in Shechem for a few years, then moved to Mamre to be with his father, Isaac.

Q. Do we know if Rebekah was able to finally meet Jacob's wives and children?

A. Though Scripture does not tell us when Rebekah died, many rabbis believe she died at age 133. The Genesis account is silent on the subject, while the Book of Jubilees and the Book of Jasher indicate that Jacob saw Rebekah again before she died.

The Bible does record the death of Rebekah's nurse, Deborah (Genesis 35:8), who died after Jacob reunited with Esau, but before Jacob moved his household to Mamre to be with Isaac (Genesis 35:27–28). Since several years passed between Jacob's departure from Haran and his moving to Mamre, it's certainly possible that he stopped to see his parents and introduce his family to Isaac and Rebekah. But then he spent several years in Shechem, where his children grew old enough to experience the events of Genesis 34.

If Rebekah died at that point, it's logical that Jacob and his family moved to Mamre because Isaac was blind, frail, and alone after Rebekah's death.

Q. Did Esau really return home to Isaac and Rebekah?

A. There is extrabiblical material that speaks of Esau's return to his parents, and the Bible does tell us that he and Jacob buried Isaac together (Genesis 35:29). At some point, the brothers made peace, reestablished communication, and cooperated.

Q. Was Esau not part of the Abrahamic Covenant?

A. God promised Abraham three things: land for a nation, a lineage of uncounted millions, and that the entire world would be blessed through him. As a son of Abraham, Esau *did* receive two of these three things.

He was blessed with a land, but it would not be a permanent possession. In Deuteronomy 2:4–5, as the Israelites were leaving Egypt, God told them, "Command the people saying, 'You are about to cross into the territory of your relatives, the sons of Esau, who dwell in Seir. They will be afraid of you, so be very careful. Do not provoke them, for I will not give you any of their land—not even a footprint—because *I have given the hill country of Seir* [Edom] *to Esau as a possession.*'"

He was also blessed with thousands of descendants. Genesis 36 lists the beginning of Esau's lineage.

Esau, however, was not chosen to be the line through which the Messiah, the Deliverer, would come. In Malachi 1:2–3, God tells Israel that Jacob was loved while Esau was hated. God is not using the words *love* and *hate* as we might use them, because while God does have emotions, He is not temperamental. Before the sons of

Isaac were born, before they *did anything good or bad*, God chose Jacob to be the branch of Abraham's family that would produce the people of Israel and the world's Savior.

As the sons grew, Jacob developed a heart for God, while Esau proved to be a godless and immoral man (Hebrews 12:16). I'm sure Esau had good qualities, but he did not follow ADONAI, and neither did the idolatrous Edomites, his descendants.

In Malachi 1:1–10, the prophet reports God's verdict upon Esau's people: "For Edom may say, 'We have been beaten down, but we will return and rebuild the ruins.' Thus ADONAI-Tzva'ot says: 'They may rebuild but I will tear down. They will be called a wicked territory, the people ADONAI denounced forever'" (v. 4). Therefore, the land Esau was given was not a permanent possession.

Q. Why didn't you tell us more of Jacob's story and his marriage to Rachel and Leah?

A. The events concerning Jacob, Leah, and Rachel will be explored in the third and final book of THE MATRIARCHS series, and the chronology will overlap a bit. Here, we will get Jacob's and Leah's points of view as they tell their story.

Reading Group Discussion Guide

1. How did this novel influence your opinion of Rebekah? Had you formed an opinion about her before reading? Did that opinion change over the course of the story?
2. As a child, did you ever feel that your parents loved a sibling more than you? If you are a parent, are there days when you feel closer to one child than another? Do you believe parents secretly have a favorite child? Why would they favor one sibling more than another?
3. What did Esau's selling of his birthright for a bowl of porridge say about his character?
4. If you had been Rebekah—knowing what ADONAI said about her sons' future—would you have aided Jacob in his quest for the firstborn's blessing?
5. Do you believe a wife should *always* obey her husband? Why or why not?
6. Had you ever given thought to what happened to Rebekah and Isaac after Jacob went to Haran? The Bible doesn't record much about what happened to them, but in Genesis 35:27, we read that Jacob moved his household to be with Isaac at Mamre/Hebron, presumably after Rebekah's

death. Do you think the events of the novel—taken largely from the Bible, the Book of Jasher, and the Book of Jubilees—are plausible?

7. The Bible tells us that when Isaac died, both Esau and Jacob buried him (Genesis 35:29). So the brothers did achieve peace, though they did not live together because the land could not sustain their combined livestock. If land had not been an issue, do you think they could have lived together in peace? Why or why not?
8. Have you read *Rescued Heart: The Story of Sarah*, the first book in this series? How does Sarah's life compare with Rebekah's? What do you think Sarah would have thought of Rebekah if she had lived long enough to meet her?
9. While she is walking with Deborah, Rebekah has an epiphany about her relationship with her sons. Do you think she was right? Do you think God needed her to fulfill His sovereign will?
10. The next book in THE MATRIARCHS series will feature the story of the remaining two matriarchs, Rachel and Leah. Of these two sisters, who do you think loved Jacob more? If she'd been given time to really know them, which of the two do you think Rebekah would have been more drawn to?

Read on for a sneak peek at
the next book from
ANGELA HUNT

DEVOTED HEART

The Story of Leah

Book 3 of the Old Testament series
THE MATRIARCHS

Available in the summer of 2027

Chapter 1

WE HAD BEEN BORN from the same womb and nursed at the same breasts, yet the gods had seen fit to pour the gift of beauty into my sister's vessel while leaving mine only half full. Though my sister and I shared similar features, her eyes, nose, and lips were like fine linen, while on me they were more like wool for everyday wear.

My stomach twisted as the incense merchant's son leaned over to whisper in my sister's ear. Rachel tipped her head back and laughed, her throat as graceful as an egret's neck. Even from across the room, her eyes sparkled like stars reflected in still water.

No one whispered to me.

The oil lamps sent flickering light against the mud-brick walls of our house, casting dancing shadows that enlivened our celebration. Rachel and I had reached our eighteenth year, so Father opened our home to half of Haran to mark the occasion. The smell of roasted lamb and fresh bread mingled with the heavy scent of the incense Mother burned in bronze censers.

I pressed my back against the brick in the corner of the main room, watching a sea of bodies move and sway in the lamplight.

Men clustered around Rachel like moths drawn to a flame, their voices rising and falling as they vied for her attention. She sat on the wooden stool Father had commissioned for the occasion, her hair gleaming like polished obsidian in the lamplight, her laugh tinkling like the silver bells on Mother's finest robe.

"Adinah?"

I turned to see a neighbor approaching my mother. The woman's silver bracelets clinked as she moved. "Your daughters are lovely," the woman said, "but tell me truly—why has Laban not yet arranged marriages for them? Surely every father in Haran has made inquiries about your youngest."

My mother's spine stiffened the way it always did when she felt the need to defend our family's honor. She lifted her chin. "My husband has high standards," she replied. "He will not settle for less than the best. We have relatives in Canaan, descendants of Abraham. Laban waits to hear from them."

The woman's eyebrows rose. "Indeed," she murmured, "but I have become a mother and grandmother while Laban has been talking about Isaac's twin sons. Surely they are old men now."

My mother's smile tightened. "My husband is certain the youngest is waiting for one of my girls, and we would not have married them earlier than their present age. Others may marry their daughters as children, but Laban would not."

The woman moved away, but her comment echoed in my mind. Isaac, our kinsman, was the son of Abraham, whose God had demanded he sacrifice his own child. Rumor insisted that one of Isaac's sons remained unmarried, yet the traders who brought news from Canaan spoke of him as if he were as ancient as the cedars of Lebanon. Seventy years old, some said. Perhaps even older.

I leaned against the wall, feeling the rough texture of the dried brick through my festival robe. The tunic was a work of art, even more extravagant than Rachel's because she needed no embellishment. Mother had worked for months on my gown, embroidering tiny flowers in gold thread that caught the light when I moved. Mother's eyes gleamed with approval when I put it on, and now it felt heavy on my shoulders, weighted with expectations I was not sure I could meet.

Clearly, Father was hoping one of us would catch the eye of a young man in need of a wife, and then the other daughter would marry his kinsman. But who would want to marry an old man? Not me.

Rachel appeared to be having a wonderful time laughing with the men around her, but I had different dreams—foolish perhaps, considering that I could never escape comparison with my sister, but mine nonetheless. I dreamed of a husband who would look at me the way those men looked at Rachel, a husband who would choose me not because I was available or convenient, but because something in his heart called to something in mine.

My husband would not possess a striking appearance. He would be like me—solid, dependable, and reserved. Organized. Hardworking. When we met, he would look beyond my bland features and spot the hidden qualities others missed, the virtues that would bind us together. Somewhere, surely, the gods had created a man who would see me, know me, and love me.

Across the room, Rachel's laughter tinkled, piercing my mood like a needle through cloth. She rose from her stool, her movements as fluid as water, and began to dance to the music of the lute player Father had hired for the evening. The male guests formed a circle around her, clapping as she swayed, her arms moving like wheat in the wind.

I could dance, too—Mother had taught me the same steps and graceful gestures—but I dared not dance beside Rachel because I would suffer in comparison with her. Who could focus on Leah when Rachel was in the room?

I folded my arms and watched Rachel spin and smile, twirl and sway. Without a doubt she was the most beautiful girl in Haran, and something in me warmed at the thought. My parents were honored to call her *daughter*, but mine was the greatest honor of all. I was her *twin*. Her shadow. Her other half.

The oil in the nearest lamp sputtered, casting deeper shadows across the faces of the revelers. In the flickering light, I glimpsed my reflection in the looking brass mounted on the far wall. My eyes held too much longing, and my lips appeared to be glued shut. Words did not come easily to me, and no one would describe my conversation as delightful. If I were to please my mother, I would have to work harder.

Perhaps my parents were right to wait for word from Canaan. No one in this room had looked beyond Rachel's brilliance to notice the steady flame burning in my heart. She would probably be wed to someone from Haran, whereas I, as the eldest, would marry first. But an old man from a distant land, bound by duty and family obligation—was he the best I could hope for?

The thought settled beneath my breastbone like a boulder, heavy and cold, as the birthday celebration swirled around me.

Angela Hunt has published more than 165 books, with sales nearing six million copies worldwide. She's the *New York Times* bestselling author of *The Tale of Three Trees*, *The Note*, and *The Nativity Story*. Angela's novels have won or been nominated for several prestigious industry awards, such as the RITA Award, the Christy Award, the ECPA Christian Book Award, and the HOLT Medallion Award. American Christian Fiction Writers and Romantic Times Book Club have presented her with Lifetime Achievement Awards. She holds ThDs in Biblical Studies and Theology. Angela and her husband live in Florida, along with their mastiffs and chickens. For a complete list of the author's books, visit AngelaHuntBooks.com.

References

Some of Abraham's prayers are adapted from Dr. John Fischer's *Siddur for Messianic Jews.* Palm Harbor, FL: Menorah Ministries, 2018.

———. The BibleAsk Team, "The Age of Jacob," https://bibleask.org/how-old-was-jacob-at-pivotal-points-in-his-life/, accessed March 6, 2025.

———. "When Joseph Was Born," https://bibleinsight.com/crn1p4.html, accessed March 5, 2025.

———. "Why Does the Bible Not Speak of the Death of Rebekah?" https://hermeneutics.stackexchange.com/questions/89510/why-does-the-bible-not-speak-of-the-death-of-rebecca, accessed February 20, 2025.

Balogh, Amy L. "Shechem, City of." Ed. John D. Barry et al. *The Lexham Bible Dictionary*. Bellingham, WA: Lexham Press, 2016.

Brueggemann, Dale A. "Gerar." Ed. John D. Barry et al. *The Lexham Bible Dictionary*. Bellingham, WA: Lexham Press, 2016.

Carasik, Michael, ed. *Genesis: Introduction and Commentary*. Philadelphia: The Jewish Publication Society, 2018.

Charles, R. H., translator. *The Book of Jasher*. Kissimmee, FL: Mccallister Editions, 2018.

Cunning, Lisa F. "God Makes Promises to Women, Too." *Global Journal of Classical Theology 2.1*, 1999.

Drinkard, Joel F., Jr. "Mamre." Ed. Mark Allan Powell. *The HarperCollins Bible Dictionary*. San Francisco: HarperOne, 2011.

Edersheim, Alfred. *Bible History: Old Testament*. Vol. 1. Grand Rapids, MI: William B. Eerdmans Publishing Company, 1975.

Feinberg, Jeffrey Enoch. *Walk Genesis!: In the Beginning*. Clarksville, MD: Messianic Jewish Publishers, 1998.

Freeman, James M., and Harold J. Chadwick. *Manners & Customs of the Bible*. North Brunswick, NJ: Bridge-Logos Publishers, 1998.

Hamilton, Matthew James. "Canaanites." Ed. John D. Barry et al. *The Lexham Bible Dictionary*. Bellingham, WA: Lexham Press, 2016.

Held, Rabbi Shai. *The Heart of Torah: Essays on the Weekly Torah Portion: Genesis, Exodus, Leviticus, Numbers, and Deuteronomy*. Vol. 1. Philadelphia: The Jewish Publication Society, 2017.

Hirsch, Emil G. Seligsohn, Executive Committee of the Editorial Board, "Rebekah," https://www.jewishencyclopedia.com/articles/12610-rebekah, accessed January 22, 2025.

Kennedy, T. Michael. "Haran." Ed. John D. Barry et al. *The Lexham Bible Dictionary*. Bellingham, WA: Lexham Press, 2016.

Kramer, Joel P. *Where God Came Down: The Archaeological Evidence*. Brigham City, UT: Expedition Bible, 2020.

Kriwaczek, Paul. *Babylon: Mesopotamia and the Birth of Civilization*. New York: St. Martin's Press, 2010.

Kugel, James L. "Jubilees." *Outside the Bible: Ancient Jewish Writings Related to Scripture: Commentary*. Ed. Louis H. Feldman, James L. Kugel, and Lawrence H. Schiffman. Vol. 1. Philadelphia: The Jewish Publication Society, 2013.

Marshall, I. H., A. R. Millard, J. I. Packer, and D. J. Wiseman. *New Bible Dictionary*. 3rd ed. Lisle, IL: InterVarsity Press Academic, 1996.

Mathews, K. A. *Genesis 11:27–50:26*. Vol. 1B. Nashville, TN: Broadman & Holman Publishers, 2005.

Mills, M. S. *Genesis: A Study Guide to the Book of Genesis*. Dallas: 3E Ministries, 1998.

Morris, Michelle J. "Rebekah, Daughter of Bethuel." Ed. John D. Barry et al. *The Lexham Bible Dictionary*. Bellingham, WA: Lexham Press, 2016.

Myers, Adam L. "Philistines." Ed. John D. Barry et al. *The Lexham Bible Dictionary*. Bellingham, WA: Lexham Press, 2016.

Qumsiyeh, Mazin B. *Mammals of the Holy Land*. Lubbock, TX: Texas Tech University Press, 1996.

Richards, Sue Poorman, and Larry Richards. *Every Woman in the Bible*. Nashville, TN: Thomas Nelson Publishers, 1999.

Singer, Isidore, ed. *The Jewish Encyclopedia: A Descriptive Record of the History, Religion, Literature, and Customs of the Jewish People from the Earliest Times to the Present Day*. 12 Volumes. New York: Funk & Wagnalls, 1901–06.

Vamosh, Miriam Feinberg. *Food at the Time of the Bible: From Adam's Apple to the Last Supper*. Herzlia, Israel: Palphot Ltd., 2007.

VanderKam, James C. *Jubilees: A Commentary on the Book of Jubilees, Chapters 1–50*. Ed. Sidnie White Crawford. Vol. 1 & 2. Minneapolis, MN: Augsburg Fortress Publishers, 2018.

Wright, Paul. *Holman Illustrated Guide to Biblical Geography*. Brentwood, TN: B&H Publishing, 2020.

Sign Up for Angela's Newsletter

Keep up to date with Angela's latest news on book releases and events by signing up for her email list at the website below.

AngelaHuntBooks.com

FOLLOW ANGELA ON FACEBOOK

Angela Hunt, Novelist